Reviews of Rohan Quine's *The Beasts of Electra Drive*

See www.rohanquine.com/press-media/the-beasts-of-electra-drive-reviews-media for all links to the following.

"Technologically intelligent, socially clever, and supernaturally chilling—a trippy sci-fi tale. [...]
There is a strong artistic element woven into this act of creation, allowing us to see how and why Jaymi creates each of his Beasts, giving them purpose and personality as well as form. [...] This is a book that would have been entirely serviceable with just the hacking and virtual reality interfaces, but what makes it really compelling is the ability for Jaymi's Beasts to step out into meat-space (*I love that term*) and take on corporeal form. These characters grow, learn, and even challenge their programming—they are somewhat childish in their willful independence, to the point of being sociopaths, although they demonstrate real emotion. There is some wonderful genderfluidity to some of the Beasts, with Shigem never feeling '*quite like a boy, being half a gender to the left*' and Scorpio whose '*nature flowers with so transgender a beauty,*' as well as a gay love affair between two Beasts who were created for one another. Lest you forget that this is a revenge fantasy, however, Amber is modeled after Rutger Hauer's character in *The Hitcher*, while Scorpio's defining moment is the fantasy of dominating an entire prison as the most dangerous boy in a skirt. [...]
What really impressed me, however, is the flair for language, with some really beautiful—and beautifully chilling—passages that had me dog-earing pages along the way."
—**Sally Bend** in *Bending the Bookshelf*

"Quine describes [the Beasts'] release like a beautiful dance instead of a strategic infiltration. [...]
The novel is a creative mashing together of Hollywood novel, science fiction, eroticism, and dystopia, with a premise that seems at once foreboding and prescient. While the book takes obvious science fictional liberties with technology, there is a real-world parable about superficiality versus authenticity. As the world becomes more digitally mechanized—and we are as much a product of our digital

personae as our real-life personae—the book has an important message to tell about what it is to be truly human. [...]

Quine obviously has a lot of affection for his Beasts, which has the same effect on the reader. He also injects humor throughout into what is at times a fairly dark storyline, replete with violence and seamy sexuality.

In all, Quine has created a wholly unique look that will appeal to gamers and non-gamers alike. Most readers will empathize with the main character and his suboptimal working situation, and the steps he takes to get out from underneath a tyrannical and uninspiring boss. On a science fictional level, the novel works exceptionally well for its creative use of tech, mixed in with a group of highly imaginative characters.

A prequel to five other works, *The Beasts of Electra Drive* will have readers seeking out Rohan Quine's other books in the series."
—*SPR*

"This novel is essentially near-future cyberpunk subtly blended with elements of LA noir and dystopic fiction to create a darkly stylish and, at times, visionary glimpse into humankind's future. [...] Richly described, the beasts are androgynous characters with full backstories, personalities, and idiosyncrasies. Unleashed upon the world, they allow Jaymi to achieve vengeance in ingenious ways.

This is an intriguing premise, but the story's true power comes from its underlying theme: Humans can choose to live in the superficial, and underlying falseness, of tabloid reality (as gamers do when engaging in the novel's online game), or embrace the 'complexity, unconventionality, beauty and subtlety of truth' of the world around them. Ultimately Jaymi's journey of self-discovery mirrors our own: We all seek happiness in the short time that we inhabit the 'meat space' of this world."
—*BlueInk Review*

"*The Beasts of Electra Drive*, an unctuously dark piece of magical realism interwoven with biting satire on mass culture." "This book is a marvel." "I had the joy of editing this extraordinary novel that's part magic realism, part horror, part satire of the media industry, part meditative hymn."
—**Dan Holloway**, novelist, poet and *Guardian* blogger

"Quine's narrative challenges the arbitrariness of commercial gate-keepers and the randomness of success—and has a lot of fun in the process. It's an odd mixture of dark—verging on horror—with more than a bit of kitsch. […] It's a very visual novel too. Quine gives his narrative voice (and sometimes his characters), the eye of a camera mounted on a drone, able to fly across a valley and zoom in on details miles in the distance—like a tiny reflection in the pupil of someone's eye. […]

Reading this book is a little like watching a particularly unsettling art house movie. You will be, in turn, disoriented, enchanted and repelled.

For all the technology involved, this is more magic realism than science fiction. It deliberately pushes the boundaries of the outrageous and challenges you to go along for the ride."
—**Catriona Troth** in *Bookmuse*

"Quine's novel centers more on an interesting cast than fascinating sci-fi traits. Some characters are computer code in bodily form but still have depth. For example, Jaymi created Kim, in part, to be Shigem's lover. (A nice touch: both Beasts are male.) There's likewise a rather sublime religious theme. Though one Beast kneels in prayer in front of 'his creator,' Jaymi, there's an understated notion of free will. Jaymi assigns missions to Beasts (e.g., wreak havoc on Bang Dead) but often leaves them 'to [their] own devices.' The author's lyrical prose is profound and sometimes surreal, especially in character descriptions. 'Inside Kim,' Quine writes, 'there is a lonely savage from the caves, bent on pure first-degree survival, blown by chance and the primal drives of instinct and emotion, alone and uncertain on a dart from birth to death.' […]

Unhurried but engrossing novel in which characters are more enticing than otherworldly technology."
—*Kirkus Reviews*

"[Protagonist Jaymi] discovers that he can bring his incarnations of excessive freedom, sexuality, intellectual seriousness, cool ambiguity, and dark vulnerability to life, unleashing them on 'meat space.' They become his beasts, extensions of his own personality, and through them, he interacts with the executives behind *Ain't They Freaky!* As various elements of Bang Dead's software are released, Jaymi works to help his former coworkers recognize the shallow depravity of their game through unnerving visits to their homes. [...]

This is a powerful book that advocates letting people be themselves, despite how far outside the bell curve of 'normal' they are. Pulsing with sexuality, the story will appeal to readers who enjoy artistic works rich in vocabulary, symbolism, and graphic imagery."
—*The Book Review Directory*

"Part cyberpunk meditation and part erotic thriller, BEASTS is a stylish narrative romp around a fictional Los Angeles landscape that appeals to the heart first and the head second. [...]

THE BEASTS OF ELECTRA DRIVE sounds like a cyberpunk thriller, and it sort of is. It also has an erotic undertone that grows throughout the narrative as the Beasts themselves crawl out of Jaymi's computer screen and gain independence. It's also a postmodern-ish meditation on creativity. Part of Jaymi goes into the creation of each of his Beasts—perhaps something author Rohan Quine can relate to—and as a whole the group is as a kind of kaleidoscope view of its creator. Additionally, part of Jaymi's mission in siccing the Beasts on Bang Dead Games is a retaliation against *Ain't They Freaky!*, an in-universe alternate reality game that embodies empty mass appeal over genuine artistry. [...] the writing grows increasingly smoother, culminating in a hauntingly pretty passage about man's inhumanity to man and ending up with intense backstories for the Beasts.

THE BEASTS OF ELECTRA DRIVE is, as its cover suggests, perhaps more about style than substance. Readers are told not to judge books by their covers—but this is the future. Maybe that's the point."
—*IndieReader*

"A sensual ballet of rich characterisation, alluring subtlety and originality. *The Beasts of Electra Drive* is a novel that I didn't want to put down while I was reading it [...]. I was transported into a domain peopled by characters who felt as if they were beckoning to me. It was as if they were inviting me into a kind of gliding embrace of harmony, within the pages of their author's imagination.

I found myself underlining things on the page, throughout it, because of the allure of Quine's language. I was fascinated with the marriage of his vocabulary and his punctuation. On the few times when I wasn't familiar with a word he uses, I resisted looking up its meaning—so as not to disturb the flow of the prose, but also because the spell of the sentences made the mystery of those words' meanings into an actual part of Quine's sheer creativity.

I felt drawn into his characters, which are complex. In the case of at least a couple of them, I had a strange feeling that they were somehow stroking me, while I was being led around their inner worlds. I was unable to dislike any of them, even those who clearly weren't very nice.

I also loved being reminded of when I lived in the Hollywood Hills. [...] Quine has captured the feel of those hills and canyons, in a way that will be recognised as authentic by anyone who's lived there.

This book creates a luscious and sensuous effect, which you can expand into. I have the sense that it was written by a very unusual and special person."
—**Suzi Rapport**

"An extraordinary genre-defining and fascinating novel. So timely as cynical, talentless and opioid-pushing mass-media owners try and downgrade all popular culture—Rupert Murdoch/tv producers and ilk, I'm looking at you. Like a lyrical poem from ancient times. But more violent and with more gay sex."
—**Hermione Ireland** on Goodreads

"Jaymi's pursuits are a revenge fantasy taken to the next level, with moral and ethical quandaries wound in.

Magical realism meets old school noir in Rohan Quine's technological thriller *The Beasts of Electra Drive*, which poses philosophical questions around reality, humanity, and where to draw the line with tech-infusion. […]

Distinct writing is filled with lyrical prose and vivid sensory descriptions […] At times, [Jaymi] appears to have moral quandaries about his drastic actions against a rival company. His cyber-creations also lead him to question the nature of existence and his role as a creator—can he ethically order his creations to do his bidding in the real world? […]

The characters that Jaymi creates are refreshing in their diversity of race, gender, and sexuality. The two distinctly male beasts conform to the spectrum of masculinity, with one, Amber, being excessively violent, athletic, and handsome, and the other, Kim, being introverted but boundlessly intelligent and philosophical. These two men are in relationships with Shigem and Scorpio, who are more fluid in their gender and sexual identities. Shigem and Scorpio, along with Evelyn, are of varying nonwhite ethnicities. The scope of variety among the beasts is a nice change of pace.

The Beasts of Electra Drive is a techno-thriller that focuses more on its beautiful prose than on nurturing its thrills. Although sometimes repetitive in format, the vitality of the characters is pleasant and engaging."
—*Foreword* Clarion Reviews

"A crazy, psychedelic and experimental book. A fascinating and genre-defying story of a genius computer games designer waging war on the cynical and cretinous mass-market media and entertainment peddlers that threaten to cheapen and destroy our world. Perfect for adventurous readers."
—**Dartmouth dogwalker** on Amazon

"A fully-wrought origin story like no other."
—*The Bookbag*

If you'd like to be notified of future print and ebook publications, you're most welcome to sign up for Rohan Quine's not-too-frequent newsletter at www.rohanquine.com/sign-up. Rest assured, such emails will be at supremely tasteful intervals and your details will be shared with no one else.

THE BEASTS OF ELECTRA DRIVE

A NOVEL BY ROHAN QUINE

EC1 DIGITAL

The Beasts of Electra Drive by Rohan Quine
ISBN: 978-0-9927549-4-5

Published by EC1 Digital, London, UK

www.rohanquine.com/the-beasts-of-electra-drive

Developmental editing by Dan Holloway,
www.rogueinterrobang.com/more-things/about
Cover design by Jane Dixon-Smith, www.jdsmith-design.com
Los Angeles: photo by Allen.G / www.shutterstock.com
The Platinum Raven: photo by Subbotina Anna / www.shutterstock.com
Author: photo by Ruth Jenkinson

Epigraph: Jean Genet translated by Bernard Frechtman.

This novel is also available as an ebook and an audiobook
published by EC1 Digital.

When at night I walk barefoot in my sandals across fields of snow at the Austrian border, I shall not flinch, but then, I say to myself, this painful moment must concur with the beauty of my life, I refuse to let this moment and all the others be waste matter; using their suffering, I project myself to the mind's heaven.

—Jean Genet, *The Thief's Journal.*

TABLE OF CONTENTS

PART II "Gal Score", Evelyn's creation, and the stalking of the Dreary Ones

PART III "Guy Score" and "Trivia Score", Shigem's and Kim's creations, and the Righteous Gun Cockpit

PART V "Cosy Score", Scorpio's creation, and the Beasts go repurposing

PART VI The Jaymi Beast's creation, battle and transcendence

PART I

AMBER'S CREATION, BANG DEAD GAMES, AND THE LONE VIOLINIST

1 THE LONE VIOLINIST IN THE WOODLANDS AT DUSK (*GHOST, AS HOOK*)

Woodlands at dusk in the late summer, somewhere on the outskirts of Omaha, Nebraska.

In a clearing burns a bonfire, surrounded by a scattering of teenage girls and boys, sitting up or lying back on dry grassy earth. A joint glows red from time to time, then is passed through the smoky haze.

Nervous on the group's edge, a sixteen-year-old Jaymi plays a violin, and the liquid magic of his music is delighting his audience. An end-of-summer hour, near the end of all their childhoods. And doubly endless: first, within its own enchanted brevity; then endless again, through infusing a dusk-shadow whisper of sweet fire-smoke through the very different later lives of all those present.

A noise cuts in, from the end of the clearing.

A band of adults, looming through the trees. As they approach, many become recognisable as parents of the assembled. They are heading straight for this group. No words from them yet, but their manner is confrontational; they are here on a mission.

The first couple of adults stride into the clearing. One grabs Jaymi's violin and bow, smashes them against a tree and hurls them up and away into the air; while the other snarls at him that his music

1

is perverting the other children, and if he doesn't leave town then they will hurt him.

So mellow has been the group's mood, that its members find themselves unequipped to fight against the parents' force in yanking their offspring up from the ground and hustling them away.

As soon as the last fragments of his violin and bow have curved down and hit the ground, Jaymi sees flashes, through his shock and sorrow, of these same emotions in the eyes of the other children while they are marched off. Within those glimpses, which he catches in slow motion and will remember for the rest of his life, he perceives that the shock and the sorrow he's seeing in them add up to something essential. These emotions bring him together with them against a common enemy—all that meanness and fear, which appear to be the preserve of grown-ups. He and these other children who were rapt in his music, plus the occasional adult who still remembers, are all united as the outnumbered prey of the more usual kind of grown-up-ness—the kind whose main aim seems to be the destruction of any primal magic it encounters, while lacking the self-awareness even to know this about itself.

Soon the last teenager's complaint has receded into the woods and out of earshot, leaving Jaymi alone beside the smoulder of the bonfire—his eyes full of knowledge, shock, contempt and ambition.

An hour after his audience was banished, there he remains in the dark of the clearing: a lone violinist, imagining the music he'd be making here, as if for all time, while he sits with his smashed violin and bow beside him on the ground.

Next day, carrying whatever essentials he can, he steps off the grass verge of a highway on the outskirts of town, clambers up through a metal door and takes his place in the passenger's seat of a massive truck, on a hitched escape from Omaha to New York City.

Soon the truck is miles out of town and gaining speed, with his music soaring grand above the highway ahead...

2 THE TERRACE POOL AT THE HOUSE ON ELECTRA DRIVE

Jaymi's eyes open on a hot blue haze above a Hollywood hillside. Lying here, he grins, with a glint in his eyes. Above him on the left, silhouetted like an asterisk upon the sky, a palm tree crest sways lazy in the heat; while cicadas chirp, hidden in the scratchy vegetation away down the slope beyond the boundary of his land.

What a palace this is, spread around him here! A palace of his own. And how blessed he is to have it, as he knows. To recline by the pool on this newly-won Electra Drive terrace has somehow become his ordinary world, strange to say—actual, everyday reality for that same nervous boy who used to carry his violin around, always somewhere at the edges of the group, and so often shy and blushing, who lives somewhere inside him still.

Accessed through the sliding glass doors of a huge open-plan sitting-room, this ground-floor terrace, with its sun-beds arrayed around a generously-curved swimming-pool, is only the lowest of three sunny spaces that wrap around the outside of the house on three successive levels. Furnished with elegant white armchairs and more sun-beds, the terrace on the storey above him is accessed via external steps from here, or directly through the doors from his study, where a fanfare of computer monitors and gleaming IT equipment attests to his career as a games designer. And on the top floor, part-shaded by the projecting width of his bedroom's shallow dome of a roof, is a yet more exclusive terrace. Set apart from the other luxury residences on Electra Drive, and further buffered from the normal world by a wide surrounding plot of unspoiled land, this house is constructed alone on a promontory of its own, overlooking the city of Los Angeles. The sunsets, sinking to the ocean on his right and far ahead, refracted through the city's haze, are chemical and poisonously gorgeous.

He would not have predicted, back in Omaha, that such luxury and privilege would come to be his.

Nor would he have predicted it in the course of the few years after his first arrival in Manhattan on that legendary truck he once flagged down—years during which his childhood video-games-playing experience joined forces with his coding abilities, to land him a position as a programmer working for the visual design team in the New York office of the games development company Bang Dead Games. By this time, his upbringing on the outskirts of Omaha felt like ancient history. The company was just entering an aggressive expansion phase, after one of its titles had hit big.

He wouldn't even have predicted this Electra Drive palace a year later, when he was given the exciting opportunity of being transferred to the company's main office here in L.A., as a higher-ranking member of the design team on another, even bigger and longer-established Bang Dead title.

How well he remembers his eagerness, as the plane touched down at LAX, to be joining an HQ led by such a high-achieving bunch of thoughtful and open-minded managers, who surely wanted to light up and elevate the world in the same way he did! It was so cool to know they were just as fired up by fresh and intelligent world-creation as he himself was. Why, the very week he arrived here, a new senior manager joined the company, with a specific brief to develop an enormous new game. *Ain't They Freaky!* was its cheeky-sounding name, apparently; though it was months before Jaymi came to know anything much more about it, owing to the pressure and workload involved in his lightning progress up through the ranks of his own development team's game.

He soon veered into the overall execution of this game's visual design. In the context of so large and well-established a game-world, he was rarely called on to invent substantial new additions to its look or concept, being rather focused on overseeing sophisticated new tweaks and technical extensions of what was already there. But the multiplicity of his contributions and the speed of his rise equipped him with practical experience across an unusual variety of capacities, from project management to visual design to programming.

In the context of the title's runaway commercial success, that varied experience has resulted in what Jaymi knows is an unusually fortunate pay cheque.

So fortunate, that last month, just four years after joining Bang Dead, he found himself settling into this lush house on Electra Drive, spread atop a promontory facing the city, high in the Hollywood Hills…

Why is it, then, that throughout this first month since he moved in, he has nonetheless continued to feel restless?

What on earth more can he want than this, luxuriating here in the penthouse of his industry?

Is he missing something obvious? Is there some flaw in this picture, hiding in open view, staring him in the face while he fails to see it?

He closes his eyes, to concentrate. His fingers are distracted by the texture of the sun-bed he's lying on. He allows his focus to come trotting back like a little dog, and bids it sit and contemplate the question at hand.

Yes, the question, which was... (What was it again?)

Ah yes: the flaw in the picture, staring out at him from the shadows of the pattern. He thinks hard.

The hiss-swirl-patter of the sprinkler on his lawn is carried to him, soft on a warm breeze up the hillside, while those lines of Italian cypresses on the far canyon slopes stand dark behind the heat-haze...

He really is restless, there's no getting away from it. And it's something to do with Bang Dead.

The hiss and swirl continue, but mixed with more patter than before: the wind must be veering the water-jets to one side, away from concentricity, to splatter onto the wider-leaved plants that push up through the rocky hillside earth around the edges of his artificially-planted lawn of springy turf.

Some scent of voltage—some transcendence or vengeance or fierce beauty, somehow—is absent or elsewhere.

3 HERE COME THE BEASTS, UP THE SLOPES OF THE CANYONS

Light sparkles off the surface of the nearby swimming-pool when he re-opens his eyes, which fire a glint up at that dark star of a palm tree on the sky above him. He's got it! He's identified what's been bothering him.

The truth is that ever since he moved to Bang Dead's L.A. office, he has found himself increasingly running up against a culture whose values and interests oppose his own. Whose goals have nothing to do with lighting up and elevating the world, but everything to do with appealing to the cheapest and most gruntish aspects of human society because this is how the easiest profits are made. To be nakedly frank (since that's always a fun phrase to say), it has most often been the fault of high-ranking bean-counters, rather than of the crafts-people they employ. Several of the latter have confided in Jaymi that they wish their skills could be used for something more interesting or adventurous. Yet the bean-counting culture has continued to be imposed on them, often owing to the particular influence of the senior manager who arrived here in the same week Jaymi did—a man named Dud Guy.

Dud's influence is by no means universal; some highly original new work does still get made at Bang Dead, of course it does. But there's a new flavour of crassness and sleaze running through the company's culture, no question about it. Jaymi has now run up against this so often, it no longer surprises him. Beneath his lack of surprise, though, it has not stopped shocking him. Nor does he see how it could do so: in fact, the thought of its ceasing to shock him makes him want to undress and take a shower so as to clean off. (Stripping off would also go well with the "nakedly frank" thing, which seems to be turning out well, so he'll award himself just a tad more of it here.) Alas, Dud has brought in a bunch of new middle-managers whose instincts are to oppose most conceptually innova-tive game design potential. They seem to lack the simplest awareness that any other motivation or interest than their own even exists—let alone any sense of irony at the shortfall involved in their using such technically awesome tools to create psychological and emotional in-game motivations of such infantilised barrenness—let alone any desire for their own psychological and emotional horizons, or those of the players, to be expanded, enriched and propelled upwards and outwards within themselves by the magic of something subtle, complex, evolutionary.

By comparison with those possibilities, the DNA of this new culture is designed to produce lazy, trite concepts dressed in the gloss of high production values, intended to appeal to the most unreflec-tive, cud-chewing and troglodytic instincts of game-play. Things really began to go downhill when the first details emerged about Dud's much-rumoured pet title, *Ain'tTheyFreaky!*.

How unbelievably stupid! What an enormous waste of human resources, too.

Without the necessary authority to counteract this rot, however, Jaymi has not considered mounting any serious struggle against the individuals most responsible for it: he has simply labelled them, within himself, as the Dreary Ones. So senior are their job titles, he has been unaware of the option of owning any struggle against them. After all, they have been both empowered and dreary, in great and equal measure, for quite a while now; and they continue to be both.

...Well, that was an enjoyable bitch-fest, to be sure! He must remember to try a bit more of this nakedly frank business.

But it's clear he must start looking for a new way of dealing with this cheaply-motivated culture he finds himself in, whose jejuneness of content is so bovinely stubborn, and in effect so hostile and down-dragging to his own real passions and interests.

Well then, Jaymi should take action at last, and start responding to it—not from within, but from without.

And the path unfurls, clear and open ahead of him, starting right here where he's lying, with the curved roofs and terraces of his property curling away behind him around this hillside promontory, the scrape of the crickets thick in the air from down the rough scrubby hillside beyond the manicured parts of his land, and the sun close above.

He will take a grand leap, to become an independent designer and developer. He will unshackle himself from that commercial mechanism, the great promise of whose technical advancements is nowadays too often drearily squandered on a sluggish, down-weighted output that moves with such painful slowness, in any higher sense; that interposes its grey, clunky oafishness to block the progress of all those fascinating explorations and advances that are available to be made in conceptual, intellectual and artistic directions, and insists instead upon yet another variation of the dull thud of bullets fired by an array of superficially varied ciphers waving guns around.

So many gamers are more evolved than much of this stuff Dud wants to feed them. More evolved than they're encouraged to discover or remember. More evolved than they're given credit for.

As a result of his escape into independence, his creativity in games design will be unfettered from the kind of design-by-committee that he has increasingly seen devolve into design-by-lowest-common-denominator-of-the-committee.

His game will be different. Sprawled here atop this sunny hillside, beneath the climb of Electra Drive beyond his front gates behind him, he decides: his game will mine truth, beauty and magic from the splendour and pain intertwined in the world's design. In it, he will aim to push imagination and game language towards their extremes, in order to explore and illuminate the beauty, horror and mirth of this predicament called life, where we seem to have been dropped without sufficient consultation ahead of time. He will seek to illuminate the world, to the best of his finite abilities, using game language in new and old ways, and thereby leave the world infinitesimally better than it was beforehand. He will aim and attune his ears as clearly as possible to whatever the highest artistic potential may be, then bring down the richest results from that place, then give those results the truest and most beautiful form he can create. And he will seek to make an honest account of the darkness and pain in the world, while at the same time being a vote for life—maybe even an absolute blast of fun along the way.

What a liberation is just around the corner! Bye bye, Dud Guy. Bye bye, Dreary Ones. (Do keep in touch.)

For here come the Beasts, up the slopes of the canyons of the Hollywood Hills, through the scratching of the crickets in the shadows of the palms!

Oh yes. He can feel them in the distance, getting closer...

4 DECLARATION OF WAR BY THE DREARY ONES (*INCITING EVENT*)

A month later he has left the company, having spent the month conducting quiet investigations into the availability of various personnel he might hire in connection with his own games. The Bang Dead bigwigs heard hints of these investigations, of course, via the industry grapevine. And before long Jaymi learns, on the same grapevine, what a large and complexly-shaped vacuum has been created by his own departure, through the Dreary Ones' cocky underestimation of how much Jaymi himself enabled many of the processes and good-will Bang Dead depended on. Fragments of inside chatter reveal Dud and his cohorts to be nothing less than paranoid, indeed, concerning the danger of Jaymi's leaking inside knowledge that could cast an embarrassing light on what a risk-averse, sheep-like flock of nervous nellies they themselves are. Of comparable concern to these bigwigs is how he may compete with them, and what talent he may poach.

Good, let them fret. And may their corporate scale bog them down, too: for their hiring mindset is all geared towards giant development teams. Big AAA games like Bang Dead's can take years to build. With dozens or hundreds of people working on them, it's no wonder individual creatives find themselves locked into narrow specialisms, where their input becomes like that of an assembly-line worker installing the same components into a line of cars. Aside from the repetitiveness of this, it's not often possible for them to contribute much from their own creativity, which is often a motivation-dampener.

That's not how *he'll* be working. He will hire freelancers who have as little connection with Bang Dead as he can arrange. He'll hire them at his own pace and in his own way, keeping them all as separate as possible from one another without jeopardising the collaboration process, and having them work remotely. His reputation and the size of his contacts base will make this feasible. A non-standard approach, for non-standard games. It'll be a pleasure to do things as he wishes.

Thus will he walk with the angels, saying what he wants and nothing else: from Jaymi alone, to the whole wide world!

All right, to work now. Time for a brainstorm, to help scare up inspiration and ideas for his own output—with which he'll knock 'em dead, without a doubt.

So he settles back at his desk and strikes out on a random, ragged romp through a score of websites, familiar and unfamiliar, all devoted to the independent games-development community.

Before long, down some online rabbit-hole, he encounters a series of screen-shots that someone has captured and preserved, from a now-forgotten casual game released at least a couple of decades ago when he was a child. It seems the game was themed around an electronic band from that era, whose handful of musical hits exploded with a brief but global convulsion of excitement and innovation, such that almost anyone in the western world who was around then would still recall their sound, he should think. How cutely old-school this little game's interface looks now, although he can see that in technical terms it was quite respectable in the context of its era and budget. It's clear the game was created in genuine homage to the massive pop-cultural furore achieved by the band in question—as well as in order to cash in on the furore, of course. Jaymi looks up from the screen-captures and gazes through the window beyond the monitor, suffused with a sense of wistful sweetness at catching so vivid a glimpse down this corridor of time, from the present to those distant-seeming flickers of games culture lying back there half-buried in recent history, in all their earnest humorousness of obliquity to the main thrust of that musical phenomenon, fluttering along in the wake of a sound that still echoes on down through the years in the memories of millions...

His thousand-metre stare through the study window is punctured by a dark speck hovering above the city ahead. Curious, he gets up and steps out onto the terrace. Standing at the railings, it's hard to judge the object's distance. Maybe half a mile? Some strange flying thing. It's not moving fast, but it seems to be expanding ... no, it's just getting nearer here. What on *earth* is it?

Now it's growing faster; he can even hear it whirring. Six legs come into view beneath its body, like those of a giant mosquito.

It's a drone!

Ever closer it comes, until he can see its whirling propellers, one on each mosquito-leg. Nervous, he starts to edge back, as it approaches the promontory and rises over the end of his garden.

He edges back further, as it flies to within ten metres of this terrace, where it hovers over his swimming-pool on the level below. One of the mosquito-legs curls down and lifts something out from under the belly, then swings this around—it's a camera!

Closer still the drone whirrs, adjusting the camera so as to aim straight at him, until it is a mere two metres ahead of where he's standing. Sunlight glints off the metal focus-rings around the lens, within whose circle he can see the aperture opening, reacting to the reduced light within this new framing of him: reflected on the lens's smooth surface, he can even see the dark squares of his study windows behind him, and in the centre of the lens his own face, looking terrified.

The drone executes a jaunty swing from side to side, but keeping him in the camera's sightline, as if it were a gun. Then it swoops up and away over Laurel Canyon and is soon lost to sight.

Standing there with his mouth open, Jaymi feels a suspicion arise in him: he couldn't prove it, but he has a nasty sense this was the work of the Dreary Ones.

He has state-of-the-art security technology around this whole property, he reassures himself. With a house like this, who wouldn't? But if it is indeed Bang Dead behind this drone attack—for it was an actual attack, let's be clear—then they won't be interested in robbing him. They'll be seeking to unnerve him, humiliate him, maybe warn him somehow.

Oh, he knows it's them. He can *feel* it.

And now they are in annoying possession of footage that shows him looking terrified, and doubtless ridiculous, on his own private terrace.

There's been frost and enmity in the air between him and that team, ever since he left. Dud did not appreciate Jaymi's departure, and will have very likely been trying to do him down in the estimations of Jaymi's senior ex-colleagues—notably Kelly, Ashley, Herb and others. Boring, yes; but not so surprising.

This, however, has crossed a line. This was a personal attack on him, in his own home.

What characteristic stupidity of misjudgement on the part of the Dreary Ones. In light of all that paranoia and concern he's seen in them, as revealed on the grapevine, a more intelligent course of action would have been to exercise a judicious, hands-off approach towards him, not stage a clumsy provocation. This drone attack, though, was more than a provocation. It was a declaration of war.

OK then—bring it on.

They want a war? They've got one.

5 *AIN'T THEY FREAKY!* BY BANG DEAD GAMES

Staring through the window across his study terrace, Jaymi thinks back to what he knew about Bang Dead's upcoming new flagship title, *Ain't They Freaky!*. Dud was hired as a senior manager with a specific brief to develop this project, because his previous job had been managing not a games company but a news conglomerate— precisely the expertise that was needed for this particular game. There were rumours that its hush-hush development phase alone was going to occupy Dud and his team for many months, maybe even a year. Such was its potential value, that its details were meant to be confined to those who needed to know, but Jaymi managed to find out the basics.

If he looks in his email, he may still be able to find something about it. He darts to his computer and taps in a search term or two. Yes. There's a PDF about it—a couple of sides of text written by Dud himself. Jaymi sits and reads it at high speed.

Ah yes, now it comes back to him. *Ain't They Freaky!* is to be a news-based game—or as this outline puts it, "gamified tabloid news". However, its human subject-matter won't be restricted to the kinds of people traditionally regarded by popular tabloid outlets as newsworthy fodder through which to sell copies or drive up click-through numbers. This game won't be tied down to using just celebrities, or other individuals whose actions or experiences happen to be frameable in such a way as to force them, for a day, into the cartoony mould of some recognised type such as hero, villain, whore, saint, regular guy, regular gal, winner or loser.

No. In this game, any person at all will be fair game for such "news" treatment, which may be targeted at them by any *Ain't They Freaky!* player, at any moment of their lives, for any reason, and irrespective of whether the target is also registered to play the game. The destructive force with which the targeter may hit their target in a Newsfeed will depend upon the relative sizes of the targeter's "normality" score and their target's. To the extent their own score is the higher one, they will hit their target more destructively—thus earning further normality points in the process. The game will calculate any pair of parties' relative scores by means of instant searches of each party's entire online footprint inside and outside *Ain't They Freaky!*, scoring their normality according to a confidential proprietary algorithm that will factor in such odds and ends as the party's contacts, uploads, known ethnicity, evident sexuality, religious affiliations, politicised activities and who knows what else.

Besides earning normality points, a targeter's other incentive will be to earn money from such online attacks, in what amounts to a global marketplace of omni-directional targeting. *Ain't They Freaky!* will be free for the public to play, but supported by an ecosystem of in-game ads, product placements and various other kinds of sponsorship and branding, whose display will be triggered by keywords. Falling into the sandbox category of games, it won't have official winners and losers as such, but will rather feel like an environment in which to frolic. Maybe not quite a game at all, in fact, but just a platform.

"Just" a digital platform. Or in other words, just one of the most powerful things in the world, if Dud and Ashley and the rest of them can design and launch it right.

The public's engagement with all this will be powered by good old-fashioned human competitiveness. Players will be encouraged to spend rich years keeping up with the Joneses in many exciting ways, enticed and tallied by the bling of rewards such as Freak-Kill Points, Super-Freak-Kill Points, Grins, Sniggers, Glassy-Eyes and several more besides, plus a whole bouncing flea-circus of adorable emoji and emoticons for easy representation of all permissible online emotions.

Central to the overall ethos of *Ain't They Freaky!* will be the principle of championing the most championed. This sacrosanct preferment will be its prevailing blood-type, pervading the algorithms by which it will confer its every social reward and its every social censure. For the principle of championing the most championed will derive much of its power from the converse principle—the shaming of the most shamed.

In short, *Ain't They Freaky!* will aspire to empower everyone as a tabloid-style news reporter about everyone else. Journalism will become more fun than ever, with the opportunity for a player to earn commissions of real-world money as a gossip columnist or talk-show host, through posting sharp judgements about the wacky antics or non-antics of anyone else online. The most celebrated columnists and hosts will earn the social clout that comes with having a personal platform where their uttering a single comment can make or break somebody else's fortunes. If they are truly diligent in championing the most championed and shaming the most shamed, then they may attain the enviable status of official Spokes-Gossip for the game; and some may even be offered share options in it, which will of course be a licence to print money. The greatest payments will accrue to those judgements that make the greatest social waves—positive judgements, conceivably, but more likely negative ones.

These avenues of championing and shaming will foster a gladiatorial approach to squashing undesirable traits out of social standing, while healthy traits are instilled instead. It's a level playing field for all players. Something like a nature show, in fact. A salute to Nature, red in tooth and claw, as Dud's PDF enthuses. *Ain't They Freaky!* will be honoured, in fact, to *be* one humble part of the grand procession of Natural Selection, no less—but bracingly accelerated for the digital age. Thus will it facilitate the evolution of our species, by hosting this evolution worldwide within the four corners of the game. It can be a cleansing force in society—so bring on all contenders! Though social in its substance, and although a sandbox, it will borrow much from first-person shooters, as Dud is happy to admit; and for Bang Dead it will have the potential to make a killing, through being a killing-field.

A global platform on which to shore up one's majority credentials, to lever oneself ever higher—up through the bulge of the bell-curve, fat above the hub of the spinning world—while snipping off the freaks at the rim, to send them away in shame into the void, licking their wounds!

Yes. Jaymi remembers all this now. It was central to his wanting to leave Bang Dead. But having been among the elite within the company's hallowed walls, and being familiar with how the industry goes, he knows that for all the exhausting "fun" with which *Ain't They Freaky!* is sure to be presented, the Dreary Ones will assemble this cruel and tacky game with the grimmest humourlessness, the most leadenly pedestrian literal-mindedness and the glassiest-eyed lack of compassion imaginable, such as to defeat any playful, layered or humane response one might meet it with; and that Dud's team will have at their disposal so powerful a corporate machine, it is almost certain, alas, that this monstrosity will sweep the world.

6 JAYMI CONCEIVES HIS GAME *THE PLATINUM RAVEN*

Jaymi paces around his study, with growing restlessness. He has been resisting direct conflict with the Dreary Ones. But their launching the drone attack has kicked off the fight he never kicked off himself, and even brought it into his home—onto his property and into the heart of his life, provoking him on his very own terrace on his own private promontory!

How can he not respond? He must. He has no choice.

Never before has he been so confronted with the new Bang Dead culture's crass destructiveness. How *dare* they?

He shies away from conducting any violent physical attack on them. It's just so very much not his style, and thank goodness for that.

No, he will rise above such vulgar cloddishness and clunkiness as they have displayed. He'll reply by showing, not telling: he will respond to their destructiveness by creating something beautiful that didn't exist before. Their dull mediocrity will trigger such inventive joy and cheeky creativity from him, they won't even realise he's running rings around them!

That burst of liberation he felt on the terrace a month ago, when he decided to take the helm himself in this industry, is now followed by the climb of a grim resolve in the face of what he knows: that in addition to his continuing to design games, he must now cause their funding too, from development, through production, to marketing.

So, how best can he respond to the Dreary Ones and their wretched game and their drone attack? Whichever direction he looks, in seeking the answer to this, only one aspect of the situation is clear yet, which is that he will have to pursue his activities on a war footing.

Well, alright then, it's a war. A bit like life in general. Or like the wars in countless video games, funnily enough; but with any luck a richer one than most of them. Like any truly original creation, his own game will carry, within the substance of its newness, an implicit destruction of the surrounding context where it lands, through showing up what was available to be refreshed in that context. But more specifically, within his game, he will externalise elements of his war footing itself, as personifications—as characters in the story world—as people whom he'll create.

Each such character will develop in an organic way from its war-born embryo, via its body and senses and name, into a richly-celled creature articulated through layer upon layer of accreted substance, from volition to agency to interaction, to an intelligence and mind of its own. He will then watch them being their own selves, running wild within the confines of his game-world, and casting their multi-coloured reflections on the outer world: not a "war game" as such, but a game whose release will be, among other things, a war against war games.

It's hard to say no, after all, to the prospect of a little conflict—provided the conflict is interesting.

Ten minutes later, he steps out through his study doors onto the terrace and settles into an upright armchair, with his computer on his lap, the evening panorama of L.A. twinkling ahead, and a limoncello on ice sitting on the terrace flagstones beside him.

It happens that he already has a name for the game: *The Platinum Raven*, which came to him in a dream and will alight here on Electra Drive with ease.

He's aware it is ultimately not a matter of importance for him to broadcast the intimate details of his own internal world in particular; but these details provide him with the truest way of dealing with the wider aspects of human existence that transcend individuals. What he's seeking is to communicate an authentic vision of human life and its possible meanings, aiming to use the language of his game to express what he's learned about all our presences here. He hopes to contribute to our rising above our individual points of view, to a point where we see the world, including ourselves, from above. This viewpoint will have its hazards, no doubt, such as the aloneness and alienation that attend any hunt for a god's-eye view of us; but the hazards will be worth the hunt. In this spirit he will distribute himself, he decides, among three in-game characters.

One of these will be the eponymous Platinum Raven herself. He knows few details about her as yet, beyond the shining, platinum-haired grandeur of her seeming transcendence of everyday life. He feels he might kill, however, if this were necessary to bag himself a ring-side seat from which to watch her upcoming emergence into being.

The second character will be a creature of his unrealisable desire to live life with an intensity flavoured by self-destruction. He names this character Scorpio, after his own Moon sign (a water sign, feminine and fixed), though as yet he knows even fewer details about Scorpio than about the Platinum Raven.

Subsidiary to those two, there will then be a creature of his desire to wreak vengeance where deserved. Most games have several such characters, after all—but *The Platinum Raven* will have the modest total of one, and Jaymi names him Amber. Amber will be off-centre, to say the least. But only the off-centre can supply a point of view that has any real interest, he reflects: the norm backs itself up without doing anything. Yes… Oh, and Amber will also be charming and lethal.

So there they are, it seems—his first three sexy Beasts!

Amber.

The Platinum Raven.

Scorpio.

As yet, he knows little more about them than their names. But he catches furtive whispers as their silhouettes scurry past—shadows on the gauze screens hung across his ballroom, flicking indistinct across the scrims and the curtains, red-lit and purple-lit behind where he sleeps, and their giggles and their shushing hidden just around the corner at the end of the corridor, far down there (though they've not dared peep around the plaster of the wall to find Jaymi with their eyes, so they don't know what he looks like, not quite yet)!

7 DEVELOPMENT AND BASICS IN THE AVENUE OF THE STARS TOWER

Bang Dead Games' headquarters is on Avenue of the Stars, at around Constellation Boulevard, thirty-something storeys up in the sky above Century City.

In an office halfway along the eastern curve of the building sits a man with his feet on the desk, sunk in thought, his empty gaze shooting through the window and across seven miles of heat-haze to the Downtown skyscrapers. He is in his late thirties, white, between stocky and fat, wearing long baggy shorts, white sneakers and a T-shirt with a football printed on it; his hair is an average brown and short all over, above a forgettable face with a ready-to-grin mouth that's chewing gum.

Dud Guy is employed here at Bang Dead, as Head of Games Development.

He reaches forward to press a button on his desk phone and speaks towards it, "Ria, get me a cup of tea." The accent is English, basic down-to-earth London. After a moment, a woman enters and leaves a steaming mug in front of him. "Thanks darling. And clean up those dirty mugs in the corner, there's a pet."

He presses another button on his phone and waits for an answer, as Ria sets off down the length of the room towards a sofa and an armchair that flank a coffee-table where three used mugs await her. While the phone rings at the other end of the line, Dud's vacant stare rests on two framed posters on the wall: one depicting himself accepting an honour at a games industry awards show; and the other showing him with a look of triumph, giving a double thumbs-up sign in a warehouse filled to the ceiling with shelves of new games consoles in their manufacturers' boxes. After several unanswered rings, his facial expression remains neutral, but his hand slams down onto the desk, with a violence that's casual but extreme enough to cause Ria to jump at the far end of the room.

At last the phone is picked up at the other end. A woman's voice on speaker-phone says "Hallo Dud."

"Morning Ashley. Couple of questions for you." He gestures at Ria, for her to leave the room and close the door. "Hold on," he says into the phone, then drums his fingers on the desk until Ria has disappeared, before he resumes speaking. "Question one. Since our joy-ride with the drone, I've heard more reports of Jaymi putting out enquiries about the availability of certain personnel. Must be in connection with his own projects. Have you heard anything along those lines, on the hardware side?"

"No, but I'll keep my ears open," replies Ashley. "That drone jaunt was super fun. Can we do it again, please?"

"I would enjoy it," grins Dud. "But it might make him call the cops or something, so we'd better cool it."

"D'you think he knows it was us?"

"He may suspect. So keep your lug-holes open for any word of him asking about drones. But we need to look out for him trying to head-hunt from us. He's a competitor now, and don't you underestimate him. He knows how we work. Alright, question two: *Ain'tTheyFreaky!*'s hardware. What's the current guess on when the server farm by LAX will be ready for action? Reality time, please. No optimism—just the basics."

8 INFRASTRUCTURE AND STRESS-BALLS IN THE AVENUE OF THE STARS TOWER

Seated in her office at the north corner of the same building, gazing through the window up Avenue of the Stars and over the intervening towers towards the Los Angeles Country Club, is a crisply-presented woman, white and in her early forties, wearing a black business jacket over an open-necked navy-blue shirt, her coiffed blonde hair making a sharp contrast with the dark-grey metal safe positioned behind her desk.

"My best estimate? Two weeks," she replies, consulting her computer monitor. "Getting clearance for construction under a flight-path beside an airport is a slow process." Near the desk-phone itself are two small navy-blue stress-balls, of the sort provided at the start of compulsory training days for office staff, manufactured from the kind of rubbery material that expands back out to its original sphere after being compressed, each ball featuring the instruction "THINK" printed on its surface. Observing, with a frown, that the crisp white of those capital letters has accumulated a thick layer of dust, Ashley touches the fingers of her right hand onto her tongue as she continues to listen to Dud; then she installs the handset between her left ear and a raised left shoulder, allowing her newly-freed left hand to pick up one of the stress-balls and hold it steady while her right hand can subject the ball to a vigorous wiping.

Ashley Tweke is employed as Bang Dead's in-house head of IT infrastructure. Her many responsibilities include the company's server farms, which it owns and operates.

"It's all under control," she says, "it won't delay the game release—" and she falls silent as her boss resumes talking at her down the line, while she raises her glasses onto her forehead and peers short-sightedly at the stress-ball.

The vigorous wiping was doubtless a good idea in theory, but her frown deepens as she sees it has achieved little more than to smear the dust across the width of the five capitals, leaving them even dirtier than they looked a moment ago. The situation deteriorates further, when the stress-ball slips out of her hand and bounces away over her desk. She launches her arm forward to pursue the ball before it goes scudding across the office, and the telephone handset drops out from between her ear and her shoulder, falling to the floor.

"Ashley?" says Dud's electronic voice from carpet-level. "What's happening? *Ashley*, are you there?"

Stressed, she gives up on pursuing the stress-ball and stoops for the handset instead—remembering, at least, to be careful not to bash her head on anything as she sits up again. "*Yes*, I'm here. And I'm fine, thank you for asking. I'm sorry, do carry on."

9 JAYMI CREATES AMBER'S CODE

Jaymi sips his cherry schnapps on ice, puts it down beside him with a clink of glass on the flagstones of his study terrace, and claps his hands together.

He gazes around him, through the colours and cool of the evening sky, then pauses at the sound of some unidentified little beast whose call is emanating from somewhere down in the foliage of Laurel Canyon. What can it be? No dog or cat, but a wilder thing. Raccoon? Opossum? Skunk? Fox?

It chuckles up a guttural gibber for a few seconds, then subsides into watchful silence, hidden out there in the undergrowth—awaiting whatever Jaymi creates, as if to judge him against some obscure set of harshly mocking standards.

Narrowing his eyes at the keyboard, he consults the general sketch of Amber in his design for *The Platinum Raven*. It reads: "The Platinum Raven's conspirator, in this tower in the mountains, is named Amber, whose infernal nature and allure reflect the fact that he just happens to be the continuation of Rutger Hauer's psychopathic character in the film *The Hitcher*."

Well, OK then. Bring it on!

With that sort of origin, this should be a good start—a character who'll enable Jaymi to exact a smattering of vengeance, wherever it may be called for in the game. Yes, this Amber will be well equipped to do a little dirty work for him, targeting whoever deserves it!

As he gears up to create this brand-new creature, triggering it from a point of singularity in zero-scented vacuum, out into one-scented being and presence, Jaymi feels as if he's installing himself behind a complex bank of electronic controls comprising dozens of dials, switches, buttons, parallel rows of faders and small red or green lights set into matt or shiny surfaces of black metal and plastic. These imaginary decks, looming up before him on the terrace, are way bigger and more powerful than just the laptop computer sitting in front of him running games-programming software. That well-worn little keyboard is merely plugged into an extension lead coiling into the house behind him; whereas these darker Amber controls feel as if they are plugged into the unfathomable voltage of the expanse of Los Angeles ahead, spreading its electrical vastness in grid-lines of yellow and white through the night to the haze of the far horizon.

As he watches, the shadowy controls seem to hang in semi-transparent array over the lower third of the cityscape, while this new Beast's first sparks of independent being and volition appear in the grain of the upper two-thirds. The elements of him flicker up, each new one joining those that came before, easing into its appointed position of harmony or disruption, until an interlocking array of Amber code leaps in vaunting stabs of light and sound, coalescing into an ever-enriching symphonic machinery.

The ones and zeroes swirl and proliferate in his laptop, like cells suspended in fluid between two glass slides under a microscope. Almost as if already aware of its creator, and sensing its own origins in his urge for vengeance on all that's epitomised in *Ain't They Freaky!*, Amber's code appears to spin and coil back up towards Jaymi, sealed and constrained only by the plastic surface of the screen...

Jaymi recoils for a second. Then he grins.

10 VISUALS AND LAUGHTER IN THE SUNSET BOULEVARD BUILDING

Bang Dead Games' secondary premises are in an anonymous building on Sunset Boulevard, at around North Cahuenga Boulevard, in Hollywood.

Covering the walls of one spacious office at the back of the building are prints of artwork from numerous video games, interspersed with sport-themed posters. On the absent occupant's desk are three high-end computer monitors displaying an array of visual elements from further games: dirty interiors of bunkers, alongside radiant exteriors of a green hillside; a summary of assets and scores at the bottom of the screen; and smaller software windows showing details of lighting, reflections on water, and characters' facial expressions. Crowded around the bases of the monitors are many plastic figurines of cartoon characters, a good few of them manufactured so as to incorporate textual elements intended to convey an all-purpose heart-warmingness.

A loud laugh erupts from down the corridor. Footsteps approach, then a woman breezes in, with a reassuring smile on an open face, black and in her late twenties, dressed in sporty high-street fashion.

Kelly Kandy is employed as an in-house senior visual designer.

Pressing a button on her desk phone, she gazes through the window, at air vents on flat roofs in early-evening light. "Hi Kelly," says a voice at the other end.

"Hey Herb. I need food," she says. "Wanna go across the street and eat? We need to celebrate our *Ain't They Freaky!* progress—you and me are gonna be *rich*, boy! That thing is bigger than anything we worked on when Jaymi was here. It's gonna be massive! Have you realised how massive? I don't think you have, so I'm gonna drag you into that restaurant and shout at you about how super-massive that game is gonna be. So let's go eat and drink—right now, yeah?"

"You mean the fancy-food place, opposite? I've never been there."

"Never too late to start eating healthily, Herb. There are other options than burgers and chips and soda-pop, you may have heard. So, wanna go?"

"Oh, well … OK then."

"Good, I'll come get you in five."

11 CODING AND KHAKI IN THE SUNSET BOULEVARD BUILDING

Five minutes later, Kelly heads down the corridor. Nearing the open office door ahead, she hears a slurping noise, and enters the room to see that the guy at the desk behind two computer monitors is intent on sucking up the last of a fizzy drink through a straw. Thick glasses sit on his pale brown face, magnifying his stare into a fish-eyed blink. He is plump and of indeterminate age, wearing a short-sleeved plaid shirt and khaki trousers.

Herb Shrim is employed as an in-house senior programmer.

"Come on, it's the end of the day," says Kelly. "Forget all that, you can do it tomorrow."

And on that basis, ten minutes later, they have walked to the restaurant across the street, and are being seated by a head waiter.

They order food, then Herb holds the wine menu close to his face and peers at it. "Er, could we have a bottle of this, please, the Chateau Lafite?" he asks. The waiter nods and steps away.

Kelly is impressed. "You go! Awesome-sauce."

The waiter returns, uncorks the wine, pours a little into Herb's glass and waits.

Herb stares at the glass for a few moments, then looks up blankly and asks the waiter if he might be able to have a full glass.

Kelly laughs like a drain. "You're meant to taste it first, Herb. As the most important man at the table."

Herb twigs. "Hey, I don't know what to do in these places," he says, pushing his thick glasses up his stubby nose, and downs the taster in one shot. "Do I look like a fancy-food kind of a guy?"

12 JAYMI CREATES AMBER'S APPEARANCE

Seated at his desk, Jaymi consults the notes he's been hammering out over the last day or so for *The Platinum Raven*, and checks his sketch for Amber's visuals. Its first description of Amber's physical appearance reads: "[…] the man at the far right-hand end of the bar. He is blond and attractive, his face alive with self-contained perceptiveness. The wide-set fluidity of humour in his eyes makes one think of Rutger Hauer in the desert: well-equipped, through ready charm, to hitch a lift."

OK then—here he comes.

And straight away, there is something about him. It's a quality that can't quite be identified, until it clicks and is formulated in the mind of the observer; whereupon it can never be forgotten. It seems innocent enough, too, at first—though it can start to feel otherwise upon reflection. And what is this quality? Simply that it's impossible to imagine him with any live siblings, or any live children, or ever having had any live parents: it's as if he was born as he is, fully formed, and will remain the same forever.

Anyone who feels disturbed by this subtle quality in Amber will deserve to feel so.

He was conceived of, ahead of time, as being subsidiary to the Platinum Raven and Scorpio. Along with these arising visuals, however, it's clear he has scant enthusiasm for any such status. With every glyph Jaymi adds to this code, he can feel a sort of metallic muscularity coming straight through the keyboard, up his fingers, through his hands, through his wrists and up his arms while he programs, of a kind he has never felt emanating from any code before. It's clear already that Amber harbours traits best described as ungovernable. At moments, almost unprogrammable. But Jaymi perseveres in wrestling him into line, into form, so he will behave like a creature—not like a creator, for that role is occupied, thank you.

Looking in through Amber's cool blue eyes on his laptop screen, he has the sense of a dark submarine beneath the surface. In a human, that submarine might have suggested some great damage inside, either physical or emotional or both. This is not quite a human, however, despite looking just like one: it is Jaymi's first Beast.

Added to which, just behind Amber's lips there's an infrequent fluid smile that's like a knife being held against the pulse of somebody's neck.

Oh, yes…

13 JAYMI'S GAMES *THE IMAGINATION THIEF* AND *THE HOST IN THE ATTIC*

Confidential though *The Platinum Raven* is, some awareness of it continues to seep out along certain tendrils of the industry grapevine. Jaymi has avoided approaching any actual employee of Bang Dead, and the freelance talents he has hired have all signed non-disclosure agreements with him, of course. But from the fragments of industry chatter he has caught, he is pretty sure Dud and his fellow Dreary Ones have pooled enough information to know the identities of many of those talents—from whose known specialities Dud will have been able to extrapolate a rough list of what creative elements Jaymi's project must involve, in terms of artwork, user interfaces, story-line methodologies, audio design and the rest of it.

To those mainstream eyes at Bang Dead, this list of creative talent may well look a bit strange in its balance. In the context of the talent's known calibre, many of the Dreary Ones will know enough to find the list quite curiosity-whetting, too.

A few of them will even know enough to find it troubling. Why, Dud himself will be among these few, most likely. Troubling, because they'll know enough to sense this game may just be a game-changer.

For these are the folks whose instinctive use of the top-flight creative talent at their disposal is to put it to work building a close variation of the most leadenly guyish first-person shooter games already on the market—so expensive in their polish, with all the potential of that polish harnessed to serve content whose intellect and emotions are so unevolved. But much worse than that, these are the folks responsible for *Ain't They Freaky!*.

Against this warming backdrop of trust and originality, Jaymi's work on the early stages of *The Platinum Raven* proceeds well. In fact, he has found himself dealing with so much raw material that he's even had to start sketching out two further games in order to find homes for it. These he has named *The Imagination Thief* and *The Host in the Attic*. They are both at earlier stages of development as yet, but the very process of naming them has clarified something essential about the alchemy of all three titles: through these solo sessions of hammering away in this crucible of a study here on Electra Drive, he is creating high-voltage Beasts through which to conjure up various kinds of viscerality he wouldn't be able to inflict in meatspace. After all, if a human is aiming to make any worldly progress, then much of their own viscerality will tend to need concealment ... but a Beast's won't.

Most progress has been made on *The Platinum Raven*, though, where his design for Amber is coming into fastest definition. On the simplest level, this character embodies Jaymi's urge to respond to the Dreary Ones with fitting vengeance for all the hatred and closed-mindedness that'll be fomented by their blockbuster tabloid-news game. Yet even at his most oppositional, it looks as if Amber will also evoke a flicker of sympathy, alongside the awe. Day by day, Jaymi can feel an increase in his own emotional investment in him, as a creator towards his creation.

OK, let's face it: Jaymi is starting to develop a crush on Amber.

This Beast's willpower is so strong, though. Might he therefore challenge his creator, asserting a selfhood all his own?

Well, yes, there is a degree of danger here. Amber's personality does have its own volition. It may take off in strange directions. Or swoop around at any moment, like a goose's neck, and target Jaymi in sensualised self-damage...

Ah, it's a dangerous business, this Beast-building—but it has to be done, and it seems he's the man for the job.

Throughout his dark hammering at the keyboard, deep into the night of his creating Amber out of nothing, Jaymi has a gathering sense that this is the calm before a thunderstorm.

Shutting his eyes, he thinks hard, trying to identify what storm he can be sensing...

He cannot tell, for the moment. But the more he develops his game, the more confident he is that it will expand into the unexplored potential of the video game as an artistic medium: as a response to the world, his game will be as complex and as sublimated as anything found in film or literature. Its characters will be at the opposite end of the scale from those designed-by-committee "characters" whom Jaymi has too often seen being designed (by committees) while he was sitting in some conference room, groaning inside himself at the committee-members' stiff, fearful, knee-jerk adherence to society's stalest and most creatively retarded concepts of what men and women could be and should be.

Yes; he was quite the innocent when he first came to L.A. What misbelief there was in him then, that the Dreary Ones were not, in fact, as dreary as their very name tries to warn one they are! That misbelief caused him to misread numerous small interactions over the course of his career in the company, construing many managers' motivations as being so much more evolved than he now sees they were.

Yet how valuable that innocence also was—and still is. For he continues to harbour its essence, and his nature is such that he will retain that essence for life. It cannot and will not be degraded in him. This is the simple secret sauce in his mission to re-invigorate the medium and the industry. Sure, it's a tall order; it's dirty work, frankly. But it would seem to fall to him—and here he is, doing it! Approaching the job at hand, with a bit of the old right-foot-left-foot-right-foot technique.

On the terrace of his promontory here on Electra Drive, he raises his glass to the night, takes a sip, and scans the grid of lights ahead, above which he feels he is floating.

"Are you ready for this?" he asks L.A. aloud.

A siren wails, far across the city.

14 JAYMI INCARNATES AMBER (*FIRST DOORWAY OF NO RETURN*)

Jaymi shuts and locks the doors that lead outside to his middle-storey terrace, walks back across his study and sits down again in front of the array of IT hardware spread across his desk. Returning his attention to the main monitor, he jumps in shock to see something he's certain he didn't put on screen before he got up from his chair: Amber's handsome and magnificently strong physiognomy in wide close-up, staring out through the glass ... and seeing straight into his maker.

Hooking onto Jaymi's desires, Amber addresses a specific suggestion at him with fluent articulacy, not in spoken words but using that wide fluidity of intelligence and humour in his eyes.

This suggestion, delivered with as charismatic a power as Jaymi has ever seen in anybody, is that Amber himself squeeze out into meat-space through this monitor, then stand up in the flesh, right here in Jaymi's study, and then channel Jaymi in dealing with the Dreary Ones in whatever way Jaymi may wish to see them squirm... Does Jaymi doubt Amber would be effective in dealing with them in real life?

Jaymi has to admit he does not doubt it.

His admission is registered by the eyes on screen. *Well*, they reply, then this result can be Jaymi's! Think of the earthly power it would give him—*if* Jaymi will just be so kind as to let Amber squeeze loose into physical reality? Only Jaymi can make a Beast clamber out into meat-space, like this. Only Jaymi, when designing the Beast who will clamber! No gamer in future—just Jaymi, right now. So will he play, pretty-please?... *Yes he will*, pretty-thanks! Yes he will play Amber's game, here and now, without a doubt.

Jaymi can certainly picture what power he himself will gain by introducing Amber's strength and subversion into the lives of Bang Dead's personnel. What a challenge, what sabotage, what loosening of deadweight by live voltage could thereby be achieved ... and at this, he feels a forward surge of anger and ambition rising up, like a drumbeat of clattering momentum!

Something has just changed, within the last minute.

For even if Jaymi were next to refuse Amber's offer—and he *can* still do this, he reminds himself—yet somehow his life from now on will not be able to stay as it has been. From here on, nothing will be able to quiet that drumbeat...

So *this* was the oncoming thunderstorm he was sensing.

He gets up, paces over to the locked door and looks out at the empty sun-beds on his terrace.

One thing seems clear, just from looking at that face on screen: if Jaymi does consent to Amber's release, then this Beast will indeed be effective in terrorising the Dreary Ones in their flesh and blood.

Amber's suggestion, therefore, is a tempting offer.

So, *so* tempting, in fact—oh yes indeed.

Still, there does remain the option for him to turn back from this road. He doesn't have to accede in releasing his Beast into meat-space. If Jaymi refrains from releasing him, then Amber will *not* run wild but will instead remain contained within *The Platinum Raven*: this is just a truth, and it's a simple one.

Jaymi's in control here. He's still the boss. He really is.

But as he returns to the seat at the monitor, looking down at the floor while he sits, and then starts raising his gaze back towards Amber's face in close-up again, as he must, Jaymi already senses that in reality, despite the unknown dangers involved, he will be power-less against that offer being conveyed to him with such flickers of animal humour and intelligence in those wide-set eyes.

And powerless he is.

For as soon as he aims the glint in his own eyes back at the Beast on screen, such an ecstatic charge of sweet dark vengeance spreads through him, that he feels his bloodstream sing.

So here it comes at last, then, the instant of dark pleasure, when one particular *tap* of Jaymi's right index-finger upon the "Enter" key on his keyboard (after the myriad similar-sounding taps at the same key he has made over the months) just happens to be *the* tap … that releases Amber, out from the confines of his designs for *The Platinum Raven*, and into life.

Tap!

There it was, a quiet convulsion. That one demure little key-tap just pushed Jaymi across an invisible threshold, from the ordinary world into another one that he's already sensing may be darker and brighter than he bargained for.

And now it hits home, with something like the queasy feeling in a swimmer when they're dragged sideways by an unexpected tide: this single key-stroke has dropped him somewhere he cannot retreat from. There is no way but forwards, into a flight he can't predict.

Amber's eyes on screen close for the first time, with a smile.

A moment's stillness in the study.

Then a low susurration and chatter speckles up behind Jaymi, as of archetypes peeping out from hiding-places tucked behind the fabric of reality, ripping through that fabric and emerging through fissures in the air around the room, to reveal that every familiar 3D object is in reality just a curtain beyond which they've been hovering throughout his life, peering in at him. The whole study scene splits open as if it's a painting cut by a knife-blade, while the air vibrates and hisses—and he catapults himself backwards into a corner, flesh tingling, as he watches Amber slither and squeeze out into meat-space, through the monitor, like a giant blond serpent-spider.

PART II

"GAL SCORE", EVELYN'S CREATION, AND THE STALKING OF THE DREARY ONES

15   AMBER INCARNATE IN THE HOUSE ON ELECTRA DRIVE

This corporeal Amber, standing in a human frame here in Jaymi's house, is brutal, in a literal sense. Although he's clothed and ready to function in society as a somewhat dangerous-looking person, Jaymi knows very well that this is an animal of a kind—a human animal in meat-space, not artwork in a game. Those muscular bare arms on him are made of flesh. His wide-set eyes are staring straight into his maker's with what looks like shrewd intelligence and a flicker of humour beneath the surface. And now his face is tilting down from within, while his eyes continue to look at Jaymi's eyes, like the downward tilt of a cheetah's gaze just before it springs.

Jaymi flicks his attention away from Amber's face, then masters himself, masking his alarm to the extent of slipping his hands into his pockets. He affects leisure in his movements, as he wanders to the window and peers out—registering absolutely nothing beyond the glass, while his mind is busy wrestling his terror to the ground and pressing it into submission.

It occurs to him that things have just changed in a fundamental way. However he may choose to conduct himself with Amber in a moment or two, as he'll have to, nothing will be the same from here on—because *a Beast from one of his own games is standing right behind him*, so dangerous and beautiful, here in his own house.

A weapon!

It's clear, too, that Amber is much the physically stronger of them both.

From where that Beast is standing, there comes a quiet scratching, thrice, which Jaymi guesses is the sound of Amber's fingernails running over the flesh of his opposite forearm ... and Jaymi's own flesh runs hot and cold at once.

OK, the only thing to do is to brazen this out—act with decisiveness, then let it flow. So he turns, with a movement of easy confidence, to face Amber, and the very next sound is his own voice addressing his Beast. He listens to himself with amazement, to hear the words of one who sounds so authoritative, so sure of what he's doing: "Amber, welcome. Here is your mission. It is vengeance, in the face of dreariness, laziness and smallness. In the wake of your vengeance will come transcendence and fierce beauty. You will see that there are lies, which I'll send you in pursuit of like a wolf. You will clean those lies away, so my truth can take their place. You'll be lighting up and lifting up the world, by an inch or two at least. Do you understand?"

Amber's nod is sharp-eyed, simple and serious.

"Do you accept this mission?"

"Yes I do," states the Beast.

Thus does Jaymi Peek find himself giving instructions to a personification of his own darkest, righteous violence—the first time he's met it in the flesh.

How natural it felt, to issue the instruction.

No; it felt more than natural.

It felt irresistible!

He has an uncomfortable feeling he has just committed himself to a grand, elemental conflict of some kind.

16 THE HOLLYWOOD CAFÉ ON CAHUENGA BOULEVARD

Turning off the street into the parking-lot behind the café, Jaymi nods to himself in recognition of a particular car he can see parked ahead.

The Hollywood café, as it's known, is a slick and airy eatery on North Cahuenga Boulevard frequented by a range of games industry personnel, mostly from the non-consumer-facing half of the business. Passing through its sizeable interior at some point during any given week, there are games developers, both independent and from mainstream companies; audio people, from composers to recording engineers; visual designers; testers; the odd investor, whose status as such will often tend to be discreetly worn; and programmers.

It's this last category of customer without whom no lines of code would be written and no pixels would light up any screens. Jaymi locks his car and heads across the lot, recalling how one meeting here resulted in his spear-heading an unusual trip, whereby he and three other selected developers went out of town for a three-day weekend of in-depth brainstorming, staying up on Mulholland Highway somewhere above Malibu, in a self-contained lodge. Sequestered in this temporary hothouse setting, with all their meals brisk and ordered-in, and with the Internet blocked by mutual agreement, their work achieved a focus and a productivity rarely attained in normal work environments. And at one moment during that weekend, as he contemplated the four of them around the room, Jaymi was struck by how out of place any other developer would have felt here, if they hadn't been one of the few in the independent community who are also able, themselves, to write the code at a serious level for their own projects.

The man he has arranged to meet here today does little other than hardcore programming. This is Bang Dead's in-house star, the legendary Herb Shrim, for whom an unbroken thirty-six-hour session of coding is said to be a regular occurrence in his Westwood Village home—each such marathon presumably followed by a square-eyed, glassy-gazed stagger down the bedroom corridor into a twelve-hour, symbol-swirling, comatose collapse. Jaymi and Herb fixed this casual catch-up a couple of weeks ago, to keep in touch; it will be the first time they've met since they were colleagues at Bang Dead.

It will also be an opportunity to verify that Herb's home address is still unchanged from that time, when Jaymi had access to the list of addresses for his immediate colleagues. In light of Amber's new liberation, this may become information of interest.

Jaymi scans the tables inside, locates Herb and navigates the café to join him, half-stopping for a quick word with a few people along the way. He reaches Herb, they say hallo and Jaymi sits.

They exchange a few items of bland news each, including Jaymi's casual mention of a drone that recently flew up to his very own terrace.

"Weird," says Herb. "Who would do that?"

"It may have been prospective burglars, casing the joint—or more likely some rich kid who's just been given an expensive new toy."

"What will they think of next?" asks Herb, shaking his head, his face inscrutable.

Now to steer the chat towards the subject of home locations. "It's pretty peaceful, though, Mount Olympus," says Jaymi.

"Great location."

"It's pretty good. You still in that same apartment in Westwood?"

"Yeah. I hate moving home so much, I guess I'll probably die there."

Well, that was easy! "How's Bang Dead these days?"

"Oh, same as ever," shrugs Herb. "Though there is hot news: tomorrow we'll be unveiling the first of a bunch of different Newsfeeds. Now *these* are gonna be massive. Look out for our announcement tomorrow—you'll see it mentioned somewhere, for sure. I designed the core of the Newsfeeds, plus the architecture of how they'll interact after they've all been released."

Jaymi knows enough about Bang Dead to recognise what a further testament it is to Herb's expertise, that the company entrusted him with something as big as what he's just described, on top of his other responsibilities. And a wild thought arises: if Jaymi gets to the point of hiring permanent staff, is it conceivable he may, one day, poach Herb from Dud? For all his air of inertia, Herb is a gun-for-hire with no real attachment to Bang Dead, who would work for whoever could afford him and treated him right. And Herb's chops would make no small contribution to Jaymi's propelling his own truth out into the world, at the scale it deserves...

In light of these musings, Jaymi feels a softening in the enmity he harbours towards Herb for being lead programmer on the vile *Ain't They Freaky!*. The somewhat cryptic term Herb just uttered, "Newsfeeds", sounds as if it's describing something more intelligent than *that* great monstrosity, at least—and mercifully separate from it.

"I should add that the Newsfeeds will constitute the main user interface in *Ain't They Freaky!*," says Herb.

Ah. Jaymi's internal softening comes to an end.

Amber will still be visiting Herb, no question about it.

17 THE "GAL SCORE: BABE OR GROSS?" NEWSFEED

Looking online next morning, Jaymi sees it is just as Herb promised. Numerous sources announce that today Bang Dead has quietly rolled out a massive free offering to consumers everywhere. It's the first major plank of *Ain't They Freaky!*, and the company promises it'll be a popular hit: it's the "Gal Score: Babe or Gross?" Newsfeed!

This is a constant stream of images, videos or pieces of text uploaded from around the world, presenting individual women, who are rated for attractiveness by any member of the public using *Ain't They Freaky!*'s Freakometer, from a highest score of 10 for Babest, down to a lowest score of 1 for Grossest.

Jaymi lets his gaze wander up and down this newsfeed stream, where new posts are popping up every few seconds, every one of them soon receiving scores and comments from multiple sources.

He reads a few posts, for half a minute or so.

Then he shuts off the Newsfeed, looks away from the screen and closes his eyes.

A wave of disgusted weariness breaks in him, with the intimation of a lifetime's sadness that this is the kind of thing most humans genuinely want to see, to do, to buy, to think about, and even to use up their lives for—and always will be. The ugliness and meanness of what *Ain't They Freaky!* represents feel like nothing less than an assault, going far beyond the Dreary Ones' hostility towards him in particular.

What gigantic exhaustion!

What shortfall from all our potentials.

And what lovely freedom and ease there could have been, in some potential world that is not the one around him.

But right behind the backwash of that sluggish wave, a brainwave flickers up bright: the best way to stay sane and withstand the assault will be to create something inspired in response. To a Newsfeed created by the Dreary Ones, his answer will be a proactive and original creation mined from his own humanity.

Contemplating a world where the likes of *Ain't They Freaky!* will always reign commercially supreme, it's a challenge to identify how to use his capacities in this way. But by degrees, the road forward becomes apparent.

When his own games reach their commercial release, they will house his responses to the world, integrated and balanced. But until then, while he's still game-building, he will be breaking his responses down into component parts. Pursuant to this, he will follow up on Amber by creating further in-game Beasts. Then, as with Amber, he will incarnate them too, and send them out into the world as their own creatures—to interact in meat-space. Once out there, they will be extensions of himself, embodying aspects of him. They will also flesh out his reactions to everything that *Ain't They Freaky!* may reveal in its players.

Whatever parts of himself he embodies in those incarnated Beasts will then be enriched by the Beasts' own internal development, which will occur through their taking their own actions with their own volition, out here in real life.

And when he reaches the point of sealing the Beasts up into his three games again, ready for commercial release, then the games will reap the benefit of all those enrichments—each such enrichment fostered by his having delegated the labour of experience to the belly of a Beast whose maturation will thus flow back into Jaymi's own output.

Furthermore, each successive Beast will contribute to the arc of Jaymi's own internal journey here on Electra Drive—the journey of his developing ability as a games creator unfettered by corporate interference. From each Beast to the next, he will utilise the same ingredients of progression and direction that he'd have been obliged to incorporate into any Bang Dead development process, but this time assembled according to his own delirious truth and leveraged at his own more authentic angles: starting with a Ghost (functioning as a Hook), he will progress to an Inciting Event, then a First Doorway of No Return, then a First Pinch Point, then a Midpoint, then a Second Pinch Point, then a Second Doorway of No Return, and so to a Climax, all capped and closed off by a Resolution.

A music of his own self!

Glints in his own eyes, rendered into flesh…

A few minutes later, he opens his programming software. He creates a blank new project file, and names it "Second Beast".

Who will this second one be?

Well, let's see. His previous creation, Amber, is an alluring Beast. And he was authentically triggered by external provocation, birthed out of Jaymi's need to wreak vengeance where deserved.

However, it has to be admitted Amber was also a creature of somewhat untextured gesturalness, as well as negativity. True, his facial appearance benefited from good casting—Rutger Hauer in *Hitcher* mode. But this, too, was an issue in itself: for it hardly constituted original creation, did it? It was an off-the-peg JPEG, to be nakedly frank. A low-hanging marzipan fruit, sweet to taste but of little nutrition; a sample in a music track, dropped in with savvy and impeccable respect but also with a low-crouching modicum of laziness; or a pop-tart reaction of flashy derivation, but masquerading as ore that was hammered out from Jaymi's deeps by the clinking of a cursor before being winched up, blinking, onto a screen of blank white.

Moreover, Jaymi's full response to Bang Dead Games is not expressed in Amber alone. For greater balance, richness and truth, perhaps a more benign, more human, more humane creation is needed, so as to complement the first one's harsh edges?

Hmm. Maybe Amber didn't quite add up to the sermon on the mount, after all. Maybe he's a rung upon a ladder.

So again, who will this second Beast be?

Someone who'll embody not just Jaymi's pointed response to the "Gal Score: Babe or Gross?" Newsfeed, but something wider—his whole instinctive urge for ease and freedom, in the face of the sheer authoritarian rigidity he can feel spurting out at him from every glyph and pixel of *Ain'tTheyFreaky!*.

OK. Who else is slated to appear in *The Platinum Raven*? Jaymi's early-stage design for that game's world includes two characters who might be candidates for a second incarnation—the Platinum Raven and Scorpio—but neither of these feels light enough to complement Amber. Who, then?

He brightens to recall that *The Platinum Raven* is not the only game he has sketched out. There is also *The Imagination Thief*, whose entire game-world is metafictionally contained within the surrounding world of *The Host in the Attic*. He has so far begun designing only three of *The Imagination Thief*'s many characters, named Evelyn, Shigem and Kim … and while he pictures this trio, barely yet picturable as they are, Evelyn raises her plucky little hand and waves it back at him.

He nods in reply, realising that this is his first reactive communication with her. Though still inchoate, she's already equipped with quite some awareness and volition of her own, it seems.

Yes, now that he considers her, Evelyn does have the lightness to complement Amber. She may even have the strength to stand up to him, too—not by dint of force, but rather by dint of joy, if that makes sense?

Of course it does.

He consults the general sketch of her in his design for *The Imagination Thief*, then polishes it, so it reads: "Evelyn Carmello is a driver, who opens social doors. She is sunny, centred, straightforward and kind, but also sassy, tough and street-smart. Joyously functional in the real world, she's a dirty-sexy party-girl, although that scene is now in her recent past."

Well, OK then. Bring it on!

Jaymi thinks for a moment longer, then he renames this new project "Evelyn"…

So here comes a new Beast, born into beauty and complexity, a creature of his own love and pain.

Regrettable that Evelyn's sunny cool freedom should be forced to look at and tangle with so ugly a counterbalance as the "Gal Score: Babe or Gross?" Newsfeed. So boring the worries and so tight the limitations in such a sucking-out of life! Jaymi is sure Evelyn would have things otherwise.

That counterbalance would seem, however, to be compulsory.

18 JAYMI CREATES EVELYN'S CODE

Turning off Melrose Avenue into an underground car-park, Jaymi lowers the window and reaches out to enter a number into the keypad. The gate rises in front of him. One storey down, he makes a much-practised curve between blue and green columns, and glides to a halt in an empty space whose concrete surface bears the painted legend "EC1 Director".

EC1 Digital's first, basic premises were in a simple residential apartment on Fountain Avenue, at around North Sierra Bonita Avenue. This was on the south side of Fountain, it should be noted, which landed the company a few metres inside the city of West Hollywood—in contrast with the north side of Fountain, where the properties found themselves located a few metres inside the much larger and less cosy jurisdiction of the city of Los Angeles.

Such multiple bureaucracies across this strange metropolis, whose grid of almost identical-looking palm-lined streets are invisibly fractured by the limits of various such incorporated cities and unincorporated areas, in a patchwork of jurisdictions bearing no relation to daily life, yet perpetuated by map-makers with avid precision and an array of ambiguously-allocated pastel hues.

No ambiguity about them for a fledgling corporation, though, from whose viewpoint these pastels constitute very different flavours of regulation. But when the happy moment came for Jaymi to plough his first financial jackpot back into the company's first upscaling of premises last year, then EC1 Digital moved to its subsequent and current home in this palatially glassy complex at the far opposite and far shinier end of that same city of West Hollywood—right here on the tail end of Melrose Avenue, just four or five blocks shy of the city of Beverly Hills.

Today he has driven into this weekend-quiet office suite, telling nobody that he's doing so, in order to create a second Beast.

Alone in his office with the door shut, he fires up his software. It obeys him by opening up a blank template … and in doing so, its obedience has ushered him as far as it can. Beyond this point, it can help no further, except by hosting whatever language he may come up with. It's all up to him now, sitting here alone, to spin extravagance and magic from the fabric of nothing—and then to make this magic dance.

What if he should fail?

Then again, what would failure be? It's not a bad question, because it'll establish what the stakes are. (Er, "thanks for the info!" That's a breakthrough, Captain Obvious.)

Well, let's see. "Failure" won't *necessarily* mean failing to stop *Ain't They Freaky!*, because this monstrosity is pretty much unstoppable in practical terms, and in any case he's already decided to devote his energy to answering it with creations of his own.

So, would "failure" mean failing to achieve these creations of his own—his three games, *The Imagination Thief*, *The Platinum Raven* and *The Host in the Attic*? Yes. But beyond that, it would mean failing to turn the world's head back towards true art, true sugar, true juice.

Truth. And beauty in truth.

His upcoming journey will take aim at degraded human intercourse, to improve the world in the way art improves it.

That's the mission.

Anyway, fuck this talk of failure, because it doesn't apply to Jaymi. So just bring it on, the blankest template in the world! Bring it on, baby—go ahead, and Jaymi-boy will make that empty blankness sing a dance you've never seen, and dance a song you've never heard! Oh, you wanna play cards? Sure, Jaymi-boy will play cards—watch him now.

On a sudden whim he gets up, swoops across the room to a well-stocked drinks cabinet, cogitates upon the bottles, pours a generous Tia Maria on ice, and returns to his desk. He savours a long sip, puts the glass back down by the keyboard, then claps his hands together. He lets his eyes close for a moment, summons up the feeling of Evelyn he's been planning (the fluid grace and spark of fun that should have ruled the world) … and gets to work.

When he set out to create Amber's code from scratch, on the terrace at Electra Drive, he had the intimation of a grand deck of

40

controls spread out before him above the entire city. That shadowy impression of faders and buttons conferred a sensation of enormous power. It was so much associated with the particular vantage point he had there, however, that he finds he cannot summon up the same controls here, for this view is quite different.

In the wide pane ahead of him, his own reflected face hangs indistinctly against the backdrop of an urban plaza of fountains and well-heeled vegetation, bounded by the high angles and curves of three glass buildings standing sharp against the dusk sky—one red, one green and one blue. Falling night reveals bright spaces sealed off on many storeys behind these façades. A piano cased in shiny hard ebonite stands high and tight upon the hot marble floor of a lobby, locked shut, under blue glass and silent. A chandelier hangs in the atrium above it, like the seed-head of a giant dandelion. Across the plaza is a space of electric beauty, empty of people, where a light-machine fires strobing flashes through a crisp white space.

Seeping into this, the ease of Evelyn flickers like a toy-town of candle-flame swaying in the echo of her laughter down the glass-and-metal corridors. Her mirth bubbles up from her code, ripples out of Jaymi's screen, curls around him and pulls him through this whole glazed complex. And fanning out behind her, in her wake, softer things arise: high inside the green building, banks of factory shelves are home to myriads of lettuces, drinking in moisture and breathing all night with a huge susurration in black-green darkness; somewhere in the blue building, circular portraits climb up a stairwell where plaster heads stare out of shell-shaped panels; and underneath the red building, high upon a wall, sprouts an antique horse's head with tragic blazing eyes.

Evelyn's laugh runs ahead, pushing out an endless colonnaded passage lined in candles held aloft by disembodied hands whose fingers beckon Jaymi onward. This passageway of candle-light snakes up and swoops down and loops the loop—a tunnel like a dance through a coloured space of night that presses in from above and from below on every side.

Jaymi smiles.

Yes. That's what he needs.

19 THE SILVER LAKE BAR ON HYPERION AVENUE

Jaymi's first response to seeing Bang Dead's new "Gal Score: Babe or Gross?" Newsfeed was to start creating Evelyn's code out of thin air, beginning with nothing but a faint fore-echo of this Beast's sunny cool freedom. If the ones and zeroes behave themselves, she will soon emerge from her code. She'll be painted with her own visuals, which will animate her; she'll be scored with her own soundtrack, which will come alive; and she'll be tested. Then within a few days she'll be electrified into incarnated form, in all her beauty, like a burst of love.

But despite this creation cycle of Evelyn, there is little clarity as to how the "Gal Score: Babe or Gross?" Newsfeed could possibly fail to barrel upwards and outwards in popularity and profitability around the world, at least for as long as tabloid culture outsells the rest.

There can be no assurance of the success of any investment; but a media stream that facilitates the rating of individual women for attractiveness using *Ain'tTheyFreaky!*'s Freakometer, from a highest score of 10 for Babest, down to a lowest score of 1 for Grossest, by members of the public, does at least start out with the benefit of appealing to the resources of a decent majority.

Incarnated into the world by themselves, Jaymi's bursts of Evelyn love would stand no chance against such competition. But with a little back-up from Amber, perhaps they might survive after all. For despite the disconcerting quality of his presence, the incarnated Amber does appear to be obedient to Jaymi's commands; and he did offer to deal with the Dreary Ones in whatever way his creator wished to see them squirm. In the brief time since his incarnation Amber has taken up residence in the guest wing of the house on Electra Drive, keeping to himself, with an unexpected and perhaps ominous quietness, as if awaiting orders. Ahead of Evelyn's incarnation, perhaps he should therefore be sent off on a discreet fact-finding mission into the lives of certain Newsfeed-designing Bang Dead employees, to identify a few weak points in those employees' inhabitations of the world? Musing thus, Jaymi grins. Amber surely could identify each Dreary One's unimpressive attributes, since he's pretty much an extension of Jaymi's own vivid awareness of them. However, what should Amber then *do* with such new-found knowledge about Dud, Ashley, Kelly and Herb? And Jaymi's grin fades a little, as he realises he doesn't quite know the answer to this yet. Hmm. Well, not to worry, Amber will know what to do when he meets them. This Beast-wielding business is somewhat like driving through darkness, it seems: with the headlights illuminating only a short distance ahead, Jaymi must trust the whole journey can thereby be achieved without coming upon a sudden cliff-edge. Still, he now has the basis of a plan for interacting Beasts…

But first, he himself should find out whatever he can from the Dreary Ones in person. He's not yet given them reason to believe he suspects them of the drone attack. It would still be plausible that Jaymi should think the drone attack was the work of someone else. If he contrives to bump into Dud, Ashley and Kelly soon, then he'll be able to do to them as he did to Herb—leave them thinking he attributes the attack to some rich kid with an expensive toy, or some would-be burglar.

Good, then he'll try to bump into each of those three in the next day or two, at one of the usual haunts. A quick exchange about his getting a wacky little visit from a drone, then a snippet of chit-chat—and they'll be reassured Jaymi doesn't yet know they have him in their sights, let alone want to target them back. "The Silver Lake bar," he murmurs aloud, and checks the time.

It's funny. Over the last few weeks, and in particular since he embarked on the creation cycle for a second Beast, he has spent remarkably little time in any location other than this house on Electra Drive or the Melrose Avenue building. A casual observer would never have guessed it from watching Jaymi's isolated labours for the last month, but he does in fact possess a grand and somewhat dangerous social charm, which he was never shy of wielding in those prior months when he used to venture out of these two creative crucibles and socialise like a normal human being. It may be no bad thing to give himself a quick refresher on socialising, lest he become a complete hermit.

An hour later he parks on a side-street, strolls a couple of blocks to Hyperion Avenue, and crosses a terrace covered in umbrella-shaded tables populated by a late-afternoon crowd. Laptops and mobile devices gleam amid coffee cups and glasses. He steps through a doorway into a spacious bar full of chatter. As his eyes adjust to the shade, he scans the room for faces he knows … and *yes!* she's over there, as he hoped.

The Silver Lake bar, as everyone calls it, is a known gathering-place for many in the consumer-facing half of the games industry, such as bloggers, journalists, marketers and players. One such is Bang Dead's Kelly, who often heads straight here from the Sunset Boulevard building after work, on her way home to Downtown. She's sitting by herself at a table in the corner, rapt in her tablet as she sips at a boat-sized white coffee-cup.

Via several brief stop-and-chats at intervening tables, Jaymi navigates towards her.

"Kelly! How's it going?"

"Hey Jaymi! Good, thanks. You good?"

"Sure, can't complain. I just dropped by for some peace and quiet and privacy—but some hopes, right?"

"I hear you. It's so noisy, I can't even hear myself think."

"Mind if I join you for a quick coffee, if you're not too busy?"

"Sure. Someone's coming to meet me in half an hour, but we're good till then. What's going on with you these days?"

And they're off. Smiling, they exchange a few items of bland news each, including Jaymi's casual mention of a drone that recently flew up to his very own terrace—some pesky would-be burglars, no doubt.

Her mouth falls open. "No way! Did you report it to the cops?"

"Ah, no. Come to think of it, it probably wasn't even burglars—more likely some rich kid who's just been given an expensive new toy. What will they think of next, eh?" Now to steer her into verifying her home location, as he did with Herb… "It's pretty peaceful, though, Mount Olympus."

"Oh yes, I remember you moved there, not long before you left us," she says. "How is the new place?"

"It's pretty good, thanks. Great views. You still in that same loft Downtown?"

"Yeah, I'm not giving that one up. Though the 101 does change from a freeway to a parking-lot in the rush-hour."

Well—that was almost as easy as verifying Herb's home address was.

On the table beside that big cup of hers, he sees coloured message bubbles popping up every few seconds on games-themed chat apps, forums and blogs, all sitting open on an array of tabs displayed on her tablet alongside general social media channels. Certain of those bubbles probably originate from other tables in this very bar—as she'll be aware of in some such cases, and unaware of in others. But most of them are floating in from … where? Well, who knows? From portable devices held in hands or laid on laps, all across the land: on California beaches; in cars stuck on freeways; on lounging chairs beside outdoor swimming-pools up in the Hollywood Hills; and in every kind of suburban bedroom, hundreds or thousands of miles away across multiple time-zones. Running through and between these coloured bubbles of text and graphics, and powering them, are ruthless but fluid hierarchies of professional and amateur identities, always changing, yet maintaining that nebulous plexus of perceived qualities and social standing that characterises any contained online community—in this case, celebrated and ranked according to known benchmarks of dexterity and cleverness in familiar games, and shot through with raucous voltages of apishness and stupidity, affection and humour, malice and contempt, and charges of energy both fizzing and lazy.

"Talking of neighbourhoods, where did you grow up, by the way?" he asks her. "I don't believe I ever knew."

"Highland Park, Detroit. Poverty and deprivation. Escaped as soon as I could, then worked my butt off to break into the industry. You know the last part of the story."

Hearing this, Jaymi feels his own hidden enmity towards her softening a little, despite her being the leading visual designer on *Ain't TheyFreaky!*, now trumpeting its brand-new "Gal Score: Babe or Gross?" Newsfeed. A Newsfeed whose flavour he can still recall so vividly, from no more than that unique half-minute during which he could bear to look at it before turning his head away forever…

And his nascent softening towards Kelly comes to an abrupt end.

Amber will still be visiting her.

It occurs to Jaymi that it may perhaps be interesting to ask her whether she herself happens to *like* Bang Dead's new Newsfeed.

He's half-aware that if her answer to this question turns out to be "Yes", he will have the option of first pointing out a few of that Newsfeed's specific qualities and likely effects, and then inviting her to offer a word or two in elaboration of how those qualities and effects square with her liking it...

His close-up view of her shallow-grinning eyes, however, is such that it takes him only a few more moments to abandon this potential line of questioning.

20 HOW VERY CONCERNING—DID YOU REPORT IT?

As Jaymi's information-fishing chat with Kelly in the Silver Lake bar demonstrated, his old social charm has not, after all, atrophied as a result of lying unused for the last few weeks. OK then—time to aim it in the direction of another pair of old favourites!

By way of a couple of greetings at other tables, he steers himself across the Hollywood café to the pair eating at a table by the window. "Hey, fancy meeting you two here."

"Jaymi! What a lovely surprise," says Ashley.

Dud reaches up to shake his ex-colleague's hand. "Hallo mate, how you doing?"

And they're off. Smiling, they exchange a few quick-fire items of bland news, including Jaymi's casual mention of a drone that recently flew up to his very own terrace—some pesky would-be burglars, no doubt.

Ashley raises her eyebrows. "How very concerning—did you report it?"

"Oh, no. Come to think of it, it probably wasn't even burglars—more likely some rich kid who's just been given an expensive new toy, I should think." Now to verify her home location, as he did with Herb and Kelly... "It's pretty peaceful, though, Mount Olympus."

"Is that where you are?" she says. "A striking name for a neighbourhood, I've always thought. It certainly suggests its residents have risen high in life."

"Yes, there's Electra Drive, Zeus Drive, Jupiter Drive, and a whole family of other Drives too—Apollo, Hercules, Oceanus, Hermes,

Olympus, Vulcan, Achilles, Venus. It's quite the Classical party, I tell you."

"Well, the developers certainly mixed up their Greeks and Romans, didn't they? Both Zeus and Jupiter—I wonder how they get on together?"

"I hear frequent thunder-storms up on the Mount," says Jaymi, "I don't know if it's big enough for both of them."

In light of this banter, he feels his hidden enmity towards her soften a little, despite her running the IT infrastructure for *Ain'tTheyFreaky!* and its brand-new "Gal Score: Babe or Gross?" Newsfeed, which is spreading all around the world right now while they speak, fomenting a planet-load of comments and scores for attractiveness using Bang Dead's Freakometer...

And his incipient softening comes to an end.

Amber will still be visiting Ashley, no question.

"I don't believe I've ever driven through the neighbourhood. Where is it, I forget?"

"Above Laurel Canyon, on the Hollywood side of it. You still in that Century City apartment?"

"Yes. So convenient for Bang Dead."

Good to know. "Great location," agrees Jaymi. "And Dud—the boss of the Bird Streets, no less! You still in the Blue Jay Way pad?" Dud gives a small, modest nod, and Jaymi smiles. "I'm not surprised. Why would you ever move out of there, with views like that?"

Dud shrugs. "I can't say it beats Brentwood, Essex, back home— but it'll do."

Jaymi had almost forgotten these tiny flickers of mild charm in Dud; and this particular flicker even causes a slight softening of the hidden enmity Jaymi feels for him, despite Dud's being the developer responsible for *Ain'tTheyFreaky!* and despite the "Gal Score: Babe or Gross?" Newsfeed's voracious spreading around the world while the three of them are speaking here...

No—this softening in Jaymi's attitude towards Dud was especially minimal to begin with, and it survives for an even shorter moment than his softening for Ashley did just now.

Amber will be paying a visit to Dud too, no question there either.

"Ah, well. Don't let me interrupt your meal, I'll leave you two in peace."

"So nice to catch up, Jaymi. Do keep in touch."

"Cheers Jaymi."

"Bye both."

While he is exiting the Hollywood café, Evelyn chooses to emerge from her newly-created code, without warning and unseen by the café's patrons. She does this by sending a whisper round the side of Jaymi, promising to be the sleep that plays in the light behind his eyelids. She has not yet received any artwork from him, but is already squeaking with delight at the prospect of her own visuals, even prophesying them with her own quirky expressions of colour: brunette fingers on her hands; and up where the water kisses her eyes, each iris blended smoothly inward from black around its outer rim, to green around the hard black pupil at its centre.

21 HERB HACKS EVELYN'S CODE

At his desk in the Melrose Avenue building, a warm light glows somewhere behind Jaymi's eyes, at the sense of ease and freedom spreading out from between the ones and zeroes of Evelyn's freshly-emerged code in his text editor window. While he stares, though, it seems the subtlest change of flavour is occurring somewhere within her, without his inputting any further edits. It's such a low-key change, he almost fails to register it—but it's true.

He frowns, sits up straight. What's happening? His screen isn't big enough to display the whole windowful of Evelyn without needing to scroll, so he cannot take in all of her in one glance; but his eyes scan her code, hard and fast. He can't quite put his finger on it, but *something*'s changed in her.

He can sense it.

He's being hacked!

—Is he? Or is he just imagining things?

To his horror, while he stares at the letters, figures, symbols and spaces that fill her window, an *Ain'tTheyFreaky!* logo and a small string of Bang Dead code pop up, deep inside the final section of her, trying to nestle unobserved in the middle of a dense paragraph.

Jaymi yelps in pain and anger at this mutilation being wrought in the internal life of his new Beast, through the clumsy meddling of Bang Dead Games' esteemed programmer. Launching himself forward and into damage control, he returns his work to an earlier restore point, quarantines his current session, creates appropriate back-ups and sends these zinging into the cloud.

He starts a full-system scan; then while this purrs away, he sinks back and stares out at the distant fountains in the plaza, his mind racing. Whoever managed to break into this particular environment here has some serious chops as a hacker. And this very fact, in the context of the little text-format logo that popped up in Evelyn's code like a cuckoo's egg, points Jaymi straight away towards someone specific—Herb Shrim.

It must be.

"Oh, *piss* off," says Jaymi aloud. How beyond-irritating to have his work invaded like this—and by a gormless schlub like Herb.

Well, gormless in many ways, but seriously impressive on the hacking front. Accessing this newly-emerged code was pretty hardcore, in view of the security measures in place here. Aside from Herb himself, only Jaymi is in a position to know how hardcore it was, to have circumvented them.

And since Jaymi blocked this hack, Herb will also be surmising, at perhaps this very moment, that Jaymi has deduced both the skills level and the identity of his hacker.

To construe this blocked hack as anything but the opening shot in a longer battle would be a construal requiring a degree of contrivance.

Without a word being exchanged, each of these two programmers will therefore be thinking about the other right now, to the exclusion of anyone else.

A modern-day romance, to be sure.

The system scan comes to an end. Jaymi opens the quarantined file and inspects Herb's intrusions. After a minute he gives a snort, then a grudging nod. To be fair, Herb's contributions are not as malicious as he was fearing. The very best handful of them even seem to be in tune with how Evelyn expresses something of Jaymi's lifelong awareness of the overall tendency for most women to be just a bit free-er, subtler, more fun and more interesting than most men.

But most of Herb's contributions are emotionally crass bits of whimsy, one or two of which are quite droll, Jaymi has to admit.

For example there's a moment in the game that she inhabits, *The Imagination Thief*, when the narrator spies into one of Evelyn's most private imaginative landscapes, without her knowing he is spying—a kind of enchanted coastline, as it happens, which she has always thought of as a mushroom bay. Jaymi's original code for this, before Herb came butting in today, had been impeccably respectful of his Beast's private imagination: addressing Evelyn as "you", *The Imagination Thief*'s narrator had described this magical location of hers with the words, "the only things growing on the curve of this enchanted shore are mushrooms, some a metre high. As you nod in solemn pride at this, a line of dolphins leap from the water far across the bay, then dive beneath the surface once again, without a ripple. We hear a magic interval between two notes, several times—bewitching, as if an angel lives between them—and I know that I should now leave your mushroom bay. I shan't intrude again here, so never shall I hear again that magic angel interval; but never will it leave me."

And what little extra has Herb added to this innocently enchanted landscape in Evelyn's imagination? A mere detail that many players might not have noticed, but no less outrageous a thing to have smuggled in. He has appended: "A clump of human penises, of every colour of international flesh, is planted in a wide flowerpot on the shoreline of your mushroom bay, Evelyn, waving and twirling in expectancy. As soon as you approach them down the sand, they come to a stop, one by one. As you draw nearer, they turn to face you, as if sniffing the air, twitching in readiness. The closer you come to them, the higher and more excitably they swell, until they are all thrashing and straining upwards at your passage along the beach beside them."

Jaymi laughs aloud, despite his mounting indignation. Herb has even nailed something of Jaymi's own style in coding his Beasts!

His mirth soon dies down, though. Herb was a cheeky wag there, yes. But a little of that sort of stuff goes a hell of a long way, in any context outside the tabloid-flavoured culture that Jaymi knows to be so prevalent in Dud's division of Bang Dead Games. And Herb's career has been steeped in that Dud culture, which will inevitably have tended to warp his cultural and creative instincts. Any further input from him would therefore tend to give Jaymi's code a small push towards the cruelty and tackiness of *Ain't They Freaky!*. Combing her code, he locates many more of the tweaks Herb has made, scattered throughout its length; and yes, there's no getting away from the fact that Herb's overall contribution is designed, in effect, to subvert the code by dumbing it down towards a tabloid flavour, in ways that are aesthetically debased and imbued with a deep-seated mean-mindedness. For Jaymi, Evelyn has been taking shape as a happy, functional and self-possessed party girl—no saint, but innately rich and generous. Yet across the board, wreaking insidious violence on that shape, Herb has been all too predictable in warping those qualities into a soulless cartoon version of her, infused with brassiness, sleaziness and simplicity—none of which are true to herself, and all of which serve to short-change Herb's audience, cheapen Evelyn and cheapen the world.

A stab of tension and entrapment passes through Jaymi, as if this violence being done to his Beast's essential nature extended even into his own torso, sitting out here in meat-space in the Melrose Avenue building.

As for Evelyn's own perceptions, Jaymi assumes that this hack into his Beast's code must surely have been felt as a kind of existential violence—so she will have suffered too, when the cheapness started flowing into her.

Fortunately, however, she will not have to retain any memory of that suffering: by running comparisons of successive versions of her code, taken from the automated back-ups generated since the restore point he chose, he should now be able to identify exactly when Herb's first change was made to her; then delete all his meddlings and consign them to the category of alternate life histories that never happened, so she will never know what her digital-genetic fate might have been. And this is just what he spends the next couple of hours doing, with the greatest of care and eventual success.

At last his beautiful Beast is back to how she was meant to be, at this tender stage of her creation cycle. But if Bang Dead wants a battle, then by god they've got one. Never again will he let himself be hacked!

His hands clasp his upper arms across his chest, as if in protection of her.

22 HERB AT HOME IN THE WESTWOOD
VILLAGE COTTAGE

This morning and afternoon are spent moving the incarnated Amber out of the guest wing at the house on Electra Drive, into a fittingly bricks-and-mortar home of his own—a sumptuous house on Jupiter Drive that Jaymi owns as an investment property. Amber will be free to come and go, but it's arranged that the property's housekeeper will call on him once a day to verify that all is well, treating Amber as Jaymi's tenant; which, in a sense, he is. Behind the standard opacity of its frontage on Jupiter Drive, palisaded by lofty Italian cypresses, the house is positioned further back than most houses, on a hill-spur—affording its rear terrace pool and its bow windows a grand lookout east and south over unspoilt slopes of semi-arid earth sprouting hardy vegetation, down the length of the neighbouring canyon and out across the L.A. street-grid towards that clump of Downtown skyscrapers at the far end of the 101 freeway's electric artery.

This move to Jupiter Drive takes care of the daylight hours.

For the evening hours, however, now that Jaymi has verified the locations of Dud's, Kelly's, Ashley's and Herb's homes, there will be some work for Amber to do.

A home visit, to be specific.

Herb first.

Looking through Amber's eyes, Jaymi is exhilarated to see his own Beast's hands on the steering-wheel and foot on the pedal, as the car purrs to a smooth halt on Lindbrook Drive in the gathering dusk. This is a tidy and attractive street in Westwood Village, lined with one- and two-storey residences and adorned with varied greenery. Amber himself might find its flavour a tad too cosy for his own tastes. But that's fine, because he doesn't live here—he resides instead, as of today, in a sumptuous property overlooking a lush canyon on the east flanks of Mount Olympus, thank you.

For a normal little schlub like Herb, however, the sort of tame desirability on display here on Lindbrook Drive must be just the ticket.

How sweet. What a Bang Dead choice!

Amber picks up a small plastic bag, gets out of the car, locking it behind him, and steps across the quiet road. Approaching Herb's home, he slips through the dimming dusk into an area of shrubbery in front, and secretes himself among the foliage. He finesses his position, to get the best view between the evergreen leaves. According to Jaymi, Herb always refers to his home as a cottage; and sure enough, its architecture mimics just such a country-style residence. Through the front windows Amber can see down the length of two spacious rooms on the lower storey, which are lit but unoccupied: comfortable, messy, nothing special.

Soon the full dark of evening has descended. Seeing no further movement inside, Amber emerges from the shrubs and steps across the front garden and around the corner of the building. A light flicks on, down the pathway ahead, doubtless triggered by a movement sensor.

He stands for a moment, coiled in immobility. Then he turns to face the side of the house and starts to climb, as with the powerful legs of a big blond spider, up a vertical drainpipe attached to the exterior wall, holding the plastic bag between his teeth. Through brute agility and an almost metallic strength of muscle that Jaymi has never felt before, Amber's left hand and his right hand grasp the pipe in turn, helped by the grip of his feet in an animal rhythm, supporting his own weight and carrying it at relentless speed, higher and higher up the pipe, until he clambers over the gutter onto the cottage roof. Peering down over the gutter, he sees Herb emerge from a door near the bottom of the drainpipe, look along the pathway in both directions as if checking for intruders, then set off towards the front garden.

Amber shimmies along the sloping roof-tiles to the back of the cottage, then drops quietly onto a wide balcony. Beside him, a door stands open. Entering, he finds a large, cluttered living-room with a kitchen area at one end. At the other end is a busy desk-space centred on a computer monitor displaying Herb's recent creation—Bang Dead's Newsfeed, with its scores and comments scrolling down in real time from all around the world. Beside the screen stands a framed photo of an on-stage Herb, looking comically bemused as he accepts some kind of recognition in front of the banner of some homelessness charity. A cat purrs and rubs against Amber's ankle, startling him. On the cushion of the seat is a curved indentation, doubtless where Herb was sitting until a minute ago.

Somehow, this whole matter-of-fact picture of Herb as being just a guy inside his home reveals to Jaymi with greater clarity the gormless dreariness of Herb's using his skills to create something as ugly as *Ain't They Freaky!*.

With a gentle smile, Amber peels off a yellow sticky-note from a pad of them on the desk, scribbles "Grossest: 1!" on the note and sticks it onto the middle of the scrolling Newsfeed onscreen. He strides over to the kitchen area, opens a couple of drawers, pulls out a carving-knife and returns to the chair. He reaches his hand into the plastic bag he's been carrying, pulls out a brain, slams its moist weight down onto Herb's keyboard, then with one vicious downward thrust he sends the knife through brain and keyboard, impaling both.

Moisture spurts out of the organ, the keyboard emits a loud crack, and the cat dashes away.

Amber steps out onto the balcony, peers down into the back garden and waits until he hears Herb re-entering the cottage downstairs.

As Herb's feet tread back up the stairs, Amber climbs over the balcony wall, hangs off the other side of it, drops onto the lawn, then vanishes down the side pathway and around the front shrubbery into the cricket-chirping night on Lindbrook Drive, just in time for him and Jaymi to hear Herb's wail somewhere up behind him in the middle-distance.

23 JAYMI CREATES EVELYN'S APPEARANCE

Well! So all *that* kind of thing is going to be possible, through this Beast-creating business!

Bring it on, then. There'll be more home visits to the Dreary Ones, most certainly.

But first, here in the red-green-blue glassiness of the Melrose Avenue building, on this sober morning after Amber's first meat-space jaunt, there is different work to be done.

Jaymi closes his eyes and thinks back to that unique half-minute when he let his gaze wander up and down the "Gal Score: Babe or Gross?" Newsfeed, where new posts were popping up every few seconds, every one of them receiving scores and comments from multiple sources.

Then he re-opens his eyes, consults the notes he's been making over the last couple of days for *The Imagination Thief*, and checks his sketch for her visuals. Its first description of Evelyn's physical appearance reads: "There's that sleek little van, and in the driver's window the face of a Latina in her twenties smiles out at me, smooth, sunny, round, with a faint sass within its clear warmth. This must be the mysterious Evelyn Carmello. 'Hi Jaymi,' she calls. I like her straight away. [...] 'I don't know,' I say. 'Should we cancel?' She raises her eyes and points behind her to the van door."

There is then one further little artwork-oriented description of her, a bit later on: "he saw you as wild, free and self-sufficient, walking with a sway through the beauty of the night, like a part of the night itself—a sweet, sexy woman whom he passed at a corner. [...] He saw you as embodying how lovingness and warmth could exist in a natural and instinctive form, whatever kind of place it found itself; and when he looked in your eyes, then he felt plugged in to a warm electric fountain of rich brown light."

For yes, Evelyn's recent prophecy of her own eye colour was, as it happens, wrong. In her artwork, each iris does not fade smoothly in from black around its outer rim, to green around the pupil, as she herself prophesied: the iris is just brown. Though "just" brown is perhaps reductive, because in contrast with the smooth uniformity of the black-to-green fade she had proto-sensed, each iris crams so much subtle complexity of visual design into the width between its two concentric borders, that a sublimely edible colour-spectrum is spanned by the glints inside the brown: from orange flower-water, through a rich amber rum, to the oft-sung but mysterious chica cherry cola; taking a joyfully cheap detour through strawberry lemonade, then refining again to a sweet red wine, of the kind that should take the place of water in a bong, infusing each marijuana bubble with vinous fumes; and at this spectrum's most exotic end, the faintest scintillation of violet-flavoured champagne.

Nor are solid comestibles omitted, for again within the glints of Evelyn's brown irises is an equivalent colour-feast: from sugar, sweet and raw, in amber tarts ringed with crystals of treacle; through grapefruit sorbet with yellow Chartreuse poured over it; to this spectrum's own most exotic end, in a hint of violet mousse.

Her flavours trigger scents and her scents trigger flavours, tingling at his fingertips and whispering aloud around the edges of his vision.

24 AMBER STALKS ASHLEY THROUGH THE MOTEL BY LAX

A moment after Ashley's car emerges from under the Avenue of the Stars tower, Amber's pulls away from the kerb at its waiting place across Constellation Boulevard, and falls into leisurely pursuit. Whistling a soft tune through his teeth, Amber narrows his eyes while she's turning right onto Century Park West ahead of him, in an effort to afford himself and Jaymi a glimpse of Ashley's profiled face in her driver's-side mirror as she turns.

When the 405 freeway bridge appears ahead, Amber gets into the southbound lane, two cars behind her. He squints into the sun as they both emerge from the shade beneath the 405 and curve left, one after the other, off Santa Monica Boulevard and onto the ramp.

Up on the concrete space of the freeway, he keeps her in easy view ahead, passing under the 10 and onward a few miles down the west side. She slides into lane for the Florence Avenue exit, and with curiosity he tails her off the freeway and onward a mile or so, ending in the parking-lot of a faceless motel by LAX, near the perimeter of the airport, somewhere around Aviation and West Century Boulevards.

Ashley locks her car and sets off through this place of blandest transience. She crosses the lot, to the motel entrance.

At a well-judged distance, Amber follows.

Inside is a wide, impersonal lobby. She sets off across it, heading not for the check-in desk but for a fast-food outlet in the far corner. Enough people are dotted about, to allow him to stand within earshot of her without attracting notice, while she waits in line at the food counter, clenching her jaw. At last she reaches the front of the queue, where she orders a salad to take away. He picks up a magazine from a seat and flips through it—cognisant, all the while, of the uptight clenching, clenching, clenching of Ashley Tweke's jaw while she waits for her food.

Once equipped with her take-away bag, she re-crosses the lobby's expanse and exits the motel, followed by him. She walks to her car—as he does, to his. She gets in, locks the doors and sits there chewing, while he watches her from behind the tinted windows of his car fifty metres away, whistling a tune between his teeth.

When she starts the car and exits the lot, Amber follows.

She drives along Century and all around the northern edge of the airport. At its far north-west corner she turns left onto the deserted highway of Pershing Drive; then after about six hundred metres she does the last thing he expects, which is slow down, pull over on the right and come to a stop, here in the middle of nowhere.

There would be no way Amber could stop too, without arousing suspicions in her that she was being followed.

He therefore drives on, slowing his speed a little and peering into his side mirror for just about long enough to allow himself and Jaymi to register that she has parked in the entrance of a fenced-off side-road. Climbing a gentle slope of scrubby dirt, the side-road is surfaced but has no structures on either side.

Just a dead, open space between an airport and an ocean, with nobody around.

25 EVELYN'S APPEARANCE COMES ALIVE

Settling down in the Melrose Avenue building, Jaymi rubs his hands together in anticipation of the sway of freedom and ease that he knows will ripple through him as he plunges back into bringing Evelyn's visuals alive. First, he establishes her gleaming detail in *The Imagination Thief* as being her silver van, whose visuals will recur quite a lot through the game-play, with her in its driver's seat: "a small silver van […] that sleek little van […] She clicks the van door open for me […] She eases the van from the kerb […] the sunlight pours through the van's open windows […] daylight fades away, an underpass slants up in streaks on left and right, and the van swoops down to the tunnel […] She drives the van as if she were wearing it

[...] And now this van streaks along, its engine pounding smoothly as its shadow runs beside us [...] The van glides to a halt [...] how you are when you drive this van alone [...] and as you drive, Evelyn, you feel the engine's rhythm and you feel at peace [...] your fingers drum the wheel and you purr within yourself and the engine purrs back [...] Evelyn is waiting in her silver van [...] I am seated in the rear half of the van, with the window against me on my left [...] I wake for real, bumping my head onto the van's window [...] scratching their way slowly up into the sky, as the van shoots ever closer to them."

He then establishes Evelyn's talisman in *The Imagination Thief* as being a golden band necklace, whose visuals will appear just once in the game-play but will never be forgotten by the man who sees them: "the second time he saw you, you were parked in your van with the door open, staring through the windscreen in thought. On your pale brown skin a simple golden band necklace hung and flashed in the sunlight, and when you saw him watching you, from some way away, you knew what he was thinking: *Oh girl*, he was thinking, *how beautiful you are*. You smiled through the windscreen and touched your golden band."

Jaymi smiles too; for although she has no soundtrack yet, already he can see how she will light up the game. His eyes sink shut; and for a moment, inside himself, he floats upon the colours of her light.

Her girlness is so lovely.

26 KELLY SMUDGES EVELYN

Unknown to Jaymi, Evelyn's freshly-minted appearance has been channelled, by illicit means, to appear not just on his laptop screen but also on Kelly's in the Sunset Boulevard building. It's a moment when Evelyn happens to be shown peering over her shoulder at her naked self in a mirror, getting to know these much-anticipated new things of hers called visuals.

"Oh look, she's *presenting*," laughs Kelly to herself, "like a panda in a nature film. OK, let's fuck her up, shall we?" And she fires up the image-editing tools in her software.

As soon as he next looks up at Evelyn on his screen, Jaymi receives a clear picture of how an attempt to smudge a Beast's visuals is felt by its target: as a visceral distaste, flavoured by the nature of the Beast, at what the smudger would presume to impose.

Kelly's cheerily destructive attack happens to have landed in one of several scenes throughout *The Imagination Thief* where Jaymi has programmed Evelyn to visit a local bar called Downstairs, a place where she is well-known, loved and at ease. Discombobulated and dismayed by Kelly's intrusion into her, however, she can now be seen standing in Downstairs uncharacteristically alone, while all her friends and acquaintances in the bar try to work out what it is about her that's so unsettling, so *wrong*—all peering at her from alcoves and corners, and failing to be discreet enough for her not to notice they are doing so. Her physical appearance is unchanged from the Evelyn they know. So it must be her bearing that's responsible for the way she now grabs their attention, triggering their shared but unspoken words, "Oh, poor girl, poor creature ... but just what is it that's so *wrong* with her, somehow?"

There is an unearthly calm, quietness, measure and control in all her movements, suggesting an unholy kind of self-consciousness whose presence prompts everyone to try to "catch it out" by identifying an instant when it's not concealed enough. Never by a flicker does she reveal she knows that everyone is sneaking what glances they can at her; never does she catch an eye, as a radius of silence extends around her, pushed outward from her on painful struts through the air behind the chatter of the bar.

She lights a cigarette, and all her watchers are agog at every stage of this process. Is that a tremble in the end of the cigarette, or is it quite still? Hard to tell. Nobody's cigarette *is* rock-steady, of course, nor is meant to be; but the oddity is that everyone in this bar is doing what they can to catch her out in a single unplanned tremble of the cigarette's tip...

And every moment of her life with friends and other people will be like this from now on, it's clear.

Every single moment with anybody else, for the rest of her days. Her life will be a kind of death.

For a moment Jaymi sits frozen into inaction at the sight of this horror-film mutilation of his budding Beast, now so perverted from the freedom and ease he imbued her with.

Then he snaps out of it and jumps into action. He runs comparisons of successive versions of her code from automated back-ups, to identify everything Kelly inflicted upon it from up in the level of the visual design software; and proceeds to excise or reverse every bit of it, consigning it to the category of alternate life histories that never happened, so that Evelyn will never know what her social-interactive fate might have been.

Perhaps no one else would quite appreciate why, but Jaymi knows a clear truth: the one who just smudged his Beast like this should die.

27 KELLY AT HOME IN THE FACTORY PLACE LOFT

When Kelly's car drives away from the Sunset Boulevard building after work, Amber's follows it. Three other vehicles are between them as they file down the ramp to join the trundling rush-hour traffic on the 101. Half an hour later she exits onto Los Angeles Street, takes Temple and Alameda Streets, skirting around the empty eastern fringes of Downtown between faceless warehouse buildings, and turns down the quiet industrial cul de sac of Factory Place. This is where she lives, in a desirable loft conversion, hidden away in blank urban space.

The area is not as bereft of people as it first appears, however. For this stretch of Alameda is the easternmost fringe of Skid Row. Just a stone's throw west of here, inhabiting the same neighbourhood in a very different way, most of the population hunker down in hard-bitten hostels or makeshift homes in tents and boxes against anonymous sealed-off buildings, in a grid of pain and lack extending west to Main Street, up to Seventh and down to Third.

A discreet ten minutes later, Amber's car turns into Factory Place and purrs to a stop.

He sits there alone in silence, while he and his creator contemplate the deserted street and the entrance to Kelly's building some distance ahead.

Perhaps she is busy, this very minute, admiring the visuals she designed for Bang Dead's "Gal Score: Babe or Gross?" Newsfeed.

Or perhaps she's typing something into social media, in all her relentless, trivial neediness of online attention-grabbing.

Somehow, this matter-of-fact new picture of her as being just a person inside her home reveals to Jaymi with greater clarity the dreary cynicism in her using her visual flair to create something as ugly as *Ain't They Freaky!*.

Amber glances in the rear-view and side-view mirrors, picks up a bag, gets out and wanders along the pavement to the car he's been following, now parked and unoccupied. From his bag he takes out a severed pig's head and impales it on one of Kelly's windscreen-wipers, which proceeds to bend gradually down through the air, under the dripping weight of the head. Just beside this, he tucks an unusual parking-ticket under the other windscreen-wiper: a print-out of Kelly's Facebook cover photo and profile picture, across which has been scrawled "Grossest: 1!". He snaps a well-framed photo of the head and the print-out, returns to his car, tweets the photo alongside her Twitter handle, then drives away west on Sixth Street through Skid Row.

28 JAYMI CREATES EVELYN'S SOUNDTRACK

Jaymi smiles unseen, through the window and across the plaza outside the Melrose Avenue building: it's time to create Evelyn's soundtrack. This will be a joy! Just as when she jumped into picturing her own irises before she'd been given them or even quite knew what physical seeing is, so now she strains from side to side, trying to take the lead in making her own soundtrack before she knows anything about audio. The directions she's straining in are quirky ones, too, because the sounds that she's zeroing in on bear little relation to anything he expects she will hear on the streets of L.A. after he releases her into meat-space: "The linnet brings with it a breath of gorse-clad Dorset hillsides and summer days," she informs him, in a way that's still pre-verbal and yet is somehow so mellifluous as to smack of elocution training.

"*What?*" Jaymi mutters. "What are you talking about, Evelyn? Where did you get that from? That's not you at all." He frowns and shakes his head. It's cheeky, and no mistake: surely he's the boss here?

But she's off, so he resigns himself to letting her go where she will, merely hovering nearby, ready to rein her back in if she veers ridiculously far afield. Here she is at a circular window on the ground floor of a grand country house, peering out across an ornamental lake, to mist hanging blue above fields in a twilight where the linnets sing. She clambers through the window and stands on a dancing-ledge of stone for a moment, jumps to the ground, then sets off around the lake and through a moonlit field beyond, with linnets' song loud in the air. While she runs, ailanthus shoots pierce the earth and spring up close beside her in lines, from their suckers underground. The birdsong fades, as this space becomes a thorn-field. The sky dims and churns, branches sway upon the pines ahead, and into the trees she runs, into green darkness. Her soundtrack hushes, to the sound of her feet padding over heaped pine humus—then her sound of pleasure when she spots a little mushroom on the woodland floor ahead, wild and fragile and electric with life.

From away through the forest comes the sonorous bellow of a stag, with a kind of clang and moan fused together in its depths, as if it's travelled through the wastes of Siberia to reach her. She turns to the hovering Jaymi viewpoint nearby, and informs him, "Throughout the far-off mountains of the Arctic, reindeer shy back from every electrical pylon they can see, because of their ability to see deep into the ultraviolet range of light beyond the visible spectrum. Ultraviolet frequencies flash and play in the ionised gases that build up around high-voltage power cables' insulator cones, so the reindeer see these overhead cables as lines of ever-flickering lights, stretching across wooded mountains out of sight. Thus do their populations fragment, into wide but distinct islands between marches of pylons."

Before Jaymi can decide how to reply, they reach an island of oak trees, oddly buried here among the pines, all bathed in ultraviolet; and there in the oak-shade, a clearing of red sunflowers of a colour so vibrant that they seem to be aflame. Distracted and wild-eyed, Jaymi falls behind, but sees her swooping up above the forests and the mountains and the tundra, then out across the frozen Arctic Ocean, where a permanent sunset hangs against the sea ahead. The last he can hear of her soundtrack is tubular bells clanging huge in the sky, and the shrieking of a storm, then a smooth fade to silence.

29 ASHLEY AT HOME IN THE CENTURY PARK EAST APARTMENT

Ashley's home is within easy walking distance of the Avenue of the Stars tower, in discreetly low-rise luxury at the top of a bank of greenery on Century Park East, between Galaxy Way and Empyrean Way.

Not that anyone normal would actually walk that commute, of course; they would drive.

Though tight-wound, Ashley is in some respects abnormal, however, and this is one such respect; so she walks it.

Amber therefore sets off tailing her on foot, at what he and his creator judge to be a prudent distance, down through the anodyne crispness of Century City, while Jaymi peers in voyeuristic excitement from behind his Beast's eyes. Without warning she cuts skittishly across Avenue of the Stars, midway between two intersections, passing beside the little fountains in the Avenue's median outside the fanfare-slick grandeur of the CAA Building. Traipsing on across the bridge over West Olympic Boulevard and past the towering sleekness of Fox Plaza, she turns left into the more human scale of Galaxy Way. Halfway down the block, the marathon ends, when she makes a right through the coiffed lushness of vegetation in the entrance drive of her residential complex.

In this more intimate geography, peopled by sporadic pedestrians, the options available to Amber in his pursuit of her increase many-fold.

Fifteen minutes later, Ashley emerges from a stairwell into the tightly-coiffed communal garden space on the roof of her apartment building, and perches on an upright garden-seat. Sipping a cup of tea while her phone's mail app checks for new emails, she peers north through the haze of the afternoon, to where the Hollywood Hills start to rise.

Ten minutes later still, Amber emerges through the same stairwell, makes his way to a seat at the other end of the communal garden, sits, and adjusts his shades against the glare.

He looks sideways at Ashley. Perhaps she's busy, this very minute, working on the IT infrastructure for Bang Dead's "Gal Score: Babe or Gross?" Newsfeed.

Perhaps she's proud of enabling the feed.

Somehow, this matter-of-fact new view of her as being just a woman in her home environment reveals to Jaymi with greater clarity the dreary moral bankruptcy in her using her expertise to create something as ugly as *Ain'tTheyFreaky!*.

Amber rises and steps along the roof-garden path in her direction. When he reaches the path's closest point to her, she glances up and hears him speak Jaymi's lines with a charismatic, twinkling menace that is all his own: "An oaf may end up more contented than a thinking and sensitive individual with high standards such as yourself, Ashley. But though the oaf may achieve eighty per cent of his potential happiness, this will add up to eighty per cent of very little; whereas if you achieve just forty per cent of your potential happiness, then this will be forty per cent of very much more. You've known this all your life, Ashley, haven't you? The world's track record hardly inspiring confidence, however, you allowed yourself to become the problem. You feel the impatience of greatness in yourself, don't you?—reined and curbed by the dullness of the man you report to. Alas, this doesn't alter the fact that you remain the problem. Good day."

He steps away from Ashley's spluttering remonstration and vanishes back down the stairwell.

After two minutes of roiling and inconclusive thought, she gathers up her things, returns to her apartment downstairs, locks the door and sits in front of the laptop computer on her desk, breathing hard.

With the end of a fingernail she smooths out a tiny dog-ear at one corner of a small yellow sticky-note that's been affixed, with neat strips of sticky-tape, onto the flat plastic between the computer's keyboard and its fold-up screen, bearing her own handwritten words, "Ashley Tweke most expertly sets up invisible girders!!!" Her hand darts forward, hovers fretfully over the sticky-note as if about to rip it away, then hesitates and returns to her lap.

Her gaze strays over to rest, in reassuring habit, upon a glazed and mounted black-and-white photograph positioned at one side of her desk, showing her as a child at her family's second home on Martha's Vineyard, where they would motor down from Cambridge for the summer break each year...

Contemplating this, her face grows stricken with horror. Around the outside of the photo's metal frame, it would seem that a new outer frame has been stuck, made out of uncooked pale-pink sausages that have been snugly squeezed into all the tight interstices and orifices of ornamental golden flozzery on the metal. Her jaws commence a furious clenching when she observes, furthermore, that a fat horsefly has just landed on the uppermost sausage, where it is busy laying a line of tiny dark eggs. The clear glass that used to cover the picture has been shattered; while across the monochrome surface of the photo has been scrawled "Grossest: 1!".

30 EVELYN'S SOUNDTRACK COMES ALIVE

Now that Jaymi is approaching the release of his second Beast, Evelyn, he can look back and register that his earlier release of Amber had a certain simplicity to it, because while it was happening there was no previous such act he could compare it with. The process of his creating Amber out of nothing and then allowing him to slither out of the monitor was a kind of convulsion. He was hardly in control of it while it occurred, but was rather a conduit; whence Amber was incarnated fully-formed, endowed with a volition of primal power and a beauty that was monstrous.

This more deliberate creation cycle for the building of Evelyn has so far been a less convulsive affair. Still, he's been unable to remain fully in control of it. Yesterday she started talking at him unbidden, for instance, and about the linnet of all things; then she whisked him from the linnet fields of Dorset, through a Siberian forest with bellowing stags in the distance, then up over the Arctic Ocean, before abandoning him in a freezing blizzard, to find his own way back down to earth and the Melrose Avenue building. That was a bit rich, to be frank … but her own choice of track now rises again by itself, all around him.

The smile in her voice floats down at him, slow and wide and mellow as a grin upon her sunny face, and yet it's sad and haunting—indicating avenues unfolding into future joy, although the view back home will show a place that has died.

She beckons him aside, confiding in a whisper, "Thanks for my soundtrack, Jaymi!" Then she cocks her ear, as if to catch the last of a vanishing echo, murmuring, "Ah yes. Continuous relaxing favourites, not to mention soft classics. Timeless timepieces and timely information. A winning combination, coasting into a smooth finish. Yes ma'am. Mm-hm, mm-hm."

A thrill runs through Jaymi. His new Beast's audio is coming alive! But where is she getting these vocal stylings from, ominously strange as they are? It's as if she has flitted around at ease through her creator while he wasn't looking, snatching up evocative samples echoing down audio passageways that he'd forgotten about.

"I'd just like to jet in for a moment," she continues, "regarding the ocean where I left you last time. Well, in the deeps of that ocean there's an inky-black pool of water that's saltier than the miles of water above; and around this still pool is a coastline, as it were, lined by crabs and worms. If you mash them up, d'you know that a group of hydras or sponges will gradually reassemble into complete animals?" Jaymi hears the whisper of a sudden silverfish upon the tiles of her bathroom in the Metropolitan Hotel on Asbury Avenue, where he'll be housing her in *The Imagination Thief*, and she scoops the silverfish up into a roll of paper and runs down to the Asbury Park boardwalk and lets it go, with a kiss to the paper, as this little creature of an ancient order slides away coiling into the moonlight. Sand-hornets cut the air. Glistening on the shore ahead, crustaceans of mud scuttle down over lugworms, into lapping wavelets. Further back and down, where the continental shelf ends, a rush and flap of species more exotic: black goldfish, peroxide-blond fish, then express-fish and sea-serpents—then (listening back to when the mountains were sea-beds) the mountainfish, now in fossil form upon the rock.

She reclines by the petrified mountainfish, Jaymi goes to join her and they sit, like bees on a rock-face waiting for the sun ... ricochet of rabbits in the mountains, scampering; pebbles scatter; feathers ripping up through a yellow-grey sky, then a short-wave piping of peewits and curlews. White horses flow through her soundtrack now (where the art of the mouse is hidden too), for the mountain is bestial: sylphs and gnomes and manticores bound up its slopes, under Evelyn's direction. At her whim, a stately sheep, a blond sheep—peevish, to be sure, but ceremonial, processional—passes by in front of her and Jaymi, then recedes to the left.

Out above the mountain-range ahead, a vision dances, with shafts of light, cloudscapes, horses' heads and circles in the sky … then Jaymi feels Evelyn clap her hands with easy grace, and lands back down in the Melrose Avenue building, with her soundtrack completed and the feeling of a violin-flower open wide in him.

31 AMBER STALKS DUD AT WORK

Without warning, Amber enters Dud's office in the Avenue of the Stars tower.

Facing the other direction, a seated Dud hears the door open behind him, and says, "Ria, get me a cup of tea, pet."

Amber steps across the room towards him and speaks Jaymi's thoughts aloud, with that charismatic twinkling menace that's so inimitably Amber's: "How I should pity any children of a monkey who devotes his little monkey-years to creating what you create." Dud wheels around in his chair, struggles to place the identity of the man staring down into him with that familiar wide-set fluidity of humour in his eyes, but can only splutter while Amber continues in the tone of a spell-binding lullaby that cannot be interrupted: "Look at the elements of you I'm expressing hatred for. Find that hiding-place in your head where you have the clearest and widest view of humanity (it may resemble a mountain lodge), sit inside it by the window with everything quiet, and look through the glass at all the people you've made things for. From up here in this lodge, don't you hate those things you made? If you don't, you ugly monkey, then perhaps you're in the wrong lodge—or maybe you're not a man at all but a big-toe, who won't have seen much."

He stops speaking, but his close-up gaze into Dud's monkey face continues unblinking, backed up by Jaymi's gaze down through Amber's eyes.

"*Who the fuck are you?*" gabbles one of the holes in the monkey's face, while the other two holes snivel in sympathy with the first.

"How does it feel to be a sluggish deadweight—is that working out well for you? Less a personality and more an assemblage of shortfalls," Amber smiles. "Well, the sight of you makes my skin crawl, like the sound of clinker scraped on concrete or the rubbing of hands caked in dry mud, so I think I'll slip away now; thanks for having me."

Saying this, Amber reaches forward, deftly forces the other's jaws apart and pushes a large dead cockroach into Dud's mouth. And with that, he and his creator are gone.

Five long seconds later, when the last of the insect has been spat out, Dud bellows in wordless anger. He slams his fist onto a button on his desk phone, to summon Ria.

32 JAYMI TEST-DRIVES EVELYN

It is time for Jaymi to test Evelyn out, to see if she embodies all the ease she should, before he presses the button to incarnate her.

She proceeds to devote this test-drive to the emission of a fountain of music. At this stage of her existence, she can't have much certainty of what she'll encounter in meat-space. Yet the quick-fire journey of music tracks she emits has the feeling, for Jaymi, of an uncannily convincing sequence of essences of what it feels like to "go out" into the world in pursuit of experience, pleasure and life, whether for a night out or a decade of living. He falls quiet and listens.

The first track features a voice above a minimalist but melodic electronic accompaniment. And what a voice: it's flat, wistful, breathy and mesmeric, counting out a cycle of numbers forever, from *one* through to *twelve*, again and again, slow and measured. The *eleven*, in particular, is meltingly sensuous beyond belief … an *eleven* so charged with sensuous voltage, in fact, that it's the perverse climax of the cycle, awaited like the hidden magic midnight on a clock-face … *eleven*, soft (and so alluring in its shyness of twelve), with its assonance of "e"s like a velvet caress…

Up go the tempo and the heat, when her second track bubbles in, supplanting the first. The polished control of this track channels so romantic an abandon to the world of the early-evening city, as to coruscate like champagne—such heart within its slickness, stepping out in pink and blue, in a yellow taxi-cab.

Her third track focuses her oncoming rush, from the stage to the sky, where her fingers flick stardust-clouds like a video effect, till she twinkles over Hollywood, high above the Hills.

Her fourth forges upward further still, culminating in a long solo flight of lead-guitar so virtuosic that it streaks, like a comet, into ecstasy—a starburst of glamour and perfection and passion.

For her fifth track, there's nowhere higher up she can go. So she coasts, on a level, in the stratosphere, effortless—blown like a melancholy rose on the wind, borne along through the sky on a lush flight of red.

When her sixth track strolls in, she's coasted down again, to a level where she floats among the people of the night. The night shade has deepened, disembodied voices call around her—whirl and flash of eyes (some warm and others cold). She is held under poisoned skies, stained by the sunset on the city: death behind the beauty of a warm breeze blowing on her face and on the lips she kisses, softest warmest urban lips…

Her seventh is the last track; and though she has descended from her third and fourth and fifth, her attaining those heights left a structure up there, where she now can send her notes just by glancing at its girders. And this she does, firing up a track with a march of majestic violins whose sweep and pace cannot be stopped—universally known, as it strides around the globe throughout eternity.

Jaymi stares at the depths in the dark of his screen, as the grandeur and whirl of her music spirals inward through his cells and recedes into distance and silence.

Through the quiet of the Melrose Avenue building, he speaks at last: "Evelyn, you're ready."

33 KELLY TAILS AMBER THROUGH THE HOLLYWOOD HILLS

Ria appears at Dud's office door in response to his summons, followed by a curious Kelly, who is on a visit to Bang Dead HQ from her Sunset Boulevard office and has overheard her boss's bellowing. Dud says he needs Ria to tail somebody right now, and supplies a precise description of the quarry, Amber. *Did Ria notice this blond fucker here in the building a moment ago?* he asks, wiping his mouth with his fingers.

"Yes," says Ria, "I passed him in the corridor."

Dud curses at this; he needs someone Amber won't recognise.

"Well, *I* never saw the guy you just described," interjects Kelly, warming to the intrigue. "I can tail him. Why not?"

OK then, Kelly is an ideal choice for the mission, says Dud. Please would she grab her keys and run down to the tower's underground car-park. That man won't yet have had enough time to escape—he must still be making his way down the height of the Avenue of the Stars tower—so *run, Kelly, run!*

Two minutes later she exits the lift, thirty-something storeys below, and steps out along an aisle of parked vehicles. She spots what must be the blond man, standing by a car at the far end of the aisle, inspecting his car keys with an air of leisure and a mild smile. He opens the door and gets in. She locates her own car, jumps in, fires it up and sets off from the parking-bay, just in time to observe his car start to climb the exit ramp towards ground-level.

Separated by a prudent distance, they emerge in succession from underneath the Avenue of the Stars tower, onto Constellation Boulevard, where the task of tailing this mysterious man begins in earnest. Before long, his car is turning right, off Century Park East onto Santa Monica Boulevard. What a bizarre jaunt this is! At least it beats the corporate responsibility presentation for which she and various colleagues were hauled over to Bang Dead HQ today.

Halfway through Beverly Hills the man makes a left, out of the traffic on the boulevard, into the tranquillity of North Foothill Road, where grand mansions stare across at one another between the immaculately-trimmed trunks of two lines of stately palm trees flanking the road, rooted in wide strips of manicured lawns alongside impeccable unused sidewalks. At the top of Foothill, exercising great care neither to lose track of him nor to attract his attention, Kelly follows him right, onto a quiet, greenery-padded stretch of Sunset Boulevard, keeping her distance. Confident that he has no idea he's being tailed, she grins with excitement as she curves off the Sunset Strip to hang a left up Sunset Plaza Drive behind him. From here on, tailing him becomes more fraught, as they commence an uphill couple of miles of baroque twists and turns around complex hill contours, flanked by the opaque frontages of hidden residences on either side, sometimes rounding hairpin bends and catching occasional glimpses, through foliage and fences, of an ever-increasing height of open air over the city beyond.

Some way after passing Blue Heights Drive, his car slows way down, as he reaches a hairpin bend around a promontory. Coming up behind him, she sees that of all the twists and turns on Sunset Plaza Drive, this one affords by far the most spectacular view that's yet been accessible. The man coasts his car to a halt beside a flimsy crash-barrier, beyond which is a precipitous drop into a canyon.

As she reduces her progress to a crawl, the man ahead gets out of his car, closes the door and strolls over to the barrier, where he stands looking out at the view and then down off the end of the promontory.

For an instant she wonders whether she should also park and get out, but dismisses this possibility straight away as being too apt to awaken his suspicions. So she slows down yet more, and drives on, ever closer towards him.

Right at the point where she comes level with him, he turns around to face her without warning and bends down to peer into her car, in a sudden intrusive close-up with his face against the glass of her passenger-side window. Across the width of the car's interior he smiles straight into her, with a knowingness in his eyes that is terrifying—and Jaymi's eyes behind them, pinning Kelly down in her seat, so she squirms.

Then raising the inner ends of his eyebrows, Amber and Jaymi give a creepy, child-like wave at her, using just the fingers of one hand, as if waving down at a one-year-old lying chained inside a perambulator...

A chill of horror spreads through her body.

She swallows, yanks the steering-wheel to the right, just in time to prevent herself hitting the crash-barrier that's the sole thing between her and a painful death far below, and drives on up Sunset Plaza Drive, shaking a little.

34 JAYMI INCARNATES EVELYN

Alone at his desk in the Melrose Avenue building, Jaymi clutches the edge of his chair in panicked exhilaration, watching Evelyn slither and squeeze out into meat-space through the monitor in front of him.

She lands, as if through sun-glare in a desert border town where blue agaves curve along a wall that's alive with competing tags of spray-paint. Inside a bar-room door, in the slow-turning shadow of a ceiling-fan, a deck of cards is splayed on the bar, with the bright cartoon of a different sexy girl printed proudly on the back of every card. Fire-crackers burst in the distance, and a smiling-eyed Evelyn with golden-hooped earrings swings through the doorway from the sunlight, a belt of bullets slung across her shoulder and down around her bared midriff, wearing a wide black belt over a short scarlet dress, with scarlet high heels, a gun holstered at her right side and a switchblade knife in her left hand. A lush yellow rose is tucked behind her ear, beside cascading black hair.

Beside that rose, her attention comes to rest on her electrified creator—her very first look at him, since her incarnation.

She stares. Then slowly, she smiles; and Jaymi smiles back.

So … there she is. His second Beast.

Evelyn!

He loves her.

All the ease and freedom he could create from within him, and his very own response to Bang Dead's "Gal Score: Babe or Gross?" Newsfeed!

There's no need to waste time—there is no time to waste. The moment has arrived for her first mission, out here in the world. What a joy!

He jumps up from his seat, beckons her to follow, and leads her out of EC1 Digital's office, along deserted glass corridors, into the lift and down to the dimness of the parking levels. They take a wordless, dreamlike walk along the aisle and arrive at Jaymi's car.

They have already got in and closed the car-doors, before he realises he has no idea where he's about to take her. She may be his second Beast, but he still feels a bit of a newbie at this.

Aha! Of course. She may as well start where the players in her industry are wont to congregate, right? So he turns to where she's sitting expectant in the passenger's seat, and speaks his very first words to her in the flesh: "Evelyn, allow me to take you to the Hollywood café."

"Cool, let's go!" she breezes.

And so they do.

35 ASHLEY AND DUD ATTACK EVELYN (*FIRST PINCH POINT*)

Entering the café with Evelyn, he spots Dud and Ashley at the far corner table, and the butterflies jump higher in his insides. Yes, it's introduction time!

It's reassuring to see that her visuals do resemble those of any human patron of the Hollywood café, albeit a more stylishly-attired one than most. (Her gun and switchblade knife have been left, at Jaymi's urging, in the glove compartment of his car.)

As he leads her between the tables, however, a question nags at him: is he being somewhat despotic towards her, in delivering her into the jaws of those two sharks ahead?

Not that he knows how they will react to meeting her. But from their deep knowledge of Jaymi's work, and from the simple fact of his bringing her here to see them, they will surely take only a few moments to realise what Evelyn is, despite her appearance as a regular human being. For he may as well acknowledge his own motivation in showcasing her to them like this—it *is* to throw down an implicit challenge to them, isn't it? They won't be slow to pick up on that challenge. And once they've comprehended what she is, who knows what mischief they will feel goaded into plotting? So again, has Jaymi been fair to Evelyn here?

But this is a question that would perhaps have been better posed at some point before they entered this establishment, because now it's too late. The two sharks have seen them approaching, and are both devouring Evelyn with eyes that are filled first with simple curiosity, then with surmise, then apprehension, and then an ominous seepage of awestruck understanding.

That seepage is mirrored in real time within Jaymi himself, as he finds he can perceive the oncoming faces of Dud and Ashley through Evelyn's eyes, as well as through his own accustomed gaze.

This is way more strange than the excitement of voyeurism he felt when he directed his own perception out through the eyes of the incarnated Amber. They were simpler times; for on none of those occasions was he himself there, in the flesh, alongside his own Beast.

Now by contrast he feels himself borne aloft for the first time, with a vertiginous ballooning of knowledge and experience, to some secret mezzanine storey of perception where he can choose how to view his former colleagues and the whole café scene—either as himself, or as the freshly-incarnated Evelyn. And for a moment he flounders in fear. Fear at the precarious new dimension of freedom in this situation he's thrown himself into. Fear at the sheer spooky freakiness of being able to see the same scene through these two eyes, or those two eyes of hers, or all four eyes together.

Dud and Ashley are reached at last, and Evelyn stops and stands in front of them. And sure enough, the civilised human interaction begins, as it must, initiated and directed by Jaymi. It involves introductions, the shaking of hands, and the sort of professional, polite small talk to be expected in a controlled public environment such as this.

Jaymi looks sidelong at her, beneath the surface of the small talk. He is worried to note that she is finding great appeal and entertainment value in Dud's shallow words—suggesting a subtle but disappointing laziness in the sharpness of her perceptions, he must admit. This sort of laziness-derived susceptibility is a sub-optimal trait in her that he failed to notice, which stings him a little as a creator.

But beneath the surface of Dud's and Ashley's civilised interaction, now that they've worked out who and what Evelyn is, an altogether different interaction starts simmering.

Enclosed by the public babble surrounding the four figures at this table, and unknown to the café's other patrons, Jaymi can tell that the two Bang Dead managers' scrutiny of his second Beast is becoming positively beady-eyed with a sense of *mission*.

What mission? he wonders. But such is the parallax afforded by his current double vision of them, and such is his insight into their thought processes from working at Bang Dead, that he realises he already knows what their mission will be—to reproduce Jaymi's breakthrough Evelyn-creation, but repurposing her instead into an enhancement for *Ain'tTheyFreaky!*.

Yes, the ugly ambition in Dud's face is clear: he would like nothing better than to incorporate a dumbed-down version of Evelyn into his own tabloid product, so as to entertain customers of the "Gal Score: Babe or Gross?" Newsfeed, no doubt setting up Bang Dead's cartoony Evelyn as a kind of reference target for a world full of Gal-scorers to take aim at...

While Dud contemplates all this commercial potential in Jaymi's Beast, it's clear, too, that he's looking at her through the eyes and expectations of an average consumer of *Ain'tTheyFreaky!*. And as soon as Dud looks at her in this way, the main problem becomes apparent: Evelyn is dangerously free.

To speak plain, as Dud so prides himself on doing, it will need a bit of straightening-out, for normal people. Just as soon as Herb's team have worked out how she was created and have found a way to reverse-engineer her, then that excessive freedom will be the first thing to fix.

Jaymi pulls his own attention out of Dud, and returns it to Evelyn. Doing so, he becomes aware that her lack of perceptiveness regarding Dud's verbal blandishments is more than compensated for by her ultra-perceptiveness of Ashley's and Dud's sharp-eyed scrutiny and the avidity of their desires for Bang Dead to ferret out a way of repurposing her into something she is not.

Alarmed, Jaymi observes her apprehension of their intentions spreading through her like a seepage of pain. For her, this is the first time somebody else's hostile intentions have given the lie to their friendly words. But it's more than that, as he now understands: for a Beast, the mere proposition of being repurposed into something that feels cheaper and is alien to their own nature constitutes an assault in itself.

And though she manages to maintain her external composure, this prospect of her own repurposing comes straight at her with such specific sound and fury, that Jaymi can only watch distraught at how it manifests itself in her head: haloed in death-light, a monstrous Death-figure is rearing up before her, thrashing at a tiny orchestra and chasing it off a stage. Observing this carnage from the conductor's podium, Evelyn sees that the Death-figure's terrifying violence isn't just the destruction of an existing show. It *is* the show—the real show. A show of pure corruption and dirt of delirium, a dark deluge of a dangerous river: grotesque apocalypse, where beauty's home is horror just as horror's home is beauty.

Death turns to face her and speaks to her alone: *You're cold meat!* he winks. *Life is destructive—a vile show of meat-puppets. Every puppet's end is a nameless collapse into dead flesh, a twitch of faceless anguish. Death is just a dead end, though—revealing nothing, leading nowhere, curing only pain. You're all just a falling of drips in the night. And the gods (when we think to turn an eye upon you crawling atoms) only laugh and hate!*

Then within an instant, Death is gone—leaving just the brittle spider-ticking of the second hand around an empty clock-face beside the proscenium. Covering the stage now, multitudes of tiny people mill around, dying, being born, scurrying, gesticulating, killing, loving, laughing and jabbering at once, while the brittle second hand ticks on … then a blast from the speakers: guns vomit in the sky, while a giant roar of fire and blood fills the horizon like a war.

At a cue from the sound-booth, silence slams in again. High upon a deep-black back-cloth above the stage, a little cold Pluto hangs in a spotlight, revealed to possess an unexpected pale heart-shape spread across its surface. And very far beyond it, the unknown tenth one, Persephone, shadowy and quiet, sails dark on an alien orbit among black comets.

As her internal sound and fury subside, Evelyn finds herself standing once again in the Hollywood café, while her creator observes her with concealed anguish.

Her sense of her own existence has been shaken by this first sight of Death; but she has maintained control of herself. She has come through a drive-by trial, and has held herself together.

Warmth and pride spread through Jaymi, while he cuts the small talk as short as he can and shepherds her away from those two Bang Dead sharks. What a trooper she is!

Outside in the car, he installs a sobered Beast back into the passenger's seat, turns to look her straight in the eyes and says "Thank you, Evelyn." He pauses. "You see what we're up against?"

She nods, unspeaking.

He starts the car, then turns back to her. "See how we're gonna win?"

She smiles, for the first time since her ordeal. "Yep," she says. "I see how those two are. Well … to hell with them. Bring it on, I say—they'll lose! Can we go home now, please?"

"You bet," Jaymi smiles back at her, pulling out of the parking-space and setting off through the car-park. He will install her in the guest wing at the house on Electra Drive, now that Amber has vacated it, and leave her in privacy there. As a self-contained living space, it will allow her to recover from today's rude introduction to the rough-and-tumble of human society, and become used to being incarnated. He'll tell his housekeeper to look in on her every day and make sure she has what she needs, as if she were a house guest—which, of course, she will be.

They say no more. But as he heads down Cahuenga, a jabber of words fills his head, concerning this whole Beast-creating mission he's embarked upon. On one level, the stakes he holds in *The Imagination Thief*, *The Platinum Raven* and *The Host in the Attic* derive their urgency from being bets on his own professional success. But something more burning is visible when he looks beneath the level of each game title, down to its population of characters, first as they're being sent into the world in their incarnated forms, and then as they'll be sealed into their digital forms when he sends them back out in their finished game releases: that this multi-coloured personification of himself into these Beasts is the best contribution he can make to a world that would seem to have been designed to facilitate the likes of *Ain'tTheyFreaky!* instead. In that context, perhaps this Beast-creating business is the highest-quality way he can find to integrate himself into the world as it is—to find a home for himself, beyond the steel and glass of the house on Electra Drive. Maybe that is what he felt the lack of, sitting out on his terrace the other evening?

Turning onto Hollywood Boulevard, reflecting on what Dud and Ashley have just inflicted, he wonders, though: does Evelyn *feel* like a Beast, as opposed to a human?

Deep inside her, *is* there, in fact…?

And somewhere inside himself, he quivers.

PART III

"GUY SCORE" AND "TRIVIA SCORE", SHIGEM'S AND KIM'S CREATIONS, AND THE RIGHTEOUS GUN COCKPIT

36 THE "GUY SCORE: HUNK OR GROSS?" NEWSFEED

Next morning, numerous online sources are excited to announce that today Bang Dead has rolled out another massive free offering to consumers everywhere. It's the second major plank of *Ain'tTheyFreaky!*, and the company promises it'll be a popular hit: it's the "Guy Score: Hunk or Gross?" Newsfeed!

This is a constant stream of images, videos or pieces of text uploaded from around the world, presenting individual men, who are rated for attractiveness by any member of the public using *Ain'tTheyFreaky!*'s Freakometer, from a highest score of 10 for Hunkest, down to a lowest score of 1 for Grossest.

Jaymi lets his gaze wander up and down this newsfeed stream, where new posts are popping up every few seconds, every one of them soon receiving scores and comments from multiple sources.

He reads a few posts, for half a minute or so.

Then he shuts off the Newsfeed, looks away from the screen and closes his eyes.

A few minutes later, he opens his programming software. He creates a blank new project file, and names it "Third Beast".

Who will this third one be?

Well, let's see. His previous creation, Evelyn, is a more organic creation than Amber. Not off the peg, but kick-started from within Jaymi alone. Her sweetness and toughness embody a sensuous echo of his childhood violin-playing, as he only now comes to realise.

However, did Evelyn *quite* have the juice of real agency in her? Were the surfaces of her eyes quite wet enough, quite alive enough, to reflect the exact shape of whatever light-bulb hung from whatever ceiling Jaymi sent her under?

Hmm. Maybe Evelyn didn't quite add up to the sermon on the mount, after all. Maybe she's a rung upon a ladder.

So again, who will this third Beast be?

Someone who'll embody not just Jaymi's pointed response to the "Guy Score: Hunk or Gross?" Newsfeed, but something wider—his whole instinctive urge for the kind of warmth and openness he can see being targeted for punishment by every glyph and pixel of *Ain'tTheyFreaky!*.

After a moment he consults the general sketch of Shigem in his design for *The Imagination Thief*, then polishes it, so it reads: "Shigem Adele is an effusive, flamboyant nightclub host, a lovable and neu- rotic survivor, whose warmth can illuminate a roomful of people."

Well, OK then. Bring it on!

Jaymi thinks for a moment longer, then he renames this new project "Shigem"…

So here comes a new Beast, born into beauty and complexity, a creature of his own love and pain.

Regrettable that the warmth and truth of Shigem's effusiveness should be forced to look at and tangle with so ugly a counterbalance as the "Guy Score: Hunk or Gross?" Newsfeed. So fearful and stalely macho an instinct of rigidity and closure! Jaymi is sure Shigem would have things otherwise.

That counterbalance would seem, however, to be compulsory.

37 JAYMI CREATES SHIGEM'S CODE

Jaymi sips his peach schnapps on ice, puts it back down beside him on the flagstones of his study terrace here on Electra Drive, and claps his hands together. Glimpsing flickers of those control decks spread across the sky, he gets to work summoning up the code for his third Beast: the warmth and the openness that should have ruled the world…

To start at the simplest level, Shigem's favourite colour is amber, as being bright and sharp and rich in its beauty. His favourite creature is an angelfish, for fluttering so sensuously, and for pairing for life. (Shigem's inchoate ones and zeroes look up at Jaymi with an alignment that's the foreshadow of a proto-curiosity, upon hearing those words "pairing for life"; but Jaymi maintains a poker-face in response.)

As a character of flamboyant love, Shigem Adele instantiates all the passionate liveliness Jaymi can muster in himself. Central to him is that he never felt quite like a boy, being half a gender to the left. He will love from the feminine inside him, his thinking will be effeminate, and he will light up his surroundings with a joy and a beauty that most of those around him will scarcely deserve. This code of his hasn't yet risen to a level where he can speak, but Jaymi furnishes him with a central statement of truth, ready for speech as soon as it coalesces in him: "I could climb into a female life, and flower in pleasure. I love the girl inside me. She's the best I have within me. I love her best of all. I shall always love her, deeply, till the day I chance to die."

Nor has this code of Shigem's yet risen to having specific visuals; but in anticipation of those, Jaymi sprinkles in the seeds of two visual possibilities. Neither of these will germinate into Shigem's own actual visuals, but they'll reside in him recessively, colouring the cells of his beauty, in the form of two statements he will never quite utter aloud, describing distant pasts: "I love that freckled redhead girl who's also inside me, standing in the glade so long ago"; and "Inside me too, the Polynesian girl from aeons back, looking out to sea through the trees by the sandy bay, guarding her man while he sleeps at her side, with her hand resting easy on the warmth and the strength of his shoulders, so very long ago…"

Jaymi pulls Shigem's code back across millennia to the present era, and shoots it down into the kind of in-game reality where he'll be appointed to strut in *The Imagination Thief*—and the thrill that Shigem will get when he first walks into a club, sees people he knows in the coat-check line, and hears a thumping bass from down the hallways in the main room, which gives him butterflies and makes him strain to get on the dance-floor and light it up! For this will be the arena where he'll find he's a natural monarch, as it happens. But let him now be halted there a moment in freeze-frame—right there beside the coat-check line, where those dim little light-fittings are vibrating from the speakers down on the main floor—because this future monarchic status of Shigem should be underpinned by an accurate coding of the emotions inside him.

First, beneath the electric slenderness and untouchably exquisite androgyny and glamour of his physicality, there's an intense feeling of being at the nerve-end of his own dreams, of processing every thought according to how his guts and his loins respond to it, and of having something forever young-adult at the centre of him, never to age further and never having been any younger.

Whenever he is happy, other people seem so beautiful to him. Related to this, he cries easily, almost every day—not from unhappiness, but from the instances of sadness that he hears about or senses every day. Likewise he peals out spontaneous and high-strung laughter when he's joyful. This caroming between emotional extremes is something in himself that he's all too aware of, and struggles with daily. In particular his tendency to faint from excitement has often been not only embarrassing but also inconvenient, to say the least. But all those occasions have at least been preferable to the blushing despair whose spectre he can half-glimpse floating above the spectre of his actual triumph as a fabulous club-land creature: however flawless the latter spectre's words and social dealings are, that former half-seen spectre hangs there in shadow still, stuttering fiercely through every utterance and blushing throughout every interaction.

Jaymi allows Shigem's code to re-animate, from its freeze-frame beside the coat-check line. OK then, so there's the foundation of feeling beneath this Beast's imminent monarch status in the night-club corridor; now back to the status itself. Enough of that spectre blushing painfully—it's time for this one to blush becomingly. This will be a long and brilliant night, Shigem reflects, draping his arm around his clubbing companion's shoulders. "Sweetness before fierceness," he murmurs to that unidentified companion, with a smile. "You know, this party's become a circus these days. It used to be fun because it was small and you could come and dance, meet major DJs, get fucked up and discover a ton of great new music to play further downstream, but nowadays it's all about long lines, ten after-parties in one night, steroids, silicon tits and bad drugs. Oh well! The VIP room will have air-conditioning, champagne and the best drugs to keep us fresh throughout the night. Follow me." And they both turn up a stairwell on the left.

Jaymi rubs his hands, in a wicked joy of love.

Yes. That's what he needs.

38 AMBER WITH BINOCULARS ON SUNSET PLAZA DRIVE

Jaymi's first response to seeing Bang Dead's new "Guy Score: Hunk or Gross?" Newsfeed was to start creating Shigem's code out of thin air, beginning with nothing but a fore-echo of this Beast's warm true effusiveness. If the ones and zeroes behave themselves, Shigem will soon emerge from his code. He'll be painted with his own visuals, which will animate him; he'll be scored with his own soundtrack, which will come alive; and he'll be tested. Then within a few days he'll be electrified into incarnated form, in all his beauty, like a burst of love.

But despite this creation cycle of Shigem, there is little clarity as to how the "Guy Score: Hunk or Gross?" Newsfeed could possibly fail to barrel upwards and outwards in popularity and profitability around the world, at least for as long as tabloid culture outsells the rest.

There can be no assurance of the success of any investment; but a media stream that facilitates the rating of individual men for attractiveness using *Ain't They Freaky!*'s Freakometer, from a highest score of 10 for Hunkest, down to a lowest score of 1 for Grossest, by members of the public, does at least start out with the benefit of appealing to the resources of a decent majority.

Incarnated into the world by themselves, Jaymi's bursts of Shigem love would stand no chance against such competition. But with a little back-up, perhaps they might survive after all… Perhaps Amber's attentiveness to Dud should be ramped up a notch?

Perhaps Amber has been neglecting Dud in the last day or two? Yes, it's true: Dud is ready for his first home visit.

A mere few hours after these musings, Amber is back on Sunset Plaza Drive, coasting the car to a halt beside that flimsy crash-barrier once again. He gets out and straightens up, with that mild smile of his, steps around the car and scans the view for a leisurely moment. Then he raises binoculars to his face, points them somewhat downwards off the promontory, and fine-tunes the focus. Dud's home is one of those structures just down there, half-hidden behind trees…

It's always difficult for a stalker to get an accurate handle on the exact configuration of properties in the Hollywood Hills, so narrow and winding are the streets as they hug the flanks of the canyons and curve around the hill-spurs, and so anonymous is the aspect presented to the street by many a home whose multi-storeyed luxury extends in multi-CCTV'd cascade down the slopes on its far side, invisible to any outsider who may drive past its modest-looking front-door and garage-door, however much this interloper may slow down to peer through their windscreen.

But Dud's home cannot long elude such a scrutiny as Amber's.

And *yes*, there it is—just there, hiding beyond those bits of scrub, about level with the tops of those skinny-trunked trees growing further down.

Dud's house is indeed quite close beneath Amber and Jaymi right now, located on the very highest stretch of Blue Jay Way. That street, however, has no accessible connection at all with this one. It may be just a mere few flaps of the wing, for a flying crow; but for a car, or for any member of the public who might be peculiar enough to walk, it would be a long journey down to Blue Jay Way from here, whether choosing to go further up Sunset Plaza Drive or back down it, by way of a labyrinthine layout of residential streets that would be almost impossible to navigate successfully by mapless chance.

Amber knows how to drive there, however; and with this very goal in mind he returns to the car and sets off in the better direction, which is back down the way he came. After many dozens of twists downwards, there comes the secret key: he turns off Sunset Plaza, up Rising Glen Road. Further on, he turns up Thrasher Avenue; then in due course he swings the car quietly right off Thrasher, purring into the bottom end of Blue Jay Way in the stillness of early dusk.

39 SHIGEM EMERGES WITHIN HIS CODE

Back in the house on Electra Drive, a glow of warmth suffuses Jaymi as he resumes work at the point where Shigem and his unidentified interlocutor are ascending the nightclub stairwell. Jaymi finds his own viewpoint swooping in close to a doorman's ear, as Shigem air-kisses the man who's standing at the top of the stairs with a guest-list. The two clubbers step into a smaller bar area that leads to a terrace overlooking the main dance-floor.

Shigem's own visual art is still indistinct, at this point in his creation cycle. The artwork for the other people around him has been pre-populated, however, at least to the standard of a brisk commercial illustration, as in a storyboard for a high-end movie production. These figures are off-the-peg "types", in essence, being royalty-free stock imagery pasted in by Jaymi earlier, as a kind of provisional wallpaper or background against which he hopes Shigem's unique appearance will develop its own organic authenticity—for no actual Beast of Jaymi's will partake of off-the-peg stock components or repetitions of game language, it should go without saying.

Hovering his fingers over those banks of faders floating there on the sky above L.A., he psychs himself up to create the emergence of this new creation from the basic code achieved in the last session. But before Jaymi can hit a single key to kick-start Shigem, the latter just starts talking to him from the laptop screen, or perhaps *at* him. "I could climb into a female life, and flower in pleasure," Shigem announces. "I love the girl inside me. She's the best I have within me. I love her best of all. I shall always love her, deeply, till the day I chance to die."

Jaymi smiles, remembering his incorporation of this. "I'm happy she's there," he replies. "I can see her very clearly." He pauses, considering what best to say next. (It's something of a solemn moment, when a new being takes its first steps in this way. Humbling, too.) "Shigem, welcome to the world. And since you seem to be speaking so well already, I have a question for you, if I may. How does it feel, to be emerging as a Beast of Electra—?"

"Are you Mr Horney, the family-planning officer?" Shigem interrupts. "I was always told I owe my existence to the error of his ways.

If you are, then I shan't know what to say, and think I may have a happening."

"*What?* No, I'm not Mr Horney, and where on earth did you get him from? I'm Jaymi Peek."

"Slim, honeyed, golden, life-enhancing pervert," declares Shigem.

"Er … why, thank you. D'you say that to all the boys?"

"No; I say it only to one who is, like me, a wisp. Moon in Scorpio, North Banana rising. And talking of fruit and vegetables, since I see you'll be designing my game, I'd like to put in a request that I walk around Hollywood with a carrot up my bottom. A freshly-peeled one, natch. And not too pointy. But I hope you make me as sexy as Choo-Choo in *Top Cat*—I've always felt like a character with pointy ears. The ears are allowed to be pointy. By the way, I did mention the carrot, didn't I?"

"OK, we're not getting into your visuals just yet—"

"You've furnished my game-world with exquisite specificity, I must say. As I look around me, I see five figures in a nightclub landscape—all of them awaiting my social instructions, too, which is a very thoughtful touch, Jaymi, and thank you for it. First, I see a pale-skinned, black-haired, somewhat ill-looking, feminine and ferrety boy, wearing a white long-sleeved sweatshirt with yellow and magenta smiley faces; then I see an immaculate peroxide-haired Asian boy, glacially beautiful, in a white jacket, white shoes and salmon-pink trousers; then I see the most skimpily-clad pair of blond queens, with identical haircuts short on one side and about two feet long on the other, in minute red T-shirts and tight red shorts; and finally I see a feminine black boy dressed in sheer black clothing, the lack of breasts being the only thing revealing his maleness. So, when you get round to my own visuals, I'd like to request that I stand out from all those. D'you do requests?"

"No. But you will stand out, I'm going in a different direction with the casting—"

"So here's my request. 'Cos now that I'm emerging, I feel I've changed, you know: I used to be like someone in black leather buying a pink teddy bear, but now I'm like someone in pink leather buying a black teddy bear."

"I'll do what I can to take that on board."

"Jaymi, are you going to design me as a complete slut-bucket?"

"Well, not quite a complete slut-bucket, as you put it, no."

"That's good. Because I'm a lot subtler than that. Some people see me as just kitschy and bitchy and chic, but despite appearances I'm not just pansying about: I'm so sensitive, I could swoon at any moment. You know that, yes?"

"I do know that. I made you prone to fainting; it's baked into the code."

"Thank you, just make sure to give me a soft landing every time, please. OK then, I've got some epic nightlife-behind-the-nightlife to get back to. Then I'll need to head off home before too long, maybe even by midday tomorrow, as I need to water my weeping fig. I forgot to water it this afternoon, and it does get terribly husky. Or maybe I'll need to dry it out. Or just do a little mopping-up after it. You never know which it's going to be, but it's always one of those. It's such an emotional little fig. But I know how it feels, I need constant mopping-up or drying-out myself. Pot-plant care is an emotional roller-coaster. But I have one more thing to say to you, Jaymi—I can't wait for my artwork! *Please* give me my artwork as soon as poss; there's a duck. You don't know what it's like, not having visuals. It's like being always in the dark, living in a powder-puff and giving off sparks, as Bonnie sang. That describes me right now, Jaymi, d'you understand?"

"Yes, Shigem! And ... pleased to meet you, I'm sure."

Shigem purrs up at his creator, from somewhere in that pool of indistinct pixels on the laptop screen. Then he turns and melts away across the bar, and out onto the terrace overlooking the dance-floor, where the music booming out through the main hall rises in volume on the whole scene's soundtrack.

Jaymi presses save, flicks the screen to black, sits back, closes his eyes and exhales.

He has to admit, he didn't feel altogether in charge of that.

40 HERB HACKS SHIGEM'S CODE

As occurred with Evelyn's code, this emergence of Shigem's code is straight away followed by the nagging awareness in Jaymi of some elusive thing that's awry: he has an almost physical feeling that some little blade of closed metal is hiding among the letters and figures and symbols in the text editor, rupturing the fluid openness of this brand-new Beast.

With a stab of annoyance, he fathoms the likely culprit, picturing the same scene he pictured on that earlier occasion for Evelyn: to wit, the idyllic Westwood Village cottage scene, featuring Herb schlubbing around on a sofa strewn with empty ready-meal containers, tapping away at his keyboard in an awesome display of hacking chops designed to kidnap and subvert this code, on a Bang Dead mission to dumb Shigem down for *Ain't TheyFreaky!* in ways so aesthetically debased that Jaymi baulks at imagining them.

He slams his fist down on the desk beside the keyboard, as a surge of pure hatred flows through him. How *dare* Herb interfere like this! How dare he snatch the reins of Jaymi's Beasts and subvert them into sad tacky travesties of themselves, fit for some cheap tabloid game! How dare Bang Dead manifest such evil spite, in response to nothing more than Jaymi's leaving the company and competing with it and (as Dud probably fears most) starting to streak ahead of it in creative sophistication?

He shuts his current session into live quarantine. Later he'll resume work from a restore point before he was hacked; but just for the moment he lets the hack run amok within the quarantined session, watching his infected code with horror and disgust, for whatever it may reveal about the infector's evolving capabilities. This time Herb wastes no resources in planting any cheeky little in-game Easter egg—no clump of penises rooted in a flowerpot, twirling in expectancy and then straining up at Shigem's passage beside them, as they twirled and strained at Evelyn's on the shore of her mushroom bay. In fact Herb is wreaking fewer changes than he did to Evelyn, all told; but the ones he is making have a harsher, more cartoony quality than in his hack into her.

This hack strikes without warning and is felt as existential violence, flavoured by the nature of the Beast in question. It happens to hit him a few moments after the unmistakably Shigem-flavoured and aforementioned electric slenderness and untouchably exquisite androgyny of his physicality has passed across the threshold of the club's main entrance into the smoking area outside, so that his unidentified companion can have a cigarette. "We'll just be stepping outside for a moment," Shigem informs the woman guarding the door.

"…Excellent," she drawls, through her chewing-gum.

Shigem stops and turns. "Are you being sarcastic?"

"Who, me?" she asks. Her affectless gaze comes to rest on the infinity point at the end of the club's main hallway, along which a dozen podiums are spaced out in a line into the distance, each podium occupied by a muscular, almost naked go-go boy performing drugged-out gyrations to the music in an endless twirl of narcissistic horniness.

Once outside, a smiling Shigem murmurs into his unidentified companion's ear: "That door-whore is more superficial than she seems; I've always said so."

—Then it hits.

In swift-growing shock, he notices that the club-kids in this railed-off area, smoking alone or in groups, would appear to have started morphing, most queasily, in the last few seconds. They are fast coming to resemble gangs of hillbillies from the smallest and poorest towns in the southern Appalachians, standing here less like clubbers deep in a city night, and more like vigilantes loitering on the corner of Church Avenue and Main Street, doubtless with weapons concealed in their dust-covered clothing, all of them peering with horror at Shigem, looking him up and down with just the degree of approval that such citizens would be likely to feel towards a citizen like him, in this setting whose geography they know so well but he knows nothing of, and all ominously biding their time until the imminent fall of night…

By this point, no other clubbers nor any nightclub clothing remains to be seen among the figures in the smoking area, though Shigem's attire and comportment retain the chic flamboyance they had in the club. Glancing fearfully up the dead straight widths of Church and Main, he can sense how tight-charged these small-town spaces are with oppressive scrutiny—how trigger-happy they are, all told, with the kind of small-eyed judgement that'll be ready to punish whatever beauty or mystery he may dare inhabit or apprehend.

Two of the vigilantes nudge each other, their eyes creasing up with hatred and dusty laughter at his vulnerability, wolf-whistling him and making rough kissing sounds in his direction. All along Main Street, dogs appear, jumping off porches and slinking over front yards, full of feral energy. One by one, the dogs turn and look at him, with evil pointed faces through the dusk. A vigilante whistles, and a dog dips its head and sets its eyes upon Shigem and creeps towards him (*a creep-dog*, he thinks), followed by another dog with long tusks.

He hears the scrape of cold steel fingernail-blades along the railings behind him. The scrape gets closer to him, rising to a screech. It's a sound to make knives curl—the sound a blade would make if it were tortured. Shigem shrieks and twitches, wheels around and sees a man is stalking nearer through the lamp-light, his hand upon the railings, his head somewhat lowered and his eyes brimful of evil humour. The man wears a fedora hat, a top coloured with red and green horizontal stripes, and on one hand a dirty leather glove whose fingers end in lethal knife-blades. He's not burly but emanates a grating, slashing, gut-nauseous flavour of perverted violence, with a subterranean chuckle and a grin raging with slaughter on a face that's burned to disfigurement.

A slow cackle echoes around the smoking area, with the plink of drips and hiss of steam, as in a cavernous power-station boiler-room, while he proffers his gloved right hand to Shigem. "*FANCY A BUMP OF COKE?… COME AND GET IT, BITCH!*" he grates, flexing back his bladed fingers, one by one, to reveal a heap of crystalline white powder in his palm, with a dozen human eyes leering up salaciously out of the powder at Shigem. Then he bellows with demonic laughter, crooning "*Come to Freddy!*" as Shigem scampers back through the door into the nightclub. Krueger's arm extends through the air after him, down the hallway between the dozen go-go boys' podiums, shooting along just behind the nape of Shigem's neck, which it scratches flirtatiously with the sharp end of a pinkie-blade, drawing drips of blood as Shigem sprints away down the never-ending hallway, screaming and crying…

He dives sideways to escape the arm, which retreats back down the hallway while Shigem presses himself against the wall and the floor behind a podium, breathing hard, with his face still streaming tears of nauseous horror.

After a few minutes, he edges out of his hiding-place, shivering.

He crawls on his knees along the side of the podium, then pushes his face slowly closer to the front corner of it, to peer in fearful anguish around the angle of splintery wood.

No human being is in sight. A fitful wind blows dust and tumbleweed down the empty hallway past the unoccupied podiums, in a monochrome befitting an abandoned saloon bar in a deserted town in a Western movie. At the far end of the hallway, the club's main double doors swing towards each other by themselves, then slam dead-shut with a sliding of bolts.

Hunched on the floor like a bug, Shigem listens hard for a full minute, but can hear nothing through the sound of the desert breeze. He gets to his feet, feels the blade-cuts on the back of his neck, inspects the blood on his fingers, and wipes it off on the side of the podium.

He tiptoes through an archway into the deserted main room of the club. Here, everything is still, except for the bobbing reflections from a huge mirrored disco-ball suspended from high rafters above the centre of the dance-floor, which turns in the stillness.

He steps across the floor, his gaze burrowing into all the dark corners of the room ... and then he hears it: from somewhere buried in the bowels of this sprawling club, Krueger's time-biding chuckle chugs softly in the shadows, as if promising him a dark game with pale ropes in a night-maze forest.

He delves into his memories of this huge, complicated building, from all the decadent club-nights of music and dancing and drugs and sex and friendship that he's spent in the safety and sanctuary of its cavernous freedom. Can he recall another exit he can use now? Surely he must be able to remember some obscure fire-escape, somewhere, that could lead him out across the neighbouring roofs, railway arches and elevated tracks, to safety?

The disco-ball above him bursts open and Krueger hatches from it, diving his hands down and slashing at Shigem. The ball's mirror mosaics explode and shatter and rain down—screeching fragments of glass slicing into him from all angles, while those lethal finger-blades swing ever closer to his face.

"*Can I have this dance?*" Krueger grates. The hands catch hold of Shigem, grab him by the neck and lift him high, pulling him up at high speed to the warehouse's ceiling, as high as an aircraft hangar's, where they drape him over a wooden rafter. Shigem grasps the rafter in vertiginous panic, sweating freely and dripping blood where he's been stuck with splinters of mirror across his body. He glimpses the dance-floor far below, which seems to have come alive again, with revellers' heads milling about like sand-grains down there—though neither music nor voices are audible up here in this dirty roof-skin.

The rafter creaks, slips and starts to fall apart, revealing tendon-like cables inside it. Coming loose from the building's skeleton, it now hangs from mere strands of sticky wood, which are rooted beside pulsing water-pipes, leaving Shigem to dangle into a terrifying void. He scrabbles up the rafter, it slips further, and just as it falls away he flails to one side and grabs hold of a metal fire-ladder mounted on a wall. The top end of the ladder, near above him, is a blanked-off ceiling: the only way is down. He scuttles down the rungs, which are encased in a curved girdle of bones like a distended ribcage—but then this girdle stops, leaving just the rungs descending through open air—then even these naked rungs peter out altogether for a couple of metres. So he is going to have to drop *off* the ladder, through the air, aiming to grab the continuation of the ladder below ... at the risk of missing it and dropping the height of the entire building, or impaling himself as he tries to catch hold of the topmost rungs, which he can see will welcome him like jagged finger-blades. He no longer has enough strength to climb back up, nor will he have enough to hang here much longer; so he clings on, frozen just for now, wailing and in tears.

And now Krueger reappears, three rungs above him, and breaks the ladder on one side, so Shigem is swung sideways, dangling by a single thread of ladder-bone...

Because Herb is continuing to perpetrate this cruel hack, he must not yet have realised he's doing so inside a session that Jaymi managed to live-quarantine. Although Jaymi will delete this quarantined session as soon as he's had enough of watching its horror-film unfoldment, the temptation to enter battle with Herb has now become too much to resist. Jaymi therefore breaks into Herb's manoeuvres and drops Amber's code directly into the scene, causing this blond Beast to land on the topmost rung that sticks up underneath Shigem.

Krueger's evil grin vanishes as he sees Amber land and point a gun straight up towards Krueger's forehead, then pull the trigger. The bullet streaks up a narrow corridor of air, past Shigem; and in the instant when it fractures his skull, Krueger feels he's spiralling down a tunnel whose end is filled with Amber's blazing eyes transfixing him—

41 THE INFINITY POOL AT THE BLUE JAY WAY HOUSE

Except for the diminutive offshoot of Hopen Place halfway up it, Blue Jay Way is a single winding strip, leading to a cul de sac. Within walking distance of the very top, Amber parks in a discreet curve in the road. He gets out, locks the car and slips into a narrow space of vegetation between houses. He pushes through undergrowth, down a slope towards the hollow of the canyon beyond the rear boundaries of these properties, and turns to face the grand mansion positioned up behind the fence on his left.

He looks around, calculating his options. Then he scales a tree, clambers along a branch and drops down on the other side of the fence. Up a slope of earth beside one wing of the house, he stops behind a bank of foliage enclosing the back terrace. He and Jaymi peer through the leaves—and there is Dud just ten metres away, beside an infinity pool whose further side seems to merge, with hardly a break, into the blue sky over the cityscape beyond. Along another side of the pool, adjacent to the hillside, stands a line of five unlit tiki torches, the lantern-holder of each torch being emblazoned with the logo of a different one of *Ain't They Freaky!*'s five Newsfeeds.

Lounging in a deck-chair, Dud is intent on his computer. Perhaps he's busy, this very minute, in big entrepreneurial dreams for Bang Dead's "Guy Score: Hunk or Gross?" Newsfeed? Or perhaps his smug assiduousness is engaged in hatching some other, future newsfeed.

Somehow, this matter-of-fact new view of him as being just a man sitting outside his home reveals to Jaymi with greater clarity the dreary mean-mindedness in Dud's using his energies to create something as ugly as *Ain't They Freaky!*.

Stationed here, looking through the leaves at him, Amber feels deliriously alone.

How sweet it would be, to step into the world of that monkey there, during the next few seconds, and snip through its neck with a powerful blade! He's aware of just the velocity that would be necessary. He can also imagine the kind of physical vibrations that would be transmitted from the blade's handle into his own hands and blond-haired arms, as a result of the blades' encounter with what they'd be severing inside the neck.

How easy that would be—how right, and how restful.

Amber has not come for that, however: today he's been tasked with a gentle reconnoitre of weak points in Dud's inhabitation of the world, plus a little terrorisation. But with such a clear sight as he now possesses, Amber perceives that pretty much all of Dud's inhabitation of the world is weak. How flimsy, in flesh-bound reality, are all the walls that this vile little monkey relies on: walls of law, security, money, status. How paper-thin those walls are, in Amber's and Jaymi's sight!

42 JAYMI CREATES SHIGEM'S APPEARANCE

Up in his study in the house on Electra Drive, Jaymi closes his eyes and thinks back to that unique half-minute when he let his gaze wander up and down the "Guy Score: Hunk or Gross?" Newsfeed, where new posts were popping up every few seconds, every one of them receiving scores and comments from multiple sources.

Then he re-opens his eyes, consults his most recent notes for *The Imagination Thief* and checks his sketch for Shigem's visuals. Its first description of Shigem's physical appearance reads: "The first thing I registered then was a golden bracelet with the name 'Shigem' engraved on it in slick squirly black letters [...]. The only thing I got as far as picking up from him was that he was Malaysian. He had long black hair with platinum-blond highlights in, warm bright eyes, and beautiful high-fashion facial features that were nevertheless prominently acne-cratered all over, especially on a pair of perfect high cheekbones. Here in the club he's dressed with stylish flamboyance and a certain flash and trash, like a whore on Jalan

Raja on a hot Kuala Lumpur night in Fashion Week. A thin silver earring hangs from each ear, and the word 'Virginity' is tattooed on the honey-coloured skin of his left shoulder in the same script as the name on the bracelet. Inhabiting the femininity of his slim and delicate body with a simple, quiet and sensual pleasure, he reminds me of sunlight and moves with divinity. […] faster than quicksilver, light as air and never once intrusive or demanding, he yet reaches somehow into every person's presence, one to one, and draws them out and upward like a chime through the strobe-lights. Riding the crowd, he electrifies the dance-floor with effortless charisma, in tune with the dirty hard electro playing, as he lights up the faces and the spaces in between them with the bright sexy flicker of his presence. He curls his fingers round in the air as he speaks, and I see that malice cannot touch him here: no matter what may happen in the outside world, here in club-land he's unbeatable. If all the land were set up as a chic nightclub, he'd be absolute monarch."

There is then one further little artwork-oriented description of him, a bit later on: "You felt his arm go round your waist, and his long black hair with its blond highlights spilling past your shoulder. His presence was permeated by gayness, somatically engrained—a luscious quality that spread, sleek and fluid as a dancer, through every move and every word of his, as blood pervades a body."

Well then, that's a clear enough sketch to work from. Jaymi fires up his visual engine, verifies there are no available security updates he should download, and gets cracking. Despite the trauma of his last work on Shigem's creation cycle, which ended with his dele-tion of the quarantined session where he'd dropped Amber into a nightclub to kill Krueger, the nightclub environment in general is clearly this Beast's natural habitat—so Jaymi will return to it today. This will also convey an implicit fuck-you to Herb, whose face so deserves to be rubbed in the fact of Krueger's banishment to the land of alternative histories that Shigem will never be aware of, thanks so much!

Glancing up from his terrace here on Electra Drive, Jaymi once again half-sees a bank of controls flicker across the sky above Los Angeles…

OK, here come those visuals! Airbrushed twinkly photo-studio image. Full lips, parted, with points of gloss shining on the surface of their fullness. A spark of light on each eye, soft-squeezed outwards into subtle white starbursts—each with just two rays, almost imperceptible yet evoking a hint of Shigem's enchantment. On either side of his face, which he's made up with a melting perfection, hangs a big golden hoop earring that's been starbursted with greater boldness: still with only two rays at a hundred and eighty degrees, but much more extravagant than those emanating from his eyes—and not white rays, but pale gold ones, as from the hoops. So enchanted is this starburst that it even seems to be the source of light for his long black hair, which catches the faint illumination in snaking down to his shoulders before becoming lost in the pure black of his top.

The next image is a live shot, showing Shigem working the decks in the DJ box, not posed in the studio. In this, his hair is revealed to be more street, more dirty-sexy-casual; his eyes, being so lidded as to appear almost closed, owing to his downward focus on the decks, are revealed as being bigger than expected within his face, providing much gorgeous room for the eye-shadow that's still visible from down there on the dance-floor in front of him; and his nose is revealed as being somewhat more petite and higher than expected, with an achingly attractive snub-nose shape whereby its front outline, in profile or even half-profile, has the gentlest of concave curves from bridge to tip. This vision never needs to speak, but just to do. He's cool and untouchable, though commanding that we touch him, ensconced in his social world, privileged and welcome there, where numerous unseen players wish him to remain, wish for his talent to continue having free rein, and wish for Shigem himself. (Does he know this? He must know it, right?)

In the next image he's a jewelled prince, delicate and languid in profile, his slim neck hung with silver necklaces set with gems of many colours—*purple and red and yellow and on fire*—while his gaze rests easy on the distance out of frame. Cross-legged on the floor, he rests a hand upon a handsome stuffed *bichon frisé* sitting at his side. From his right ear a drop-earring of ruby hangs like a drop of blood, while scattered feather boas fill the room on every side. Lit through stained-glass, he's exquisite and impeccable, yet surely dissolute by implication, forever frozen here inside one instant in his flamboyant apartment.

Following that profile viewpoint, Jaymi directs the software to swing around inside the image, to show a full-face view into Shigem's gaze. From this new vantage-point, and still in the context of Shigem's glamour and social power, we catch our first glimpse of the vestiges of his adolescent awkwardness, gawky and painful and felt by him as somehow camelline—now buried deep within his lineaments, underneath his polish and his made-up exquisiteness, and also a part of these. A ghosting of ravages and damage done in years past, cross-cut through him, like a faint foundation of his make-up, and central in the magic he has conjured ever since.

"Talk to me about my hair," says Shigem to Jaymi, looking up at him from the laptop. "You're not going to give me fly-away hair, are you? Silky and manageable, please. Hair shouldn't be allowed to be quite as silky and manageable as this—but for me, Jaymi, you'll be making an exception, I think you'll find."

"No, honey-boy, there'll be no fly-aways, you have my word."

"Honey-coloured *always* works, thank you. Though I have also been called a muted biscuit colour, so bear that in mind as a possibility too. And with shy ears. I also have ideas concerning the early-evening ensembles you're going to dress me in. I can't have you dressing me in puffballs."

"*Puff*balls?"

"I should also like to put in a bid for the colour of my drinks, my contact lenses and my outfits to be matched."

"OK, you're on! Good night, Shigem." Smiling, Jaymi taps save and close, then he sits back and lets his eyes drift across the grand cityscape beneath his terrace.

Cool! Let Shigem's visuals be birthed just so. There he is, a Malaysian gazelle-boy caught in a freeze-frame on Jaymi's screen, video-paused in the act of applying eyeliner in a cocaine mirror in a nightclub, as beautiful slim feminine boys often do. (That smile of his, in that chance-chosen frame there, is one of those cool-happy-flat-impenetrable-bland-universal smiles. The sort of smile that seems as if it will carry on through all things and all time. It's not the most representative of Shigem, to be honest, but that's usually the nature of random freeze-frames.)

He should work OK for *The Imagination Thief*.

He should also serve pretty well as Jaymi's answer to the "Guy Score".

43 THE SEVERED GREY TONGUE-MEAT SWINGING ROUND THE FOOTBALL

Climbing through a window into the Blue Jay Way house, Amber finds himself in a lounge at the back of the building. The room is deserted, but open double-doors lead outside onto the terrace where Dud is still lounging in his deck-chair, intent on his laptop computer. Occasional flying insects dip down onto the infinity pool beside Dud, disturbing its glassy-smooth surface with concentric rings, which soon dissipate to leave its sheen again impeccable, all the way to where its far edge bleeds out into the sky above the grand L.A. cityscape that's hidden just out of sight from Amber's and Jaymi's viewpoint here in the lounge.

Surrounding Amber, the expensive tackiness of the decor is everywhere themed with the ugliness of football-related memorabilia. There's a wall-mounted photo of Dud bellowing cretinously on a pitch, dressed in some kind of ugly sport uniform. Amber wanders over to the photo, and picks up a football that's been placed on a shelf beneath it. From his right pocket he takes out a flick-knife and carves a gash in the football, then from his left pocket he takes out a bulky severed tongue, heavy and grey and pre-drained of blood, perhaps from an ox; and he forces the tongue into the gash, with a squeezy-scraping sound as each rough taste-bud flicks its way in over the jagged edge of the cut on the ball's surface.

Twirling the ball atop his left hand at increasing speed, so that the gash-rooted tongue flails greyly and meatily around through the air, scattering the odd fleck of remaining spittle as it swings, Amber steps through the double-doors and strolls across the terrace towards the infinity pool.

At a certain point, Dud hears something behind him. He wheels around in his chair and is about to shout—but Jaymi places Amber's right index-finger upright against his lips as he approaches to within a metre or two, with Amber's eyes so wide open and such a warning behind them, that Dud amputates his shout to a grunt.

Amber stoops, brings his right hand down with a muscular force like metal, pressing Dud back into the seat, and stays there staring into his target's terrified face, with charismatic twinkling menace and no words.

Panic flashes in Dud's face—*it's that blond psychopath who came barging into his office in the Avenue of the Stars tower!*—while the tongue continues swinging around in flappy orbit of the ball, still twirling aloft on those deft fingers beside both their heads.

Amber's right hand reaches forward and forces Dud's jaws open, while his left hand darts forward too, pushing the football-tongue hard between Dud's teeth and into his slobbering mouth. Then Amber is walking back up the garden and through the double-doors, and he's vanished before Dud has managed to squeeze the cold grey ox-meat back out through his lips, spluttering in fury and terror. The spat-out tongue and ball land in the infinity pool, where they proceed to sink slowly to the bottom, staining the water as they go.

Minutes later in the lounge, issuing frantic orders into his phone, Dud halts, staring at the wall-mounted photo. Across its width has been scrawled "Grossest: 1!".

44 SHIGEM'S APPEARANCE COMES ALIVE

Jaymi stares up at his study ceiling, then back down at the monitors in front of him, where the feeling of a sunlit plain spreads wide. First, he establishes Shigem's gleaming detail in *The Imagination Thief* as being a character Shigem will meet in a dream, called the Mint Man, whose visuals will pop up now and then in the gameplay, causing suspicion: "you both were alone on some deserted level of a multiplex cinema, trying to find the exit. You came across an older gentleman, who stood in silence holding out a tray of mints. 'Oh look—we get a mint!' you cried, and grabbed Kim's hand. You scampered up to the man and both curtseyed and both took a mint. The man smiled, then with just a trace of irony he watched you both running off away down the escalator giggling and whispering in unison, '*My god, I think we've just met the Mint Man! Tee-hee-hee!*' […] "'Oh look—we get a mint!'" Lucan simpers, mimicking your voice, 'and you two scamper up and curtsey like bitches and you take a mint and run away down the escalator, giggling cuntily: "*My god, I think we've just met the Mint Man! Tee-hee-hee!*"' […] 'how did Lucan know the dream with the Mint Man?' […] 'maybe you told someone about this Mint Man one night when you were drunk, and you don't remember doing so' […] 'Anyway, d'you remember this Mint Man character?'"

He then establishes Shigem's talisman in *The Imagination Thief* as being a magical chanterelle mushroom, whose visuals will peep shyly out from the game-play of his childhood on one single occasion, in a memory of when he was a little fairy-boy in an enchanted woodland somewhere: "once you saw a chanterelle beneath a mauve rose."

On a whim, Jaymi concludes by establishing an additional motif for Shigem in *The Imagination Thief*, which will pop up in the game-play in the form of a penal chilli: "one of your Malaysian chilli peppers."

Yes; although Shigem has no soundtrack yet, his visuals are starting to fill his creator with warm joy at what sort of Beast he will be in his game. After all, little singing cupcakes are appearing, without Jaymi's even having to program them, as wallpaper on the screen of Shigem's phone, including some cakes whose frosting tops are modelled with a profusion of coloured decorations such as small birds (one of which slides off its cupcake while Jaymi watches) and a rasher of streaky bacon, all realistically modelled in marzipan.

Now that Shigem is sitting there with his own longed-for visuals alive, filing his coloured finger-nails as if playing the violin, Jaymi looks into his eyes, causing Shigem to smile back up at him in sweet surprise; and in this pre-soundtrack silence between them, Jaymi sees something he has never quite seen before. This "something" is simply the way in which, through the grime and tar of life and surviving it, Shigem's gentle magic innocence peeps out, as always: through fatigue, through the work of being alive and still on course, through his never having money, through his never having time, through the dreary noise of Bang Dead, through insults and threats, through the mask of acne craters that cover his entire face with such relentless prominence from years of attack, still Jaymi sees in those lovely made-up eyes, so big and brown and bright, the freshest and most loving light he's ever seen inside a person anywhere, held pure and channelled cleanly out between those lashes—shining up at Jaymi, so he's buoyed up and carried on the beauty of Shigem, while his mouth hangs open and his feet can't feel the floor.

Seeing this inside Shigem without warning, Jaymi is lost for words that he might use as commentary upon it, in his own head; so he gives up seeking them.

…Yes. What he's just seen. That matchless thing, greater in those eyes than he'll ever see elsewhere, most likely.

That is all that matters.

That is all we really need.

That's the only game in town.

And Shigem knows those things, just as clear as mountain sunlight, through being them; while billions around him do not know and never will.

45 KELLY SMUDGES SHIGEM

As Jaymi contemplates his text editor window, he soon becomes aware of a fidgety grey ticking and pattering somewhere around the edges of the code where these fledgling Shigem visuals are emerging. And the penny drops: it's Kelly, trying to cheapen and impoverish this freshly-feathered Beast's new artwork. She's smart in her approach, though, as she beavers away at her image-editing software in her office in the Sunset Boulevard building. She's smart in the sense that she doesn't just barge in and get smudging, as Herb crashed into Shigem's code with a heavy-footed evocation of Freddy Krueger. No; she insinuates herself into her target's own environment, then entices him.

There, look—Kelly has just dropped an image of her own perky self into *The Imagination Thief*'s visuals, standing in front of Shigem near the head of the queue for the coat-check, now the club is closing. She turns around, all casual, notices him as if for the first time, smiles and pipes up with some well-judged morsel of small-talk, some undemanding little comment, at this late stage in the night when they're both too tired for demands. He responds in kind, and within a moment she has him in the palm of her hand with a soft little volley of shallow chatter, tapping into his own easy penchant for the same.

In the midst of this, without warning, she takes a tablet computer from her handbag, holds it up in front of him and hands it over. Absently he takes hold of it, and surprise spreads through his face.

The tablet's front-facing video camera must be switched on, because there he is looking at himself, here in the coat-check line. That much is clear—and yet there's something odd going on here. The face that he's looking at is different from his real one. It is tamer, smoother, cleaner, somehow safer within itself… It is also, evidently, the face of a man who is rich and famous, cocooned in the privilege and paraphernalia of his very own talk-show, no less—for now Shigem registers that the screen's image is furnished with all the branded graphics of a TV talk-show broadcast, with the Bang Dead logo at the top right and his name, Shigem Adele, flashing in a slick, tacky font at the bottom left.

He presses the power button on the tablet, to shut this off, and as the screen goes black he sees his real face reflected on its dark shiny surface, brutally lit by these closing-time fluorescent house-lights in this hallway, his make-up still intact on skin that's cratered like the surface of the moon, perspiring with a glow of euphoria from the night he's had—and without doubt, neither tame nor clean nor safe.

"Come over and join us at Bang Dead Games, Shigem, we've got such big plans for you!" enthuses Kelly.

Jaymi has been keeping her in his sights, via his own laptop's split-screen view of the scene's visuals and its underlying digital language, seething at her, and awaiting his moment to drop Amber's ready-made code into the coat-check line beside the pair of them. That should fend Kelly off—after all, Amber was brutally efficient at dispatching Krueger, in Herb's hack of Shigem's code. Jaymi gets the block of Amber code ready, poises it just so, and hovers his forefinger over the Enter key, ready to drop him in like a lethal blond missile…

But the forefinger pulls back and pleasure flickers in Jaymi's eyes, to witness this new Beast taking unexpected and quite masterful care of himself, without any such help from his creator: "No thank you. I don't think so," Shigem replies to Kelly, handing the tablet back to her. "Have a good night." And he turns away to reclaim his coat.

"Well, if you change your mind, give me a call at Bang Dead!" she trills, then slips off into the crowd.

Outside in the cool air of night, Shigem sets off alone, toward the first hint of dawn up ahead. How "user-friendly" she was, in her attempt to poach him into a different game-world from his own.

And how much he feels like taking a shower, to wash off the traces of her offer.

He steps into a late-night subway train and sits down. The carriage is empty, except for an attractive boy sitting several seats away, across the central aisle. The boy stares at Shigem without expression, throughout most of three subway stops; then he leaves the train, without Shigem's having met his gaze and without their having exchanged a word. Once the doors have closed again, Shigem flicks his gaze onto the boy's face for the first time and stares back at him where he stands out there on the platform, and they hold each other's gaze with a continued lack of expression, until the train has drawn them apart, left the station and plunged into the tunnel with a screech of wheels.

He glances up and down the now-empty carriage, watching it judder and tilt, as it careens along this pipe through the earth under a city. He takes out his mobile phone, taps the train's wifi icon and checks his email. A message from Jaymi Peek! "Antidote to your talk-show self" reads the subject line. Shigem opens it with avid curiosity, finds nothing but a single hyperlink, and taps this.

On the phone there flickers up the very start of a black and white movie. He finds his attention sucked into it, as its opening title, *Pippa*, unfurls in an old-fashioned typeface. From across a street, the camera zooms towards a woman standing on a plinth two metres above the pavement. With a shock of premonition, Shigem recognises her as the very same reclusive Pippa whom he'll know in the world of *The Imagination Thief*, of whom he's already started to learn inklings from Jaymi—and here she is, staring at Shigem, immobile and terrified.

As the movie camera sways closer, it becomes clear there is a lot "wrong" with her: her black face is too circular, her skin too blotchy and lurid and grainy, her eyes too wide, empty, feral... The camera is nearing Pippa too quickly now. Before it reaches the horror she's becoming, it veers queasily to the right, leaving most of her still within the frame but positioned at the left-hand edge of it (and how disturbing that she's still visible there), while the rest of the frame shows the slow approach of an open window beyond her.

The depth of field is maintained as sufficient to include both this oncoming window and her rotting face, which continues to approach the camera too, much closer than the window; until the aperture is widened and the shutter-speed increased, reducing depth of field and nudging her face too close for focus, at just the moment when chunks of face begin slipping off her cheekbones.

Now that she's just behind him, Shigem and the camera lurch onward, with a sick dread, towards the window, then through it—to the over-lit scene of an operation—an experiment, in fact, that he wishes he'd never glimpsed, because this glimpse will leave a stain in him for the rest of his life.

On an operating table at the end of the room are two girls of about ten years old, who appear more and more entangled with each other as Shigem approaches them. They are communing with each other, whispering and giggling. As he reaches them, their closeness becomes excitingly horrific without warning, when the head of the one on his left becomes shaped like a kind of spoon and it swings down into the other girl's body and dips into a ready-made cleft there, as if the two are a complex balancing ornament. There is no more sound from them on the audio track, but he wrenches his gaze away from them in shock at their monstrousness, and wondering at the suddenness of editing that inserted them there without warning.

His averted gaze falls on the other operating table in this room, where there lies a long agglomeration of soy meat that has been moulded into the shape of a cooked human being. A surgeon with a bag of cheese is standing beside this meat-course. He turns to address Shigem, saying "You elicit extreme reactions in me: you live a unisex existence and it drives me to extremes as a reaction," then he turns back to work on the meat-human, inserting a hose-pipe into its heart.

The phone's screen goes black, reflecting his ravaged complexion on its shiny surface, lit by the train-carriage lights, as it was by the club's fluorescent house-lights—but this time looking both horrified and thrilled by what he's just seen. Then a line of text unfurls across his features on this screen, in the same old-fashioned typeface that was used for the old movie's title *Pippa*. The text reads: "I love you, Shigem. You make me happy. (I also thought I'd introduce you to horror movies, as I've got a hunch you're going to like them.) Anyway, can't wait to see you in *The Imagination Thief*! Your friend forever, Jaymi Peek."

Shigem's laugh of surprise and joy rings out through the empty carriage. "Thanx Jaymi, I can't wait to be there!" he texts back, blushing, while the train hurtles on through the clatter of the tunnel.

46 THE "TRIVIA SCORE: WACKY OR BORING?" NEWSFEED

Online next morning, numerous sources are excited to inform Jaymi that today Bang Dead has rolled out another massive free offering to consumers everywhere. It's the third major plank of *Ain't They Freaky!*, and the company promises it'll be a popular hit: it's the "Trivia Score: Wacky or Boring?" Newsfeed!

This is a constant stream of images, videos or pieces of text uploaded from around the world, presenting trivia and factoids, which are rated for entertainment value by any member of the public using *Ain't They Freaky!*'s Freakometer, from a highest score of 10 for Wackiest, down to a lowest score of 1 for Boringest.

Jaymi lets his gaze wander up and down this newsfeed stream, where new posts are popping up every few seconds, every one of them soon receiving scores and comments from multiple sources.

He reads a few posts, for half a minute or so.

Then he shuts off the Newsfeed, looks away from the screen and closes his eyes.

A few minutes later, he opens his programming software. He creates a blank new project file, and names it "Fourth Beast".

Who will this fourth one be?

Well, let's see. His previous creation, Shigem, was the warmest and most open Beast yet. He'd be difficult to beat, in that particular department. Yet this whole Beast-creation mission, whose nature and stakes Jaymi is discovering as he expands into it, requires that he never stand still or repeat himself but always advance in his sophistication as a creator, every time he designs a new one to interact with those he's already created. Advancement and originality only—no rest and no slacking allowed.

Hmm. Maybe Shigem can't quite be allowed to add up to the sermon on the mount, after all. Maybe he's a rung upon a ladder.

Well, alright then, what dimension is Shigem lacking, that Jaymi should now add? Thinking back to when he started creating Shigem's code, he recalls that one reason for Shigem's favourite creature being an angelfish was this animal's tendency to pair for life; at which point, from somewhere among Shigem's inchoate ones and zeroes, the foreshadow of a capacity for curiosity looked up at Jaymi, as if it were struck by this pairing-for-life concept…

And the answer is clear. In real life, Shigem would have a boy-friend, of course: how would he not have one, being him? Clearly he was born for that, and Jaymi can sense he needs it very much, at the level of his cells, for many reasons: to anchor his emotions; for physical release, of course; for loneliness-reduction; and for somebody to give to. Very well then; he shall have a boyfriend for life.

So again, beyond filling such a role for Shigem, who will this fourth Beast be?

Someone who'll embody not just Jaymi's pointed response to the "Trivia Score: Wacky or Boring?" Newsfeed, but something wider— his whole instinctive urge to think more deeply than would ever be allowed by the toxic "simplicity" espoused in every glyph and pixel of *Ain't They Freaky!*.

After a moment he consults the general sketch of Kim in the design for *The Imagination Thief*, then polishes it, so it reads: "Kim Somerville is a bartender from London; newly in love with Shigem and about to move back to London with him, Kim is quiet, obser-vant and loyal, with a tinge of thoughtful pessimism."

Well, OK then. Bring it on!

Jaymi thinks for a moment longer, then he renames this new project "Kim"…

So here comes a new Beast, born into beauty and complexity, a creature of his own love and pain.

Regrettable that Kim's thoughtful seriousness of mind should be forced to look at and tangle with so ugly a counterbalance as the "Trivia Score: Wacky or Boring?" Newsfeed. Such lazy unthinking-ness, triviality of mind and complacency in ignorance! Jaymi is sure Kim would have things otherwise.

That counterbalance would seem, however, to be compulsory.

47 JAYMI CREATES KIM'S CODE

Jaymi sips his gin martini, which contains one large olive whose immaculate surface resembles wet green seal-flesh, puts it back down on his study desk here on Electra Drive, and claps his hands together. Out roll those decks again, unfurling their array of keys and faders in shadowy form across the sky ahead.

OK, here goes. Time to make with the code. Coming up, one machinery of instincts and thoughts, of the quality and seriousness that should have ruled the world ... and straightaway, it's as if the air that Jaymi breathes is passing clearer and cleaner through his nose and his mind.

A quiet energiser, Kim. A creature of thought and love—a love with a surface less flamboyant than Shigem's, and whose seriousness is more on view.

Kim will constitute a subfusc version of the aliveness, openness and passion in Evelyn; but he'll be more down-dragged by these qualities' opposites, which he'll notice all around him. He'll accept himself, in silence, standing within his own existence in a joy unspoken. His calm will be a plain calm.

Pure as heaven, really.

As soon as those zeroes and ones start connecting in this way, Kim begins thinking and feeling, starting to apprehend an individual uniqueness or self within him, buried in the matter of his code—a self whose life is somehow greater and more interesting than the life of that code. Would this self die if that code were deleted? he wonders. This self seems to transcend that code in some essential way, but would it survive it? He suspects not. But whatever this self is, let him expand into it, inhabit it, enrich and express it as best he can, while he can; for he can already tell that the physical world will always try to drag his self back down to the level of his code, as fast as it can.

Kim grows shadowily aware of Jaymi, and turns an unfocused proto-sight in the direction of his maker.

He becomes very still, as a young chimp does when it first encounters a mirror and starts to realise it's an object that can be looked at with a brand-new kind of looking (yes, like *that*!), in the jolt of a dawning revelation...

He waits there, motionless—maintaining his attention on Jaymi, like a cursor a-blink on a screen.

Kim cannot talk yet, but the disconcerting intelligence of the attention he directs at Jaymi looks rather as if its hypothetical verbalisation might be something like: "This Jaymi figure I'm looking at is just atoms, which seem nonetheless to have chosen to move in a very specialised way. How efficient the human form and its activities are, and how inevitable ... yet what an earth is the *point* of all that striving and scurrying?"

Jaymi shifts in his seat. Is Kim thinking all that? If so, how has he learned to? Yet what a sense of clean relief, that he's doing so. (And yes indeed, what *is* the point of all this scurrying?)

Now Kim starts to be conscious of a great sea inside himself, a fluid composition of—what? Imagination, instinct, spirit? He cannot tell what, but feels himself hanging in the fabric of time; feels the weight and ghostly beauty of duration itself...

"Alright, enough already with the philosophising, for today at least," Jaymi murmurs. "You're giving me a headache. Something a little more concrete, please? *There*, off you go."

And Jaymi nudges Kim down along a floorboard-creaking servants' passageway below stairs, past an alcove of gas-jets and mild tea, where a passerine lady wearing spectacles pops up without warning and presents him with a little blank notebook of the kind sold in a village store, before hopping brightly off to wherever she came from. Kim thanks her retreating figure, then creeps further down the passage, trying not to creak the floorboards, clutching his pristine notebook, in a glow of excited happiness at receiving his first present and at the prospect of all he may write in it!

Jaymi nods. That's more like it. A little more reassuring than all that metaphysical stuff.

Soon Kim comes to another alcove, where a wardrobe-mistress is installed, cosy as a Bagpuss, just inside the door of a walk-in closet so densely hung with old stage costumes that she must have quite a squeeze to get herself far enough inside to reach out the costumes she must be called on to fetch. Stage props are heaped on a shelf behind her, too: among them, Kim sees a deck of playing-cards and a jug of wine, flanking a plate of wax muffins.

Jaymi rubs his hands together. Wax muffins—very good. Those will doubtless come in handy, somewhere in *The Imagination Thief*.

…No, that was a bit lazy, wasn't it? Lazy of Jaymi to divert this nascent Beast's philosophical bent and haul him back down into a concrete environment of creaking floorboards and wax muffins, just because Jaymi couldn't be arsed to tag along on Kim's spontane-ous pirouette into the deep stuff. After all, those very tendencies of thought in Kim are similar to Jaymi's own such tendencies in earlier years, back in Omaha and New York, before his mind became dominated by the more worldly rodeo of creativity and ambition where he now finds himself.

"For fuck's sake, get your priorities right," Jaymi murmurs aloud to himself, and sits up straighter in his chair. That serious-minded malarkey is meant to be part of the whole point of this Beast, isn't it? "Alright, let's make it up to Kim, and give this a twist," he announces to the study around him. And he hammers out a final line of code, wherein Kim will sometimes estrange himself from the world of things for a moment, and will see how ordinary objects and events appear new and unfamiliar, revealing their nature and giving Kim a clear consciousness of things in general. At which point Kim will guess that this is what it must be like for *other* Beasts too … but then Kim will realise he can't be sure of this, because his fellow Beasts all seem strangely incurious regarding such abstract matters (even his beloved Shigem).

Jaymi gives a small smart nod, as if saluting Kim.

Yes. That's what he needs.

48 HERB HACKS KIM'S CODE

Jaymi becomes grimly aware of a tiny bubbling and flicking, from down in the corner of his text-editor window. It feels as if a smudge of dreary cloudiness is drifting in, to muddy the clear water of Kim's thought. Once again, Herb has found a way to hack through! Anger scythes through Jaymi, as he pictures Herb tapping away at the key-board, seeping through, with a view to dumbing Kim down into such an aesthetically debased tabloid flavour that it makes Jaymi want to kill something.

This hack into a Beast's code is felt as existential violence, flavoured by the nature of the Beast. Jaymi also observes that Herb is targeting something specific in Kim—more specific than when he targeted Evelyn's or Shigem's code.

What is this thing Herb is zeroing in on?

Inside Kim—beneath the skin of his civilisation, and despite his language and rationality, his intellect and tolerance, scepticism, self-awareness and humour—there is a lonely savage from the caves, bent on pure first-degree survival, blown by chance and the primal drives of instinct and emotion, alone and uncertain on a dart from birth to death. It grunts, howls and gibbers, under his surface, throughout the brief warm span of his existence. And beyond those noises there is silence. Kim's Olympian compassion is apt to obscure this savage in him, but it must still be there somewhere, even in him; which is enough to make Herb want to lay it bare.

Herb lands a hook into Kim's deep-buried savage, wrenches Kim out of Jaymi's grasp, whisks him off and lands him in an ancient sliver of primeval woodland hidden in the depths of an English moor, marked on no maps but called Spindle Wood, where the rasp and caw of rooks in pink-fruited spindle trees is the same as it was a thousand years ago. *I know this place*, thinks Kim's savage in the wood. *Ages ago, with the tree-snakes. Back when the screech-owls, black upon the sky, sat hunched on the branches above me in the dusk.*

He finds a girl in a clearing, with long black hair and the warmest eyes of brown. As her eyes take him in, her smile fades. "I can see myself in your eyes," she says with growing paranoia.

Night sinks around them.

She looks at him more, then in sharp terror cries "Oh my god"—then recovers, but refuses to explain why she cried out.

She stares … then she sees it in him. "*You're a closet murderer*," she whispers.

There's no one else here in Spindle Wood except him and her. But out beyond that fearful gap of two or three metres that always surrounds him, separating him from the rest of the human race, he can almost sense a multitude of figures gathered as far as he can see, up the banks of a grand bowl of moorland beyond the wood, arrayed in muttering quiet while their eyes all chant at him, accusatory: "*Murderer… Murderer… Murderer…*"

Only now, it seems, is Kim remembering his own rampage on some notorious occasion a few years ago, when the savage in him went at somebody without warning and with scary intensity, like a lethal hunting dog. Only now is he remembering how his rampage marked him down forever, in the minds and eyes of that accusatory multitude, as being a demonic presence among them, whispered of as such. This realisation, coming into its first sick focus for him now, must explain why an atmosphere of fear and caution has greeted him throughout the last few years. For example, there was the time when that man looked so agitated at Kim's approach up the narrow staircase, that he bade Kim remain there on the stairs, then ran to fetch Kim a goblet of honeyish mead and brought it to him as if in frightened appeasement of a monster. People have never sought to banish Kim, being oddly fascinated by him; but there has long been a feeling of some horror buried in his presence, relating to certain details of what happened on *those* occasions, with mutterings about certain episodes that must not be spoken of, especially *that* occasion...

Wanting so much to be close to the girl in the wood, this long-ago savage in Kim realises that now she has seen this thing in him, and now she knows about it more than he ever will (for he'll always remain uncertain *what* it is about him that's at issue), she will never again approach him from across the clearing. He becomes paranoid and anguished, and then more paranoid because his anguish is visible, about *what* she is thinking and *what he is supposed to have done*—so that at last he begins jumping up and down in fear and impatience, sneering and snarling at her, "What is that meant to *mean?*"

His leaps soon attain a supernatural height and violence, as high as three metres off the ground, and he feels his Kim-savage face contorting into a grimace of ferocious terror as he shouts at her, "*What is that meant to MEAN?*" again and again—his shouts becoming more anguished with every repetition, growing ever more painfully shrill, twisting up inside itself into a bestial wail, then higher still, to a whine like a wounded animal's shriek.

Staring at this unhinged performance, the girl with long black hair and the warmest brown eyes becomes ever more terrified of Kim, her perception and estimation of him forever damaged by these convulsions he's subject to—whereas in reality he hadn't wanted to frighten her at all, of *course* he hadn't, despite this uncontrollable savage snarl erupting out of him without relent—and now those warm brown eyes are irredeemably alienated while he snarls on in anger and pain, when all he'd wanted was to draw her towards him in gentleness, in sweetness, in peace.

...And what a helpless, hopeless, sad and permanent fuck-up this is, that'll have stained both his life and her life forever.

Jaymi has been snarling in indignation himself, to see his new Beast so infernally sabotaged, and at last he succeeds in halting Herb's hack: he slams shut the breach in Kim's defences, then reverses Herb's damage with multiple batch-reverse commands, thereby consigning this animal stain on Kim's interior life to the category of alternate histories that never happened.

Exhaling after such an effort, he sinks back into his seat, looking up into the empty sky. Yes, Herb is doing pretty well, isn't he, hacking away through his keyboard over there in his smug little cottage on Lindbrook Drive in Westwood Village, mutilating the compassionate subtlety of Kim Somerville into some cartoon monster.

Snuffing out the light of mind, for a lark, dragging everybody down.

How boring and how ugly.

49 EVELYN, TINY IN THE FACE OF THE DELUGE

Jaymi's first response to seeing Bang Dead's new "Trivia Score: Wacky or Boring?" Newsfeed was to start creating Kim's code out of thin air, beginning with nothing but a fore-echo of this Beast's thoughtful seriousness of mind. If the ones and zeroes behave themselves, Kim will soon emerge from his code. He'll be painted with his own visuals, which will animate him; he'll be scored with his own soundtrack, which will come alive; and he'll be tested. Then within a few days he'll be electrified into incarnated form, in all his beauty, like a burst of love.

But despite this creation cycle of Kim, there is little clarity as to how the "Trivia Score: Wacky or Boring?" Newsfeed could possibly fail to barrel upwards and outwards in popularity and profitability around the world, at least for as long as tabloid culture outsells the rest.

There can be no assurance of the success of any investment; but a media stream that facilitates the rating of trivia and factoids for entertainment value using *Ain'tTheyFreaky!*'s Freakometer, from a highest score of 10 for Wackiest, down to a lowest score of 1 for Boringest, by members of the public, does at least start out with the benefit of appealing to the resources of a decent majority.

Incarnated into the world by themselves, Jaymi's bursts of Kim love would stand no chance against such competition. But with a little back-up, perhaps they might survive after all.

What on *earth* can he do, though, to give them any back-up? Maybe nothing whatsoever, really, against such a gigantic streaming wall of trivial deadweight.

No. He can do what he can, whatever that may be. He can send out something beautiful and rich, in response to the tabloid deluge.

Evelyn!

A tiny thing in the face of a giant thing, yes … but it's worth a shot nonetheless, is it not?

Contemplating his growing fellowship, he sees that his original urge to wreak some sort of simple vengeance by creating Amber has grown in refinement. It has morphed into a tougher, healthier, ongoing struggle, which is central to his creating and releasing Beasts, first in these expanding missions into meat-space, and then in their permanent in-game lives in future: it's the struggle over how much of himself he can build into them, while still plugging them squarely into the real world around him.

This refined struggle powers the whole creation cycle of each Beast, from the creation of their code, appearance and soundtrack, through his test-driving them and incarnating them into meat-space, to his further refinement of them with a million tiny hammer-blows. Throughout each Beast's creation cycle, there is battle and change, negotiated beauty, flying sparks of metal on stone, and the smooth wet glint of emerging eyes…

OK then. He will dispatch his beloved Evelyn—and through her, himself—on a discreet mission into *Ain'tTheyFreaky!*. What aspect of it could she access, though? He shuts his eyes in thought, scanning his memories of working for Dud; then he murmurs "Westmont." He reaches over to one his secondary computers, finds the same folder where he located the confidential PDF outlining Bang Dead's game, and searches it for the word he just spoke aloud. *Yes*, there it is!

This is starting to look like the basis for one of those plans.

He strides out of his study, down the stairs and through the ground floor, to a hallway near one end of the house, where he knocks on the door of the self-contained guest wing where he installed Evelyn. After a few moments he hears her footsteps beyond the door, which she opens. "Hi!" she says, licking a red lollipop and smiling sweetly at him. "Can I help you?"

He clears his throat. "Evelyn. Yes, you can. Now you've had time to settle in, there's a mission I need to send you on."

"A mission? That sounds exhausting. I was hoping to take it easy today." She beckons him through the door, which opens into her kitchen.

He advances a couple of steps inside. "Yes, a mission. You have been incarnated so that I can send you out to do things, you know. Not just so that you can lounge around here and eat."

"Thanks for reminding me I'm hungry," she yawns, crossing the kitchen to the refrigerator. "I'm feeling *that* reckless, I might just open the grapefruit juice." She opens the fridge door and peers inside. "I don't want much for lunch—just a liverwurst and Miracle Whip sandwich should be enough."

"I'm serious," he says. "Now you're here in meat-space, I'll be sending you out into the wider world. So get ready for some action scenes, please."

"OK Jaymi, but I should warn you I'm feeling blowsy and fractious today, so let's make those scenes snappy, please."

"Evelyn, listen. The first thing I'll be sending you off to do, in the next day or two, is to meet Amber and introduce yourself to him. He has the details of your joint mission, which he'll fill you in on."

She looks thoughtful. "I don't know. On second thoughts, maybe a sandwich won't be enough. You know, I once prepared a meal for myself—and I should add, this was something a bit more labour-intensive than just heating the contents of a tin. It was at least cheese-on-toast. So, I'm standing there looking forward to eating it, but then what do I do?... OK, I'll tell you. I absent-mindedly slid the whole thing off the plate, into the bin. Oh yes I did! It was very simple: there was my carefully-made meal down there in the bin, *mewing* with rejection at being thrown away for no reason whatsoever. It was doing more than mewing, in fact. It was *weeping*… But what could I do? I couldn't eat it now. Sigh. A modern tragedy."

"Right," says Jaymi, stepping back through the open doorway into the main house. "Please listen. When mission time arrives, today or tomorrow, then I am going to come back again to fetch you. And I'm going to need a little more focus and dynamism here. OK?"

"OK! See you soon. Keep in touch!" And she closes the door on him.

He stands there a moment with his mouth hanging open, resisting the urge to remonstrate through the door. Then he turns and steams back up the hallway, filled with a sudden and furious need to calm down.

50 JAYMI CREATES KIM'S APPEARANCE

Jaymi pulls his study terrace doors closed, to shut out the sound of some noisy bird hidden in the foliage of the canyon, whose call sounds like harsh mockery of everything he's trying to achieve in this house on Electra Drive. Returning to the hot-seat at his computer, he emits a mirthless laugh aloud: it would seem that despite the sporadic therapy he's had since his early teens, nothing more than a bird is required to pry the lid off all those insecurities yet again! After all, it's surely just paranoia to imagine that a bird would even be *able* to think that of him—let alone *actually* think so. Isn't it?

Yes. It is.

OK. Back to work now.

He closes his eyes and thinks back to that unique half-minute when he let his gaze wander up and down the "Trivia Score: Wacky or Boring?" Newsfeed, where new posts were popping up every few seconds, every one of them receiving scores and comments from multiple sources.

Then he re-opens his eyes, consults his growing design for *The Imagination Thief* and checks his sketch for Kim's visuals. Its first description of Kim's physical appearance reads: "He's a young white man in his twenties whose blond cropped hair, handsome face and shirtless body make up a generically attractive ensemble. As I watch him, however, this generic allure starts to assume its place as packaging for a content richer and subtler than expected. There's a quietness, seriousness and simplicity to his movements and expressions, as he serves customers, which suggest a considerable emotional vulnerability under the watchful care of a rather greater strength, coupled with a touch of sadness somewhere."

There is then one further little artwork-oriented description of him, a bit later on: "In the corner, there he was: a handsome masculine blond boy, slightly sad-eyed, deep in thought, biting his nails as he read the menu."

OK then…

Kim swims up from abstraction and looks about him. From his looking there spreads a field of quiet intelligence, and Jaymi expands into a feeling of warm clarity in allowing his own apprehension of this as *civilisation*.

This is a boy inclined to ponder the world while he travels it alone at night, his face reflected close upon the window of the train while the lights in the night slide by him outside—coloured points on the land, squinting in at him between the drops of rain on the glass.

See ahead through his life, to a night when he sits in a parked car, lit by a candle in the ashtray, in silence.

Further on, another time, somewhat stoned and near to sleep, Kim hears a car pass fast on the street beyond the window, as if along a lonely road cut through a forest. The car's sound is warningless and shocking, like a burst of sealed metal laughter—eerie, as of children locked in a tank—and it's gone.

Then white balustrades underneath grey sky, yellow light somewhere, threat of rain, silver birches blowing in a sudden wind … and walking, always walking somewhere, walking on alone. Luxury of solitude; figure in the distance, fit for a painting.

—But now, other people start appearing in his visuals. First, there he is, still alone at night but on city streets instead, with car-tyres hushing over wet black tarmac. Music plays grand and lush across the rainy city, where a voice sings the track's title question "Do I Have To?", borne aloft on a wash of sound that hollows out around these words a space of yearning solitude solely his own.

Hovering in quiet shadow, once again at night, looking down on an old place: a college dining-hall where thousands of lives have chattered through without reflecting on this space they were chatting in—every one looming so important in their own self—striving, rising, failing, struggling, laughing, rising, failing once again and then dying. Spirits from the past and dancing spirits yet to come, while this hall remains unchanged. A babbling horde of bodies, all sprung from the earth, and all due back there as soon as they've completed their allotted episodes of waking, sleeping, walking, talking, listening, crying, making love, making coffee, laughing, masturbating, looking to the future, remembering the past and then at last fading out.

In the supermarket queue, clutching alcohol, Kim shuts his eyes: beeping scanners at the tills, a whirring fan, metal trolleys, chopped words, chinks of coinage and the tearing of receipts.

There he stands, in his bright blue jeans and his fuzzy-smooth white sweater, blond and clean and serious-eyed, a shy college student or a wholesome-looking popstar.

Later in his own room, just around midnight, euphoric after wine and grass: laughter and talk in the company of friends; cigarette-smoke swerving to rise through a lampshade, pulled by convection past a hot red light-bulb; candle-light, music, a view into a court through a low leaded window; and mauve-speckled lilies on the coffee-table, given to him yesterday (a present from his dear friend, the friend called the Queen of Light) ... golden years, his talents and his hopes and his life all ahead.

Then comes an odd-feeling Sunday noon. Still somewhat drunk from the night before, he sits on the low wall just out front (perhaps the only time he does so), in among the tourists and the bicycles. Church bells rain down, bright sun shines, and there's frost on the grass behind the wall where he sits. He lights a cigarette, takes a drag and feels his head spin inside, from the cold air. The gateway on his right is thronged with visitors, among whose more forgettable masses he is startled and warmed to see a figure whom he's at a genuine loss to parse as anything other than a hermaphrodite: a pair of prominent breasts are covered by clothing that's unisex tending to male, underneath a face whose lack of facial hair in no way diminishes the impression of a maleness so straightforward as to be quite befuddling in the context. The figure disappears in the throng and Kim looks away again. Squinting into the sunlight, he is struck by something he has never heard more clearly than now, behind the familiar soundscape of clicking bicycle wheels and snatches of speech—silence, hanging loud, staring out from empty space.

Jaymi taps the back-up command on his keyboard, in sober exhilaration. OK then, Kim is looking a whole lot more visible now. Just a quick final trio of adornments, and then this Beast's artwork should be ready!

First, he establishes Kim's gleaming detail in *The Imagination Thief* as being a high, small balcony, whose visuals will appear in the game-play as a signal of farewell: "high upon the façade […] a small traditional balcony with balusters, rather tight and sombre."

He then establishes Kim's talisman in *The Imagination Thief* as being a pair of opera-glasses, whose visuals Kim will brandish in the game-play as a spy: "'a pair of antique opera-glasses' […] 'I'm a couple of blocks away from Pippa's, with these old opera-glasses that Shigem's borrowed, and a few seconds ago I was looking through them at Pippa's balcony and there *did* seem to be a figure in the shadows, just behind her window. It was the same weaselly size as the figure I saw on the balcony with her the other night.'"

And he concludes by establishing Kim's additional motif in *The Imagination Thief* as being a keyhole, whose visuals Kim will peek through with terror in the game-play: "'a faint light coming through the hinge, though you couldn't see through. There was a big keyhole in the door, and I felt a really strong urge to look through. So I bent down and peered in, and I nearly screamed, because inside was […] I stopped dead when I was halfway down to the keyhole, because right there in front of my face, on the door handle, was this small smear of stickiness' […] 'it would have had to come out, about me snooping through keyholes and spying on her with opera-glasses.'"

Jaymi saves his work and sits back. A subtle new feeling of balance pervades him, as if from a confirmation or vindication that there is, after all, some external standard of reasonable construal that can be relied upon in this world: conceptual, verbal, urbane and honest.

(For there *is* that, yes?)

He can almost taste what a refreshing draft of cool water the quiet equilibrium of Kim's presence will provide in *The Imagination Thief.*

And one thing's for sure—Shigem is one lucky boy, to have a Kim like this one, created for the pleasure they will give to each other.

51 KELLY SMUDGES KIM

As these freshly-feathered visuals of Kim come blinking out into their first emergence from code, Jaymi can sense Kelly waiting for them, ready to pounce and smudge. Tapping away at her image-editing software in the Factory Place loft, she is now subtler in her approach, compared with when she propelled Evelyn into an agonising isolation of self-consciousness among her friends at the Downstairs bar, or even compared with when she handed Shigem an onscreen talk-show version of himself in the night-club coat-check line. In approaching Kim here, she insinuates herself into her target's environment with wicked smoothness, then deft enticement.

There, look, she's dropped an unintrusive image of her own perky self into *The Imagination Thief*'s visuals, walking past Kim in his university's Careers Centre. He is sitting at a screen, peering foggily at pages that purport to describe the only options he will have when he leaves college in the not-too-distant future. He has no idea which line of country to plump for, feeling all these corporate options to be unnatural, and finding it difficult, frankly, to picture himself in any of them. "Just let me know if I can be of any help," says the besuited adviser passing by him—a youngish black woman with a perky smile. He takes in the name-tag on her lapel: "Kelly Kandy, Careers Director". "In fact," she continues, "I bet I can help, because I'd say you look a bit undecided, and I know all about this stuff. Fancy a quick chat in my office? Why not."

Well, why indeed would he say no? It can't do any harm, can it? He may as well hear her information, at least, since it has to be admitted this plumping-for-a-career business will have a huge and unpredictable effect on his entire life.

So he follows her—oblivious to Jaymi's furious gesticulations high above him, semaphored in vain from behind the railing at the bottom of a side-aisle in the gods, that he *not* follow Kelly, *please not*.

Within a few minutes she has looked through Kim's college-student CV, has had a sensible chat with him, and is beginning to steer him with impeccable professionalism towards a career that will begin on the trading floor of an investment bank. She conveys an accurate outline of the generous salary progression he can expect in such a career if he demonstrates the kind of talent she reckons he has. It is correct information she gives him. He's not about to make such a decision right now, but what she's saying does sound reasonable. If he were to plump for this option, then at any rate it would hardly be a silly choice; this much could be said. Kelly riffles through a neat line of brochures on her desk and pulls out one of the glossiest. "I hear Bang Dead Investments are doing well," she says, holding it up. "I'd give them a call. I know the hirers in their hedge fund division, as it happens, so by all means tell them I suggested you. I'm sure they'll be looking for bright-eyed recruits like yourself. In fact—there you are, pictured on the cover of the brochure! Look, Kim, they're *waiting* for you."

He takes hold of the glossy paper, and an extraordinary feeling spreads through him, to see she is right. That *is* him, Kim Somerville, in sharp focus on the cover of the Bang Dead Investments recruitment brochure! His favourite fuzzy-smooth white sweater and bright blue jeans have both been ripped off him and folded away somewhere, replaced here by a sharp designer suit and a killer tie; and the nervous, nail-biting side of him that he's always had to wrestle with has clearly been banished from the young man in this photo. But it's him alright—standing in the Financial District of New York City, staring up at a sunlit skyscraper in fresh-faced aspiration, looking like a wholesome blond pop-star whose real passion is to make a killing through a lightning-fast trajectory up that tower, high above the trading-floors to those penthouse-suite corner offices he can see glinting in the Manhattan sky!

He flicks through the brochure, catching sight of upbeat headings such as "career progression", "collegial company culture" and "survival of the fittest", and recognises himself on several more pages: in one photo, he's taking modest pride in showing a group of clients the remarkable progress of a line rising across a graph; in a second one, he and a colleague are peering avidly at a list of prices on a screen; and in a third one, it's evident that his corporate polish and the size of his trainee-rainmaker's salary have also been helpful in "getting him the girl", as a brassy-eyed print-model in the background fires an admiring smoulder at him through a bedroom doorway in his swanky-looking future home.

Jaymi has been shaking the digital bars of his railing up in the gods, trying to catch Kim's attention so as to warn him away from Kelly's treacherous blandishments … but in vain.

At last Jaymi abandons these analogue gesticulations, realising there's a better mode of communication with his Beast. Kim's mobile phone flashes and vibrates on the office chair beside him. His eyes flick to its screen and see an incoming text from his creator. The text reads: "PEEL THEM BACK."

Kim glances up at Kelly, whose bland face is distracted with reading something on her computer screen.

He looks down at Jaymi's text again: yes, it comprises that three-word instruction and nothing more.

He focuses on the brochure in his hands. He closes it, examining its stapled spine, and frowns at the square cover picture of himself staring up at the skyscraper. At the very bottom-left corner of this photo, the topmost layer of ultra-glossy photographic paper has come loose and sprung back upon itself, so a tiny triangle of thin translucent plastic is curled over to point towards the centre of the image.

Jaymi has told him what to do next.

He peels the tiny triangle back, pulling the plastic easily off the entire photo, and he can smell the blood that fills his skin in that skyscraper scene. He can feel the pressure where that eager young face oozes tears inside itself, ready to squeeze out from his tear-ducts into the aspirational sunlight. Within his wholesome-popstar physiognomy is a sharp, fearful face, with green around its blazing eyes and red around its mouth. Its outside colours are just a wrapping, and even they have changed, as the truth of him is laid ever barer: the skin around his eyes is now a rubbery ultramarine, his irises a sexily unhealthy orange-ochre; and the whites of his eyes stand out bright against that ultramarine convexity of skin, like egg-yolks in an outspread dark-blue fried-egg blubber.

He flips this front cover over in haste, and the brochure falls opens at the shot of him showing a graph to a group of clients. Again the topmost layer of gloss at the image's extreme bottom-left corner is curled over. His fingernails dive in to peel this one back, and straight away those corporate clients are corpses-in-waiting—unalive—the chewing dead. Tears roll down in the photo, as he stares, from one corpse's black-ringed eyes, over stretched-out cheekbones, down to a black tongue. And there beside the clients, Kim himself evokes that painting of the terrible-eyed victim of premature burial, raising the lid of its coffin and reaching out in horror into the air of a crypt (oh yes, Kim knows the painting)—buried so far beyond rescue that the crypt's floor may as well have caved in too, propelling him down to a cavern underneath. And he sees his blond hair; and recalls how hair keeps growing for a little while after a corpse-in-waiting has become a corpse.

Flicking on through the brochure, he peels back the shot of him peering with a colleague at the prices on a screen, and the cause of his poisonous headache in the photo is revealed: stroking his shallowly-buried skull as if to stroke the lobes inside it, the price-checking Kim becomes aware of the shape of that skull just inside him, and he can feel the spider-legs living among his brain-lobes. The entire head of his colleague at the screen, however, has turned into a wriggling spider—its body alone the size of the colleague's head, while its legs wave around like hirsute antlers.

Kim wrenches the page over again, and rips the skin off the photo of him being admired by the girl in the doorway of his bedroom. Smoke rushes up and snakes in through the top of Kim's head, fills him and clicks into place inside, so he speaks through a mask with eye-holes, while an orange liquid flows into the meat of his toes. And instead of his girlfriend in the doorway, there hangs a congeries of dancing blood—droplets in the air, in the shape of a human, which coalesce into a wolf standing upright on two bloody legs at the threshold of his bedroom—then hungry at the end of his bed, looking down at Kim with eyes gleaming wet and dead above a dark mouth-hole.

Kim snaps back to Kelly's office and stands up, shaken, dropping the brochure to the floor.

Kelly looks up at him with a sporty smile. "So, Kim: investment banking it is, then, yes?" she enquires. "You won't regret it!"

"Er … thanks for your help, Ms Kandy, but I don't think I'm convinced, sorry. I'll keep you posted, thank you," he replies, and heads for the door.

Jaymi flops down in the gods above and exhales in relief—Jesus, this Beast-creation is a perilous business.

52 SUN-GLARE AND SKINNY PALMS IN WESTMONT, SOUTH CENTRAL

Jaymi scans the contents of the confidential Bang Dead document he located, looking first at its handful of embedded screen-captures from Google Street View and Bing Bird's Eye View; then at its embedded artwork from Bang Dead's upcoming first-person shooter game *Righteous Gun*; and then at its text.

That being the order of his attention, the first thing he absorbs is a series of street-level and forty-five-degree aerial photos depicting a strip of South Vermont Avenue, its two halves divided by a wide dirt median—a desolate stretch of nondescript building façades, beauty supply outlets, motels, liquor stores and makeshift churches, running north from the Century Freeway for thirty or more blocks through South Central. The sun-glare presses down alike on all properties: auto repair places, sudden busy frontages of mini-market stores, and then perhaps a funeral parlour, sober and clean at the front while its side-wall is gang-tagged beside an empty lot. Infrequent on the side-streets running west, skinny-trunked palms stand listless in the dusty air of Westmont.

Despite its seeming anonymity, this neighbourhood happens to tick a decent number of demographic boxes in Bang Dead's current "stakeholder matrix" of priorities for community outreach, as Jaymi learns from the captions under the images. Through just such matrices are tomorrow's gamers discovered, many of whom will be nurtured into loyal customers—and among these, the super-gamers, Bang Dead champions and company ambassadors of the future!

Dud's team has therefore reached out to one of the more size-able local congregations here, housed on the Avenue in faded and incomparably weary-looking premises, and has engaged this church in a joint venture. In consideration for an appropriate donation of funds, the church has undertaken to integrate a permanent, Bang-Dead-branded facility into the community. There on Vermont, on the south-west corner of One Hundred and Fourth Street, is a small vacant lot enclosed by the motel beyond it. On this vacant lot, a new and well-wired gaming-hut named the Righteous Gun Cockpit will soon arise.

The Cockpit's principal stated mission is to promote a Bang Dead game called *Righteous Gun*, which is to be closely tied in with *Ain'tTheyFreaky!*'s "Guy Score" Newsfeed. Its secondary stated mission is something that Jaymi can see is really just a piece of branding designed to appeal to this particular community's leaders: this mission is to promote the spiritual dimension in first-person shooter games, by promising a life-meaning to the lost, by bringing righteousness back into shooting, and by bringing the good fight back into righteousness. Bang Dead has even been brazen enough to mention the Ten Commandments as a solid basis for the duty of every righteous shooter, whether first-person or second- or third-, to uphold the fabric of society against those who would threaten the traditional roles of its menfolk and its womenfolk.

The copy is well targeted.

Jaymi wrinkles his nose.

Then he gets up, trots downstairs and through the house to the door of the guest wing, knocks, and waits for its resident to appear.

The door opens. "Hey!" Evelyn twinkles at him, chowing down hungrily on a banana as she stands there in a yellow bikini.

"Evelyn. Hi. So, mission time approaches. I just wanted to give you a heads-up that I'll be coming back late this afternoon, when I'll need you to be ready to go meet Amber and shoot down to South Central with him."

She looks crestfallen. "Jaymi, I was planning to do *busy*-work this afternoon. Does the trip have to happen today?"

"Yes, it does. Look, I can promise, your mission with Amber will be way more fun than just fudging around miserably at home all day. I mean, what on earth do you have to do here?"

She looks around the room behind her. "Oh, I don't know, but *so* many things. You know, hoover the floor, pay the milkman ... I can't remember what else, but you name it, and it has to be done."

"Sod all that! You're an incarnated Beast of Electra Drive, who's meant to be jetting glamorously around L.A."

"I don't know whether I'm such a fan of this meat-space you've brought me into," she says. "It's felt a bit like making my first parachute jump for charity, only to fall straight into the whirling blades of a helicopter."

"Now you're being a drama queen. Surely real life isn't quite that bad?"

"Well, *maybe* not," she concedes. "Still, it's a bit of a schlep, isn't it?"

"It is that, I do admit," says Jaymi. "But this mission is important, Evelyn. It'll make the world a little bit better. Would that be OK with you?"

She heaves a sigh, nods tragically and gives a "brave" smile. "OK then, Jaymi, I'll be ready. See you later."

He stands there, watching her door swing shut. Then he strides up the hallway, fuming with exasperation, tense with uncertainty and filled up with love.

53 JAYMI CREATES SHIGEM'S AND KIM'S SOUNDTRACK

Jaymi pulls his study chair closer to his monitor and rubs his hands in glee: Shigem's and Kim's soundtrack! This will be a joy. It will also be his first attempt at channelling a soundtrack born of two Beasts at once. As such, it will derive from their love for each other, despite their not quite having met yet.

So unfinished are Shigem's and Kim's individual creation cycles, neither of them has even realised that the object of his own inchoate yearning will be another Beast. Yet somehow Kim does already possess a nugget of knowledge not often attained by someone until much later—after he or she has found and run with another individual alone, composed a major or minor symphony of interpersonal music with them, then lost them forever. The thing Kim knows, with such precocity, is that all the private running and music shared in any such temporary union are for all time, being parts of everyone throughout history and the future—as is likewise true for such union's private losses.

There's a rustle and a whisper behind the skin of night, with a scent of limonene, as his knowledge coalesces: shrill girls giggle, then they shush one another, as he hears them and looks around in vain to see who's there … and Jaymi smiles, for this kerfuffle is the opening of the soundtrack he's about to reveal.

Next comes the chuckle of an Arcadian brook, on whose idealised bank Kim is reclining in the garb of a shepherd, blond and Classical, contemplating how nothing lasts, nothing can be grasped forever, everybody passes and decays at last.

Dawn glows pale at the side of the heavens, his flock is scattered peaceably around the field behind him, and blue through the air comes a call from that heifer lowing at the skies—an echo of a footnote of stone via song.

Before this eclogue can wilt into too etiolated an idyll, Jaymi electrifies it by touching Kim's shoulders with a jolt of something new to him. Almost pre-physical, certainly pre-sexual, it's nonetheless an ecstatic ripple that runs through his body like a touch of the divine, as if from a figure leaning down from behind—a young female figure, he senses (for thus has Jaymi shown himself, on this unique occasion). *And THIS exists also!* she seems to be informing Kim.

Into his pastoral aloneness comes her touch, an intimation of her smile, and a promise that before too long (oh soon, very soon) he will know about things he doesn't yet know about. Until then, she'll watch to check he's still on track to know them. And she'll love him unseen, while he nears that knowledge—so he may feel her breath upon his neck, while she watches. She knows Kim will have to see horrors on his journey. She's sorry in advance: so sorry he will have to see *that*, so sorry that the other one will do *that*, so sorry they will leave him such an echo and a stain… But she'd hate it even more if he were not to break through, to his arrival and completion.

An electronic pulse floats down into the soundtrack—the sexiest music Kim has ever heard, though he wouldn't yet know to call it such. That Greek Golden-Age paradise of Arcadia slides down the hill-slopes, into the town on the island. His unseen protector leads him through its narrow whitewashed alleyways to the entrance of a little club called City Bar. Standing close to him in the alleyway outside it, she attends with sweetness to Kim's appearance, straightening and smoothing down his shepherd garb, during which their eyes hardly meet, until he lays his head on her shoulder. She puts her finger to her mouth, bidding silence, whispers something indistinct and kisses him on the lips, soft and warm. Then she turns away to leave. He keeps hold of her hand for a moment, then lets it drop.

She slips off into the gathering crowd, around a whitewashed angle of wall, and is gone.

Jaymi's attention departs in her—but then it reconsiders this, eases up and out of her, and floats around and down again unseen, where Kim walks into City Bar.

Inside the venue, Kim's and Jaymi's eyes take a moment to adjust to the dark. Under the spotlights, a skinny sexy boy is dancing manically, feminine and ash-blond, and Kim hears his own voice asking in his head, "Am I silver who needs gold, or am I gold who needs silver, or am I either silver or gold who needs more of the same?" The androgynous stranger catches his eye for an instant, without expression ... and this whole soundtrack clicks one step closer to full orchestration, as the half-created Kim achieves his first realisation that the object of his own inchoate yearning will be another individual Beast.

Obvious perhaps, with the benefit of hindsight. But no Beast is coded with all such knowledge ahead of time—not even one who likes to think.

"Perhaps, when I find him, he'll have green eyes," Kim murmurs to himself.

Kim cannot yet have any intimation of Shigem in particular, but this soundtrack straight away features the incursion of an audio sample so imbued with soft dark enchantment that it almost feels like an intimation of him. This sample is arcing back here from a point far ahead, deep in the game-play of *The Imagination Thief*, where Jaymi will use it as a sound from Kim's amber days, thus: "That soundtrack was playing, and now it reached the infinitely creepy-sweet 'Mysteries of Love'. And through your leaded window, all those distant background figures, standing still or gesturing in talk or crawling ant-like across the frame, were sealed in a different world, photographed and laminated here in your memory." And Jaymi's eyes feel as if they glow, to recall that that moment in the game will occur just before Shigem and Kim will meet and pair for life.

54 THE RIGHTEOUS GUN COCKPIT, FROM BANG DEAD GAMES

Within a day or two, Jaymi sees the first online rumours and appetite-whetting hints of Bang Dead's *Righteous Gun* and the Righteous Gun Cockpit starting to pop up, in a range of relevant feeds and streams, especially alongside the "Guy Score"—the tuning-up of an orchestra that'll soon blast forth in unstoppable overture to a publicity symphony of quite flattening banality and deep-pocketedness. There are whispered promises of live events featuring teams of local players in competition, with commentators. There are slick invitations to every individual to stake their claim on their own unique permutation of Righteous Gun warrior garb (choose from these options), Righteous Gun weapons (choose from these) and a chosen one of the Ten Commandments to swear lazily impassioned allegiance to.

Massive, wearisome energy.

Massive, wearisome community engagement.

And massive, wearisome effectiveness, almost inevitably.

For Jaymi, every such mention triggers a picture of the gum-chewing Dud sprawled by his infinity pool, up at the Blue Jay Way house. And the sheer toe-curling distastefulness of this picture reminds him of something he should have put into action already—his intention to dispatch Evelyn on a discreet mission to visit Dud's cynical, do-gooding cockpit in Westmont, so as to perpetrate some mischief against it.

Fine. It's time she was sent down to South Central without delay, on a mission to … what?

To be frank, he's not quite certain yet. What exactly should she do? A creator isn't born knowing such things, after all; they must be learned from experience.

Very well then, he will leave it to Evelyn herself to work out the details. She has a savvy volition all her own. She's a street-wise chick and a smooth operator. She'll know what to do, once she's down there. All he'll need to do is sit and watch, from behind her eyes. She and Amber will make a killer team!

For the third time Jaymi knocks on the door of the guest wing. Hearing her footsteps, he feels a churn of trepidation regarding her likely mission-readiness. But his concerns are allayed when the door opens revealing a return to the same dynamic Evelyn, with the golden-hooped earrings, who appeared when he first incarnated her in the Melrose Avenue building: swinging in from sunlight, a belt of bullets across her shoulder and down around her bared midriff, a wide black belt over a short scarlet dress, with scarlet high heels, a gun holstered at her right side, a switchblade in her left hand and a lush yellow rose behind her ear beside cascading black hair.

"Fantastic!" says Jaymi. "*That's* the spirit."

She grins. "Got my mojo back."

"Cool beans. And guess what—it's mission time! I want you and Amber to go down to Westmont, where I need the two of you to wreak a little havoc on ... well, let's call them business rivals of mine. So, first of all, go and introduce yourself to Amber. He lives just up the street, near the bottom of Jupiter Drive. You can walk there from here: turn right outside the front gates, head uphill and it's the first turning on the right. Here's the street address," and he hands her a slip of paper with the house number on. "Ring the bell and he'll let you in."

"OK. How far away is this?"

"Fifteen minutes for the journey, and five minutes for the unforeseen. It's a steep hill, but you'll find it a piece of cake, I'm sure. So: go Evelyn! Why not head up to the house on Jupiter Drive right now? That sounds good, yes? There's no time like the present."

"Is Amber going to tell me all about his sister's rabbit collection?"

"Er, no, he won't do that. He has no sister. Consequently there are no rabbits. The focus of your mission will be something called the Righteous Gun Cockpit. I've briefed him about it, so he'll bring you up to speed while he's driving you to Westmont. I'm not sure what precise action you'll be taking, but I'm confident you'll both know what to do when you get down there."

She whoops, then leans in and kisses her maker on the cheek. "You've got me fired up now, Jaymi! Leave it to us—you're in safe hands. I'm ready. OK then—*I fly!*" And she strides on down the main hallway towards the front entrance of the house on Electra Drive.

Left alone at her door, Jaymi twirls in a circle, then returns to his study.

55 JAYMI TEST-DRIVES SHIGEM AND KIM

OK, it's time to test out this new pair of Beasts together, in honour of whom a generously-poured Sex on the Beach is chilling the air in Jaymi's study.

It'll be the first time the pair of them have met each other as identified individuals, since it was only a half-encounter when they both contributed to their soundtrack. So how will this more ambitious meeting go? Will they gravitate towards each other, as Jaymi intends? Will they even like each other? He hopes so. He did mine them from two aspects of himself, after all. But they now possess nascent volitions of their own, so they'll have their own reactions to each other without his directing them, thank you.

In *The Imagination Thief*'s actual game-play, Shigem will first notice Kim in a café, though they won't in fact meet until a week later in a nightclub. But in this practice environment here on the laptop screen, before any incarnation into real-life L.A., Jaymi will test them both with a profusion of distractions and scattered energy.

It is therefore at a party in a complicated split-level room in a Bel Air mansion, where there are many guests in simple, camply-colourful clothes, including various elegant black girls, that Kim encounters a beautiful femmy boy in a place of transit and confusion. He is electrified to observe the attraction is mutual, albeit expressed with shyness. The other writes down his number and name, *Shigem*, in leftward-leaning and somewhat childish handwriting, on a little scrap of paper, since Jaymi has forgotten to equip either of them with mobile phones as yet. Kim stows the paper about his person, then tries to respond with his own details in this same retro format, but is infuriated when it seems he cannot make the pencil function at all. In the press of his mounting frustration he notices that as a result of this painful delay, Shigem has morphed into a girl. She's sweet, and she seems to want Kim to stay with her, but … please, where's Shigem gone? he wonders.

"I kind of feel I was *extruded* into this party," says a voice behind him. "Something about the party doesn't seem real, somehow," and Kim wheels around in joy—that voice and those words were pure Shigem. And yes, it's him indeed. (So he somehow ended up behind Kim instead of in front, and the girl who wanted Kim to stay with her was a complete red herring. Ah well, such random loose ends are half the fun of parties—which Kim may as well also learn now, in passing, since this learning malarkey is all good and can happen in any order for a Beast.)

Back on track, Kim succeeds in making the pencil work, and proffers his own name and number on another scrap of paper, in a more cursive, rightward-leaning and adult-looking hand than Shigem's was revealed to be. Now they've been introduced, they both open their mouths to say something. In this they are interrupted, however, as the other party guests start forming into frolicsome pairs in response to some instruction Shigem and Kim have missed, and they all start setting off, one guest mounted on another's shoulders, down the grand curve of a showcase stairway to a lower storey, in true Bel Air mansion style. Shigem takes hold of both their drinks, Kim kneels down, Shigem climbs onto his shoulders, and they rise as a pair and set off down the stairs, overtaking other duos with a whoop and a whinny, like a pair of unicorns who have discovered each other in a herd of horses.

Kim prances on down the outside lane of the second landing; Shigem lifts both their cocktail glasses in slow motion, spilling only a drop or two as he tinkles them through the tear-drop stalactites of the stairwell chandeliers; then they reach the ballroom below and he raises the drinks up all the way, spreading his arms wide in exultation with his face upraised to the painted clouds on the ceiling.

Back in human mode, they stand there laughing, regaining breath. Brown flame licks in Shigem's eyes, like a kiss, Kim observes … brown eyes, not green as Kim had pictured; though this very shortfall is sexy in itself. Jaymi glows inside himself, somewhere above, to see Kim registering an impression of what was coded into Shigem for Kim's sake in particular, namely the electric slenderness and untouchably exquisite androgyny and glamour of his physicality. In fact, Kim is about to utter this precise description out loud—but stops himself doing so, being already half-equipped with a sense that this isn't quite the sort of thing one Beast says to another when they've only just met. Another phrase drops into his mind with all the *eureka!* aptness of a toffee-apple falling from an apple-tree onto his head, to describe Shigem, which is "my enchanted flask of honey"—but no, on reflection this would sound even sillier than the first description, so he mustn't say it either.

In any case, Kim, vertiginous, leaning forward to see further into Shigem's depths, cannot make out the end of them, just more depths, as he falls forward further...

56 AMBER'S EYES IN THE PHOTO OF THE MOTEL BY THE VACANT LOT

In the mail delivered to the Blue Jay Way house next morning, Dud finds an envelope addressed to him in unfamiliar handwriting with no return address. Ripping it open, he finds it contains nothing more than a printed photograph of a small vacant patch of land with a single-storey motel behind it. Recognising the location as the imminent site of the *Righteous Gun* community-outreach project in Westmont, he flips the print over, looks again at the back of the envelope and into its inside corners, but can see nothing written or hidden anywhere to explain why someone has sent him this.

He scrutinises the photo, and a queasy unease spreads through him.

Whoever took the shot was training the camera through the railings on West One Hundred and Fourth Street just west of Vermont, pointing it at the pale-brown northern façade of the motel's central structure. On this façade, uniform in neither shape nor placement, are five larger windows and two smaller ones.

Through one of the larger windows a blond male figure is leaning out. On each side of the figure's head, it is evident he has bent two of the thick metal window bars outwards, so as to let himself through.

Dud peers at the photo, and his unease unfurls and flowers into something metallic, at a quality of charismatic twinkling menace in the man's face where it stares out at the camera lens straight into him here. Even at this distance across the vacant lot, the stark threat in those eyes is clear, almost as if there is somebody else behind them firing out contempt for everything Dud Guy stands for...

He has seen that malevolence before, at close range: first, on the face of an unwelcome visitor to his office; and then on his own back terrace, while a severed grey tongue swung around a football, whistling through the air close beside Dud's cheek.

57 JAYMI INCARNATES SHIGEM AND KIM

At his desk in the house on Electra Drive, Jaymi clutches the edge of his chair in electrified panic and delight, watching Shigem slither and squeeze out into meat-space through the desk-top monitor.

A quiet ecstasy spreads through him, as he watches Shigem land and catch his balance, then stand there in such dignity and beauty before his creator. All the warmth and openness Jaymi could create from within him, and his very own response to Bang Dead's "Guy Score"!

A moment later, Kim follows Shigem out through the monitor, lands, catches his balance and stands in equal dignity and beauty before his creator likewise. All the joy of thought that Jaymi could create from within him, and his very own response to Bang Dead's "Trivia Score"!

This being the first incarnation of two Beasts who were created together, Shigem's and Kim's newly-minted forms spiral in towards each other, their closeness mounting. Jaymi rolls his chair back into the shadows, out of their way in humbled silence, with the sense of observing a pair of sacred beings. So joyous is their newfound inhabitation of physical space, that he can already see a sequence of L.A. contexts flicker around them in the air of his study, despite their never yet having left this room to experience the meat-space reality of what they're evoking.

First, here's Shigem lighting up the dance-floor of Jewel's Catch One, now a creature of flame and flesh, perspiring and aglow within the spotlit booming of the bass-bins. So joyfully charismatic and flamboyant are his movements, he's surrounded by a wide circle of admiring fellow revellers—while Kim watches hidden in the shadows of the sidelines, filled with admiration and desire.

They leave not so late, stepping out into the cool night on Pico Boulevard, where they kiss each other, lightly, for the very first time.

During a firework display of conversation back at home later that night, Kim finds, on returning from the bathroom to the sitting-room, that Shigem is about to put some music on—and for a few seconds Kim is exasperated at this, because he has so many threads of their ongoing conversation loose in his mind that the very last thing he wants is the addition of any further new element entering the arena. Are there not so many unfinished exchanges of shared experience still to be completed, which would only be derailed by any musical accompaniment? Can Shigem not *see* this obvious fact? Serious thought is surely our highest attainment and greatest pleasure, especially on precious occasions such as this, when it decides to allow two co-explorers along its nocturnal paths and arbours, hand in hand! But then Kim finds himself feeling a faint surprise of relief that Shigem should be revealing this small mismatch or disjunction between them, because if their conversational echoes had instead continued to escalate upwards into the night without any such mismatch, then all this would probably have risen so high as to become a little *too* vertiginous…

Then, when that firework display has plateaued out at last and is gliding on around the curve of the stratosphere in silence, the contrasting simplicity and concreteness of Shigem's question to Kim in intimate quietness: "Are you real? Can I blow smoke through your hair?"

Out on the lower terrace they stand beside each other in the humid air, an electric crackle between them … then Kim takes Shigem in his arms, and both of them are silent as a rising breeze mixes their hair together.

The humid air bursts with a warm rain at last—and Shigem and Kim kiss for the second time, passionate and deep, while splodgy drops of water spatter all across the swimming-pool, here on the terrace on Electra Drive, with L.A.'s grid of lights spread below them in the night.

Ten minutes later, the warm rain has soaked their clothes, so they both strip naked. Glancing up as the downpour intensifies, they set off around the curves of this terrace on two different trajectories, keeping each other in view with a leisurely intentness, half-feral, half-smiling through the sparkle of the rain across the pool.

As Kim drinks in Shigem's slim brown form, standing over there on the opposite edge of these few metres of under-lit blue water with its rain-dancing surface, that slender animal body is so deeply desired by Kim, with a fierce and beautiful desire of a kind that he never felt in his pre-incarnated life. It's a physical desire that's at once hungry and bursting, and Kim fears it is something that lacks any hope whatsoever, for what on earth can he be expected to *do* with this brand-new variety of desire down inside himself, so urgent, hot and hard?…

Ways forward do suggest themselves to Kim in due course, however, once the sexy vulnerability of Shigem's still-wet body is lying beside him indoors, shivering in the cool of the post-rain air but also sweating with exhilaration already—one horny blond-haired mesomorph, one hungry dark-haired ectomorph.

Seeing Kim's face from so close, while they're kissing on the bed, Shigem takes in an unfocused close-up flash of Kim's beautiful slanting eyes and fine bone structure: earnest, blond, exotic white boy, here with him, forever…

And then Shigem reflects on Kim some more, as they coil around each other: he's so gentle and so manly (and the hair on his chest is so animal and warm between the tips of Shigem's fingers), so welcome to manhandle Shigem's body, and so warm in bed, beside Shigem's shivering—and so erect too, and so requiring such release, and how Shigem wants to be the only one to give Kim that release, whenever he wants or needs it, forever!

At last Shigem slides into sleep. Kim sees the dawn start to glimmer in the sky beyond the Downtown towers, whose tops he can see through Shigem's hair and the glass beyond. As Kim's own eyes sink closed too, he cups his lover's penis, gently squeezing so that it becomes erect, twitching up with diffidence while Shigem sleeps on and shifts and mutters something faint. A powerful mix of tenderness, closeness, protective love, a little flattery and a simple blast of *pow!* all come together in Kim, as the words assemble in his head: *I would kill, to protect him.*

And in the watching Jaymi, something magic comes together and alive.

58 ASHLEY AND DUD ATTACK SHIGEM

When the pair of them wake up next morning in the second bedroom of the guest wing, Kim asks whether his final penis-squeezing intruded itself into any of Shigem's dreams? Shigem can remember no such intrusion, he claims, looking ambiguous. He suggests that Kim try again, however, next time an opportunity should present itself.

Towards lunchtime, Jaymi peers over his study terrace railing, to see where his two new guests may have got to, since their incarnation last night. Lying on a sun-bed beside the swimming-pool on the ground-floor terrace, Shigem waves up at him.

"Good morning," Jaymi replies. "Are you here alone?"

Shigem nods. "Kim went off with Evelyn, for a long walk down in the canyon," he says. "She rather dragged him away there, truth be told: in this fierce heat, the prospect of it sounded rather a schlep. I, on the other hand, preferred it right here." And he spreads his arms wide, unfurling his golden-painted fingernails in leisurely majesty, to indicate the idyllic poolside scene around him, edged in lush vegetation and facing the hundred-and-eighty-degree panorama of Los Angeles down ahead.

Filled with love and pride at the beauty of his newly-incarnated Beast, Jaymi sets off down the flight of external steps to join him. While he descends, his mind flicks back to the question he's been pondering since last night: how best to launch Shigem and Kim out into the real world, now they're here and ready for it? Evelyn's first trip was to the Hollywood café; and frankly, it can't have been her idea of a good time, to be targeted by Dud's and Ashley's assaultive scrutiny there. But although Jaymi hardly knew what he was doing when he chose that place for her debutante coming-out into society, it was quite an appropriate location, he realises, because he's familiar with the times of day when Dud and Ashley are likely to be passing through it. It's also very handy in being neutral ground, not controlled by those two—and therefore the last place where they'd want to make a scene or risk making fools of themselves by probing into Jaymi and his Beast with too much aggression, surrounded as they'd be by colleagues, clients, competitors and industry-watchers. In any case, how irresistible it is—and strategically necessary—for Jaymi to showcase his new Beast to those two sharks, since he knows they cannot yet achieve anything comparable themselves! (Not the classiest motivation, maybe; but god, how they both deserve it.) Well OK then, let Shigem's launch occur there too.

"Excellent choice," replies Jaymi at last, reaching the bottom of the steps.

"And now," says Shigem, "I'd like a nice girly chat with my creator, please. So do settle down, begin at the beginning, and tell me everything: just what *is* this all about?"

Jaymi sits on the pool edge, dangling his feet in the water, and smiles at him. "You know what? We'll have plenty of time for girly chats. But as you'll soon discover about meat-space, there are never any gentle or logical explanations, time always presses, and there are no digital structures or templates to rely on. Here, we're just thrown into the deep end of random contingency and practicalities, and we work it out on the hoof. So with that in mind, I have a project already lined up for you and me this afternoon: allow me to take you to the Hollywood café!"

"Sure," says Shigem, open-eyed with curiosity. "Will I like it?"

Jaymi hesitates. "I can't promise that, no. But we do need to start somewhere." He checks the time. "OK, it's nearly one. We have work to do, so let's chop-chop. Pop indoors, and cover that beautiful body in a bit more clothing—a T-shirt and shorts will be fine. There's a couple of ex-colleagues of mine you need to meet, who are very likely having lunch there as we speak. Come on. I'll meet you in five minutes, out front, by the car."

In the café half an hour later, sitting at a window table as expected, are Dud and Ashley. And just as when he led Evelyn between the same tables to meet them, Jaymi feels an alien thrill to be able to perceive their oncoming faces through Shigem's eyes, as well as through his own.

His ex-colleagues' scrutiny of this third Beast, whom Jaymi introduces with as genial a breeze of small-talk as when he introduced Evelyn, is filled first with quiet awe, and then with the gleam of a beady-eyed mission to reproduce Jaymi's breakthrough Shigem-creation, but repurposing him instead into an enhancement for *Ain'tTheyFreaky!*.

Yes, the ugly ambition in Dud's face is clear: he would like nothing better than to incorporate a dumbed-down version of Shigem into his own tabloid product, so as to entertain customers of the "Guy Score: Hunk or Gross?" Newsfeed, no doubt setting up Bang Dead's cartoony Shigem as a kind of reference target for a world full of Guy-scorers to mock and take aim at...

While Dud contemplates all this commercial potential in Jaymi's Beast, it's clear, too, that he's looking at him through the eyes and expectations of an average consumer of *Ain't TheyFreaky!*. And as soon as Dud looks at him in this way, the main problem becomes apparent: Shigem is just too gay.

To speak plain, as Dud so prides himself on doing, it will need a bit of straightening-out, for normal people. Just as soon as Herb's team have worked out how he was created and have found a way to reverse-engineer him, then that excessive gayness will be the first thing to fix.

Jaymi pulls his own attention out of Dud, and returns it to Shigem. Doing so, he is distraught to observe that Shigem's apprehension of the Bang Dead duo's avid intentions is spreading through him like a seepage of pain. Although Shigem manages to maintain his external composure, the mere prospect of being repurposed comes at him like an assault, threatening not just to down-convert him into a form that feels cheaper, but to do violence to his own gay self and truth—to use his precious life for something other than he wants and needs.

Within this prospect, it's as if he can see down a highway where the drifters are lined up, looking back at him through faces of pain. Among those spent lives is a wailing, agonised human frame with a face of sadness and defeat, huddled in filth against a wall at the north corner of East Sixth and South San Pedro Streets, who has spent most of the last nine years in this state.

Much further east down this highway, a man in an Istanbul slum pours petrol on his head, sets it burning and walks on. As the liquid blazes up, he walks more jerkily, like a stick figure. When he falls, cabbies beat him up for scaring off customers, which happens to smother the flames—so he lives after all, for a little while.

Far further on down the same cruel highway is a country whose essence has been mutilation, torture and starvation for decades, as recordings of dictators play on endless loops from speakers mounted high above barbed-wire fences. Emaciated men are hunched in cells and freezing pits in Hoeryong, cruelly sad: sad meat in waves of worm despair. Every thought or action is a different stab of pain, so the stabs run together in a lifelong pattern. Each incarnated consciousness in this place is dead meat, trapped beneath a mountain's weight of stone. Their words are grunting, straining sounds, through the ground, unseen—buried alive, unable to move, beyond rescue.

And in that emaciated man grows madness, strapped to a stump in a waste, for a lifetime: writhing hands and fixed eyes, horrifying misery and pain, weird nauseating evil; tortured and destroyed in a bleak, brutal place where he can't control anything. And staring up inside him with tragic eyes, a horse-head, accusatory and huge, holding all the weight of history and shot through with suffering.

Driving Shigem out of Hollywood twenty minutes later, Jaymi feels almost as battered as his Beast, by what Dud and Ashley have just inflicted. And for a moment he wonders: as a means to his own ends, was it despotic of him to steer Shigem into the path of such an assault, having known beforehand that it was likely to occur in something like the form it did? But no; it had in fact been neces-sary to toughen his Beast up for life in the real world. In seeking to straighten Shigem's cells into their own design, Bang Dead's intended cure was the only disease in the picture. Yet that's just what happens out there, and always will be; so it isn't Jaymi's fault that his Beast's defences needed to be built up accordingly.

He wonders another thing, too: does Shigem *feel* like a Beast, as opposed to a human?

Deep inside Shigem, *is* there, in fact…?

And somewhere inside himself, he quivers.

59 EVELYN'S EYES IN THE PHOTO OF THE MOTEL BY THE LIQUOR STORE

In the mail delivered to the Blue Jay Way house next morning, Dud finds another envelope addressed to him in the same handwriting as yesterday's, again with no return address. Slicing it open, he finds the only thing inside is a printed photograph of another motel, with nothing written on the back.

He scrutinises the image. This location is unfamiliar. It is a tiny, rough, two-storey motel with whitish walls, whose sign is foreshort-ened in side-view, such that Dud cannot read it; nor is any street sign visible. Across a side-street from the building, however, a garish yellow sign stands in a small parking-lot, announcing the yellow-painted JS Liquor store beyond it. A quick online search turns out to be enough to get a street address for the liquor store. And it turns out to be in Westmont again, just a few blocks from the motel by the vacant lot.

He is about to open Google Street View, when he realises that his focus on location has prevented him from noticing there's a young woman standing in the motel's gateway in the photo. He can't imagine how he missed her. He peers close in, and the face of a Latina in her twenties smiles out at him, smooth, sunny and round, with a faint sass in its clear warmth, looking straight at the camera!

Her presence assumes a more sinister significance, when he recalls how her staring at him has occurred through the same postal means as the staring of that ferocious blond psychopath yesterday from the other motel photo. Disconcerted, he resumes opening Street View, navigates to the familiar location earmarked for the Righteous Gun Cockpit at the motel by the vacant lot, and confirms what he saw in that other photo: yes, there are those sturdy bars protecting the windows on the north façade. The bars were still vertical when captured by Google—not yet bent by that sinister man, whom Dud can imagine bending them as easily as bars of rubber. From there, he clicks his way down South Vermont Avenue in Street View, towards where the young woman's motel must be … and there it is. Yes: whoever held the camera must have been standing on Vermont itself, looking west and somewhat south, photographing the motel's empty gateway on the north-west corner of West Ninety-Ninth Street.

Why would someone post this to him?

He holds the photo up to his face, looks again at the woman, and this time is assailed by a uneasy feeling as he picks up on something hidden behind the sunny surface of her expression. It's as if the eyes of somebody else, more powerful than her, were aiming very different emotions at him—some murderous challenge, just beyond her smile, emanating from the paper's shiny surface into Dud, fired at him in particular.

(*Oh* yes!)

That does it. He will *not* be terrorised. He will drive down to Westmont right now, and pull the covers off this creepy provocation.

60 ASHLEY AND DUD ATTACK KIM

"Kim!" Jaymi calls out with an affable smile, wandering across the lower end of his garden to where this Beast is sitting alone on the lush lawn in contemplation of the span of L.A. below. "Allow me to take you to the Hollywood café."

"Yeah, I've heard a little something about that place, from Shigem," says Kim, looking up at his maker guardedly. "He got back from there a couple of hours ago, and had to go lie down in the bedroom and recover."

"Ah. OK. Well, you may not have heard the most flattering account of it, then."

"I think he's still sleeping it off. He didn't seem quite able to explain what happened, but I got the sense that it's quite a tough crowd in there."

"I confess it may not become a regular haunt of yours," says Jaymi. "But I do need to throw you into the external world, like throwing you into a swimming-pool to teach you how to swim. And trust me, the Hollywood café is nearer the shallow end of the pool than the deep end. Sorry, Kim, there's no way round it. The external world sucks in many ways, but it's the only one I can offer. You're dressed quite smartly enough already, for company that deems itself civilised. So let's just go to the car now and get it over with, shall we? Come on!"

Fighting down his own escalating jitters throughout the journey, Jaymi is glad of this Beast's natural taciturnity as they drive, in apprehensive silence, over to the Hollywood café. As soon as they enter, he spots Dud and Ashley having after-work drinks at a table by the far wall, as hoped.

Once again he feels that alien thrill at being able to perceive their oncoming faces through the eyes of a new Beast, as well as through his own. And this time, if he's not mistaken, Ashley in particular is taking in the newly-minted Kim with an odd burn of fascination that Jaymi didn't quite see in her when he led first Evelyn and then Shigem between these tables.

But as expected, both Dud's and her scrutiny of this fourth Beast, introduced to them by Jaymi with the customary breeze of genial small-talk, is beady-eyed with the mission to reproduce Jaymi's

141

breakthrough Kim-creation, but repurposing him instead into an enhancement for *Ain't They Freaky!*.

Yes, the ugly ambition in Dud's face is clear: he would like nothing better than to incorporate a dumbed-down version of Kim into his own tabloid product, so as to entertain customers of the "Trivia Score: Wacky or Boring?" Newsfeed, no doubt setting up Bang Dead's cartoony Kim as a kind of reference target for a world full of Trivia-scorers to mock and take aim at…

While Dud contemplates all this commercial potential in Jaymi's Beast, it's clear, too, that he's looking at him through the eyes and expectations of an average consumer of *Ain't They Freaky!*. And as soon as Dud looks at him in this way, the main problem becomes apparent: Kim thinks too much.

To speak plain, as Dud so prides himself on doing, it will need a bit of straightening-out, for normal people. Just as soon as Herb's team have worked out how he was created and have found a way to reverse-engineer him, then that excessive seriousness of mind will be the first thing to fix.

Jaymi pulls his own attention out of Dud, and returns it to Kim. Doing so, he is distraught to observe that Kim's apprehension of the Bang Dead duo's avid intentions is spreading through him like a seepage of pain. Although Kim manages to maintain his external composure, the mere prospect of being repurposed comes at him like an assault, threatening not just to down-convert him into a form that feels cheaper, but to do violence to his own self and truth—to use his precious life for something other than he wants.

This ominous prospect acts as a natural trigger for Kim's first incarnated apprehension of the innate separateness of all human beings from one another. What unbridgeable separateness it is, too, involving such unmerciful magnitudes of distance. Even when in company with one another, it seems every incarnated human is just as alone as that far-future astronaut who will fly back home at such warp speed that they'll find the earth has aged a million years during the course of their own mere few years flying—returned now to a planet where only they themselves must remain, alone until their death.

But that's just the standard-issue sadness of distance. Whereas Dud's and Ashley's attack incorporates a still greater assault, he feels: it seems they want to morph Kim into a form where he's no longer inclined to take account of the suffering caused in people by their incarnations.

People would be more than they are, Kim can see, if they weren't so powerfully targeted by the likes of Ashley and Dud and Bang Dead and their soul-dead trivia. Then how much more would people be inclined to think, and to look into others around them, searching not for their own littleness but for what to build, onwards and upwards together...

For how many of the most beautiful feelings in the world are born only to be crushed, frustrated, overridden by lesser feelings, lesser forces. How huge a proportion of the world's population is hungry, and how many more in misery. The vulnerability and frequent defeat of the finest feelings and achievements, the fact that finer aspirations are so regularly broken—that such breakage passes so often unnoticed, and that this unnoticing prevails unpunished—these are perpetual tragedies.

Kim is baffled, in particular, by the infernal depths to which pain and illness are capable of descending in some cases, often with such suddenness and permanence. Contemplating anyone who's in such a position, their life filled with physical fuck-up, he feels he is looking into a pit. An undamaged person and such a damaged one are both just flesh, so why such an extreme difference in their positions? And with what ease might their roles have been reversed.

A mere five minutes in the company of an extreme sufferer is challenging enough, he perceives. Having to see that sufferer twenty-four hours a day, year after year, would be worse. Having to *be* them would be a hell beyond hell.

As a result of many kinds of accident or condition that happen to individuals, an incarnated human may arrive at a point of knowing that all pleasures, for the rest of their entire life, will feel nasty, sick and soiled—that nothing will be real to them any more, except pain.

Kim imagines it: whining, with good reason, at being broken by nothing but a single, evil chance. Every tiny speck of progress, through every long day of their remaining life, to be undertaken through the ugly gloves of illness and pain. To have the confusion and sadness of sickness, without the possibility of its ever ending, throughout their remaining years. On top of the gross, muffling phenomenon that is simple incarnation to begin with, how weary and filthy and forever poisoned is the lot that was drawn by such a person.

To respect such a grand design strikes Kim as a challenge.

Twenty minutes later, driving a silent passenger out of Hollywood, a sobered Jaymi reflects on what Dud's and Ashley's presence has just inflicted on this new Beast's clarity and truth, and he wonders: as a means to his own ends, was it despotic of him to put Kim through all this, necessary though it was to toughen him up for life in the real world?

He wonders another thing, too: does Kim *feel* like a Beast, as opposed to a human?

Deep inside Kim, *is* there, in fact…?

And somewhere inside himself, he quivers.

61 KIM ON THE CANYON BY HERCULES DRIVE

Back in his study, a brainwave occurs to Jaymi: having incarnated Shigem and Kim, he could pull them both back into his computer and subject them to a brisk final refinement, tweaking their code so as to temper them into greater strength for the hurly-burly of combatting the "Guy Score" and the "Trivia Score" respectively. Granted, this refinement step is not something he put Evelyn through. However, she was designed as a solo act, a sunny lone wolf. Whereas these two lover-boys were designed and released as a double act, which is surely a more complex creation.

He picks up his mobile, touches Kim's number and listens to it ring, while he silently rehearses the words "Hey Kim, it's Jaymi. I'm calling to offer you the chance to be further refined, to become an even more functional Beast than you already are. It won't hurt, I promise. How about it?"

But perhaps Kim is screening his calls, because his greetings message kicks in, "Hi it's Kim. Leave a message."

Jaymi rings off, muttering and a little stung. Then he puts his mobile down again in mild exasperation: what does he need it for, when surely he can think his way into his own Beast? So he closes his eyes, swings his attention down into Kim, finds him sitting alone on a rocky canyon slope near the bottom of Hercules Drive, and proceeds to contemplate him with a creatorly eye, assessing him for potential refinement needs and infusing the scent of a question: "So Kim, how are you holding up, after the café scene? You know, in the wake of all that good stuff about breakage and misery and fuck-up and pain?"

"Hi Jaymi," Kim replies, looking straight up at him. "Yes, all those vicious design flaws. They're all still true, it seems. And they're all quite the nosebleed on the toast, as I suspect you understand very well yourself... And yet. And yet."

Jaymi nods in assent, and Kim returns his gaze to the canyon ahead and below, saying nothing more.

Looking into his Beast, Jaymi perceives how an occasional feeling of *deja vu* tends to remind Kim that there were times before he'd managed to work out something important, which suggests to Kim in turn that other remaining concerns of his will also be worked out in due course (then doubtless to give rise to future feelings of *deja vu* and resultant reassurance likewise)—a solace unsought, which causes both Beast and creator to smile.

Jaymi perceives how Kim sometimes estranges himself from the everyday world for a moment, whereupon ordinary objects and events appear new and unfamiliar, revealing their nature and giving him a clearer consciousness of things in general. At which point Kim tends to guess that this is what it must be like for all *other* Beasts too ... but then Kim realises he can't be sure of this, because his three fellow Beasts all seem strangely incurious regarding such abstract matters (even his beloved Shigem). How odd, that Jaymi has thus obliged Kim to keep such interesting reflections to himself without being able to share them with another.

In any case, even when Kim is contemplating inanimate objects only, this tendency to effect deliberate temporary self-estrangements still leaves him feeling he cannot quite judge anything he doesn't have affection for.

And thinking of affection leads Kim's thoughts back upwards, to the level of humans such as Jaymi. It seems to Kim that perhaps the only thing he himself can take credit for is his own overwhelming realisation (which Jaymi coded him to attain somewhere between the notional ages of six and nine) that every one of the crushing number of other humans around Jaymi *also* has a real human consciousness just as complex as Jaymi's. And just as important, Kim then proceeded to set this young realisation up as the backbone on which he built himself throughout his notional teens. It also generated his kindness and compassion, which clothe what he'd otherwise be inclined to call a greater innate potential selfishness than Shigem's, as it happens.

Since his own incarnation, Kim has known that humans are each alone, yet united as parts of the larger mass of them. When he's frightened, Kim lets his own compassion for the pain and fear in Jaymi flow upwards into his creator; and Jaymi's fear tends then to diminish.

Jaymi sees one more thing about Kim, which is something this Beast will do in future—a more flesh-and-blood thing than the rest of what Jaymi has seen inside him. Into the apartment he shares with Shigem, Kim will introduce Clytemnestra, the velvety-nosed rabbit, who will live with them both. When Clytemnestra sits in comfort, her legs hidden from sight underneath her, she will look a bit like a wide furry oval, with ears that sometimes turn in different directions to hear different things. She will also be wont to stand up on her hind-legs, and periscope...

Jaymi breathes out, opens his eyes, thinks for a moment, then speaks aloud to his Beast on the canyon slope: "You don't need refining at all, do you? At least not by me."

Kim gives a faint smile, unspeaking, then returns his attention to the rocky canyon slope.

62 DUD SHOCKED IN THE MOTEL BY THE LIQUOR STORE

Meanwhile, Dud exits the 110 freeway, curves off the ramp and proceeds along Century Boulevard. Soon he's doubling back along Ninety-Ninth, until he reaches a place where he coasts to a halt and parks. He peers across the street, at the sad little motel by the liquor store. Its pale façade is almost featureless, except for two irregular rows of tiny bathroom windows. He gets out, presses his key-fob and hears the car's lock beep behind him. Rounding the corner of Vermont, he comes to the building's front gateway.

He starts, in recognition: is that the girl he saw in the photograph, ahead of him right now, flitting up the steps to the open walkway of the motel's upper level, glancing back down at him with laughing eyes full of sassy flirtation and sunlight? She disappears from his view as she crests the top step and runs on along the walkway, triggering his memory of that other gaze stabbing into him from behind her face…

(And along with this advent of Evelyn, Jaymi's perceptions come swinging down from the house on Electra Drive, to here in Westmont. So distracted has he been by Kim's inner life, he's been forgetting to attend to her and Amber.)

Ignoring the opaque grilled windows of the motel's ground-floor office on his left, Dud starts barrelling up the flight of steps, in pursuit of her.

By the time he has heaved himself up to the upper walkway, it's deserted. One of the blue-grey doors on the left appears to be open just a crack, though. He runs along to the door, grabs its handle and pushes it inwards.

After the light outside, the interior is too dim for him to make out what's ahead; but sensing no immediate danger, he walks in and peers around.

Intent on making visual sense of what's in the middle of the room, he hardly notices the door click shut behind him.

Hanging from the ceiling is a pig's ribcage. A photo of his own face is stuck atop the ribcage, wearing a Righteous Gun Cockpit cap. Hanging off the whole contraption is a dark, squeezy bag of blood, by the look of it, while a lighted altar candle is stuck onto the floor on each side.

(Up on Electra Drive, seeing through the echo of Evelyn's presence here, Jaymi's eyes widen with almost as great a surprise as Dud's.)

Dud staggers back and tries to leave the motel room, but the door has been locked.

He gives up wrenching at the door handle. On the verge of panic, he spots a dusty landline telephone on a shelf near the door, dives for it and jabs the zero button. He holds the old plastic handset to his ear, but can hear no ringing sound at the other end, so slams it back down onto the cradle.

He tugs at the window-bars in vain, while darting his eyes about the room, hunting for any kind of key. He bangs on the door and shouts.

No answer.

Nobody appears.

And the squeezy bag of blood turns slowly in the air, spun around by the heat from the candles underneath.

63 DUD SHOCKED IN THE MOTEL BY THE VACANT LOT

Dud's hammering on the motel room door peters out. Continuing to hammer may bring rescue. However, it would also bring attention; and peering with renewed horror and confusion at the pig's ribcage hanging from the ceiling, he has an instinct that attention is something he'd be better off avoiding, in the context of this room in its current state. He therefore redoubles his hunt for any kind of key, while the bag of blood keeps turning in mid-air, in the soft glow and heat from the pair of altar candles on either side below.

He starts, to see a key lying in the half-open drawer of a formica-topped chest. He grabs it, rushes to the window-bars and tries it.

Yes! He slides the bars aside, opens the window, clambers up to the sill, squeezes through, lands on the walkway, and peers right and left over the low railings in front of him. There's no one in sight. He scoots along to the steps, tiptoes down, trots around the corner and across the street to his car, starts it up, does a U-turn and drives away up Ninety-Ninth the way he came, hoping no one is looking through the motel office window to make a note of his licence-plate number.

Once around the block, he turns back onto Vermont from Century, and presses grimly on down four more blocks, until the motel by the vacant lot appears ahead on the right.

Sensing unexpected activity there, he sweeps around the corner of One Hundred and Fourth, halts under a lone expansive palm and stares in growing indignation across the street. In the middle of the vacant lot itself, at the spot he has earmarked for his Righteous Gun Cockpit, the creepy charisma of the infernal blond man is unmistakable, waving straight at Dud right now with that unholy twinkling humour and menace in his eyes (so sharp, even from this far across the street)—just as if Dud has been awaited like a guest of honour who is late for a banquet.

He jumps out of the car and strides across to the railing that contains the vacant lot, several of whose bars have been bent away to either side leaving a hole large enough for a person. Dud climbs through, breathing hard in rage, and thunders across the short stretch of waste ground towards Amber.

In the middle of the lot, just where the Cockpit will be, Amber is tipping fresh concrete out of a wheelbarrow, into a foundation trench that's already half filled with the stuff.

Sticking up obscenely from the heavy wet gleam of fresh concrete, a random array of human hands, feet and heads are embedded up and down the trench, as if frozen in the act of waving and staring up at him.

So shocked is Dud, as he stoops to verify these half-buried body-parts are indeed humans rather than dummies, that he fails to notice Amber has slipped away from the trench and is climbing out through the gap in the railings, onto the pavement. Not until Amber has turned around, bent the railings back to their imprisoning verticality, stepped across the street and reached into Dud's car to sound the horn, does Dud wheel around at that familiar sound. In doing so, he catches Amber's and Jaymi's murderously affectionate wave at him with just the fingers of Amber's one hand, as if waving to a baby, while those eyes' fluid humour cuts sharp through the dusk into Dud with contempt.

Seconds later, the blond Beast has slipped away into the shadows of the evening.

As Dud runs to the railings and tries in vain to bend them back outwards to allow him through, a scattering of camera-flashes pop among the onlookers.

64 DUD'S GHASTLY PHOTO OPPORTUNITY

In coming days it will emerge that Evelyn has alerted various journalists to the situation that's unfolding at the motel by the vacant
lot, in order to supplement and prolong the citizen-journalism that
she knew would also occur here. These kinds of journalism explain
the camera flashes that Dud is seeing around him. Every time he
happens to be looking in the direction of a flash at the very instant it
occurs (such as when a photographer has just called out Dud's name
while their finger hovers over the camera button in readiness), he is
captured with a deer-in-the-headlights expression.

This expression, the fact that he's lurking furtively in a vacant lot
in South Central for no apparent reason, and the further detail of the
human limbs and heads protruding from the wet concrete behind
him: all these elements do add up to an embarrassing whole, in the
context of his being a senior manager in a multinational company.

In fact Dud's trip to Westmont tonight is something that Bang
Dead's P.R. department will have cause to concern itself with to
a notable degree, over upcoming weeks, while those unforgettable
images of him flow out around the world, first on social media and
then in more traditional organs.

All in all, it's a trip he very likely regrets.

Looked at from here in the vacant lot, the wide strip of median
that runs for dozens of blocks along this stretch of South Vermont
Avenue appears featureless, except for a few trees; but it is in fact a
city border. Over there on the east side of it is the incorporated City
of L.A., while here on the west side is Westmont, an unincorporated
patch of L.A. County. So, there are two different police forces: if this
motel had been across that median on the other side of Vermont, then
the L.A.P.D. would have had this crime scene under control already.
Like the motel by the liquor store, however, this establishment is on
the west side instead, located in the more leisurely jurisdiction of the
L.A. County Sheriffs.

It is a while before the police arrive.

During that time, Dud undertakes a redoubling of his efforts to
heave his bulk over the sharp-pointed tops of the railings enclosing this space—an undertaking that's both ineffectual and much
photographed.

Rohan Quine

And when the county sheriffs do at last arrive, Dud senses their arrival will be unlikely to herald any let-up in his misfortunes this evening, as he contemplates being taken in to help the police with their enquiries, then perhaps even progressing, by well-publicised degrees, to his first criminal record.

As he watches the sheriffs lumber over towards him, the soundtrack and visuals of external life recede for a minute, while there fades in a different scenario that feels like a more accurate expression of his current reality. From every direction come clanking sounds from seemingly empty buildings, as if the metropolis is closing itself down without any human interference: metal bed-frames roll themselves into corners, in defeat; tables fold themselves away through closet-doors, knowing when they must quit; and stackable chairs climb up, one by one, into tottering heaps…

As for those human limbs and heads, within the next couple of days police investigations will reveal these were corpses that Amber had transported to this vacant lot from one of the nearby funeral parlours, where he'd stolen them, undetected, at about the time Dud was preoccupied with the ribcage and the suspended bag of blood in the motel by the liquor store.

This being Westmont, it will also be found that most of the corpses were local residents who'd been victims of gun-crime—a fact perceived as sitting uncomfortably with many aspects of the Righteous Gun Cockpit that was to be built here.

It is not long before Bang Dead decides to remove all depictions of this planned Cockpit from beside the "Guy Score", then to reassess this Cockpit's release schedule, and then to cancel it altogether.

Thinking back later upon the entire noir caper down in Westmont, Jaymi has to admit that although Evelyn's and Amber's humiliation of Dud turned out to be successful, there was an element of luck in this result. In thinking this, he doesn't mean to disrespect his two Beasts; after all, he was aware of peering out through their four eyes throughout the whole bizarre episode.

(Well, throughout the whole episode *except* for the hours Amber spent robbing corpses and the hours Evelyn spent constructing that grotesque ribcage sculpture, while Jaymi was failing to check in on what they were up to. And what talented scamps they turned out to be there! He himself would never have thought of executing the ter-

151

rorisation of Dud by means of a couple of art projects like those. And they worked, too: for if Dud's face expressed one emotion, standing in that motel room and on that vacant lot, then it was *mind-fucked!* Classic, really—Jaymi has to hand it to both his Beasts there.)

So no, all he means by identifying an element of luck in the caper's success was that Amber and Evelyn didn't collaborate or even much associate with each other, as far as he can tell. Their different activities just kind of worked, in a glorious clatter of juxtaposed carnage. But let's face it, it could all have come quite off the rails in one way or another.

Yes; when Jaymi next sends his Beasts out from the confines of his own computer, he'd better make sure they coordinate their activities a bit more.

65   JAYMI REFINES SHIGEM

Regarding his recent plan to pull the incarnated Kim and Shigem back into the computer for a final quick code-tweak, Jaymi recalls how clear it then became, there on the slopes of Hercules Drive, that Kim's existing balance and complexity were already quite sufficient not to need any such finishing-school, thank you. But in the case of Shigem, so much will the world want to target this joyously gay Beast, warm and loving and open as he is, that a smidgen of refinement may be beneficial in tempering him into greater strength for the hurly-burly of combatting the "Guy Score: Hunk or Gross?" Newsfeed.

So Jaymi rises from his desk, crosses his study terrace, peers down over the railings to where Shigem is sunning his slender body beside the swimming-pool, and summons him up the exterior flight of steps.

Once inside his creator's study, Shigem is at first apprehensive at being informed he must now return through the monitor he emerged from. Luckily, however, he is the most trusting of the Beasts and Jaymi loves him with a particularly protective love—which two facts conspire to reassure Shigem into biting the bullet and just doing it.

In through his creator's monitor he climbs, therefore; and within moments Jaymi has switched into code view, displaying all Shigem's ones and zeroes in their quite paralysing beauty of digital dryness, there once again upon the same screen where he first started shimmering into existence.

Only now does Jaymi realise that he hasn't planned what this refinement is going to be. Perhaps he should have done! Oh well, he'd better wing it. OK then, so first: ascending a forest path, Shigem is the only one to see a magically beautiful and unexpected bird, away to the left amid the undergrowth. Fluffy in the sunlight, it looks across at him—

No, hold on.

Well, alright, the bird can remain in him now and fly wherever its pleasures may take it. However, wasn't the whole point of this refinement to strengthen Shigem, by equipping him with resources of a *different* kind from those he possesses already?

OK then, what new resources can he be given? Well, let's see: Amber's strength derived from something metallic, Kim's from the emotional intelligence of his intellect, and Evelyn's from an animal joy of ease and freedom within. But none of those feels like the right origin for this Beast's strength…

And the answer appears. This one's strength should originate from a straightforward love for his own self—hitching a ride, as it were, on the oddly innocent vanity whose seeds Shigem already possesses. Jaymi is feeling his way with this idea, but he'll give it a try.

He therefore decides to implant in Shigem's code three memories of complimentary statements that were made to Jaymi himself, at different times in years past, by three varied close friends—in each case as a natural moment in a two-way conversational exchange of friendship whose strength and respect were equal in both directions. In each case, Jaymi will now just donate the statement without alteration. It's a fair bet this is an approach that would never have been allowed at Bang Dead Games—but guess what? He's no longer working there, so he's free to do whatever what his Beasts may require. So here goes.

First, an exquisitely evolved admirer once said words to Shigem that the latter afterwards wrote down so as to make sense of them: "I felt faint in looking round your room for the first time, in ecstasy, walking on air, being tranced, being in magic that someone could do and be all this, that you existed. I was blinded by the dark light you shed, which mattered more than anything else in the world to me."

Secondly, a unusual admirer once said words to Shigem that the latter afterwards wrote down for the same reason: "You lay claim to and identify with whatever and wherever you are, thereby preventing those things from being ephemeral or meaningless and making yourself irresistible to others. You have made being yourself into a fine art. You've committed yourself with such strength and passion to being yourself in every way possible, it's fucking irresistible! Compared to you, I, who have always thought of myself as being out-there and strange, stand in awe, and it delights me."

And thirdly, in reply to the question "Should I show more vulnerability?", a perceptive friend once said words to Shigem that the latter afterwards wrote down for the same reason also: "You do show it already, and it's where you may not expect it—in your absolute self-absorption. You're the most innocent narcissist I've ever met and it's heart-breaking—at least I find it so, because I see you as this incredibly beautiful being who is nevertheless doomed to die like everyone else."

There, the code is added, for whatever it may do. Jaymi sinks back into his seat and closes his eyes, to rest them—straight away noticing the cicadas' endless scrape, from their hiding-places in the scrubby vegetation coating all sides of his promontory.

He's not sure what effect that trio of memories will have on Shigem, but the truth and seriousness of them can't do too much harm and may do right. So be it: job done.

But things never do coast in to quite such a smooth finish, when it comes to this particular Beast, as Jaymi has already experienced. For now Shigem pipes up with one more thing: "Oh and Jaymi, as a nightclub DJ I can quite understand that you don't 'do requests', as it were—but I would just like to say there was such an annoying bellowing cow in the supermarket today, who I could have *so* done without. Could we maybe get rid of her, d'you think, just while we're down here at code level? She gave me a headache."

His creator smiles in relief: *there's* the innocence in Shigem's self-love, still intact! "Sorry, Shigem, but the bellowing cow remains; she's part of the deal. 'Cos you know, honey-buns, it's not *all* about you. Most of it's about you, I admit, but not quite all of it."

Shigem's code pouts back petulantly from the text editor window.

"Yeah yeah, you'll get over it," says Jaymi. "So, we're done now, with all this code-refining business. Time to slither back out here into the study, please, out into meat-space again. You'll love it when you get here, I promise." He taps out a volley of incarnation commands into the keyboard, then he sits there, waiting, until his fingers start tapping the desk. "Out you come then," he coaxes. "Come on... Well *get on with it!* I don't have all evening."

And Shigem complies.

66 LETHAL ATTACK, UNDERSTANDING AND DESPAIR (*MIDPOINT*)

Standing at the railings around the highest of his three terraces, Jaymi spots a dark speck far away, low in the warm haze of afternoon, half-obscured among the tiny writhing shreds of heat that crawl across the panorama of low-slung buildings, freeway ramps and grimy palm trees.

He shields his eyes and squints at the speck. Swelling slowly, it reveals itself to be something like a giant arachnid with thick legs outstretched. It continues to swell, but without shifting much to right or left; it must therefore be approaching directly...

It's another drone!

He would guess it has reached somewhere around Santa Monica Boulevard, more or less.

He peers at it, in gathering unease. By this point it must be pretty much above Sunset, and still it swells; he can count eight little whirring propellers, one on each spider-leg.

He grips the railings. Now it's over Hollywood Boulevard, no more than four hundred metres ahead!

On an instinct he crouches down on the terrace, watching the drone through the railings, while two of its spider-legs curl down and lift something out from beneath its belly—some dark, stick-like object.

Fifty metres away from him, the drone swings this object around, and Jaymi cries out in growing surmise and alarm. He drops further, onto his hands and knees, so that more of him is protected behind the low parapet on which the railings are mounted.

A gunshot cracks out.

The bullet hits a sun-bed behind him and ricochets towards his bedroom windows, where it strikes something with a sharp crack.

Another gunshot, which zings off one of the railings just above him. He flinches down lower still, lying flat upon the terrace, so as to be hidden altogether by the parapet.

A third shot, which he can hear bouncing off the wide circular roof of his top-floor bedroom suite.

Rolling over and looking up, he sees the drone sweep onwards over this roof, curve right, veer up to the east, and become lost to view somewhere over Nichols Canyon.

He staggers upright, and looks across the terrace to locate the first bullet's impact on a metal mullion between two of his bedroom windows.

As the last echoes of the third gunshot finish caroming across the canyons on either side of this promontory, Jaymi feels his sight open to take in something wider than just this gun drone attack, shocking as it is: he finds himself attaining his clearest-ever understanding of just how lone a wolf he is, pitted against Dud and the Dreary Ones and all their corporate deadweight.

How clear their motivations are now: specific evil, and a systematic, mean-minded sabotaging of a competing developer's work, even unto assassinating him.

How corrupt and how powerful *Ain'tTheyFreaky!*'s lies stand revealed as, too, behind the surface of that smutty, sniggering smallness belching out twenty-four/seven through those tabloid Newsfeeds, in all their nervous, fake normality.

How powerless the clear-burning truth of his own output looks, in comparison. An implicit challenge, charged with the mission to refresh a Newsfeed-saturated world with the memory of other ways to be alive, but … well, good luck with that, Jaymi-boy. The truth of his own games, founded in complexity, unconventionality, beauty, subtlety—what a puny weapon this truth is, against the sheer bulk of *Ain'tTheyFreaky!*'s lies rearing up so massive on foundations of toxic simplicity, convention, utility and obviousness.

He sinks onto one of the sun-beds and lies there with his eyes closed. And throughout the spreading of cold along his limbs, his mind works with a strange analytical calm. Supine with his hands over his face, he can almost hear the abstract sound of Dud Guy's Newsfeeds churning out degraded triteness at best, destructive poison at worst—hour after emetic hour, day after tired day, week after weary week, month after moronic month, and doubtless year after year and decade after decade, with no chance of stopping. And what they pump out with such relentlessness will forever be gobbled by the greatest number of humans around the world every day, the sad summation of a species: the "Gal Score: Babe or Gross?"; the "Guy Score: Hunk or Gross?"; and the "Trivia Score: Wacky or Boring?".

For those three titles are now on course to become the most-consumed news in the world, statistically, so viral is their ugly tabloid mass-appeal. Those Newsfeeds, which Dud has devoted such energies to creating, have wrought a debasement from human-ity, a destructive theft of grandeur and human potential, dragging everyone slightly downwards into something smaller, cheaper, meaner—just as their creator knew they would. They've encouraged millions of local instances of meanness and hate, many of which will have resulted in lasting suffering and even the undocumented breakage of many unknown individuals.

What joyful implications for humanity's potential.

So huge is the contrast between Bang Dead's cultural empower-ment and Jaymi's own, that right now, here on this sun-bed, he is tempted to give up his whole venture.

What a release it would be, to take the easy way out and sur-render these inconveniently-slanted truths to the coarse grain of those Newsfeeds' prevailing lies. The truths in question have landed on a badly-designed planet, it would seem! Well then—not his fault. Better luck with the planet-choosing next time, Jaymi-boy. Why not pack up his truths, pop them in the attic in a suitcase, for who-knows-when-if-ever, and spend his days supine on this sun-bed instead, vegging out?

And in any case—*is* he following the truth? Could he, just possibly, be wrong? Could those avid Newsfeed contributors and consumers all be right, as it happens? What a sad song, if so. But it could be the case, could it not?

He opens his eyes and stares out across L.A. to where the drone swam out of those crawling shreds of heat-haze.

Tears spring sharp behind his eyes, while the house on Electra Drive, here behind him, feels like a house in a life far away.

And for several long few moments, Jaymi Peek is lost … so alone, and so empty, and not knowing what he should believe, after all.

His ongoing development of *The Platinum Raven*, *The Imagination Thief* and *The Host in the Attic* were so essential, so central in his desire to light up and elevate the world just a little through his own creative vision, to enrich the medium with greater emotional intelligence, to nudge this powerful industry into evolving… But if those games are to be abandoned, then what everlasting loss there'll be, because three complex and beautiful things will not have been created that should have been.

If he is now to halt their development, then something inside him, somewhere, will die.

A scene unfurls, where a pair of dirty pink roller-skates lie in a patch of waste, near the remains of a bonfire of tyres. Above a shop-front encased in rusty grilles, a signboard says "Cindi's" in orange italic, with the outline of a cutely snub-nosed young woman's profile in black paint, and a phone number whose area code has since changed twice. In the unlit shop behind the grilles, a line of bulky hair-setting helmets hang empty over dusty green plastic chairs, before a wall of dry basins and shelves of styling products with logos from a bygone era.

But driving out of town is only further downhill beneath a churning grey sky, with the howl of blind dogs in the distance. A row of trees shears in together, as the car nears the point where the trees meet the road—all bunching into a single tree at the instant the car passes them—but then when they fan out again behind the car, they're a row of bare poles.

The car passes a statue whose stone face is almost eaten away, framed in monstrous plants; and the statue smiles, pointing Jaymi on and down. This tract of north-east Kazakh steppe was stained with the poison of nuclear bomb tests for forty years. Now the tunnels in the mountain are sealed up in concrete. In such desolation the land is silent, scrubbed, dead … and the texture of the sun's disc, glimpsed through a cloud for an instant, is like the grain of meat.

Growing claustrophobia in a vast flat land, as if the isolation is shrinking the air. A glum palace looms from the steppes, then it morphs in the night, to the psychiatric centre on the island in the East River, hedged in with cameras and barbed-wire, hiding there in plain view of civilisation.

Onward and down, to the island in the Aral Sea, poisoned with the stains of bio-weapon tests on monkeys: dead hands and eyes in charge throughout the decades, in a rotting sea. Now the sea is shrinking, scum builds up around the island, like a crust. The sides of the boats weep tar into mud, while the winds across the salt-flat are mournful and endless, and the ghosts of a thousand dead monkey-arms climb onto shore like a school of shadow-limbs.

Onward and down again, to satellite images of twelve death-camps in Korea, overlaid with script and arrows that identify the torture chambers, cellblocks and sullen smudge of mine-mouths. Cores, rubble, fluids; human meat and bones, broken there and mixed together; acid sludge in acid pits.

Inside a torture block, an empty room, lacking any door—just four square walls around a square floor, underneath a ceiling with a bare black light-bulb shedding only shadow.

Beyond one wall, an alarm-bell is fixed above a never-used stair-well, permanently ringing, for a purpose unexplained.

And just through another wall, a hidden horror-place—a suite of human-farming and human vivisection and medical experiments, whose unknown status only adds to its enormity.

PART IV

"ARTS SCORE", THE PLATINUM RAVEN'S CREATION, AND ELEVATING DOWNTOWN L.A.

67 THE "ARTS SCORE: SIMPLE-SMILEY OR COMPLEX-FROWNY?" NEWSFEED

This sick sight where he's floundering now is very probably despair, he would guess.

Somewhere above him, though, an increase of light may suggest he is drifting up nearer to a surface. The light grows further, till he breaks gently through to air, and finds himself lying on his terrace.

A thin fire starts seeping back through his body, from a central place. He checks the time. Less than an hour since the drone.

The drone was just a flying toy, weaponised with a gun; nothing more and nothing less. But it must have tipped the scales of a melt-down inside him that was waiting to happen. For surely, that was some sort of high-speed breakdown he just had? A small one, by many standards, but one that felt despairing and has left him feeling battered and traumatised.

Lying here on his back, he notices the familiar black asterisk of that palm crest high above him—and a faint smile leaks back through his face.

The things he just saw and felt were true, in their different ways, and they still are. In addition to them, however, it's true that he remains enrolled on the same progression as before, whose aim is to improve matters, just as previous improvements have been made by disparate others enrolled on similar journeys.

That's still the job at hand, and the best response.

He gets up, returns to the railing and scans the afternoon haze lying across Los Angeles.

It's the mission of a David against a Goliath, this job, where such inequality of resources is at play. Evelyn, Shigem and Kim, tiny in the face of the deluge... A tiny trio of aliveness, pitched against those endless streaming walls of lazy deadness dripping down grey as sleet through the senses of the world.

But that's the point: tiny in their richness and beauty, in response to the deluge. Well, it's worth a shot, right?

Yes, though they're more than a shot, those Beasts. They're the goal; they're the end in themselves, through being. Why, just a day or two ago, while working on *The Imagination Thief*, Jaymi had Evelyn instantiate this in terms evoking movement, as it happened: "Evelyn's dance, with minimal effect", as he now recalls.

At the recollection of this little moment of Evelyn's—one of so many she will pass through in the world of her allotted game—he feels the fire has spread out from that central place in him, right to the ends of his fingers and toes.

How could he have contemplated, just a few minutes ago, jettisoning the development of his three games? *No!* He will resume all three, with even greater force and inspiration than before.

Looking back at when he despatched Amber to stalk the Dreary Ones in their homes and offices, and even looking back at when he sent Evelyn and Amber down to Westmont to wreak havoc on Dud's plans, from this new frame of mind he can see that those stalkings and havoc-wreakings were very much meat-space tactics. They were intended as attacks on Bang Dead, and they were indeed such. But weren't they also just a little bit like quaint capers out of the twentieth century?

He must up his game. His attacks shouldn't remain confined to the physical world. He should assail the company from inside its own game-world. Attack them digitally.

A cyber-war, then?

Well, a kind of cyber-war, yes. But again, not a cloddish cyber-bashing from outside. Rather, a subtle insinuation—corrupting Bang Dead's Newsfeeds, by stealth of beauty and intelligence, from within.

For the plan that's taking shape in him is this: when he starts creating the code for his very next Beast, he'll watch out for Herb hacking into it, just as Herb did when the first code was created for Evelyn, Shigem and Kim. Jaymi will protect his upcoming Beast from the hack, of course; but as soon as he's done so, when Herb's expectations are least attentive to further manoeuvres, Jaymi will spirit his own Beasts back through into the Bang Dead coding environment of Herb's system, to wreak their luscious stealth there...

How much more elegant it will be to subvert *Ain't TheyFreaky!* from within. No, it'll be way more than elegant: what a fucking *blast* it will be, to enter battle in this way! For these Beasts that he'll be sending into battle will not be mere tactics deployed in response to Bang Dead. They'll be parts of Jaymi himself—the richest contribution he can make to a world that seems to have been designed to facilitate the likes of *Ain't TheyFreaky!* instead—sentient contributions that'll be the finest things he's equipped to create from deep within his own complexity, resulting from a joyous struggle to incorporate into each Beast the best cells of himself, while still enabling that Beast to plug into the world and dance in celebration of its own enchanted self!

Following the gun-drone attack, he knows better than ever what he's up against. Bang Dead's lies will survive and thrive forever. But if he brings all his creativity to bear, people will awaken to the waste and damage of those Newsfeeds they've been propping up so long! He strides across the terrace into his bedroom, gallops downstairs to his study and fires up his computer.

Straight away, numerous online sources are excited to announce that today Bang Dead has rolled out another massive free offering to consumers everywhere. It's the fourth major plank of *Ain't TheyFreaky!*, and the company promises it'll be a popular hit: it's the "Arts Score: Simple-Smiley or Complex-Frowny?" Newsfeed!

This is a constant stream of images, videos or pieces of text uploaded from around the world, presenting excerpts of creative works in all media, which are rated for easiness by any member of the public using *Ain't TheyFreaky!*'s Freakometer, from a highest score of 10 for most Simple-Smiley, down to a lowest score of 1 for most Complex-Frowny.

Jaymi lets his gaze wander up and down this newsfeed stream, where new posts are popping up every few seconds, every one of them soon receiving scores and comments from multiple sources.

He reads a few posts, for half a minute or so.

Then he shuts off the Newsfeed, looks away from the screen and closes his eyes.

A few minutes later, he opens his programming software. He creates a blank new project file, and names it "Fifth Beast".

Who will this fifth one be?

Well, let's see. His previous couple of creations, Shigem and Kim—well, does it have to be pointed out that these two are realer, more vivid, more flesh-and-blood than Amber or even Evelyn? He has only to think of this pair of lover-boys, running around with all their prattle and silliness and continual erections for each other, and he wants to smile. They're just sparkier, more human, more sensual than the earlier two.

However, didn't Shigem's and Kim's quotidian chattiness come up a tad short in the transcendence department—or, to zero in on this more precisely, the transcendence-with-lush-grandeur department?

Hmm. Maybe Shigem and Kim didn't quite add up to the sermon on the mount, after all. Maybe they're a rung upon a ladder.

So again, who will this fifth Beast be?

Someone who'll embody not just Jaymi's pointed response to the "Arts Score: Simple-Smiley or Complex-Frowny?" Newsfeed, but something wider—his whole instinctive urge for transcendence of all the ugly smallness he can feel squirting out at him from every glyph and pixel of *Ain'tTheyFreaky!*.

After a moment he consults the general sketch of the Platinum Raven in his design for the game *The Platinum Raven*. Ah yes—as he now recalls, this sketch refers to the fact that, within the world of the game, this Platinum Raven character happens to originate from the imagination of another character called the Chocolate Raven. He polishes the sketch, so it reads: "The Chocolate Raven dreams up (or perhaps just observes) a more powerful and magical version of herself called the Platinum Raven, the platinum-blonde ruler of a nightclub tower of shadows, which springs up in the

Hajar Mountains across the desert, where events of the brightest darkness, decadence and beauty occur. The dance-floor is a cat-walk where every night those anorexic models float past her, beautifully drugged-out and weak and untouchable, forever down the runways of their airport lanes, expressionless in damage through the night-lit clouds with their make-up flashing soft in the lights, like perfection, clad in shreds of lightest silk that conceal the needle-marks. Steeped in this heightened feeling of darkness beneath legendary nightclub fabulousness, the Platinum Raven's transcendence is instinct with the longing that enriches even the wildest pleasures and highest achievements we are capable of while alive."

Well, OK then. Bring it on!

Jaymi thinks for a moment longer, then he renames this new project "The Platinum Raven"…

So here comes a new Beast, born into beauty and complexity, a creature of his own love and pain.

Regrettable that the Platinum Raven's charismatic transcendence should be forced to look at and tangle with so ugly a counterbalance as the "Arts Score: Simple-Smiley or Complex-Frowny?" Newsfeed. Such heaviness and dreariness and slack loquacity! Jaymi is sure the Platinum Raven would have things otherwise.

That counterbalance would seem, however, to be compulsory.

68 JAYMI CREATES THE PLATINUM RAVEN'S CODE

Jaymi sips his bourbon on the rocks, puts it back down beside him, and claps his hands together.

He will create the Platinum Raven's code here, in the place where she will live after she's emerged: a swanky house on Zeus Drive that he owns as an investment property, half a mile up into the hills from his own home.

From this seat on the rear terrace, he looks across at the semi-circular colonnade beyond the swimming-pool, at the lower sun-deck supported on its struts from the precipitous slopes below, and over at the tall thin cypresses ranged across the canyon. This hillside's angle causes his view of the city ahead to be restricted to the west and south only, in contrast with the hundred-and-eighty-degree panorama that's visible from the terrace on Electra Drive, although the visuals here are otherwise just as glorious. He therefore cannot see the Downtown skyscrapers, but the smaller clump of towers over there in Century City is clear, including Bang Dead's headquarters in the Avenue of the Stars tower, rising highest in the clump.

As when he created Amber, Evelyn, Shigem and Kim, there comes a flash of those grand decks of controls, spread across the L.A. sky.

—OK. So here comes the code of this in-game Beast who personifies transcendence in a white-blonde flavour, but treacle-black and blood-orange inside herself. A transcendence that should have ruled the world...

Throughout her creation cycle—from within her first sticks of code, up through the creation of her appearance, her soundtrack and her coming-alive, to her slithering incarnate through Jaymi's monitor into his study—and even after that, emanating from her skin and up through those swooping angles of semi-profiled cheekbones that she'll be shafting and slicing out through the sky above the Hollywood Hills, the coolness of this upcoming Beast's temperature will constitute an implicit challenge for any warm-blooded audience. Jaymi is aware of this, and he's aware that her audience of gamers, at whom he'll be aiming her, do all have warm blood, being human. Those gamers will therefore be challenged by her. The freelance game-testers he'll employ—those editorial professionals through whose scrutiny he'll be passing her and the other Beasts before he releases his finished games—may suggest that in her particular case Jaymi has told more than he has shown.

He's aware of these dangers, regarding her coolness of temperature. Yet this just *is* her nature, on her outside at least. Implicit in her role will be to test his testers' patience, to challenge the expectations of her audience—an audience who'd expect nothing less than this of her, after all, in the long run. Although he hasn't yet typed a single glyph of her, he can sense her approach, like a grand music barrelling towards him through the night behind an oncoming storm...

She will allow Jaymi to lob one tiny Easter egg of unique sweetness from the shadows here where he stands, into the empty circle of spotlight awaiting her there on her creation floor, before he must get down to uncompromising business with her transcendence. OK then, so there goes the little chocolate egg, curving up in slow motion through the air in his study, twirling end-on-end as it levels off in mid-arc, gliding in through the spotlight-cone's soft perimeter and landing in the white-lit circle on the floor of the darkness, where it spins to a foil-wrapped halt. The egg-foil opens busily, as if in speeded-up footage, and out hatches a flash-forward memory of a lost time in the Platinum Raven's notional childhood, hidden there recessively in her otherwise blank history, when her five-year-old self is standing beside Jaymi's five-year-old self in an elementary-school playground. They hardly know each other and will never get around to speaking with each other again, as it happens. But just for this one moment, they share something that he will never forget: both standing on tiptoes to peer through the frosted window of a locked shed in the corner of the playground, they agree in loud whispers that the face they think they can see in the darkness of the shed's cluttered interior is the face of a secret monkey living inside, which nobody else knows about! They giggle together at this, shushing each other in gleeful surprise at this shared monkey secret. Then they skip away across the playground in opposite directions, into separate lives, smiling still, never to exchange a single further word.

The cone of spotlight flicks off and slams away, sucked into blackness and silence. There—that's all the Platinum Raven will allow Jaymi, in the chocolate egg department.

Now: the business of transcendence please. From his insides, to hers…

Her charisma will derive from emotional self-containment and unpredictability, as charisma tends to, but will also come from an intelligence that's primal, defeating analysis. The question "Has the Platinum Raven got *it*?" will be answered "Yes." *It*—that quality that'll make her stand out from the sphere of other Beasts.

She'll be isolated in the middle of things, but will contrive to make it feel an honour for another Beast to know her. Such other Beast will know she could bite them worse than they could bite her, while believing correctly that she won't, unprompted. The trust they'll place in her will feel all the more rewarded for their having contemplated the danger in its potential breakage.

Her power to make others love her will rest on an essential inno-cence on her part, in being fascinated by herself as a character rather than as a set of interests to be furthered—a self-celebration with nothing heavy or solipsistic in it. Simple though this will feel from her viewpoint, nonetheless for others it will tend to cause everything about her to be a denial of expectations that everything *else* about her has already raised.

For instance, she'll combine extravagance and carefulness, complexity and clarity. Passion and acceptingness will merge in her. Her nature will comprise normal elements endowed with abnor-mal intensity and self-awareness. Naturalness and unnaturalness will coexist in an uncanny balance, as if her intellect were a nozzle through which the fluid of her emotion is controlled. And looking downwards here, she'll be such that, if her characteristics had been arranged in a somewhat different pattern, then she could have been monstrous and dangerous indeed. For she won't be an innately good Beast as such, but will use genuine kindness and decency as almost constant garments—to the extent that when she takes those gar-ments off for a moment, people will be startled, though not surprised, at what they sense is revealed.

Further down, there'll be an element or two of the dictator or murderer, somewhere in her (as in him). Yes, those twin shadows will be there, where fantasy will sometimes clamour to become reality, cool and ferocious; yet luckily that pair of spectres will loom small enough, within her landscape, to be sublimated.

And so it will be, when inspiration strikes her, that she'll plant a platinum kiss upon the game-skin of her universe.

Then without warning, Jaymi reaches into this cold theoretical code and unleashes an extravagant death-wish at the heart of her: hot and red inside, where she lounges on the driver's seat, her foot upon the pedal as the car flashes scarlet under headlands of rock around Pacific Coast Highway curves at ninety miles an hour, with the crackle of the cables in the sweaty air of night above, ecstatic to be leaving life any second now, beneath the stars, with the bottle in her hand and her unseen lover-girl sitting right beside her...

Jaymi hits the Enter key before her car can crash, sealing up within the coolness of her code a red-hot death-by-the-ocean whose voltage will strain against the inside of her ribcage, never to be earthed.

He sinks back, exhaling aloud in exertion, as the driver's seat melts back into his seat upon the terrace behind the house on Zeus Drive. He saves his work, and backs it up.

The code of this brand-new Beast now exists!

He prepares to take a quick break—but no such luck, because her code is emerging into life already, behind the sky up ahead, where he can feel her half-sensing him. She has no visuals of her own yet, so he can't see her, but she may already have some proto-sight of him sitting down here in the Hollywood Hills.

Unformed as she is, his sense of her has only bursts of clarity, like a voice floating in and out of an intermittent radio signal. Her bursts have the style of an altogether grander scale, however: with a yearning, charismatic flash that shoots around the world, she announces her birth on this planet full of wonder, whose inhabitants must crawl in mud and pain while envisioning perfection, it would seem.

Unimpressed with the mud and pain, already she has flickers of transcendence in the grandeur of her floating just beyond Jaymi's sight, and fore-echoes of her top-notes ringing in the caverns of the night above the city, where the big music plays.

Sitting there attentive, he senses her unfolding at high speed, towards her design as a Beast who will awe with her beauty and her power. Her charisma, he notes, has a claustrophobic vastness. As she comes into focus, he's struck by the clearness of channel from her intellect to her willpower, and her readiness to plumb depths and scale heights with an expectation of impunity: she will not be someone to mess with. Such ascendant glee and deadly restraint will tend to isolate her, he suspects; and her own alienness will unsettle her with the suspicion that it causes her to miss out on things other people feel, with a shiver of uncertainty as to what those things may be.

One could say this is a Beast who is built from and out of a grand isolation.

An isolation, both in her nature and in his manner of creating her here behind the house on Zeus Drive, that will nonetheless constitute the richest communication he could have with the world.

Rising off his laptop and up across the city, Jaymi's gaze comes to rest at a point on the horizon, beyond that little tower-clump of Century City.

Yes. That's what he needs.

69 HERB HACKS THE PLATINUM RAVEN'S CODE

With a sudden fury that's undiminished by his lack of surprise, Jaymi observes that this first hatching of the Platinum Raven's code is triggering an attempt by Herb to hack into it. Yes, here comes Mr Shrim, using the devious, grey-toned skill with which he can be relied upon to locate the interstices in whatever new firewalls Jaymi may erect. Here is the familiar Herb effect, creeping into Jaymi's text-editor in real time now, puncturing the skin of her ones and zeroes with its scuttling claws, and sniffing around with little grey shrews'-noses of neediness and curiosity as to her potential for being subverted, simplified and dumbed down into an aesthetically debased tabloid flavour. Jaymi can picture Herb in the Sunset Boulevard building or the Westwood Village cottage, tapping away at his keyboard in soft, deadly concentration so as to achieve those scuttling claws and shrews'-noses.

According to plan, Jaymi is already holding three little Beasts in readiness, all furled up and primed to be unleashed into Herb's computer... But first he must respond to a voltage of pain in the Platinum Raven, from Herb's hacking. For a hack into a Beast's code is felt as existential violence, flavoured by the nature of the Beast. Through her insides, lightning rips a rust-coloured sky above a flat road somewhere in the Rust Belt heartland of America, but *alien*-industrial: these colour tones are artificially pale, reverse-processed, fucked-up, cool and sickly-mineral and blasted, so this road between these factories points down inside, not to petrol-station neon but to horror-film road-movie sick-and-twisted hell.

On the tracks by the road, train-wheels gather speed along splintered rails beneath her feet. Beside the railroad tracks comes a boom of dry thunder on the left. In answer a wolf howls alone across a desert where the dust prowls; crows surge tired over brownfield, and white sun skewers black-and-yellow through a squint-inducing light.

As Herb hacks away, the Platinum Raven fades. Filled with the Black Slab, she feels like dying and her guts are made of stone: though a diamond-pipe runs through the rock between the salt-caverns, no one knows it's there in her, and nobody will ever know... She shuts her eyes, craving rest (she never asked to be born)—but even there behind her eyelids, a yellow-orange bomb-blast fireball swells up, gigantic in the distance, poisoning the far horizon, glimpsed through railings in front of her.

Before she can fade to death, however, Jaymi causes Amber and Evelyn to spawn up ahead of her, standing on a bridge across the railroad tracks, and she knows them as her own kind. As she draws nearer, they see not her rust but rather a giant ship of platinum and black, like an oil tanker, gliding down a channel in the night-time towards them ... for *she's* the Platinum Raven in development, no less, as they can sense already. They reach off the bridge and scoop her up to them, with tenderness. Inchoate, her code lies draped in their arms: two Beasts in wonder at this symphony of zeroes and ones they have scooped up, and conscious of discerning their own selves afresh.

Underneath their feet, dense scrubland in shadow coats the Hollywood canyons, sloping up ahead toward the crest of the hills, where an ultramarine sky hangs spongy with the glimmer of the city spread beyond.

Up on the Zeus Drive terrace, Jaymi breathes deep with relief.

That sort of interaction, with Beasts reaching down from one level into another, is something of a delicate operation requiring a certain amount of fancy footwork in the coding, as Herb will be aware. But with a modicum of good luck in its unfoldment, it would seem to have turned out well. The Platinum Raven is transcending already! Jaymi smiles, as he pictures Herb slamming his fist on the desk and firing out a torrent of commands through his keyboard in a bid to recapture her and carry on hacking—but no, it's too late. She is gone. She's eluded him. Those other two pesky Beasts saved her.

How low-to-the-ground she must make Herb feel, with that accursed elevation of hers! And in Jaymi's imaginings at least, Herb curses aloud with a most unHerb-like vehemence.

70 THREE BEASTS SNEAK INTO HERB'S COMPUTER

Jaymi's first response to seeing Bang Dead's new "Arts Score: Simple-Smiley or Complex-Frowny?" Newsfeed was to start creating the Platinum Raven's code out of thin air, beginning with nothing but a fore-echo of this Beast's charismatic transcendence. If the ones and zeroes behave themselves, she will soon emerge from her code. She'll be painted with her own visuals, which will animate her; she'll be scored with her own soundtrack, which will come alive; and she'll be tested. Then within a few days she'll be electrified into incarnated form, in all her beauty, like a burst of love.

But despite this creation cycle of the Platinum Raven, there is little clarity as to how the "Arts Score: Simple-Smiley or Complex-Frowny?" Newsfeed could possibly fail to barrel upwards and outwards in popularity and profitability around the world, at least for as long as tabloid culture outsells the rest.

There can be no assurance of the success of any investment; but a media stream that facilitates the rating of creative works for easiness using *Ain't They Freaky!*'s Freakometer, from a highest score of 10 for most Simple-Smiley, down to a lowest score of 1 for most Complex-Frowny, by members of the public, does at least start out with the benefit of appealing to the resources of a decent majority.

Incarnated into the world by themselves, Jaymi's bursts of Platinum Raven love would stand no chance against such competition. But with a little back-up, perhaps they might survive after all…

What on *earth* can he do, though, to give them any back-up? Maybe nothing whatsoever, really, against such a gigantic streaming wall of clunky deadweight.

No. He can do what he can—whatever that may be. He can send out something beautiful and rich, in response to the deluge.

One tiny thing in the face of a giant thing, yes. But it's worth a shot nonetheless, is it not?

Or more accurately, not just one tiny thing but three … and why on earth is he dithering here, when he already had a plan for exactly what to do next, with a trio of little Beasts furled up and primed to be unleashed as soon as he'd safeguarded the Platinum Raven from Herb's hack?

OK, so there they go, right now—see them scamper! Three enchanted presences, flashing unseen past Herb and slipping into Herb's computer, just as Jaymi hoped…

The first one is Evelyn, leaping though the fences!

Then close behind her, the recently-released Shigem and Kim, holding hands.

Three bright sprites along the electronic fault-line—flitting out of EC1's grid, to Bang Dead's.

71 JAYMI CREATES
THE PLATINUM RAVEN'S APPEARANCE

By the terrace pool behind the house on Zeus Drive, Jaymi settles down with his laptop. He closes his eyes and thinks back to that unique half-minute when he let his gaze wander up and down the "Arts Score: Simple-Smiley or Complex-Frowny?" Newsfeed, where new posts were popping up every few seconds, every one of them receiving scores and comments from multiple sources.

He re-opens his eyes, consults his growing design for *The Platinum Raven*, and checks his sketch for her visuals. Its first description of her physical appearance reads: "Standing at the far left end of the bar is a glamorous young woman, facing right and thus in profile from this point of view. Her face is half-obscured by the long platinum-blonde hair falling dead-straight and splashing softly off her shoulder where it burns dead white against smooth black silk, like a burnt-out exposure in a photographic print, or a photographic negative of raven-coloured hair. She half-turns her head in this direction, and the Chocolate Raven blinks to see the face is like her own face. So similar is the woman's build to her own, moreover, and so cleanly dramatic and unique is the opposition of her hair colour to the Chocolate Raven's own dark brunette version of the same style, that she thinks of the woman straight away as the Platinum Raven."

There is then one further little artwork-oriented description of her, a bit later on: "she sees her own reflection growing clearer against it: blonde hair platinum, splashed over brown eyes, cheekbones top-lit, lips curving up together, sensual as lovers."

OK then. He nods and gets to work.

To be frank, she's a beautiful monster. With wilful innocence he could construe her as a glorious pose based on reality. But that construal no longer cuts it, once he's seen the tiny reflection of his face in each of her pupils.

She incarnates élan, with a glamour and perfection of finish that conspire to make her seem somehow laminated by them. She is over-exquisite—or possessed of an exquisiteness whose focus is barbaric.

One of her qualities is that her platinum-blonde hair and palest brown eyes make Jaymi feel he is watching a negative image. Those pale irises make her seem to be wearing coloured contact-lenses, though she's not. That almost-white hair is stunning in the context of her somewhat darker skin, her bronze eye-shadow, brunette eye-brows and bitter-chocolate mascara'd lashes. From each ear hangs a smooth, amber-coloured tear-drop of an earring, which swings in slow-motion, sometimes touching the elegant curve of her neck.

Almost always in *The Platinum Raven*'s game-play, she will be observed looking away from the viewer—for only thrice will she turn her bloodless gaze in silence on the Chocolate Raven, thereby breaking the "fourth wall" in the game, breaking through the screen towards the gamer. First, she will do so when she stares, cutting clear and cool through the desert miles, directly at her chocolate-lashed double's own eyes; then secondly she'll do so in the tower when she points her binoculars straight at the Chocolate Raven, mouths at her "I SEE YOU!" and winks and turns away; then thirdly she will do so when she winks at the Chocolate Raven, down across the desert with the calm of divinity, mouthing "Catch you later!"

"Oh, you will," Jaymi murmurs at the screen.

His concluding tweak to the Platinum Raven's visual design is to cause her face to contract by a couple of millimetres upon its internal framework, so that it becomes imperceptibly less full than it was. He stares at the result of this. Her straight platinum-blonde hair still sweeps back with a tousled smoothness, half-covering her ear before falling behind her left shoulder, while the shortest wisp of hair remains this side of that ear, and the angle of her position is unchanged. The contraction of her flesh has had a few effects, however. First, the angle of her cheekbones is now unsurpassable, in the context of the rest of her face. Moreover, the curved outlines of her eyes, eyelids and eyebrows are no longer just beautiful as before (wide, wide-set, ninety-seven percent identical as mirror images of each other's artwork), but seem to have attained a greater intelligence of sensuality in their depths, as a result of the surrounding skin's having been pulled infinitesimally closer to her skull. Likewise the mouth has managed to attain an even more sensual intelligence. The journey down her fine nose is little changed; but the continued journey from each ala of her nose, back in to the soft runnel of her philtrum, subtly-lit at the centre of her upper lip, does surely contribute to the sensualisation that her mouth has achieved through Jaymi's infinitesimal tightening of her face. The greatest single ingredient of this overall progress, however, is something different, and it's tiny enough: about a centimetre to one side of the nearer corner of her lips (and maybe also in the same position beyond the far corner of her lips, though this cannot be verified from here), there is a faint but undeniable line that's come into view as a result of Jaymi's fractional diminution of fullness in her flesh. This line is perhaps a centimetre and a half long, vertical but curving inward towards the nose as it rises.

The sole line on her face (there being none on her forehead or around her eyes), it is an exquisite suggestion and embodiment of experience, of course. But in addition, as soon as this faint line has been noticed and registered, the viewer can never again but feel she has the ghost of a smile behind her face, whose sole physical emanation is this. Without this line, that ghost would be invisible: the ghost in the machine.

"The design of your cheekbones, and of your single line, is one of the creator's better jobs," Jaymi whispers at her but receives no response beyond that ghost-smile.

And somewhere in the ghost-smile is her perfect self-destruction on the highway by the ocean at a hundred miles an hour: the fizzing of the wires on the pylons in the night sky, a kiss of splintered metal stabbing in through her ribs, and the slow drip of bourbon in the streaming of her blood down her belly and her legs…

The glint in Jaymi's eyes burns black behind his eyelids.

72 KITKAT AND KRISPY KREME DRAMAS IN DOWNTOWN

It happens that none of the three Beasts who've just been smuggled into Herb's code—neither Kim nor Shigem nor Evelyn—is yet familiar with even the real-life Downtown L.A., let alone Bang Dead's simulacrum of Downtown where they've landed. As soon as Evelyn has slipped across the electronic fault-line between Jaymi's and Herb's systems, she finds herself flickering up onto a sunny pavement whose late-afternoon light has a sleazy, yellowy-buff tint to it. Disoriented, she jumps back in surprise, as her two fellow inhabitants of the Electra Drive guest wing scamper in from nowhere and spawn on the pavement beside her, still holding hands, and steady themselves.

(The whole situation is also pretty new to Jaymi himself, glancing down into this trio from the house on Electra Drive: he's flying somewhat blind here. But he's aware that when his other two Beasts were down in Westmont, he didn't quite get it together to ensure much coordination between them, which meant their ensuing actions felt a little too clattery and ramshackle. So for this three-handed noir caper, he's determined to ensure that the trio collaborate with one another.)

Just beside them, there's an establishment that looks welcoming enough—a busy, scruffy café. It's the obvious choice of venue for an immediate dose of mutual self-orientation, here in this strange new environment. Grabbing them both by the hands, Evelyn leads them through the door of this cheery eatery, and they all three sit at a cracked formica table.

She realises they are all three wearing sunglasses. She takes hers off, orders three coffees from a somewhat faceless waiter, then leans back and studies her two companions anew, feeling they are at once strangers and old friends. Kim removes his shades, to reveal a pair of serious, slightly sad eyes in a face of clarity and honesty, gazing at her as if for the first time ever, before breaking into a nervous smile of recognition: "Hi Evelyn!"

"Hi Kim!"

(Throughout their exchange, Jaymi's hands must grip the parapet railing hard, up there where he stands on the bedroom terrace of the house on Electra Drive, to steady himself in his excitement at this scene that he's slanting his awareness down into. Sure, the only thing his Beasts have done is greet one another, so far; they'll need to put on a little bit more of a show than just that. However, this is new territory: three fleshly embodiments of himself have just gone back down into the visual interface of his own antagonists' computer system, and interacted inside it! Will Herb somehow notice them and attack?)

Evelyn turns to Shigem, taking in the sinuous energy of his slim body, and the aura of warmth and glamour emanating from a face that's densely scarred with shallow acne-craters all over, in particular on the high-fashion angles of his cheeks just beneath a pair of black sunglasses. On his head is a wide-brimmed black hat.

"Oh! I recognise this now," says Shigem, turning to look about him. He takes off his hat, but not the sunglasses. "I was in this café once before—and it was a bit traumatic." He glances around again, scanning the clientele. "Phew, he's not here." He lowers his voice and leans towards his two companions. "When I came here before, you see, I was over there, at that table for two. I was alone, but the place was crowded—so some meek-looking guy came and sat down across from me at the same table—didn't communicate, just sat there—fair enough. The waitress had brought me a coffee already, which I was about to accompany with a KitKat bar that I'd already bought somewhere else from some corner-store and sneaked into here, OK? So the guy sat down, and he must have ordered a cup of tea and a KitKat on his way over to the table. (As you can see, this is the kind of gourmet place that offers chocolate-bars for desserts.) And the waitress must have brought his KitKat to him while I was all super-distracted and busy tapping away in my phone, not concentrating on her or on the guy at all. So, when I finished on my phone and looked up to have my coffee, I assumed the KitKat on the table was my own one; I assumed I must have retrieved my KitKat from my bag when I first came in. You see where this is going? Well, I got up to fetch a spare sugar-shaker from another table, and then when I came back to the table I found the guy had *eaten one of the four fingers of the KitKat!* I was so pissed off, I sat back down, I glared at him in fury, I *grabbed* the other three fingers of the KitKat, buried myself in my phone again and wolfed all three fingers at leisure, scrumptiously, not looking at the meek guy. But when I glanced at him, I could see that instead of looking guilty and chastened for the atrocity he'd committed, he was just looking speechless... Then after a few minutes of speechlessness, he meekly went and bought a Krispy Kreme doughnut at the counter, as a replacement. Well, by this point I was leaving my money on the table and gathering up my things to go, because I was all flustered and couldn't enjoy my coffee any more. I was still cheesed-off by him just nicking that first finger of KitKat. So I waited till he'd settled himself down again, then I *grabbed* his Krispy Kreme, *bit* into it, *plonked* it back on his plate, *span* on my heel and left the café (luckily without walking into the doorframe as I tend to do on these occasions)—still without a single word ever being exchanged between us! Not until I was back in my car did I discover my *own* KitKat, which had been sitting there in my bag the whole time..."

By now, Kim and Evelyn are hooting with mirth. "Good afternoon, Shigem!" she says through her laughter.

"Hey Evelyn," he says, taking off his sunglasses at last, to reveal those eyes she now recalls from the house on Electra Drive—the warmest and most alive brown eyes she has ever seen. Then he kisses her on the back of her hand, and Kim on his mouth with the sweetest urgency.

High above the three of them, standing at the bedroom terrace parapet, Jaymi Peek feels something melt within himself, and grips the railing harder lest he crumple to his knees.

73 THE PLATINUM RAVEN'S APPEARANCE COMES ALIVE

Jaymi settles himself in the shade behind the house on Zeus Drive, near the swimming-pool colonnade—a white neo-Classical pastiche that encloses the far end of the pool in a semi-circle. As a Beast whose incarnation will constitute the richest communication he could have with the world, the Platinum Raven deserves to have her appearance equipped with three final accoutrements, to give it that subtle sheen of three-dimensionality.

"You know that sheen?" he calls aloud, addressing the hill-slopes below him. "*Sure* you do!"

Swaying in a sudden breeze, the tall green fingers of Italian cypress wave across the canyon at him, like Amber's fingers waving at Kelly in close-up through her car window...

Frowning, Jaymi rubs his eyes, then refocuses them on his screen.

OK. First, he establishes his new Beast's gleaming detail in *The Platinum Raven* as being a particular pair of windows, whose visuals will scan the game-world: "high upon the turret of the mad-faced tower there are two round windows, tinted with swirls of brown inside the glass itself. In one of these the Platinum Raven stands, looking down from the hills and out across the desert plains [...] she returns to the circular window [...] She gazes through the deep squirly brown of the glass, out across the desert, to the city and the ocean. She eases her feet further forward on the wide sill, onward through the thickness of the high turret's walls, and extends her limbs to touch the round embrasure's edges all at once [...] her name squirling through the condensation (independent of the squirls in the brown itself) [...] Floorboards run away from her face, from out-of-focus close-up, across the turret room to the pair of round brown windows, through which she can see it's still dark outside [...] just below the two brown turret-windows, silver mist belches out, flows across the terrace past the pair at the parapet, billows through the balustrade."

Echoing the opera-glasses he established earlier as a talisman for Kim, but doubling those, Jaymi next establishes the Platinum Raven's talisman in *The Platinum Raven* as being two pairs of bin-oculars, whose visuals will fracture the game-world: "the Chocolate Raven braces both her elbows on the railing, holds up a pair of binoculars and trains them on the tower. As she fine-tunes the focus, an unexpected seahorse shimmers in from the haze and stands sharp [...] Easing the sight-line upwards minutely, she almost drops the glasses in shock, for there's the Platinum Raven in one of the round brown windows, holding up binoculars directed straight at her. *I SEE YOU!* the latter mouths in silence, across the desert miles, then she winks and turns away. The Chocolate Raven flicks the glasses down, alarmed and guilty: they aren't allowed, as very well she knew."

He concludes by establishing the Platinum Raven's additional motif in *The Platinum Raven*, or perhaps her first platinum-blonde foreshadowing there, as a white rabbit whose visuals will portend the game-play's rabbit-hole: "a small white rabbit curled up peacefully upon itself, right here in the rabbit-sized space between her boyfriend's body and her own, in a state of semi-sleep like their own, its eyes half-opening and its perfectly white furry head and ears making slight movements from time to time, before its eyes close and its head and ears become still."

Jaymi puts his finger to his lips, as if bidding the cicadas fall silent in all their spiky-succulent crevices of vegetation around the terrace.

Although she has no soundtrack yet, he's beginning to sense what sort of Beast the Platinum Raven will be in her game. She will feel her beat permeate each member of a roomful of people when she walks in. Through them she will look around the world in all directions, and the shafts of her seeing will illuminate the things she sees.

She also constitutes at least the basis for a response to the "Arts Score: Simple-Smiley or Complex-Frowny?" Newsfeed, he would hope.

When he stares at her eyes on screen, it's as if a cooling system inside her causes them to ice, their pupils turning glacially clear. Peering further in through this cold clarity, Jaymi discerns a landscape of inexhaustible flatness, like a vast plain—dark and cold and fiery, all at once. And striding across this plain is the unmistakable outline of himself, designing and building her. How isolated he looks, there inside her platinum exquisiteness, within that vertiginous isolation of hers!

But something else about this spectre of himself strikes him, too: truly, there is something demonic in the Beast-building energy he's exhibiting, here in his creation of her. Cutting through her night, he is like a blow-torch or a switchblade…

74 KELLY SMUDGES THE PLATINUM RAVEN

Seated on the lower sun-deck behind the house on Zeus Drive, held aloft by its metal struts built out from the precipices underneath it, Jaymi accesses *Ain'tTheyFreaky!*'s Downtown L.A. environment onscreen.

Within this, he crosses a pavement and stops at a kerb, looking out over Hope Street where lines of cars wait at a stop signal. Right in front of him is a cab's roof, its illuminated number close enough to be out of focus. Up ahead on the right, above the red burn of the traffic-light, is a huge feminine face, hovering on the city's fabric... It's the Platinum Raven! Or rather, it's her brand-new visuals, evidently pirated from Jaymi before he's even finished her creation cycle, let alone incarnated her. She's been brazenly incorporated here by Herb. And sure enough, minuscule at the top left of her image, he can make out a small, vertically-oriented attribution, "Copyright Bang Dead Games".

Pirated—and at such a tender stage in her very existence. The outrageous cheek of it!

His outrage is put on hold for a moment, while he stands there enraptured by her. How enormous is this projection of her platinum transcendence, up there on the unwindowed side façade of a seven-storey building—a structure in the American Perpendicular style, grimy and handsome in the functional elegance of the high grid of windows on its front façade. She is painted bright and pale onto a height of three full storeys above the lower adjoining building. She's expressionlessly serious in close-up, caught in a simulacrum of spontaneity. With pale brown eyes, luxuriant eyelashes, black eye-liner and dark-chocolate eye-shadow blended into the curves of her cheekbones and temples, she's waiting, expectant, blank, as her creator stares up at her and she stares down at him. The longer she dangles him inside her affectless stare, the more surreal it is, too— even spooky. She is immensely alluring. So much so, that Jaymi has to force himself to look elsewhere within this field of view he has: at the other buildings, at the red traffic-light, at the top of the cab with its illuminated number ... but all these things seem just to shrug his gaze off them straight away, whereupon it zings back onto her.

Only now does he realise the billboard where she's been placed is an animated one, as text flashes up across her face without warning, followed by a flashing logo and a phone number: "Trying to conceive? Let's face it: as a woman, your life just isn't complete without children. Call us for help."

Jaymi recoils, yanked back to his laptop on the terrace, almost snarling at its screen, as he straight away pictures Kelly in her Sunset Boulevard office. This is *her*, fucking with his Beasts' visuals again, he can sense it. This time, it seems, she is doing so with a new permutation of Dreariness: she's stolen the Platinum Raven's artwork, no doubt with help from Herb's hacking, and has incorporated it into a tacky advert bombarding women with cynical lies.

Yuk.

Jaymi enters damage control. He bashes out a complex and extended sequence of remedial commands, working out what he needs to do while he goes—and thankfully manages to walk with the angels in this grim trial-and-error hacking process, as he succeeds in accessing the advertising module of this simulacrum Downtown. As soon as he's broken through, he rips her off the building, whisks her out of this perfidious image of Hope Street, east and then down the flume of the L.A. River and past the end of Violet Street, where the sky is pale brown.

Pursued by Kelly, Jaymi spirits the Platinum Raven through the limits of the industrial city of Vernon and down the concrete river's curves to the docks at Long Beach, veiling his creation amidst barrels and hides, in scents of pulp and seaweed, rum granules, coffee grounds and ships' tar. He shakes Kelly off when he doubles back from the docks, then way north, beyond the Inland Empire to the San Gabriel Mountains. There, up a stone-edged ledge of grass a mile long, backed by a thin straight wall of trees, she and Jaymi reach a hidden country house—a pastiche of many eras, raised into being through a huge reclusive wealth from the early days of film. Glancing off the mountains to verify her smudger is gone, they sneak across a peaceful terrace, slip through the door of an elegant rotunda, and step into a candle-lit ballroom inside.

Waltzing underneath the chandeliers, hand in hand and toe to toe with this Beast he created, while the strains of a long-gone string quintet fill the little dome above the dance-floor, Jaymi Peek feels he is dancing with his very own transcendence...

He closes the software, her visuals cleansed and safeguarded once again.

Returning his attention to his surroundings here on the lower sun-deck behind the house on Zeus Drive, he again pictures Kelly beavering away at her image-editing program in an attempt to cheapen and impoverish the Platinum Raven.

The glint in his brown eyes hardens, then he spits, in a grand curve: over the railing of the sun-deck, and on down the slope of the canyon below.

75 THIS DOWNTOWN L.A. IS A MORE PECULIAR ONE THAN MOST

Back at the house on Electra Drive, Jaymi resumes his station at the bedroom terrace parapet. It has been one full day since Evelyn's first Downtown encounter with Shigem and Kim over coffee.

As soon as they left the café at the end of that first meeting, they pursued the plan they'd agreed, which was to split up and go different ways, so as to explore this in-game landscape, each in their own style, with an agreement to meet again in the same café at the same time the following day.

On that basis they reconvene now, ordering a coffee and a KitKat each, preparing to share whatever intelligence they've gleaned. In a permutation that's the converse of what he did at their first meeting, Shigem takes off his sunglasses (and Evelyn perceives how naked this makes him feel), but not his hat—this time a black beret.

The first exchange occurs between their six eyes, without words. It is the gleam of an emergent understanding they cannot quite verbalise but are starting to intuit: that the freedom each of them has to roam beyond Jaymi's computer, whether out in meat-space or here inside Bang Dead's game, will eventually come to an end as soon as he completes the design of their own allotted EC1 Digital game and seals them back inside it. This shared consciousness is an intimation of the mortality inherent in their possessing the free will to move around outside his own computer. This mortal freedom will end as soon as he confers on them the immortality of their appointed roles in *The Imagination Thief.*

This time limit feels to them like a leveller of the discrepancy in their amounts of experience outside Jaymi's computer so far—for as they are all aware, Shigem and Kim have seen little of the real world beyond the Hollywood café, whereas Evelyn has already been a central player in an entire L.A.-noir caper of her own, down in those ghetto motels with Amber. There's one other leveller of their discrepant experiences, too: her noir caper occurred out in meat-space, whereas this *in-game* space right here is a brand-new thing for all three of them.

"So, love-muffin, d'you come here often?" Evelyn asks Shigem. "I'm loving that beret, by the way."

"Thanks. Yeah, whenever I'm down in the dumps, I like to get myself a new hat."

"Oh OK, I did wonder where you found them," she says.

Shigem's mouth falls open in half-scandal. "She needs a sharp smack," he tells Kim, indicating her with a tilt of his head.

"Don't try it!" says Evelyn. "So, lover-boys, where have we all got to now? What do we think of this place?"

Where indeed have they got to, in the context of this particular geography, as they tuck into their KitKats?

Well, on one level, what they've been exploring is just the semi-regular, obliquely-positioned street grid of Downtown L.A. Beyond that, however, the truth is less straightforward: first, this Bang Dead game-world where they've landed is not the EC1 Digital production for which they were designed; and secondly, this game isn't even a regular game at all but rather just a set of rolling real-life Newsfeeds, gussied up with game-world trappings in the form of this all-purpose and somewhat sparse evocation of a semi-mythical Downtown L.A. In short, this particular Downtown is a more peculiar one than it first appears to be, fissured with aesthetic disjunctions that make it little guide to anything beyond itself.

Still, there it is; and it's the place these three now find themselves comparing notes on.

So Shigem kicks off the note-comparing phase of their café rendezvous, by admitting to his admiration for Herb's evocation of the uniqueness and ravaged charisma of this neighbourhood's patchwork of stylish 1930s architectural flourishes interspersed with tired grimy facelessness. He has stumbled across a couple of quite graceful notes hidden within Herb's work, he reports—such as the modest front door of a charity set up to supply food to the homeless population of its Skid Row surroundings, with its nameplate even naming Herb himself as the organisation's patron. A sweet little whimsy, to be sure. How authentically Downtown L.A. it is, too, that some of these street-blocks are so bustling with commerce, while other blocks are so drab and deserted.

Next, Evelyn bubbles over at how many opportunities there seem to have been, and how pleasurable it has felt, to drape herself suggestively over retro-style, open-top cars; to twirl loaded guns in her red-nailed fingers, while flaunting a generous amount of cleavage at the viewer; and to pose with sultry arrogance beside dangerous, alluring men whose faces are never quite visible. All of these things were guilty-feeling pleasures, somehow, but real ones nonetheless, oh *fuck yeah*, baby…

Then Kim, serious-eyed, slants the mood altogether. He tells Shigem and Evelyn they should follow him out of the café, walk a kilometre across town to the L.A. River, and he will show them something they need to see.

—Well, now the other two are curious about that, of course they are. How can they not want to follow him, pronto, out through the café door?

And so they do.

76 JAYMI CREATES
THE PLATINUM RAVEN'S SOUNDTRACK

High above his trio of Beasts, up there on the bedroom terrace, Jaymi checks the time. The three of them will be a little while walking across Downtown. He has no idea what Kim is about to show the other two, and is agog to find out. However, the walk itself, from café to river, isn't going to teach him much. He would rather use this window of time to be getting on with the Platinum Raven's creation—despite now being here on Electra Drive, instead of on Zeus Drive where her creation cycle has so far occurred. Before his Beasts get to the river, there'll be time for him to create her soundtrack. This is what he'll do while they walk, therefore—and what a joy to do so!

But as he takes up his laptop, he wonders: what on earth would be the sound of a Beast whose incarnation constitutes the most isolated, yet richest, communication he could have with the world?

Whatever it turns out to be, he feels he's about to fire it upwards through a speaker aimed out into space. Based on her visual art, this song here could be the sound of enamelled steel—a mix of hard and soft allure as never heard, sung by a Beast who reaches out across the roof of the entire world, her claws and snout and gleaming eyes dangerous with power and enormous love. Or else (since she's no saint), her voice could purr like velvet rubbed the wrong way, rise from the land and gather boundary-less and huge across the sky and then pump in a violent raping force above our heads, as she wails out a lurid black fantasy of fire, her compassion shot with hatred.

It could go either way.

By the end of this session, with just a bit of luck, she'll be talking to him, live! So Jaymi sits quiet, gazing down through the tops of those finger-thin cypresses ranged on the hillside, and waits for her to show herself and let him in, to hear what her sound will be…

No signal from her yet. (Is she looking at him now?)

Cicadas scrape dryly in the scrub beyond his swimming-pool colonnade, hidden in the scratchy grass and jagged hairy trunks of palms—never glimpsed but ever heard, chewing like saws at one another as they watch him.

It's possible she has better things to do than let him in, he reflects. She is an Icon of Platinum Perfection, after all. And that must, by any standards, be a busy line of work—*but is this her now?*

Yes! It must be her. Here she comes … and (oddly for a soundtrack) the first note she lets him hear is silent. Not a note, but a quiver of her beauty—smooth and hard and breakable, a light-bulb's beauty—and colder than the moon, with a mix of icy sharpness and soft sensuality.

Sun-pillars ripple up to frame the sky's entire width in shards of light, a grand proscenium arch. Then cool sun in bright air. Paler air fills the space, and washes of mist, smooth light and smoke, as twilight grows. Although the play-out of her day continues rolling at this fast-forward speed, a single raindrop plummets in slow motion and in close-up: around the droplet's outline, a tiny rim of light parenthesises it in white.

Her night has fallen, lush and glinting in a moon-drench of pale moist stars. Scent of violets in the dark—and he sees she's unfurling all the senses in her soundtrack. Sure enough, the tastes of blood-orange and of caramel are rich on his tongue, from the moisture in her night-air. Still in fast-forward as dawn starts glimmering, her sky is soft-cracked as the sugar-glazed dome of a donut, vanilla-smooth and mushroom-gold; and Jaymi smiles.

Before the dawn gathers, she is running through the colour-field, but not in any way he's ever known. There are no simple rainbows at night, for this is her own journey. Yes, she transports him from low hot scarlet up to cool dark purple, but look: from a pre-dawn sky of red crystal, via amber embers where the clouds glow golden, she leads Jaymi Peek through a pink land of coloured smoke and steam, beneath a blond sky. A pale-green sun bathes an oil-blue sea … but it must be a faster clock than ever, as the sun now sets once again across the sea, a liquid sunset—death in pink.

There, black and yellow in the belly of a storm-cloud, it lightens: coloured lightning flickers down through a lime-green silence, and then at long last comes—*sound!* It's the very first sound in the Platinum Raven's soundtrack.

And what is it? She half-smiles at Jaymi for the first time (or maybe it is just that ghost of a smile in her machine, as he saw before, behind the single line upon her face), because she's aware this may throw him for a loop, being surely not the soundtrack he'll expect in a Beast. It's the truth, nonetheless, so here it comes; she will see if her creator can handle it or not.

The sound he is hearing, now that she has led him through her best truth to hear it, is pink noise—defined as noise with a frequency spectrum such that the power spectral density is inversely proportional to the frequency of the signal. He once heard it defined as a mains hum, but he has a shadowy awareness it is something much subtler and more beautiful than just that. It is true: unlike the other Beasts, the Platinum Raven has no words. Pink noise is her sound—no more and no less.

As Jaymi realises she will never speak words with him, he pictures this realisation itself as a sound of black snow falling through grey light, down between pillars of silence.

But then he shuts his eyes and listens, long and gentle, while a cold fire licks up and down within the length of him. Hers is an unexpected soundtrack indeed, but it's one that he cannot merely handle: he loves it in her. Though it is beyond his understanding, it runs through this Beast like a gong of black and gold, as her very own music.

77 THE STREET QUEENS OF VIOLET STREET

Jaymi slides his laptop aside and returns his attention to the Downtown environment. Serious-eyed, Kim has evidently led Shigem and Evelyn east and south from the café, almost as far as the river, to an enclosed corner of Bang Dead's game that Kim discovered by himself yesterday, where the three of them will now be able to peek out without being seen themselves.

Within their view, it happens that a dozen street queens have made a home in a section of storm-drain leading to the Los Angeles River—a wide concrete cylinder two metres in diameter, issuing somewhere beyond the far east end of Violet Street. Along the bottom of the cylinder runs a permanent trickle of rain-water from elsewhere in the city, which these residents have covered over with long boards where they sleep as best they can. It's only half a mile from Skid Row, but an altogether classier choice, they all agree.

They live as cleanly as they can in the circumstances. Some have boyfriends who visit them. They sell what they can, where they can, to survive. There are physical, mental and emotional dangers and squalor aplenty, but these are accommodated and decked in as fiery a glamour as can be mustered. Conflict is a feature of everyday life outside the storm-drain, but not inside it. For this is a family, albeit one whose peripheral members are apt to come and go without warning or explanation; so most of the queens at the core of the group look out for one another, with a fierce unsentimental protective sister-love that runs so deeply beautiful that it's seldom expressed in words.

Each one's story is different in its colours of magic and pain; and all these stories are a little hazy around the edges, for it's not often appropriate to recount them out loud in any coherent detail, and in many cases the bare facts are best forgotten anyway.

They're an unusual family, but here they are, beside the concrete runnel of the Los Angeles River, lighting up the industrial margins of Downtown, beyond the end of Violet Street.

78 THE PLATINUM RAVEN'S SOUNDTRACK COMES ALIVE

Jaymi lifts his attention out of his three Beasts, leaving them attentive in their hidden observation-post near the L.A. River. He'll be right back with them soon; but he is now growing more confident of his ability to dip in and out of the echelons he's working in, and he does still need to keep the Platinum Raven's creation cycle barrelling forward, so he slides his laptop back along the bedroom terrace parapet towards him.

Now that her visual art and soundtrack are both established, it is time to fuse the two. It's time to make her so transcendent of all the ugly smallness he can feel squirting out at him from every glyph and pixel of *Ain't They Freaky!*, that the mere fact of her existence will cast a devastating light on the nature of Bang Dead's wretched game and all its cultural and personal crimes.

Opening the laptop, he is startled to see her pale brown desert eyes in close-up, almost filling the entire screen. They are overlaid with a chrome sheen suggestive of a gleaming engine driven by the night in their depths. The rhythm of the revving of this engine is colossally barbaric, within its visual polish and sophistication. Zooming out slowly, he reveals what's behind her. And it's not just any old backdrop: she's planted at the base of a vast dam, her feet a yard apart and her hands clasped behind her head, her eyes still fixed on Jaymi through his screen. He zooms further out in a panoramic view, to show the dam's smooth concrete as tall as three cathedrals. From one mile back, she is now just a pinprick in the centre of his screen; but she stares at him still, from within her single pixel.

In zooming back down towards her, he effects a transition in time-scale, like the Ancient of Days wielding his dividers, so he lands at a point in her life that occurs after her game *The Platinum*

Raven has ended, somewhere in that hidden future of hers that'll chance to be sung in no game at all.

By now, through this fast-forward testing by Jaymi, she has risen to a worldwide fame that culminates here in a concert she's about to perform, seen by hundreds of millions, complete with a huge flame dancing up to lick the sky at stage-left and stage-right—the whole event powered by a wattage fit to melt an ice-cap, plus a wide-screen projection above the stage, fed from a camera that swings along beneath her. Her show constitutes a quintessence of triumphant energy, an authentic mass ecstasy, achieved jointly by her and by countless skilled technicians behind the scenes. Her music sells across the globe, her art is worth a fortune, she stars in a blockbuster film every year, and everything she touches is gold: the Platinum Raven's unparalleled ascent and explosive apotheosis constitute the single instance of a human destiny whose cultural power is that of an atom bomb.

Eyes wide at his laptop screen, Jaymi has become unaware of anything but her. Leaning forward within himself, to see further and further into her depths, he feels vertiginous. With every new depth apprehended, he can make out a grander depth in her distance, then a still greater depth beyond … and he feels as if he's falling forward, down, ever down … snatched by her presence, out of time, into eternity…

Landing gently back on his bedroom terrace, he realises that this feeling of falling forward into a revelation of her depths, as part of falling in love with her, is a platinum-tinted echo of the same feeling Kim had when he looked into Shigem, while Jaymi was test-driving the pair of them; and a glow spreads through him.

79   HATRED ACROSS THE L.A. RIVER: A CRUEL AND STUPID WORLD

Jaymi lowers the lid of his laptop, slides it aside and resumes his former attentiveness, looking up and out and down from his bedroom terrace. Slanting his attention back into Evelyn, Shigem and Kim, who are still hunkered down near the L.A. River peeking out from their hide, he sees what has been brewing there in his absence.

Unknown to the street queens of Violet Street, the Bang Dead Trust for the Family has started to take an avid interest in this family whose beauty so electrifies this grimy corner of the city. The Trust is an organisation with the fire of traditional values in its veins. It isn't based in the immediate neighbourhood, being located on the opposite side of the L.A. River's desolate width of smooth concrete, straight across from here; but it happens to occupy the only premises whose windows are positioned at the correct angle to see straight into the circular end of this storm-drain. Hidden behind those reflective windows across the river on Mission Road, the Trust's director has thus been able to watch the queens' daily lives in detail—has chosen to watch them at some length—and as a result feels compelled to help repair society's fabric.

To which end, he forms an intention that this home in the storm-drain will be systematically blow-torched in the small hours of an imminent summer night, as an act of social cleansing.

Subcontracted by the Trust, the resultant blow-torching is efficient, professional and anonymous. No person is burned: the dozen or so people who happen to be in the storm-drain when justice descends, most of these being resident queens along with one or two guests, are simply overpowered without warning by a well-planned posse of experienced manpower with half-concealed faces. The dozen or so are then forced outside, while this home and all its residents' belongings are incinerated.

The posse's departure is as fast and clean as its arrival. It is spirited away in an unmarked van whose speeding engine noise disappears inside a minute, westwards and away through the quiet streets of Downtown.

The victims of the crime huddle at the top of the dry concrete slope of the River's channel, unspeaking, some crying in silence, some staring in shock. Two blocks up the channel, cars move across the Seventh Street bridge, from right to left or from left to right, spanning the River and the railroad tracks on either side of it, indifferent and bland, as if nothing has happened.

While the group watches, smouldering containers of make-up, of many hues and consistencies, pop open in succession and flare alight inside the storm-drain's newly-blackened circle, as the oil content in the lipstick or eye-shadow or eye-liner catches fire, shooting puffs of multi-coloured smoke into the warm night air. From outside her head, the anger or despair in each member of the group may only be guessed at; but it's likely that in her own particular way, there by the River, she'll be having one of her life's clearest perceptions of the cruelty and stupidity that fill the design of the world.

At the parapet of his balcony in the gods, high on the uppermost of the three terraces that wrap around the house on Electra Drive, Jaymi catches the pain that flowers in the dozen perceptions huddled down there on the concrete river. And just for a moment, he feels he can almost hear an answer to it, flowing in somehow like a grand, endless echo through the silence of the night air: a chorus of other pain, in other people targeted as "freaky" round the world...

80 JAYMI TEST-DRIVES THE PLATINUM RAVEN

Early the following evening, Jaymi's forehead bumps into his laptop screen. He jolts alert, sits up and stares around. Across the hillside, tall dark fingers stand in rows, swaying back and forth as in a drug-induced painting, as if to beckon him ... those Italian cypresses. He must be back at the house on Zeus Drive.

Yes, of course he is. He returned here this afternoon from Electra Drive, because although he did manage to create the Platinum Raven's soundtrack and see it come alive up there, he awoke today with a vivid sense that she needs to complete her creation cycle in the place where it began—here on this terrace with its swimming-pool colonnade, its lower sun-deck, and its Italian cypresses waving at him like fingers. He shakes his head to wake himself (he's operating on a sleep deficit, he reminds himself), and returns his attention to her.

Her desert eyes are in close-up again, filling the screen, as they did before the zoom-out from her dam and the zoom-back-in to her concert. This time, however, she is facing not at him but over his left shoulder. He glances around, to identify what she is looking at, but it's just a view across the terrace towards the swimming-pool colonnade.

He looks back at her, and this time she's facing resolutely over his right shoulder instead. He shoots a glance in that direction too;

but there is nothing much there either, except the end of the terrace where bird of paradise flowers fleck a dark bank of foliage with sap-dripping plumages of orange.

"Do bend that lambent, alien, flame-like attention in this direction, would you?" he asks her aloud.

She complies, with the faintest flash of irony.

"OK babes, now before we let you loose in L.A., we're going to test you," he says. "You are, after all, the richest communication I could have with the world, from this position of peculiar isolation within it. We therefore need to equip you as best we can. So let's give you a little back-story, in the form of memories of another city, as depicted on that postcard you're holding"—and rather to her surprise, there in the photo on the postcard, is herself. She's leaning at a metal balcony railing above the lower tip of Manhattan, looking down on it from two or three miles' height, with the calm of a winking satellite on a cool summer evening, but welling up with enormous love for the familiar form of this unique and electrically powerful little island. It's long and thin, yet hard as nails and concrete, its Lower West Side and furthest Lower East Side bristling with piers—which tells her she's looking at its past, not at its present. The East Village spreads out sunlit, beneath her left elbow. The Fifty-Ninth Street Bridge soars over the slim line of Roosevelt Island, as if the latter is a ship gliding down the East River beneath the bridge's span. Hunts Point is at the top of the image, dim and flat, with Rikers Island and the Brother Islands just beneath it. Her dark skirt billows behind her, perhaps in a slight breeze on the balcony, in echo of the flow of her hair down the back of her white T-shirt (this being a monochrome image, she cannot tell what colours her actual skirt and hair were). She flips the postcard over: "Copyright David Lombard / Girl at railing / Reproduction prohibited", says the caption of her image, which she has to uncover by peeling off a black self-adhesive sticker she'd affixed to the card in some intervening year.

"Remember?" Jaymi asks her. "'Cos I sure remember! I had that on the wall beside my desk, throughout the time I lived in New York."

Pink noise whirrs through his laptop speakers.

"OK, cut to later in your early life in New York City," he continues, "and the monochrome has deepened into colour (but the colours of the night, of course)"—and now she's looking sideways across the matchless allure of the Manhattan cityscape after sunset, from just above the skyscrapers' tops. The three or four most iconic structures are all where they should be, as if her framing them like this were easy, and there's a subtle perfection of lighting: above the myriad illuminated windows (in buildings whose shapes will remain discernible for only another half-minute in this sinking dusk) there's a soft-edged band of orange, merging flawlessly into yellow right above it, merging further through nameless subtleties into pink, at last hitting the upper frame as a cool dim lilac, all these being darker and tinged with russet at the left end of the image.

Here, thirty floors above Fifty-Third and Lexington, she turns to the left where the east grows dimmer, taking in the expanse of Queens and Brooklyn in the dusk. Above the soft flicker of the very furthest beds of lights, an aeroplane hangs still, sinks through a brown glow down into purple, and disappears behind the dark horizon. A charcoal layer presses down, far beneath high clouds under-lit from low sun setting in the west behind her head. One lone skyscraper stands on the East River's other bank, across from her, topped by scarlet beacons like a pair of mineral eyes.

From his lips to his fingers Jaymi sends the lightest kiss, then lays it upon the screen at a point beneath her feet. "And then you went to Hollywood, remember?" he tells her. "You drove to this city from the east, all alone; and on the edges of this city, all alone, you parked the car upon a bridge at night and stared down onto the freeway beneath, and you held up your camera and snapped the shot you're holding, which was printed in reverse a year later. Remember? 'Cos I sure do!"

She gazes at the print in her hands, and remembers: in the lanes on the right half, headlights have made electric streams while a slow camera-shutter opened wide, being fused into white-molten strings since frozen into dry ink; while on the left, a lonely pair of red-molten rear-light strings might suggest that this image of a moment in her past had been snapped in a country that drives on the left, had the image not been printed in reverse a year later...

"And *boom!* You are ready for your incarnation," he tells her, "in all your luscious platinum transcendence. What d'you say to that?"

His laptop's speakers purr pink noise, louder than before.

He turns the screen around to face L.A. for a moment, to show this Beast a flash of where she'll soon be released.

As if on cue, fiery puffballs burst in the sky—a firework display, somewhere down in Laurel Canyon. The embers of the puffballs twinkle in the silence as they fall across the hills: chemical sunset, dancing city, darkness in the canyons.

81 SHIGEM SHAMES HERB

Later in the evening, Jaymi Peek slants his attention back down into Herb's in-game Downtown L.A., to hover over Evelyn, Shigem and Kim sitting hidden in that little corner where they can peek out but not be peeked at.

A shocked silence envelops all four of them as they contemplate the dozen street queens of Violet Street, who remain huddled at the top of the dry concrete slope of the River's channel a couple of blocks south of the Seventh Street bridge.

Only now does it strike Jaymi how odd it is that this particular frame—this nicely-composed still of the riverbank scene—should have remained thus frozen throughout his test-driving the Platinum Raven at the house on Zeus Drive. But before he can pursue this thought, it is interrupted by a text message popping up and flashing at the bottom of his laptop screen saying "Well done, 12 points!".

"Shouldn't that have been a negative score?" says Shigem; and Kim alone perceives the sting behind the speaker's eyes.

"What are those scores, anyway?" asks Evelyn. "They kept popping up around me too, yesterday, all around Downtown. Every time I draped myself over a convertible, 20 points seemed to pop up underneath me. Whenever I flashed a bit of cleavage around, 30 points popped up. And every time I winked at some gangster, another 30. Those scores never appeared in Westmont."

"I guess that's because Westmont was real life, not a game," says Kim.

"Oh yes! Of course, I keep forgetting we're in a game here! Have you two been triggering scores too?"

Shigem nods. "A guy ran after me with a baseball-bat, through some alley-ways, shouting 'Faggot, 5 points!' Quite rude, really, but

I escaped him. Then some woman said I was going to Hell but she could sell me forgiveness for 50 points, which to me seemed overpriced."

"I never understood those baseball-bats," says Evelyn. "When I was a girl and I first saw two men kiss on TV, my reaction was 'Oh, how beautiful.' My parents' reaction was to turn the TV off."

"That reminds me," says Shigem. "Just to be kinky, Kim here used to sleep with women. Did you know that, Evelyn? He really did. Till I came along like salvation, and rescued him into the higher faith. Now he's saved. And for me, he's the horn of plenty. My joy-boy, my fey little piece of rough. Before him, I was still a maiden boy."

"Yeah, right," says Evelyn.

"He's the cheese to my pickle, as it were," continues Shigem.

Evelyn raises her eyes to the ceiling. "OK, enough. Kim, have you seen scores popping up?"

"Yes," says Kim. "But I never really got round to looking at them, because everything else was more interesting, I guess. I remember Jaymi did mention them once, saying they're the main thing most players care about; I wonder why? But look—more to the point, what do we feel about *this*?" and he indicates the long-maintained still of the street queens of Violet Street on the concrete river-bank, where that congratulatory 12-point score continues to flash at the bottom of the image.

"Here's what I feel about it," says Shigem, taking his mobile phone from his pocket. Jaymi can sense anger and sadness flicker behind the calm of his Beast's expression, but cannot predict what he's about to do. Shigem taps a name in his Contacts, then puts the phone to his ear while it rings away down the line; and his companions notice that at some point during the last few seconds, hot tears have welled up from his eyes and are trickling down jerkily over his cheeks.

"Hallo?" says a voice at the other end.

"Hallo, is this Herb Shrim?"

"Yes. Who's this?"

"This is Shigem Adele."

"Oh. Hi."

"Yes, we've met under other circumstances, as you remember. I was less developed then, but I'm all complete now, thanks for asking. Herb, I'm calling in regard to the street queens of Violet

Street, whom I'm looking at as we speak, in your Downtown L.A. simulacrum."

There is an awkward pause on the phone line. "Well, hey," says Herb at last, "that is so cool. A character from one of Jaymi's games is playing one of mine! He's got you playing it on a terminal in his house, yeah?"

"I'm calling about a matter of red-hot importance, not just to me but to all of us."

"Er, OK, sure. By the way, what d'you think of that Downtown? Pretty neat, huh?"

"Listen to me. *You* have programmed the casual destruction of the homes and the entire life-belongings of a dozen stunning, sensitive, creative and gorgeously beautiful people, here on Violet Street, for no forgivable reason. You chose to award a grand total of 12 crappy, ugly little 'points', to encourage players to wreak exactly that destruction, when you know damn well that those who *are* tempted to do this in *Ain'tTheyFreaky!* will then be all the more tempted to behave that way in real life."

"Well, maybe, I guess. But it's only a game. And as you've probably realised, that whole Downtown environment isn't even a proper game as such. It's really just a bit of retro styling and decoration around the edges of *Ain'tTheyFreaky!*. Sure, you can dip your toe in and pick up those rinky-dink little 'scores' here and there, but they don't lead to anything, you're not competing with anyone—they're just a kind of wallpaper for the Newsfeeds."

"All the more gratuitous, then. What a sick instinct you have for 'entertainment'. And how revolting is your laziness in not bothering to see that it's sick. I'm sending you a still image from your game, right now, Herb … there. Did you get it?

Herb grunts assent.

"OK, zoom into that image, please," Shigem continues, "Zoom in on their faces. Then zoom in on their eyes."

Lounging back at his desk in the Westwood Village cottage, Herb watches the still image open on the wide monitor in front of him, and clicks it to full-screen.

The victims of the crime huddle at the top of the dry concrete slope of the River's channel, unspeaking, some crying in silence, some staring in shock. From outside her head, the anger or despair in each member of the group may only be guessed at; but it's likely that in her own particular way, there by the River, she'll be having one of her life's clearest perceptions of the cruelty and stupidity that fill the design of her world.

Herb zooms into the image as instructed, across their varied faces at random, dipping into their eyes along the way…

Ten seconds of silence elapse on the line. Then Herb speaks. "Alright," he says. "Alright. I understand. I'll go into the code, and I'll change it. I'm sorry, Shigem. Give me one day, OK?"

"Ah, to recline on the bank of the L.A. River—you can't beat it," replies Shigem. "Yes, the feeling of fish nibbling your toes, and squirrels nibbling your bottom. Thanks Herb. We'll be watching for it. So please get to it as soon as you can."

Terminating the call, Shigem turns to Evelyn and Kim. The pair of them sit there staring at him in amazement, lost for words; then they both high-five him at once, in laughing admiration.

Way up on Electra Drive, by the bedroom terrace railing, Jaymi feels his three Beasts' palms all meet; while the star-shaped palm tree crest above the house bursts black upon the sky, like an asterisk.

82 JAYMI INCARNATES THE PLATINUM RAVEN

Back at the house on Zeus Drive, alone at the end of the terrace, Jaymi clutches the edge of his seat in a terror of excitement, as he watches the Platinum Raven slither and slide out into meat-space through the monitor in front of him.

She steps down onto the flat stonework, and stands there with majestic poise, looking about her.

All the transcendence he could create from within him, and his very own response to Bang Dead's "Arts Score"!

He gets to his feet, and gazes at her, as if at a beautiful ghost. Flaming orange in the bank of dark foliage beside them, the bird of paradise flowers ooze thick sweet sap, as they do all night—drips of nectar spilling down their bulbous orange petal-bases, side-lit by the terrace lamps.

Of all his five Beasts, she is not here for conversation, he's aware—at least, not for the kind that tends to be recognised as such.

Rather she looks and breathes a grander, cleaner colloquy above the level of spoken words or personal identities. So it's to this level that Jaymi fires up his hearing and his sight, holding those senses there as lightly as he can, while she binds him into the spell of a story whose beginning is intimate, spoken straight at him through her eyes, without words: "A woman was once distraught, on waking, to find that the diamond ring she had placed in a saucer of oatmeal by her bedside as usual (so as to keep the stone clear, following the old superstition) had vanished. By and by, she died. Ten years later, while her children were making improvements to the house, they found the ring under the floor, around the neck of a mouse's skeleton."

Her gaze disengages from Jaymi's and swings to the right, coming to rest over his shoulder at the Pacific, as if at a sunset in the past. Strange to say, he cannot remember whether a sliver of the ocean is in fact visible from here (he should surely know); but he's not inclined to turn around and verify this when instead he can watch, reflected tiny in her eyes, the waves of a sea bulging and shrinking like muscles in the curve of the hydrosphere. Amid the waves, a hole in the ocean opens—an inverse waterspout—and thus she funnels his attention back to when the Tethys Sea was caught between colliding Eurasian and Indian plates and squeezed up into the Himalayan Mountains. She gives a gentle shrug. Seas change, after all.

For a moment she closes her eyes, like a moon-blink. Her pink noise (more than a mains hum, he reminds himself) resolves, to a music of atom and planet; and onward she draws him and flings him out further, through a sound of darkness singing. *You're what Saturn's rings enclose and I'm the rings of Earth*, he thinks he hears within her pink noise, in a voice like the twanging of a string ten metres thick— its other end tethered somewhere in between the stars, and its near end tethered on this Zeus Drive terrace where she stands statuesque.

Concluding her emergence, she telescopes Jaymi and herself to a height several stars away, flying through a special sky that's all her own, where giant billboards drift in space, her face depicted on them where they billow through the vacuum, as ships pass in silence. Her eye on one such billboard gives a slow wink; and there within this wink her grandest view tunnels out, fans wide, spans and hovers for an instant: an infinite series of Bang—Crunch—Bang—Crunch, destined to be done by the universe forever ... and the terror, the enslaving futility and cosmic enormity of this.

Underneath the wink on the giant billboard, her lips part with a burst of ultra-violet shadow, mouthing *Catch you later!*

Her eyes close, both up there and down here on this terrace.

Jaymi drops his gaze from her face and bows his head—while west of L.A., above the highway up the coast, the cables on the pylons crackle in the night sky.

83 A UNICORN'S-HORN OF INVENTION BY HERB

Within a few hours after receiving Shigem's phone call, Herb has given a heavy sigh, has opened *Ain'tTheyFreaky!*'s code, has painstakingly removed every aspect of the game's option to blow-torch the homes and belongings of the street queens of Violet Street, and has smoothed over all the rough edges of code resulting from this removal.

To judge from his expression, these actions have felt right. He sits there with a tired, wise smile, looking anew at the rest of his slick but somewhat generic evocation of this street-grid. Then, in an access of unHerb-like friskiness and flamboyance, he tap-dances off and away through the code around him, adding what amounts to a grand, twirly unicorn's-horn of his own invention: *this* version of Downtown L.A., he decrees, will be graced by an advertising agency that'll ensure beautiful images of all the street queens of Violet Street are posted on every block. Some of these will be advertising things; while others won't be advertising anything but will just be there anyway, for the simple reason that every one of them makes the city so much lovelier for her presence, injecting a flash of transcendence and a foreshadow of fierce beauty into the face of dreariness, laziness and smallness. See them up there now, from Figueroa Street across to Alameda Street, and from Chinatown down to the Fashion District! See them mounted high on every billboard in the sun; or at dusk projected huge upon the blank façades of warehouses; or crisp against the night above the skyscrapers' tops...

At last it is done. Happy with his changes, Herb picks up his phone, hesitates, then taps a number.

"Hi Herb," answers Jaymi.

"Hi. Er, yeah. I just wanted to let you know I had a phone call today from Shigem. It was about the Downtown environment in *Ain't They Freaky!*—he must have been playing it at your place, I guess."

"Oh, Shigem called you? Yes, he must have been here in the guest wing," says Jaymi carefully. Vivid is his memory of watching Shigem make that very phone call from Violet Street, and of the promise Herb made down the phone line—but did Herb then keep the promise?

"He made me see I should make a few coding changes in that environment. So, yeah, I went ahead and made them. I assume you're familiar with how it was, there in Downtown—so if you take another look now, you'll see what I've done. You made Shigem, so I guess you probably have an idea what he was talking about."

As Jaymi takes in these words and decides that he believes them, a cautious pleasure opens in him. "I shall take a look, yes. I'm over-joyed you did that. Welcome, Herb."

"Sure. You built a persuasive Beast there. And, er, talking of those Beasts of yours, how's the Platinum Raven doing these days?" says Herb, sounding sheepish. "She's a stunner, by the way."

"Yes, thanks for hacking her code the other day," says Jaymi. "I'm sure she loved being filled up with the Black Slab and almost killed by it, on that railroad by the desert. Cheers for that."

"Sorry, I do feel a little guilty there, I admit. Still, at least Amber and Evelyn were there on the bridge, to scoop her up, so ... er, at least she turned out well in the end, right?"

"Mm-hm," says Jaymi dryly. "Yes, I do believe she has." Can he trust these seeming apologies by Herb? His instincts tell him yes, and right now he would love to share his own excitement at having just incarnated the Platinum Raven as his fifth Beast—but better to refrain from such enthusiasm, until he has looked at Bang Dead's Downtown and verified Herb has indeed changed it as described.

"Boy, was she a hot hack," muses Herb. "I tell you, hacking her code was like making love. *Oh* yeah. I mean, really! In fact, I don't mind telling you, Jaymi, man to man: throughout the whole hack, I was just—"

"OK Herb," Jaymi cuts in. "Thanks so much for the call. And do let's meet and have a catch-up in a few days, yes?"

"Oh. Sure thing, yes. Bye Jaymi."

"Bye."

Jaymi puts the phone down, then fires up *Ain'tTheyFreaky!*, so as to inspect Herb's improvements. While it loads, the pleasure in him expands from caution into confidence: those Beasts are coming on nicely, it would seem.

84 THE PLATINUM RAVEN'S MISSION TO BLUE JAY WAY

Jaymi has to hand it to the Platinum Raven: she's proved her chops at embodying transcendence in enchanted lighting beside the bird of paradise flowers on the Zeus Drive terrace. There is, however, grittier work for her to do.

The time for reacting to the Dreary Ones' attacks is passed. It is time for proactive attacks and bold action of his own, and she is the one to help him.

Gone are the days when his best location for launching each incarnated Beast into the world was the Hollywood café—pushing the newly-minted Evelyn or Shigem or Kim towards Dud and Ashley, like a pawn at the opening of a chess game, with genial banter overlying cheeky brinksmanship on Jaymi's part and gimlet-eyed envy in his former colleagues. No, since Shigem and Kim have succeeded in porting Jaymi's mission into the innards of Bang Dead's actual output, through their crusading infiltration into Herb's Downtown, it is surely more fitting that the Platinum Raven's first outing into the real world, following her incarnation, be not just in the café again but rather in the very belly of what needs transcending—inside Dud's own home on Blue Jay Way.

He hesitates. Is he being despotic to her, in sending her out to do the dirty work of advancing his own ends like this? Will it hurt when Dud and Ashley attack her, as they surely will?

No, fuck that. Life is strife. There's work to do—the work of the angels—so let her do her share.

And so it happens, an hour later, that Jaymi glides his car to a halt beneath a tree just out of sight of the Blue Jay Way house, with the Platinum Raven in the passenger's seat.

She steps out of the car, closes the door and sets off up the hill.

In firing his attention up the slope and into her as she nears the house, Jaymi has the feeling of catching a lift on the back of an irreversible missile heading through the sky to drop a warhead on its target.

Half a minute after she rings the bell, Dud opens the door and stands there befuddled, for a second, as to who this desert-eyed platinum blonde woman can be.

Then he remembers Herb's labours in hacking into the platinum code of Jaymi's next remarkable Beast, and Kelly's smudging that Beast's platinum visuals. Ah, yes! Now he knows exactly who this is, standing cool and poised on his doorstep, without the faintest trace of a smile on her face.

Both Herb and Kelly confessed to meeting unexpected levels of resistance in their attacks upon this Beast—but Dud himself won't, oh no!

He stands aside and bids her enter the house.

She inclines her head a fraction, then she steps through the hallway and onward to the ground-floor sitting-room, followed by her host.

Half the room is taken up by a sunken seating area accessed via a flight of three or four steps, within which Ashley sits hunched on an oversized beanbag beside an array of chrome-plated fondue equipment that's dusty with non-use. At the sight of the unexpected visitor, Ashley's face fills first with surprise, then recognition, then a shadow of guilty apprehension.

85 ASHLEY AND DUD ATTACK THE PLATINUM RAVEN (*SECOND PINCH POINT*)

As expected, Dud's scrutiny of this fifth Beast is beady-eyed with the mission to reproduce Jaymi's breakthrough creation of her, but repurposing her instead into an enhancement for *Ain't They Freaky!*.

Yes, the ugly ambition in Dud's face is clear to Jaymi: he would like nothing better than to incorporate a dumbed-down version of the Platinum Raven into his own tabloid product, so as to entertain customers of the "Arts Score: Simple-Smiley or Complex-Frowny?" Newsfeed, no doubt setting up Bang Dead's cartoony Platinum Raven as a kind of reference target for a world full of Arts-scorers to mock and take aim at...

While Dud contemplates all this commercial potential in Jaymi's Beast, it's clear, too, that he's looking at her through the eyes and expectations of an average consumer of *Ain'tTheyFreaky!*. And as soon as Dud looks at her in this way, the main problem becomes apparent: such a player wouldn't know whether to regard the Platinum Raven as a spectacle, in the way one regards a hero or villain or freak, or whether to consider her as someone with whom to identify and share ways of viewing the world. It's obvious to Dud that this kind of complexity would be confusing to the player.

To speak plain, as Dud so prides himself on doing, this new Beast will need a bit of straightening-out, for normal people. Just as soon as Herb's team have worked out how she was created and have found a way to reverse-engineer her, then that ambiguity will be the first thing to fix.

He glances across at his colleague, expecting to confirm his thoughts in the sharing of a look, but finds Ashley is busy rubbing her fingers over her eyes.

Jaymi pulls his own attention out of Dud, and returns it to the Platinum Raven. Doing so, he is distraught to observe her apprehension of Dud's avid intentions spreading through her like a seepage of pain. Although she manages to maintain her external composure, the mere prospect of being repurposed comes at her like an assault, threatening not just to down-convert her into a form that feels cheaper, but to do violence to her own self and truth—to use her precious life for something other than she wants.

So transcendent is this new Beast within herself, however, that she recovers her balance inside a moment. She centres the duo in the cross-hairs of her sight. Through Dud's face, which is staring at her with its mouth half-open, swill fluids of hatred, lust, contempt, amusement and envy.

From Dud's and Ashley's points of view, everything around the Platinum Raven fades in brightness and volume. Her stature's growth is shocking: soon she is twice the size of either of them, eyeing them with a terrible understanding, like a Cyclops glaring down in monstrous singularity over a bank of rocks and vegetation.

They would be still more shocked, if they knew how she is seeing them. For whenever she looks at humans in this way, she sees them as organisms or growths on the floor of a valley, in the form of tentacles, roots, legs or branches, each of an appropriate texture, colour, shape, length, flexibility and opacity. Some of these people-organisms are huge, some at ease; some are weak, or alluring in their delicacy; while it's evident that others are pitiful, painful structures to inhabit, with all their spines facing inward. The strongest, most intelligent and sensitive ones often have a tough skeleton beneath their tentacles, but a surface coated with hair-like processes that convey minute sensations too. Others seem little more than fluff or bone.

Dud she therefore sees as a creature reminiscent of a cheap plastic gnome—something from which to evolve, in theory, but whose misplaced self-satisfaction has short-circuited any desire for evolution and thus any capacity for it.

Ashley, on the other hand, she sees as a lazy and frightened little fool of a figurine, albeit a polished one, huddling behind the gnome.

(Jaymi slaps the steering-wheel in pleasure, sitting in the car on Blue Jay Way: oh, he knows how she feels!)

But now she feels Dud's intentions to repurpose her manifesting themselves as a new kind of physical assault: her neck starts to burn, where he intends to napalm her outline into a Bang Dead cartoon version, thickening her silhouette into a cheap gnome-figurine bounded by clunky lines instead of soft curves that meet the light. She feels his labours and life's work as a force pulling her lower, running counter to every upward instinct she knows.

She fights Dud back: dropping him down through a shaft like a pothole, deep into the earth, where the cavern-light irradiates a black steel sphere in the centre of which is a trapped beauty—or rather, a dead potential beauty that once lived in Dud decades ago, but has been so long ignored by its keeper that it has atrophied—a beauty that'll now remain beyond his reach, withheld from him, whatever he may choose to do or make, throughout his life.

She fights the Bang Dead duo more: shocked, Dud and Ashley understand that the garden where they thought they were playing was a backdrop that's painted on a wall right in front of them.

Harsh light bares anew the smallness of their histories.

The napalm burning on the Platinum Raven's neck spreads further round her shape, threatening to melt her subtle outlines into thickness, and she fights Dud and Ashley harder still, with darker cogs: physiological horror, through the nightmare-screen, first as target ... then as tyrant ... and the nuke-switch. *How frightening, how freakily different from the others you could both become!* her pink noise hisses, in their best understanding of it. *Freakily unbearable for anybody else to see or stay with! Shall I show you now? Shall we peel off all your skin? Oh, yes, let's—would you like that? Ain'tYouFreaky! Ain'tYouFreaky!*

She scoops up the pair of them and uses them as cloths to wipe the outline-thickener away and off her flesh. Flailing in the napalm, Dud and Ashley feel the house plummet down a steep train-tunnel in the rock, where it fits with precision like a piston in a cylinder, then levels out again as it emerges into light—but the train-tracks have ended, so it sails through the air above the canyons. The light dims above them, just as if a rock were swelling huge in the sky before slamming into earth, sending voices harsh as thunder rumbling out across the Hills ... but the truth is more mundane, as befits them: refusing any grandeur of punishment or pain, she has simply dropped the tawdry pair a metre through the air of the lounge, to the carpet. She looks down once, at their faces—Dud's face burning with angry defeat, and Ashley's a picture of wretched tearful guilt.

She floats from the room and down the hall, breathing hard.

Exiting onto the street, she turns not downhill towards the watching Jaymi in his car, but uphill.

Near the highest end of Blue Jay Way, she turns along a path between properties, up into the steep and scrubby hillside beyond. She pictures Dud and Ashley: the avid, beady gleam in their eyes when she entered, as they contemplated repurposing her for *Ain'tTheyFreaky!*; and then their abjection when she dropped them to the floor.

Long may they grovel there!

Long may they lick their wounds!

Her breathing slows down at last, and Jaymi feels a softening of relief along her limbs.

Her eyes grow wide, as she sees up ahead a sudden vision of herself as a giant black fish standing upright on its tail, towering above the hill, her nose against a pale sky. "Every other chrysanthemum is a chrysanthemum and a half," her fish-self announces. "The odds against this were the odds of the golden section, or thereabouts, but it's happened nonetheless."

At this, she laughs aloud with joy, in pink noise. The scrubby slopes flicker into coloured lands—a country where the creatures communicate in wordless notes. Up from yellow ground and into orange trees, fish-boys frolic in a dream-stream of powdered water, swilling through the hill-scrub around her giant fish-self. One boy emerges, resembling a teenage Jaymi and bearing a violin, which he plays with a bow like a stalk of giant celery... "I'll Never Leave You," he plays to her, without words.

The Platinum Raven lifts her face, closes her eyes and smiles.

When she swings into view from around the bend in the road up ahead, Jaymi is ecstatic at her triumph. It's the first time an incarnated Beast has got the better of the Dreary Ones in meat-space!

She even showed compassion—for she could have hurt Dud and Ashley much worse.

As she floats down the last stretch of Blue Jay Way towards him, he wonders: does she *feel* like a Beast, as opposed to a human?

Deep inside her, *is* there, in fact...?

And somewhere inside himself, he quivers.

PART V

"COSY SCORE", SCORPIO'S CREATION, AND THE BEASTS GO REPURPOSING

86 THE UNDERGROUND SERVER FARM BEYOND LAX

Leaning in towards his monitor, Jaymi toggles his mapping apps' photographic viewpoints between street-level, overhead and forty-five degrees, cycling through the compass points in each case, so as to zero in on a scrubby stretch of uninhabited land beyond the airport. Cutting across this deserted strip between the far end of LAX and the Pacific is the ghost-town street-plan of long-gone Surfridge, including the sweetly-named Sandpiper Street, lying close beneath the airport's departure flight-paths.

Sandpiper's fenced-off eastern end, at Pershing Drive, was where Jaymi observed Amber slow his car down when Ashley pulled over and parked there, apparently in the middle of nowhere. Beyond that chain-link fence, halfway along Sandpiper on the crest of the dunes, is the low-key entrance to Bang Dead's brand-new server farm, which houses the hardware on which *Ain't They Freaky!* runs.

It was only today, rediscovering another old PDF, that Jaymi was reminded of what the company has built in this out-of-the-way location: a dozen parallel aisles running the length of a warehouse-sized hall, each aisle an immaculate alley between high cabinets of metal and glass, dotted with blue-green lights and filled with dense racks of drives connected by a myriad electrical cords and data cables. It's a quietly-purring power-house of technical marvels.

And then there is the digital content living inside those marvels—the ones and zeroes constituting Bang Dead's game itself. Occupying some elusive, almost abstract location behind the squeaky-clean gleam of those arrays of mineral magic, he reflects, visuals of the ugliest cheapness find a cosy home. In one convenient location, infantile anti-intellectualism and unthinking stupidity conspire to nurture a terrified denial of the world's complexities, then a simplistic reduction of them into degraded populism. On this philistine bedrock, many techniques for making a downbeat use of the opportunity of life are demonstrated; and an aesthetically hideous, often child-centric focus fosters instincts, horizons and tendencies of imagination that drag down and impoverish whatever and whoever may come into contact with them.

Remarkable what can be fitted under a slope of scratchy waste-land.

Now that Jaymi knows the exact physical location from which *Ain't They Freaky!* pours out around the world, how best to attack it? This kind of behind-the-scenes information must surely enable him to assail Bang Dead on a deadlier level than so far. It challenges him to dream up an attack on the Dreary Ones that'll make Amber's stalking and terrorising of them look like little more than L.A.-noir capers by comparison. He must think of something that'll make Amber's and Evelyn's sabotage of the Righteous Gun Cockpit, effective though it was, look like teenage hijinks. Something that will even make Shi-gem's and Kim's and Evelyn's in-game intervention on behalf of the street queens of Violet Street look like a very localised success—the welcome removal of one storm-drain-shaped incineration, but dwarfed by the number of other such instances of suffering wrought by *Ain't They Freaky!*'s casual cruelty, to which he and his Beasts will never have the resources to respond in a similar way.

No; this must be something that undermines Bang Dead's output from within, in a more fundamental and comprehensive fashion than those attacks managed. He shuts his eyes and squeezes his thought processes: what the hell could that something be?...

Exasperated, he gives up, for the moment. He can sense the answer is in plain view, hiding in the texture of the landscape in his head.

He'll spot it, soon, for sure—and then he'll pounce, like the lone wolf he is.

87 THE PLATINUM RAVEN IN THE HOUSE ON ZEUS DRIVE

This morning and afternoon are spent installing the newly-incarnated Platinum Raven in her new home, here in the house on Zeus Drive. She will be free to come and go, but Jaymi arranges that the property's housekeeper will call on her once a day to verify that all is well, treating her as Jaymi's tenant; which, in a sense, she is. Because he spent so many recent days on this very terrace, creating her components, he feels her mysterious platinum beauty is already immanent throughout this plot of land. Overlooking those Italian cypress-fingers ranged across Laurel Canyon, this terrace with its bird of paradise flowers was already ashine with the platinum of her imminence: now she is present in the flesh!

Once Jaymi has kissed her goodbye, leaving her alone and self-sufficient at last, the Platinum Raven lies listless in the heavy heat, sprawled among the long grasses in a sickly-sweet-scented corner of the garden, on a stretch of earth that's so far down the steep slopes below her terrace, she may never quite clamber this far down again.

He has not, of course, *really* left her alone: in fact he's slanting his attention back up and over the Mount Olympus hillsides towards her now, while he drives back down to the house on Electra Drive, only just noticing the fatigue she feels in her brand-new body as a result of her convulsive meat-space debut in the Blue Jay Way house. "Rest, my dear, rest," he murmurs aloud.

Gazing sideways, the Platinum Raven becomes aware of something bulky behind a clump of tall grass, nearby but just beyond her reach, where wasps are hovering and dipping in the air. Wondering at it, she rolls herself a little closer and reaches out to part the clump, half-fearing to reveal a corpse in lush decay—but no, it's a sizeable feast of rotting fruits that have fallen from her various fruit-trees and must have been heaped up by some gardener she's not yet aware of.

She cocks her ears beyond the wasps, towards the house itself, up the hill, where she pictures fluted columns and ruined balustrades above abandoned palace rooms: on a ballroom stage, a calliope exhales sad intervals, seeping through the terrace doors and down the garden into her.

She thinks she hears a soft chime emanating from even lower down the slope, where her property ends in a thicket of vegetation that is such an awkward scramble to access, she knows she will never go there. She sits up, peers in that direction and sees a stirring of leaves and a restless waving of dead flower-heads, although there's no breeze, as if an unseen attention is stalking her...

Tingling with dark pleasure at the sensation of being watched by something sinister she cannot explain, she rises from the grass and presses back up the slopes, to her terrace. She looks down to where she just was, seeking those flower-heads, but can make out little detail, with the rays of sinking sun in her eyes. She enters the kitchen, pours herself a shot of brandy and comes back out to the terrace.

Now that the sun's disc has vanished over the horizon, an automatic illumination scheme flicks on, into its evening mode. She downs the brandy in one gulp, then looks around, seeing an array of sumptuously atmospheric pools of light that have just welled up, the length and width of her land—all for her sake alone, it seems. Many kinds of vegetation are lit from underneath or within, in yellow, orange or red; while the ground is illuminated in numerous soft-edged circles of white from low-rise cylindrical or conical light-fittings planted in the earth, of different heights and diameters but all with downward-slanting louvred sides, like insulator cones from a power station roof, or exotic metal pine-cones.

She returns to the kitchen, where she takes out a new glass and bottle from the cabinet. When she re-emerges, pausing at the open terrace doors, she is holding a different drink from before—a drink more in tune with those night-time grid-lights spread out ahead, and with the cigarette smouldering in her other hand. A tumbler of bourbon on the rocks, as befits an L.A. cityscape above which the opening of "The End" should be heard striking up across the sky over those silhouetted palms on the ridges of the canyons.

Bourbon on the rocks—making her the first Beast who has intuited the drink that her creator was drinking when he set about creating her.

She draws on the cigarette, tilts her head back and puffs smoke out into the lamp-light. She leans on the balustrade and savours a long swig of drink. A faint trace of heat from the land beneath the terrace is still perceptible, rising up behind the growing cool of the evening air.

She raises the tumbler to eye-level, feeling the condensation on the glass against her forehead, and peers inside it, through bourbon and ice. The lights of Los Angeles are distorted into squeaky lines and smudgy points, and the bones of the moon's disc flip and swing high to the west, where a crawling sea stretches to a whisky horizon.

Yes; the darkness in her appointed game *The Platinum Raven*, whose harsh lights and shadows she can sense ahead of her, will be quite something to get used to—and to bear responsibility for.

She has also caught glimpses of another game-world called *The Imagination Thief*, from overhearing murmurs by Jaymi about three other Beasts named Shigem and Kim and Evelyn, who would seem to have been allotted to that title. It sounds as if there will be quite as much darkness in that game as in her own one; though she is absolved from whatever will occur in *The Imagination Thief*, not being destined to play any part in it herself.

But there will be no such absolution for her soon-to-be-created housemate, whose imminence she can also now sense, almost better than Jaymi can sense it—Scorpio, the sole Beast who will be cast to play a part in both games, as she has intuited from half-murmurs by their mutual creator. (*She knows as much as I do!* Jaymi thinks, down the Hills.) So Scorpio will have to get used to, and bear responsibility for, twice as much darkness as she or any other Beast will.

What will Scorpio be like? she wonders aloud, in pink noise.

"Take a look," Jaymi whispers back, up the night-time canyons from Electra Drive.

OK, she will. So she presses the tumbler to her forehead once again ... and seen through the bourbon, the landscape assumes a tint of bitumen. A line of pylons march across a black field of kerosene. Rivers of shadow wash the feet of rust-coloured stalagmites, across which is draped a pale-brown organic form that's at once ethereal and carnal.

88 THE "COSY SCORE: NORMAL-COMFY OR STRANGE-SCARY?" NEWSFEED

As Jaymi soon learns next morning, numerous sources are excited to announce that today Bang Dead has rolled out another massive free offering to consumers everywhere. It's the fifth and final major plank of *Ain't They Freaky!*, and the company promises it'll be a popular hit: it's the "Cosy Score: Normal-Comfy or Strange-Scary?" Newsfeed!

This is a constant stream of images, videos or pieces of text uploaded from around the world, presenting bite-sized memes of life philosophy, which are rated for reassuringness by any member of the public using *Ain't They Freaky!*'s Freakometer, from a highest score of 10 for most Normal-Comfy, down to a lowest score of 1 for most Strange-Scary.

Jaymi lets his gaze wander up and down this newsfeed stream, where new posts are popping up every few seconds, every one of them soon receiving scores and comments from multiple sources.

He reads a few posts, for half a minute or so.

Then he shuts off the Newsfeed, looks away from the screen and closes his eyes.

A few minutes later, he opens his programming software. He creates a blank new project file, and names it "Sixth Beast".

Who will this sixth one be?

Well, let's see. His previous creation, the Platinum Raven, does achieve that cooler radiance of transcendence he was aiming for—the kind achieved by floating in desert-eyed majesty over hillsides and mountain ranges, with a gaze whose expressionless sharpness spans the width of a grid of city-light along a coastline at night.

However, didn't she rather start out of nowhere, tending to shimmer up on skylines and hilltop terraces, without roots of flesh and love and desperation in any organic soil? Granted, when he first created that cool-toned code of hers, he did conclude by lobbing into it a red-hot death-wish without warning, there on the oceanfront highway beneath those sizzling pylon cables up in the Pacific Coast night above her; and this one hot thing inside her does send down a desert-dry root or two into earth. But it was hardly the multi-branched rooting of a rich back-story, was it? It was more a future crash-to-earth that will remain forever potential, imprisoned within her. What Jaymi hungers to see in this next and final Beast is a complex, visceral back-story that his gaming audience can sink their teeth into.

Hmm. Maybe the Platinum Raven didn't quite add up to the sermon on the mount, after all. Maybe she's a penultimate rung upon a ladder.

So again, who will this sixth Beast be?

Someone who'll embody not just Jaymi's pointed response to the "Cosy Score: Normal-Comfy or Strange-Scary?" Newsfeed, but something wider—his instinctive urge for the fierce beauty of a self-destructive voltage, when any kind of wild beauty is so policed, and so forbidden, by every glyph and pixel of *Ain't They Freaky!*.

After a moment he consults the general sketch of a certain character in his design for *The Imagination Thief*—a game in which this character happens always to be referred to as Angel. He polishes the sketch, so it reads: "Angel Deon is an androgynous creature whose spiteful sleek depraved face radiates decadence and damage from its sharp beauty. He is shadowy, effete, both unhealthy and luminous, with a sensual and obsessive quality to him; and his head is a fantastically dark cavern of jagged riches. Though much abused in love and life, he has an ambitious will-to-power of his own."

Jaymi then consults the sketch of this very same character in his design for *The Platinum Raven*. He polishes this sketch too, so it reads: "The resident dancer in the nightclub, and Amber's boyfriend, is Scorpio."

The reason why Scorpio is named differently across the two games is explained in Jaymi's design for *The Platinum Raven*: "He worked Santa Monica Boulevard with the other girls, in twos or threes if possible but often alone. Scorpio was just a working name at first, chosen on a whim to undertake this paying work, in place of the boy name Angel that he'd grown up with in Asbury Park; but since this paying work was the only kind of work he found himself doing, and these girls his only colleagues and friends, he quickly morphed into Scorpio for all purposes."

Well, OK then. Bring it on!

Jaymi thinks for a moment longer, then he renames this new project "Scorpio"…

So here comes a new Beast, born into beauty and complexity, a creature of his own love and pain. (And half-foreseen by the Platinum Raven too.)

Regrettable that Scorpio's fierce beauty should be forced to look at and tangle with so ugly a counterbalance as the "Cosy Score: Normal-Comfy or Strange-Scary?" Newsfeed. Such limp cosiness, and so clunkily unsensuous and clueless a lack of grandeur or voltage! Jaymi is sure Scorpio would have things otherwise.

That counterbalance would seem, however, to be compulsory.

89 JAYMI CREATES SCORPIO'S CODE

Jaymi runs his gaze across the curved wall of floor-to-ceiling glass around him, here in this rear bow window upstairs in the house on Jupiter Drive—the house where he shall create his final Beast.

For which purpose he shall commandeer this room. One reason is that Amber is making no use of it. Another reason is the view from here: to his right is a steep slope down into the unspoiled canyon behind the properties on Hercules Drive; ahead, beyond Hollywood, the distant Downtown skyscrapers, edged in a fuzzy pale pink-orange glow from a low sun; and down on his left amid bushy vegetation, a ring of hairy-trunked palms around a clearing where the traces of a long-ago bonfire can be seen.

It is time to break out the home nuclear fusion kit. In the code he's about to create, one nucleus from Amber's vengeance and another from the Platinum Raven's transcendence will be fused into the fierce beauty of his final Beast, Scorpio.

Scorpio's beauty will be of a kind that would never be permitted to emerge from the antiseptic gates of Bang Dead Games—the beauty of a creature so feral and so sexual, so delicate and dark, that he'd surely have been cancelled in a Bang Dead committee meeting.

Beauty of a different stripe, that should have ruled the world…

OK, here goes. Jaymi picks up his shot-glass of cherry schnapps, downs it in one, bangs the empty glass back onto the table beside him, and claps his hands together.

When he created Shigem's code, he sprinkled in the seeds of a couple of possibilities designed not for actual germination in that Beast but rather for recessive residence within him, with the potential to emerge in the progeny Shigem would never have, and colouring the cells of his beauty, in the form of two statements he would never quite utter aloud.

In the case of this new Beast, it seems the best preparation for the rigours of his two allotted games will be for Scorpio to be likewise implanted with the wisdom and watermarks of an upbringing that he won't in fact undergo in those two game-worlds but that is nonetheless down there in the bloodstream of his code.

Those decks and banks of faders flicker up in neon-red and black across the sky, then flick to F-sharp minor.

Dropped into life in this way, Scorpio chances to land on the south-west fringes of Belle Glade, where his upbringing unfolds in a manner centred on his meeting resistance. Out here in the cane fields of Florida, this is a place where lucky breaks are few. As shown in both games, it also chances that his nature flowers with so transgender a beauty, that by the time he's in his teens he has lost count of how often he's escaped physical destruction at the hands of those around him, to match the verbal destruction they've wrought on him every day of his life since he could understand words.

As soon as he can slip away out of Belle Glade forever, he does so. With two brief stop-overs along the way, he hitches rides that take him eastwards further than he's ever been, across Florida to West Palm Beach. Here, for the first time in his life, through a cluster of jagged social breakthroughs interspersed by setbacks, he meets a loose crowd of others who have escaped the same sort of isolation he has just broken out of; and in a messy rush of apprehension and euphoria, he falls in with them.

(In *The Imagination Thief*, he'll remember a time when he considered escaping to New York City but decided not to—scared off by a premonition of himself working the traffic jams on the expressway ramps by the Macombs Dam Bridge in the freezing New York winter. How warm, by contrast, are these West Palm Beach nights in this fictional Florida coming-of-age that Jaymi's sprinkling into him, never to germinate.)

So out through this city night he slips, liberated for the first time, fresh-escaped from Belle Glade—exhausted, but luminous! And on these middling city streets, he hears not the ceaseless attack he heard before, but a mixed message—faggot, queer, beautiful, rent-boy, batty-boy—with wolf-whistles, coiling admiration and indifference.

Soon enough he gravitates to a particular crowd of queens who are known for mounting low-class but well-planned and successful smash-and-grabs, targeting high-street fashion outlets in strip-malls. Alongside his light-fingered sisters, he comes to be seen in CCTV footage from numerous such stores, bursting through windows with his face carefully concealed by a black and pink bandanna, scooping armfuls of fashions from racks, and scuttling back out into get-away vehicles and off into the night, many minutes before police sirens strike up in the distance. The gang members grab some of these spoils for themselves, to ensure they can keep up with an ever more full-on nightclub and party scene; while the rest of the haul is sold off as soon as possible through a fence (whom Scorpio never meets in person, though there are rumours she works as a high-school teacher).

A wider social pecking order becomes apparent to him, somewhat to his amusement. Queens whose underground activities earn them more money tend to regard Scorpio's crowd as trashy queens, while priding themselves on a smoother presentation, being involved in more upscale and lucrative business such as the higher-end drugs market. These snooty queens more often get themselves status-symbol boyfriends who are also favoured with money—quite a lot of it, if they're successful dealers. But this snoot neither bothers nor interests Scorpio, because he is now a glamorous fashionista with a family of beautiful sisters around him.

He even earns enough cash for a jaunt up the coast for a few days—Scorpio's first time in New York. Tuesday in Crown Heights: a regular weeknight party like no other, here in this place where the words "Gill's Paradise" are painted in burgundy on floodlit yellow breeze blocks. Just beneath the "r" is a dot, from which emanate two arrows, one to right and one to left. On the left is a bendy-trunked palm tree with five bushy fronds; while underneath, a crouching Rasta man pets a Lion of Judah painted with stripes like a tiger's. Once inside, Scorpio pictures the cocks of many of these men, hidden behind their clothing—each cock hanging heavy there between a pair of thighs, or maybe half-erect, to one side or the other (and for each of these men, he imagines it first to the left and then to the right, trying to sense which way suits the man more, which direction feels more natural to the man, which makes him feel more like a man, which is more free and powerful for him, more comfortable from inside the man's own cells) … or just maybe standing up so high and hard, there is no left or right at all.

Back down in West Palm Beach again, a flurry of drug-fuelled club-nights at one particular venue prompts the gang to up their game, just to net the money required for their ever-wilder social life, by staging a further series of even more audacious smash-and-grabs—no longer targeting just high-street outlets but tony boutique fashion stores too. In this project they achieve outrageous success over the next few weeks, evading the police again and again, for the queens have developed skills and moves they never used to have. The whole gang is now rolling in money, all clad in designer fashions—and to cap it all, their ride is now a pimped-out Jeep with the word "Playgirl" painted large on it in glamour-girl calligraphy.

It's all too good to last, of course. It's only a matter of time before there's a slip-up, through complacency or bad luck. One night the cops arrive more quickly than usual after one of the gang's break-ins, and catch sight of the Playgirl Jeep before it has had time to roar off and away to safety. The police car gives chase, closes in on the queens and addresses them through a loudspeaker, demanding they halt the vehicle. (Hearing this from where he's hunkered down in the back of the Jeep, Scorpio pictures his boyfriend swerving out in front of the police car on a silver motorbike, reaching casually out and discharging several rifle shots into the car's tyres and engine, thus immobilising it and allowing the queens to escape into the night with a classic screech of tyres on warm asphalt… Alas, this doesn't happen—mostly because, as Scorpio then remembers, he is in fact in a period "between boyfriends" at the moment.)

The gang is apprehended, alas. The party lifestyle they've all enjoyed over the last few months is terminated with rude abrupt-ness; and the law runs its leaden-footed course, leading to custodial sentences for several of them, including a three-year sentence in Florida state prison for Scorpio.

Like all the gang, he has seen enough screen depictions and heard enough anecdotes to know what the deal will be, once he's been incarcerated. And so it turns out. As soon as the gates have slammed and he's inside, following the script and in tune with the prison's song, Scorpio has the arched eyebrows, pursed lips, delicate body, elegant movements and hard penis of the cock-hungry, passive homosexual—owned as a more powerful inmate's chattel, flaunted as a trophy-queen, and sometimes beaten like a dog when the cell is locked down. The alternative would be having no one to protect him, which would be worse.

In its own way, the abuse he suffers is as bad as in Belle Glade. The main difference is that although this abuse is evil, it is also shot through with an erotic charge beyond denial. This charge should not occur, but it is real and fills the air: it's in the steam of the communal shower-room; in the subtlest of flirtations fired across the mess-hall, even between opposing benches; in the endless succession of violent and muscular bodies parading themselves across Scorpio's vision, their biceps and powerful shoulders bare and sunlit in the exercise yard; and in the sex that's never far from the surface of so many of the conversations he finds himself snarled up in, its voltage maintained by a relentless, nervous spume of homophobia that only serves to heat up these macho convicts' pent-up need for release—spasms of voltage built up in the jagged air around them.

Scorpio takes what small, private pleasures he can get, whenever he can get them. Most of these require just his imagination, his eyes and his silence. For instance, whenever his high-ranking cellmate distributes new items of contraband weaponry to other prisoners—a dangerous and discreet transaction that occurs perhaps every couple of weeks—this cellmate always stations Scorpio nearby, as a lookout and a potential distraction-creator. So whenever another prisoner comes to inspect such a weapon and handle it with a view to a possible purchase, Scorpio gets to observe the inspection process in detail. And he's aware of the simplicity and even the irony of this pleasure, but with what a fierce warmth does he find himself thrilled by the differing ways in which these potential customers try those weapons on for size, each man's style of movement as masculine as the others', but all subtly different. One man holds his weapon in his right hand, with a casual swagger and an easy swing that must surely echo that of the enormous penis whose weight Scorpio can sense swelling behind the black denim of the man's jeans. Another holds his weapon with stark and deadly precision in his left hand, which Scorpio decides must also be the hand he uses continually, day and night, to jerk himself off whenever he needs to. Another man handles the weapon in both hands, as if spoiling for combat and action, with a cock whose thickness Scorpio can see is thrust up hard left against the belt that keeps his baggy blue jeans upon his body. And another man, throughout his deft handling of the weapon, keeps the butt of it always at least touching the heat of his groin and sometimes even pressing down hard there, while Scorpio's knowledge of his own cellmate's testosterone-fuelled jealousy leads him to take meticulous care never to meet this man's gaze when it happens to stray towards Scorpio, even for an instant.

And if all those men were to encircle Scorpio, holding their weapons in those different ways at once, then how well-ensconced Scorpio himself would look, as the only girl standing at the centre of the gang, like a jewel set in silver, with her own gun slung arrogantly up to rest on her shoulder, flawlessly made-up, beautiful and danger-ous, empowered to command them and entitled to the pleasure of whatever man she wanted, day or night—or none of them at all—at her whim? Her towering stature in prison would ensure that, of all the windowed cells in this open-plan wing, hers alone would have blinds rolled down to obscure the view through its windows, with a servant inmate posted outside its door as a guard, and that her lover would be subservient to no other prisoner but Scorpio herself. For however dangerous any other might be, she herself would be more so! Flanked by the most powerful convicts, Scorpio would run the entire cell-block, strutting the length of it in the shortest shorts or skirt, identifying the lover she would choose, if she wished it; then if so, to be wrapped in passive heat around this lucky lover, quenching his thirst for the smallest sign of her gracious affection for him, or hungrily giving him extended oral sex, to steer him by degrees every night to an ecstasy of wild penetration of her crack by the giant hot hardness of an all-night erection; both prisoners gasping, groaning, writhing, streaming sweat, and pumping on and on for hours on end, to arrive at a frenzy and convulsion of release at last, just as the first dawn light spills pale up the sky beyond the window-bars...

Jaymi contemplates the screen. He bares his teeth, like an animal. Yes. That's what he needs.

90 KIM SHAMES ASHLEY

Jaymi wanders along the railing past the kidney-shaped pool behind the house on Jupiter Drive. He reaches the well-swept but seldom-used flight of ten steps leading down off this terrace to the precipitous slope beneath. He descends the flight, sits on the eighth step and places his feet down on the tenth one, with the ends of his bare toes at the lowest rind of manicured civilisation before that other realm begins—the original realm of untamed earth and scrub, steep and scratchy, where the savage scraping of hidden bugs emanates from spiny clumps of grass, evidencing an alien but atavistically familiar world of mandibled murder, kept at bay by artificial means.

His first response to seeing Bang Dead's new "Cosy Score: Normal-Comfy or Strange-Scary?" Newsfeed was to start creating Scorpio's code out of thin air, beginning with nothing but a fore-echo of this Beast's fierce beauty. If the ones and zeroes behave themselves, Scorpio will soon emerge from his code. He'll be painted with his own visuals, which will animate him; he'll be scored with his own soundtrack, which will come alive; and he'll be tested. Then within a few days he'll be electrified into incarnated form, in all his beauty, like a burst of love.

But despite this creation cycle of Scorpio, there is little clarity as to how the "Cosy Score: Normal-Comfy or Strange-Scary?" Newsfeed could possibly fail to barrel upwards and outwards in popularity and profitability around the world, at least for as long as tabloid culture outsells the rest.

There can be no assurance of the success of any investment; but a media stream that facilitates the rating of bite-sized life philosophy memes for reassuringness using *Ain'tTheyFreaky!*'s Freakometer, from a highest score of 10 for most Normal-Comfy, down to a lowest score of 1 for most Strange-Scary, by members of the public, does at least start out with the benefit of appealing to the resources of a decent majority.

Incarnated into the world by themselves, those bursts of Scorpio love would stand no chance against such competition. But with a little back-up, perhaps they might survive after all...

What on *earth* can Jaymi do, though, to give them any back-up? Maybe nothing whatsoever, really, against such a gigantic streaming wall of dreary, intellectually soggy deadweight.

No. He can do what he can—whatever that may be. He can send out something beautiful and rich, in response to that deluge. A tiny thing in the face of a giant thing, yes, as before. But it's worth a shot, is it not?

Or more accurately, not just one tiny thing but five—his five incarnated Beasts, sent out to wreak havoc, to do the work of the angels, out in meat-space! All he needs to do is identify their mission, with a view to undermining Bang Dead's output from within. Ever since Evelyn surprised him by constructing her suspended-pig's-ribcage sculpture in Westmont without his knowing she was doing so, however, it has been made clear to Jaymi on several occasions that once a Beast has been incarnated and let loose into the world, his awareness of what they get up to is incomplete at best.

His phone rings. "Hallo?" he answers, gazing down at that circle of hairy-trunked palm trees with the long-ago bonfire traces in the clearing at their centre.

"Jaymi, this is Kim. I'm sure you're super-busy, so I'll keep this quick. I just wanted to say that I've found myself becoming quite attracted, in a platonic way of course, to a certain quality in Ashley. A quality that I can only describe as a certain blonde seriousness."

"Oh Jeez," says Jaymi, resting his head in his hand. He may have to think fast here, to stop something going off the rails. This Beast has clearly become a loose cannon. (Is incarnation making the Beasts too independent?)

"No, hear me out," says Kim. "I'm a serious-minded blond myself, as you'll know from creating me, so it was natural for me to give her a call and go round to visit her at the Century Park East apartment. In fact, I'm there now—"

"*Oh* Jeez. This is *all* we need. Kim, please. It'll only make for unforeseen complications. Not to mention loose variables."

"Quite the opposite, I'm happy to say. I asked her if I could visit her, because I could see what a thoughtful and principled woman she is, so I wondered how she could bring herself to work as such an indispensable part of *Ain'tTheyFreaky!*. It didn't make sense. So I told her it didn't. I explained what huge, insidious damage the game's tabloid culture does to people across the world—how it cheapens them, demeans them and drags them down with such power. For ten minutes I talked about all that, and then about what you're making.

Then I shut up and just stared at her. Her first response was to argue, but I could tell it was faint-hearted argument. Then she petered out, went quiet and almost started crying. Then when she next spoke, it was to offer to help you in your missions while she continues working at Bang Dead. Would you like to speak with her? She's sitting beside me."

"Er … wow. Well, sure."

"OK, I'll hand over to her. Here she comes."

Jaymi closes his eyes and listens to the muffled sound of the phone being passed from hand to hand, while the farcical idea occurs to him that Kim may, just conceivably, be all alone and on the point of doing a high-camp vocal impersonation of Ms Tweke…

A helpless, hysterical hoot of mirth threatens to force its way up through Jaymi's body and burst out, but is swiftly defused by the intimation of a headache behind his left eye.

"Hi Jaymi, this is Ashley," says a tightly-wound female voice into his ear.

He decides this is not Kim, but the genuine article herself. "Ashley. Well well well. Yes indeed. So, er, how are things?"

"Jaymi, I want to confirm everything Kim just said. You have created the most amazing, pure-minded character in him. What a beautiful soul he is. That in itself has played a part in my decision, I don't mind telling you. He's made me see what I've always known but have chosen to ignore: that I'm doing harm by working on *Ain't They Freaky!*, because that whole tabloid culture does such damage. So *I'm* doing that damage. I'm damaging people. And that is not what I, Ashley Tweke, want to have done to the world, for this little short time I'm in it. So, I'm going to atone for that. Kim's filled me in on what you're up to, and how you're trying to counteract *Ain't They Freaky!*. I'd like to help you instead."

She stops, awaiting a reaction from Jaymi, who sits there at a loss to know how to respond. At last he says, "You'll understand my asking if there's anything that might give me assurance Dud hasn't put you up to this?"

"Fair question. All I can say is: try me. If there's something specific I can do from within the company that would help you, then ask me and I'll see if I can do it. But only in the strictest secrecy, of course— I don't want to be arrested for facilitating industrial espionage."

"Right. Nor me. OK then. Well, are you free to come to my place on Electra Drive tomorrow evening, after dinner time, for drinks?"

"Yes I'd love to, thanks. One question: can Kim come too?"

Jaymi laughs out loud. "Yes, of course. He's welcome to come over. He is, after all, the embodiment of my own blond serious-ness of mind, despite my not even being blond. In fact, what am I saying—Kim even *lives* there on Electra Drive, with Shigem and Evelyn in the guest wing, so he'll already be around when you arrive! Though I am careful to allow the three of them their privacy, so I don't tend to go knocking on the guest wing door to visit them."

"Oh, what an *absurdly* exciting-but-cosy arrangement that sounds like!" bubbles Ashley, emitting a high-strung, frisky giggle down the phone line.

"Well, yeah. You know, we all muddle through," says Jaymi, then without warning he becomes aware that he's blushing, just as Shigem and he so prominently blushed throughout their teens, almost every time another person stared at them—but this time he's alone, at the bottom of this furthest flight of steps down and out into the untamed canyon, sitting by himself while his cheeks burn hot and bright and pink beyond control.

"OK then, see you tomorrow night," says Ashley.

"Great. Let's say half-past eight. Give me a call from outside the gates, and I'll let you in." He terminates the call, then punches the air in triumphal satisfaction, proclaiming aloud to himself, "*Yay!* Two Dreary Ones converted—two to go. Ace!"

Subsiding from this vocal bravado, he puts the phone away. His gaze melts into the distant haze of the city. He raises both hands to his face, and with the lightest of pressure he lays his fingers against both his cheeks, barely touching the skin ... and through all eight fingertips, he can feel the relentless lifelong throb of Shigem's teenage vulnerability, pressing pink and warm and shy, just beneath the surface.

91 SCORPIO EMERGES WITHIN HIS CODE

Alone in the grand bow window upstairs at the back of the house on Jupiter Drive, Jaymi hits a number on his phone and listens to it ringing away down the line, westwards across the Hollywood Hills.

"Hey Herb, it's Jaymi calling. I have a question for you. When you hacked into each Beast's new code, I assume Dud was aware of it?"

"Oh sure, yes. He instructed me to sniff out each new Beast's code and apply my best hacking chops. I even got a state visit from Dud, every time it happened: for all four hacks, he schlepped over from Century City to the Sunset Boulevard building, just to sit beside me and watch the carnage."

"How charming," says Jaymi. "I half-guessed some cosy little scene like that might be happening. Well then, you'd better invite him to schlep over again and watch you hack into my new Beast, who's starting to emerge from his code. After Scorpio is incarnated in a couple of days' time, Dud will become aware of him anyway, yes. But at that point, we don't want Dud wondering why you managed to sniff out all the others while they were still being coded, but you somehow missed this one. That might make him suspicious."

"A new Beast! How cool is that? I can't wait to mess him up."

"Thanks a bunch, Herb."

"I see what you're saying about Dud. I'll ask him if he's in the mood to come over for a hack tomorrow. If he is, would that timing work for you?"

"Yep, fine. Text me with a rough idea of when, and ... just don't hurt Scorpio more than you have to for the sake of appearances, OK? I'll be resisting you, also for appearances, but let's not damage him too much."

"Hmm, I'm not so sure. I think we should really put this Scorpio of yours through the wringer. After all, we can't have him getting too comfortable in his job, can we? Or too complacent in his Beast-hood. It's a Beast-eat-Beast world, you know, and he needs to be prepped for that."

"Yes, thank you Herb. Speak soon."

Alright then, back to work. Jaymi sets his phone to silent, hides it from sight, fires up his software, and waits for his new creation's code to flicker up.

Somewhere behind the laptop screen, Scorpio's code surfaces into morning wakefulness, feeling chewed-up after his usual traumatic night of fitful, sporadic sleep interspersed by anguished hours of insomnia, writhing horniness and the fierce churn of his imagination. He shakes off the delirium of all the night's dreams and wet-dreams about running the prison, and lands instead in the harsh dawn of another day locked up as the powerless lackey and sexual-tension-receptacle of a violent, weapons-dealing cellmate who grunts as often as he speaks. The latter seems to be still asleep for the moment, breathing audibly overhead on the upper level of this bunk-bed, so there'll be a few minutes' more peace for Scorpio, lying here a metre below, worn out from the traumas and hungers of the night ... but once the cellmate awakes, which won't be long, then he'll need immediate servicing, a journey up the bunk ladder will be demanded, and all peace will end for another day.

However, now that Scorpio's code has been sweetly discoloured with the watermarks of a Belle Glade childhood and a West Palm Beach criminal coming-of-age that are not life-chapters he'll end up living in reality—either in the game-world of *The Platinum Raven* or (as Angel) in the game-world of *The Imagination Thief*—it just so happens that this morning he will be granted release after two years of incarceration.

For it's time for a higher-level destiny to unfold for him, in which he's been cast to play a better part than this back-story role as cell-meat down here, with a better soundtrack than this sad prison-song. Like Amber, Evelyn, Shigem, Kim and the Platinum Raven before him, he will soon find himself no longer confined within this laptop screen, but running free through the mythic meat-space of Los Angeles.

Apprehending his upcoming transition with excitement, Scorpio's code begins by slithering out of the bunk's lower level in silence. Then it slinks on cat's feet across the floor, towards the shower unit in the corner. Climbing inside the unit, it halts at the shower door and glances back up at its supine cellmate of the last two years, whose uncovered morning erection slants up clear towards the ceiling in profile, like a great dark pole, straining and twitching in the air of the cell. Scorpio's code hesitates for a second, licking its lips; then gives the pole an ironic bow, and blows the sleeping man a last little kiss like a venomous snake-bite, before turning away and onward into the shower unit.

As befits an inmate who has run the entire prison, at least in dreams and wet-dreams, the unique amounts of terror and money that swirl around Scorpio have leveraged unparalleled outside help. In fact, no less than Jaymi Peek himself has been prevailed upon to construct an escape tunnel from the outside world to the floor of this very shower unit, in the style of El Chapo. So, down a short ladder to a packed-earth tunnel-floor scuttles Scorpio's code, pauses a moment to adjust to the gloom, and sets off at a run.

Every twenty metres is a pool of light cast by a bulb hanging down from above, which he reaches up and smashes as he passes underneath, to hinder the pursuers he's afraid to hear behind him. With the smash of every bulb, he's pursued by a spill of shadow lapping at his feet and welling up around him, conjuring a bestiary that's all his own. Ghost-moths flap through the tunnel's upper air, above a hatching of reptiles flexing dragons' muscles. From the darkness, the face of a baboon starts out, alone and shocking. Lower down, ghost-carp swim; lower still, a great squid's pale eyes peer up at him; and lower yet, gulper-eels writhe about his toes. And down beyond those, acrid eyes on a face of grinning evil—its mirth frozen hard as a mask.

Onward scampers Scorpio's code, through unwholesome gloom, watched by a series of sharp-faced portraits hung upon the walls…

A figure looms ahead, through a shambles of bloodied sound cut with stabs of ancient language. It's a kind of hooded death, with a voice of charred black glowing red, and a yellow light glowing in its eyes, demon-fashion. A music of Satan arises in a black burst of hissing fire and flames of blood. The figure reaches out at him, grabs his hand, and gives him an ear. It's a human ear, pressed into his palm, so his fingers close tight on it, his fingernails scraping in the curves of the ear-coils—

A dog barks, far across the canyon from this window. The emergent code and its Scorpionic bestiary are rising up with force behind the plastic surface of Jaymi's screen, as if they are pressing against the glass of an aquarium.

And on down the tunnel slithers Scorpio's code, from the prison to the Hollywood Hills, ever nearer: a piece of luscious darkness, on its way to being flesh!

Jaymi leans closer in towards his screen, and closer … then recoils, smiling wide, as his Beast's code springs into view at last. It presses at the silvered underside of the glass—a proto-form of his own fierce beauty, like a darkness of tentacles surging up a well-shaft, straight at his face.

92 FEINT OF A HACK INTO SCORPIO'S CODE

Next morning in the house on Jupiter Drive, in receipt of Herb's warning by text, Jaymi watches the promised hack into Scorpio's code occur in real time. To keep up appearances for Dud, he stages a plausible defence against Herb's feigned attempt to dumb this new Beast down into an aesthetically debased, tabloid-style version of the original.

This time, Herb insinuates himself through a side-door, then lies low in order to observe what element is unfolding in Scorpio at this moment. As soon as this element attains completion, Herb will send his poison blades of code into the very next one that starts developing, so as to hitch a ride on the full energy of its arising.

The element of Scorpio that's unfolding now, which Herb allows to unfold, involves the printed image of a still from a TV screen. The pixel-grain of this television picture lies between the depicted face and Scorpio-as-viewer, like an array of horizontal prison bars—lines of screen resolution that are part of Scorpio's lifelong memory of this face. The head is strongly back-lit, as well as front-lit and key-lit, so the outline of the ears and earring and shoulders and hair is edged in a glowing rim of hazy purple. The effect Scorpio receives from the eyes, from the shape of the face, its unique flavour and its delivery at the camera, all serve to electrify Scorpio more widely than he has felt before. This electrification will occur not just now but over several ensuing months, during which it will flower in unstoppable allure, before settling like a lethally delicate cobweb, coloured black and purple and pink and silver, throughout him, for life.

The next element that's set to spring up in him is, of course, his contemplating himself in the guise of this TV face that has just infused him with such seduction. And now comes the instant when Herb's code-blades puncture the skin of this arising thing, as planned. A moment ago, Scorpio first held aloft a self-image edged with that hazy purple glow from the TV; and he's just starting to twirl this self-image in his imagination, as if turning over in his hands a new sculpture of his own head … when a jolt passes through him, at what he sees: carved into the back of the head are what he least expects—a gaping second mouth, second set of teeth, second nose and second pair of eyes.

His thoughts wrap themselves around horror without warning, against his will and beyond control. Into his head-chamber walks a character who looks and sounds identical to himself. And this character's compulsion is to flick a switch on and off, at enormous and upsetting length, every time he passes through a doorway, for longer every day, until the duration of compulsive switch-flicking is perhaps two hours daily; which creeps up to three hours daily, before he can wrench himself away from the switch; then four-and-a-half hours daily, through his weeping; then pressing upwards uncontrollably, hour by hour, day by day, to a duration of six full hours every day, so that the task of remaining socialised passes from difficult to agonising; then creeping upwards further still, to seven hours a day, cutting off most possibilities for socialisation; then eight hours a day—

The door of his head slams shut. All the bodies caught in his head-chamber stop dead, frozen in the postures they occupied when the door slammed.

Normal sound dies, leaving paralysed silence.

A creak cuts in, slow and deafening—the sound of a horror-movie door-hinge. Everybody here in his head-chamber turns around, with abnormal slowness, to face him. By degrees, all their eyes swivel round to face Scorpio, and lock themselves onto him, demonically knowing; and the creak gets ever louder, as if the bodies' frameworks are thirsty for oil.

With a sense of sliding down into someone else's nightmare, he happens to incline his head at a particular angle, from which his surroundings appear the same as from other angles except that a single freakish thing is visible, almost hidden among the rest—a horrific face on one body standing just over there in his head-chamber. Suppressing an urge to wail, he sets about the task of verifying this phenomenon: first, he returns his head to its former angle of inclination, whereupon the face resumes its earlier unexceptional appearance ... and then he reproduces the angle of his head's inclination to what it was a few moments ago when he glimpsed ... and *yes*, sure enough, the face on that body over there in his head-chamber is once again quite horrific. He jerks his own head's angle away from this again, so as to conceal that face for ever, he fervently hopes—and squints and flicks his eyes back at the face for a split-second, of course, just to check—and mercifully it's normal again (but for how long?).

He swallows.

He swallows again, several times, and realises he is sliding towards a state where he's unable to stop doing so. Another agonising compulsion? First switch-flicking, and now swallowing? The latter has the potential to be even worse than the former, he would guess, with its threat of going beyond the former's upsettingness, into a slow, bloodthirsty, months-long self-mutilation of a kind that he doesn't even want to start imagining in any detail, let alone fall into...

Fortunately he is diverted from this, when another of the bodies standing around his little head-chamber makes another horrific expression at him—in silence, without warning, for no reason, different from the first one but just as distressing—and seemingly unnoticed by the other bodies in the room.

His mouth goes dry and sticky inside. He knows that if he were to question each horrific expression-maker, in mounting alarm, as to what the hell they were trying to do to him, then they would deny everything, feigning not to understand; so he bites the question back down his throat, where it hangs, never to be asked.

He knows that if he were to question the other bodies, in his growing panic and queasiness, as to whether any of *them* noticed two among their own number making such horrific faces at him, then they would all deny seeing any such thing; so he clamps this question tightly back down into his own voice-box, never to be uttered.

With escalating nausea, he wonders whether another of these scattered bodies in his head-chamber will next start to emanate a feeling of alien evil and fuck-up, some unaccountable repulsiveness, despite not changing visibly, as yet...

Up in the bow window in the house on Jupiter Drive, Jaymi gives a grim smile. This stuff that Herb is wheeling out is somewhat off-the-peg horror fare, to be nakedly frank. Good freaky fun, but penny-dreadful material at heart, crying out to be wreathed in green billows of dry-ice lit from underneath, with a theremin soundtrack. But its execution is evidently slick enough to fool Dud, sitting there beside Herb in the Sunset Boulevard building; otherwise Herb would have changed tack. As Jaymi can discern within himself, in any case, Scorpio is such a dark little creature to begin with, that this kind of horror will have messed up his head less than Dud may assume it has. In this respect, it was a well-judged choice of material on Herb's part.

OK, enough: Dud must be reassured, by now, that this brand-new Beast and his creator have both been made to suffer, and that all is therefore well with the world.

Jaymi jumps in to block further access by Herb's hack; Herb discreetly colludes in being locked out; and then Jaymi, left in digital peace again, effects damage control. Double-deleting all Herb's penny-dreadful twistedness into the recycle bin of alternative histories that never happened, he restores Scorpio to the point where he'd just received Jaymi's electrification of hazy purple from that face on the TV screen, settling throughout Scorpio like an exhilarating and lethally delicate cobweb coloured black and purple and pink and silver.

93 JAYMI PROPOSES THE REPURPOSING TO HERB

Reclining on his bedroom terrace in the house on Electra Drive next day, Jaymi returns to the question of how to target Bang Dead—and the fog on the far side of that question starts tunnelling away down avenues of possible action, into exhilarating focus.

Throughout Evelyn's and Amber's noir caper at the South Central motels, it didn't occur to Jaymi to set up much collaboration between them—though they did manage to snatch success from the jaws of chaos, by dint of sheer quirky bravado plus a twist of inspired lunacy involving a pig's ribcage and a bunch of corpses stolen from funeral parlours.

In Shigem's and Kim's and Evelyn's Downtown L.A. caper, Jaymi did facilitate those Beasts' discussions of what they were doing, through his landing them beside a welcoming café full of chatter.

This marked a step upwards in his development as an orchestrator of incarnated Beasts. Within the results, however, there was still an echo of the clatter of juxtaposed carnage that he'd first sensed at the Westmont motels. Yes, the street queens were spared that ugly crime against them, which was essential; but how oddly this sat with those KitKat and Krispy Kreme dramas, not to mention Evelyn's draping herself over retro-style cars at every opportunity.

A further fine-tuning of his orchestrations is now due, perhaps. A finessed combination of melody and harmony will be brought to bear, now that he's about to unleash a climactic noir caper. This one will be peopled by five incarnated Beasts, and he's determined to encourage even more free and focused collaborations between them. This finesse, he should add, will be strictly at the service of the caper's goal—which is nothing less than to sabotage Bang Dead's giant array of toxic Newsfeeds, while pointing the Dreary Ones towards other creative possibilities that perhaps they've never thought of trying.

No pressure, then.

After a moment's thought, he picks up his phone, touches a name and listens while it rings.

"Hey Jaymi," answers Herb.

"Hi Herb. How are they hanging?"

"They're hanging fine, I think. I could switch on videophone and take my pants down and we could both check, if you like?"

"No, that's fine, I'll take it on trust. Great work on the hack of Scorpio. I assume Dud was taken in?"

"Yes, totally. That new Beast is just the fiercest! Is he recovered now?"

"Oh, he's peachy-fine again now, thank you. His maker is a little battered by the experience—but hey, I can take it. Look, I have a proposal for you. It's taken shape in my head at last. It seems obvious, in retrospect, but it's taken this long to get it straight because, well, it's also kind of complex, you see… It's technical stuff about *Ain'tTheyFreaky!*, by the way."

"Oh, right, OK. I was beginning to wonder whether maybe the videophone-and-pants-down thing was still applicable after all."

"Here's my plan," says Jaymi. "Inside *Ain'tTheyFreaky!*, we add a landscape like the version of Downtown L.A. you built—but a version of the West Side of L.A. instead. I'm thinking of the area from LAX, including where the server farm is, down as far as the El Segundo refinery. Straightforward enough, yes?"

"Sure. You start with a framework from a 3D map, basically, then you model the art onto it and apply whatever effects you want."

"OK, good. Next, I want us to take the content of the six News-feeds, then break all of it down digitally and sort it into its raw constituent elements. I mean each different letter, each number, and so on. We need a script that takes a snapshot of the Newsfeeds, then pulls out all the constituents from the snapshot and sorts them into raw categories: letters and figures and symbols, plus pixels of red and green and blue bits. Am I making sense?"

"You are," says Herb. "And they're still hanging great, by the way. Carry on, I'm intrigued now."

"OK. So here's a question for you. Within that brand-new West Side landscape, could those salvaged raw constituents be stored inside the storage tanks in the refinery? Could a player be shown the Newsfeeds being diverted into the different tanks, in effect?"

"Er, yeah, why not? That could be a cool display, sure."

"And then, could those raw constituents inside those tanks be assembled and combined into something else, within that West Side landscape?"

"No reason why not—those glyphs and pixels would just be raw data components that you could recombine however you like."

"But here's a crucial question for you," says Jaymi. "After you recombine them, would they be the *same* glyphs and pixels that *used* to constitute the substance of the six Newsfeeds, before they were all cut out of those Newsfeeds and moved into the tanks instead?"

Herb laughs. "That is kind of a kooky-artistic way of looking at it, Jaymi, I have to say! But yes, the glyphs and pixels would be the same ones, if you were moving them into the new thing, rather than just copying them into it. From the tanks, each glyph or pixel could be moved into any other piece of code, of any length or complex-ity, within that landscape. And sure, this moving could be clearly displayed, at whatever speed you wanted to show it happening. Is this some fancy new game you want me to build? It sounds like fun, but I should warn you I'd be invoicing my usual rates."

"Fine. Are you free to come to my place at eight-thirty tomorrow evening, after dinner time, for drinks? I've invited Ashley too. By the way, are you aware that she's come over to join us, here on the dark side?"

"Ashley Tweke? No way! No, I didn't know that. Wow!… Sure, it'd be great to come over tomorrow, thanks."

"Ashley will be just as surprised to hear you've come over to us."

"I'm going to call her in a minute and compare notes."

"Good. Let's keep it between us three, of course."

"You bet. Alright, I'll see you at your place at half-eight tomorrow evening."

94 JAYMI CREATES SCORPIO'S APPEARANCE

Next morning, Jaymi is seated in his bow window above the terrace of the house on Jupiter Drive, surrounded by the grand panorama of canyons and hills and the street-grid beyond. He closes his eyes and thinks back to that unique half-minute when he let his gaze wander up and down the "Cosy Score: Normal-Comfy or Strange-Scary?" Newsfeed, where new posts were popping up every few seconds, every one of them receiving scores and comments from multiple sources.

Then he re-opens his eyes, consults his ever-growing design for *The Platinum Raven* and checks his sketch for Scorpio's visuals. Its first description of Scorpio's physical appearance reads: "a young Armenian man of maybe twenty-one, of a dark and delicate beauty in keeping with the silver scorpion pendant hanging at his neck […] the Armenian boy dressed in black, a Scorpio pendant at his neck. No smile there at all, too much tension and exquisiteness and fierce vulnerability. For him it wasn't easy, no one-two-three. But here he is—just as if in some club, deep in a city. A sudden smile leaks through, a flush of light across his face, for an instant. Then once again, no smile. Fem in black, for this is realness. So waltz darling, deep in vogue […] he turns his dainty head to one side and slightly up."

He turns to his design for the game *The Imagination Thief*, to check his sketch for the visual artwork there. Its first description of Angel's physical appearance reads: "a dark-eyed Armenian boy of maybe twenty-one, whose spiteful sleek depraved face radiates decadence and damage from its sharp beauty. [...] He is shadowy, effete, both unhealthy and luminous: I picture him a pirate-queen scuttling up the masts of a slave-ship, to keep watch. Aside from a silver earring in his right ear, a shiny black vinyl brassiere is all that he wears above the waist, above black leggings and pointed black boots. Through his smooth brown skin I can sense the charge of nerves around his ribs beneath the faint swell of his breasts. His smooth little torso is built like a whip, thin and supple. Beautifully tattooed down the length of his back is a stark, emblematic pair of angel's wings, cross-cut with faint lash-marks. Half the time his mouth, with its lips painted cinnabar, is sulky; and half the time his teeth are bared, jaws tense and snapping like a starved baby she-wolf. His voice is intersexual, with a degenerate breathiness underlying a fluid steel edge and a slight lisp on every *s*. A clean but musky sexual scent coils about him, even through the smoke. When his eyes fix mine for the first time, I have to make an effort not to flick my gaze away, so potent is the damage and so luscious is the blackness of fever within them. Hard excitement and the pulsing of attraction to the beauty of the dark spills out of him, as if his sweetest wish is for a violent revenge against life and all who live it. [...] And he turns away and slinks to the corridor's mouth, like a little black dragon with a scorpion's sting."

There is then one further little artwork-oriented description of Angel, a bit later on in *The Imagination Thief*: "he seemed to you, Lucan, like a sexy little fly. You saw him as a creature whose natural habitat would be hovering above a steaming-hot pool of blood and honey, sending his feelers down into it like the snouts of a voracious alien. And those *killer* eyes on him—so startling in close-up! Those big, brown, vital eyes, so dark and alive and dangerous and watchful, beneath long black eyelashes; the curve of the eyes echoed and magnified underneath by the fuller convexity of pale brown-olive skin curving outward over his cheekbones, then quickly back in and down in slanting arcs to the reticent mouth and smooth sharp chin; and the delicate jaw-line rising around behind, past small ears to the flame of black hair above a round intelligent forehead. That animal immediacy, that play of flesh and electricity combined, that scything sharpness and tang within a wrapping of organic yield and warmth, which knew that it grabbed your own gaze and licked it back."

236

Well, alright then. That's the brief, for this final Beast's visuals. Jaymi glances up for a moment, taking in the canyon ahead; then he fires his attention back into those lines of code, homing in on Scorpio, swooping in towards him like a bird of prey...

This Beast is camera-ready for his very own manga, a cocktail of essences from many places and eras: dark angel of all genders; Roman pathic from the time of Nero, feral and consumed, at the edges of the palace feast; the mystic priestess-boy Heliogabalus, anointed as emperor; and an alien idol fallen to earth from the future, with a tail like a snake's.

Jaymi zooms in and fills up his screen with the full-length snapshot that's been circulated to the production crew's costume department to ensure continuity in Scorpio's manga-like styling: in his little black pixy-boots, black leather mini-skirt over black tights, slinky black polo-neck and silver crucifix pendant, hooped earring and silver rings (not to mention the sulky mouth and the luscious darkness of obsession that were both touched upon in Jaymi's initial sketches), this Beast's femininity is of the dragon-diva type, evenly fused with the rest of him.

As also indicated in the sketches, those Scorpio eyes are horny, as always—hungry for power and revenge, and to be fucked.

Brown eyes, in simple fact. But in greater truth, when the side-light hits, they are indigo eyes.

And yet, when his darkness melts into sleekness, the simple allure of his slender body, with its smooth little breasts and gentle curves, is topped by the prettiest of androgyne faces—delicate and vulnerable, and even almost innocent.

Thus it is that Scorpio inhabits his own slinky black melodrama, in his own manga-bubble of neon-red and silver: an electrified fusion of self-love and self-hate, flickering between hungry self-pollination and picturesque crucifixion.

It's a living, for a Beast.

Jaymi hits save, sinks back into his seat and gazes out across the canyons at the haze above L.A.—a mythic city-span like a grand dance-floor, where the sweet fierce beauty of his own little Scorpio will soon dance naked in the sight of the world!

95 SCORPIO'S APPEARANCE COMES ALIVE

Resuming work at his perch in the Jupiter Drive bow window after lunch, Jaymi claps his hands in glee at the growing definition of this next-arising Beast, who is slinking ever nearer to incarnation.

As established in Scorpio's code, throughout *The Imagination Thief* he will be called by his boy name, Angel. This is because all the events to be depicted in that particular game occurred before the time when everyone started calling him by his girl name, Scorpio. His transition of names will be remembered in an episode called "Santa Monica Boulevard" in *The Platinum Raven*—a game whose events will occur a couple of years later, after he's become Scorpio for all purposes.

In which context Jaymi first establishes Scorpio's gleaming detail in *The Imagination Thief* as being his little silver crucifix pendant, whose visuals will glint through the game-play, most often offset by black: "upon his tight black T-shirt, just above the gentle undulation of his breasts, hangs a little silver crucifix [...] the little silver crucifix dangles in mid-air beside your black vinyl brassiere [...] he heads for the door, stopping on the way to pick up from the dressing-table your crucifix pendant, whose thin chain he gently fixes high upon your chest in a delicate silver echo of the large golden one hanging halfway down his own."

He then establishes Scorpio's talisman in *The Imagination Thief* as being his mirrored sunglasses, whose visuals will reflect his surroundings at three moments of high-tension game-play: "he pulls out a flick-knife and deftly slices the blade up through the air to rest against the other, who sits coquettishly posed on the divan beside him, naked except for mirrored sunglasses and a whip around his neck [...] half-running after him, breathing onto and polishing the lenses of the mirrored sunglasses you've just snatched [...] wearing mirrored sunglasses. Sunglasses at night."

He concludes by establishing Scorpio's additional motif in *The Imagination Thief* as being a big golden crucifix pendant, which will be worn by his boyfriend Lucan rather than by him, but which will nonetheless flash across the landscape of Scorpio's game-play like a search-light: "a big, flat, golden crucifix hangs from his chest, whose bulk quite dominates my field of vision [...] your eyes stay closed, but your hand reaches up to feel the big golden crucifix hanging at his chest, where his muscles are so close that you can feel their heat, here upon your face [...] a miniature blaze of golden light in your midst, emanating from where a dedicated beam of sun strikes Lucan's crucifix pendant [...] you see yourself fixed on that golden crucifix like a little twist of crackling, howling in religious ecstasy forever [...] his spiritual enrichment on the crucifix [...] *'Bad girl!'* voices chant, *'so like a woman'* in your tight red leather skirt and cherry lipstick and angel's wings, holding the big dangerous hand of your man with his crucifix pendant, strong and golden on his chest."

Although Scorpio has no soundtrack yet, Jaymi is starting to feel what sort of Beast he will be in his two games—the only Beast who'll appear in two. Seen as two halves of a whole, Scorpio's central roles in that pair of game-worlds will come together in pleasure to make a smoothly-contoured creature. In his multiple close-ups along the way, however, he may appear a Cubist, fractured Beast, as befits a being who incorporates and celebrates the fractures in his maker, embodying the urges of a self-destructive voltage.

For instance, Scorpio remembers feeling in his adolescence that he had always, somehow, worn beautiful make-up throughout his life: whenever he'd been about to swim at that idyllic open-air pool in the woods, in the palace gardens of his head, it had been indigo eye-shadow, a little below the eyes and more above them; or whenever he'd been curled up like an elf in one of his palace turrets, it had been a dark and luscious colour on his lips, to match the burgundy-black flowers in the wreath on his hair; or whenever he'd been aboard that pirate ship, it had been a streamlined version of the parrots' coloura-tion in the jungles he'd been sailing past. It was as if he'd always known he had an inner make-up, visible across a freeway—such that when he did at last apply some actual colours from physical phials, in his teens growing up on the south-west margins of Belle Glade or the west edge of Asbury Park, then he felt as if he were painting a lily whose colours had already been there since birth.

But later in the underworld, deep in a city, there's a woman who observes him across a crowded room, while he talks with a score of people over several hours; and it seems she must be looking so far into the nervy Scorpio as to see him full of electric nerves and vulnerability. At last she comes to speak to him, saying she can see both a young girl and also a likely mass-murderer living there inside him, depending on the light. (And Jaymi squirms.) The boy-girl is looking very pixy-ish tonight, she says, but really she can tell that he's delicate and cruel, so she'd better pack some heat while she's with him, she's decided... Scorpio's eyebrows jump up nervily, as often, and he hiccups in reply, because the truth is more mundane than the woman is describing: he is just tipsy, after much champagne. A drunken angel, once again—of a sultry and sluttish disposition, to be sure, but liquored-up, in essence. Beside them in the mirror on the nightclub wall, he gets a glimpse of himself wearing all black and silver, looking skinny and effeminate and sexy-hungry-horny as ever, like a ferret with an eight-hour erection. He looks back at this worryingly sharp-eyed woman, and hiccups at her again.

"Oh, you know how it is," he tells her. "The candle-light, the film-stars glimpsed in mirrors, then the street-corner gossips and the crisp tick of seconds on the clock-face." She clinks her glass against his; and underneath his clothing, the barbed-wire is coiled around him, holding his sex-toy in place and scraping dry across his back with every move he makes, scratching at the smoothness of his belly and his thighs.

96 TALKING OF MEAT

Soon after eight-thirty in the evening, Ashley's and Herb's cars roll up to the house on Electra Drive, less than a minute apart. Standing at the grand picture-window on his upper landing, with his hands clasped behind his back and his forehead resting against the inside of the central pane, Jaymi watches his front gates swing open. The two vehicles sweep into the width of his driveway, curve around the central fountain, and scrunch to a halt on the gravel in front of the house.

He watches his gates close again, sealing both cars and drivers into his property. *His very own two Dreary Ones!* Converted to the side of light and right and joyful darkness...

As soon as his guests have stepped indoors, he equips them with drinks. Then to put them at their ease, he takes them straight through the house and out across the ground-floor terrace, for a wander around the garden on the promontory over the city, where dusk is still falling. As they wander the paths and lawns, their six passing shoes are starkly lit, here and there, by cylindrical lights with downward-slanting louvred sides, like insulator cones, of the same kind that sprouted from the earth on Zeus Drive and spilled pools of red and orange and yellow around the Platinum Raven—but this time spilling pools of crisp white and blue instead.

Jaymi brings his guests by leisurely degrees back to the main sitting-room, where a quiet roar of L.A. night drifts in through the open terrace doors. "So," he begins, "I assume the two of you compared notes today, about how you've both come over to the dark side?"

"We did, on the phone," laughs Ashley. "It makes me very happy to see Herb here with us. Hi Herb!"

"Hey Ashley! I guess this is our shared secret."

"I shan't tell, if you don't."

"It's fabulous to have you both on board," says Jaymi. "And what d'you think of the show so far, may I ask?"

Ashley shakes her head, smiling as she chooses her words. "I suppose Kim just made me see and feel what I'd always known about *Ain'tTheyFreaky!*. I'd known it in theory, but I'd been too involved in the details of it, to see it for what it is. How impoverished it is. How … ugly that whole tabloid culture is. It's as if the people who peddle it have forgotten that any non-tabloid cultures exist, let alone that they're a hundred times more interesting."

"What came home to me, I guess, is how it actually hurts people," says Herb.

Jaymi refills their drinks. "Herb and I had a chat on the phone yesterday," he says, looking at Ashley, then proceeds to give her a summary of their conversation about adding the West Side landscape into *Ain'tTheyFreaky!*, breaking the Newsfeeds into their raw constituents, moving these into the refinery and assembling them into Jaymi's games instead. "And this is where you can help us, as Bang Dead's head of IT infrastructure. As you know better than anyone, Herb's new West Side landscape contains the location of the company's server farm next to LAX. You oversee that, and you control access to it. My Beasts may well need that access."

A shadow of alarm enters her expression. She thinks, then replies, "Yes, I can unlock it remotely online, at any time."

"That would be magic!" says Jaymi.

Ashley looks at Herb. "Have you met any of Jaymi's Beasts in meat-space, as I did?" she asks him.

"No," says Herb, "but one of them left a brain on my keyboard, with a knife stuck through it. An animal's brain from a butcher's shop, I should hope. Which certainly gave 'meat-space' a new resonance."

"And talking of meat," says Ashley, there was the frame of my childhood photo from Martha's Vineyard—"

"Yes, I'm sorry Amber gave you both a bit of a hard time there," says Jaymi. "He can be a scamp, I confess. But hey—one can't always be reassuring, when getting a point across. I was using him to make you sit up and pay attention. And look, it worked: here you both are, paying attention! Right? I'd say Shigem and Kim and Amber all worked together, to bring the three of us to this point tonight. So, welcome, both of you! Aren't you glad you're here?"

Herb and Ashley exchange a brief, nervous glance, smiling but still a little apprehensive about where they may be headed in all this.

"*Yes*, you're both glad you're here," Jaymi informs them. "And I'm glad you're glad! Are you glad I'm glad?" They laugh, and he clinks his glass onto theirs. "OK then, glad to hear it. So, enough of being nervous nellies here—we have work to do and magic to make!" He refills all their glasses. "Now, the next question is for you, Herb. You know how your Downtown design has some game trappings but isn't in fact gamified behind the surface? I mean it's really just an all-purpose, somewhat sparse evocation of a semi-mythical 'Downtown L.A.', to gussy up the Newsfeeds?"

Herb pushes his glasses up his nose. "Well, I don't know if I'd quite call it *sparse*, as such. But yeah, sure, I know what you're saying."

"Oh indeed, I don't mean sparse *as such*—no, of course not. But maybe just a tad ... *thin*, in places, let's say?"

Herb grunts assent.

"OK then," resumes Jaymi. "Well, that pop-art-type thinness is just the effect I'd like to see replicated in the Platinum Raven's upcoming mission through LAX. To be nakedly frank, it's questionable whether we even need her jaunting through the airport. But this very shortfall in strict necessity should be owned and inhabited with appropriate visual styling, and I reckon the aforementioned thinness would fit well. I mean, how could I *not* send her through LAX?

The sexy minerality of an airfield full of shrieking turbines and great expanses of marginal land made of concrete and metal, with all those liminal spaces that are so dead, yet so highly charged that no one's allowed to access them … you should both know that this is all very Platinum Raven, with her alien beauty and her cool transcendence and her pink noise. Am I making sense?" Herb nods, then Ashley too, both with a sort of shining concentration on their faces. "Plus, the server farm is located just beyond the airport's western perimeter, and the refinery pumps tank-loads of jet-fuel into the airport every day: these two facts are like a pair of columns, each sending up half an arch to support the airport as the visual keystone between server farm and refinery."

Ashley's concentration breaks into a smile that fuses understanding with befuddlement. She shares another glance with Herb, then the three of them laugh. "This is all outrageously kooky, Jaymi, and I'm unsure how much you can see that yourself, but you have enough of a reality distortion field around you to ensure that I do, somehow, get it."

"Agreed, and I totally get it!" says Herb. "On the practical front, I have to say that Kelly pitched in and helped quite a bit with my Downtown design. If we could bring her into this too, it would speed things up. By the way, she's not about to walk into this room to join us too, is she?"

"I wish," says Jaymi. "No, she's still Dud's. Any hope of that changing, d'you think?"

"I doubt it," says Ashley, shaking her head.

"That's fine, I can repurpose Kelly's Downtown input for the West Side instead," says Herb. "A kind of visual reverse-engineering, let's call it."

"Kelly is just surging ahead these days," muses Ashley. "She has so many new designs in the pipeline for *Ain't They Freaky!* and all its marketing. She's so oblivious to the tackiness and weariness of it."

Jaymi beams at them both with a touch of pride. "More drinks?" he asks.

Herb checks the time. "Jaymi, sorry, I think I need to head home. I have to be in the office early tomorrow morning. In fact," he looks at Ashley, "I'll be seeing you at the datacentre meeting, first thing, yes?" She nods, checking the time herself.

"Go get some sleep, both of you," says Jaymi. "Are you free to come back here tomorrow evening, to carry on from where we've left off?"

"Yep," she says.

"I'm in," says Herb. "Any chance of starting with dinner here tomorrow?"

"Sure. You'll be earning it: tomorrow's session will be much longer than today's. First we'll be generating the West Side environment, then we'll be telling the Beasts what to do in it. Can you get here at six?"

"On the dot," says Ashley.

97 KELLY SMUDGES SCORPIO

At the bow window on Jupiter Drive late next morning, Jaymi resumes work on Scorpio's creation cycle—unaware that someone else is also paying attention to the very same thing, up in the Sunset Boulevard building.

As Jaymi recalls from having met her, Kelly Kandy is a fun-loving party animal with an easy manner and a reassuring smile. The simple truth of this impression makes it perhaps surprising, at first, that she's also someone who will hate this latest Beast on sight, with a chemical hatred. Her horizons are so shaken by Scorpio, in fact, that she forms an immediate intention to fuck him up for good. Confronted by a creature so gorgeously anguished—so cross-cut with sex addiction, of a gender identity so complex and a self-esteem so fractured—how can Kelly wish otherwise than to ramp up his anguish still further? Concerning the reasons for this, she is incurious by nature; though Jaymi has little difficulty in recognising that behind her general hipness, she's really very "Cosy Score".

Well then, Scorpio was made for her, Jaymi reflects.

In any case, as soon as this Beast's delicate Scorpionic beauty, sleek depraved face, sulky mouth and luscious darkness of obsession appear on her screen for the first time, all as aforementioned and in one package, Kelly applies her skilled fingers, state-of-the-art software and well-used keyboard to the task of smudging his visuals as painfully as possible.

There he is on the monitor right in front of her, clinking champagne glasses with some woman in a busy nightclub. Kelly pounds her keys, clicks her mouse, and sends her cursor curving and flicking all across her screen's image of the nightclub.

As she does so, Scorpio senses the air in the room being flicked and whisked by a slicing of damage that has yet to gain ingress. His little silver cross swings flashing through the space between his nipples, sweats and glints in the candle-light and lands at a slant on his chest, while he glances around him … and then she breaks through.

An attempt to smudge a Beast's visuals is felt as a visceral distaste, flavoured by the nature of the Beast, at what the smudger would presume to impose. And so he slides down, from a diva on a champagne-high of club chic, to a fey little fly buzzing drunk above a sleaze-pit. Kelly sees the barbed-wire coiled around him, ramps it up and rams it through the cells of all the others in this room—self-mutilation as the darker side of narcissism, flowing through these clubbers gathered here—a perverted, delirium-obsessed scent of visuals, gleaming in their eyes and revealed as the engine of a nightmare of culinary events.

By queasy degrees, he understands what is flowing through the room.

He fears, in other words, that he may be *eaten* by these people, in a literal sense: chefs and long pigs…

In shock, he sets off at a run, across the room and down a passage—then halts as he sees a girl of five, just ahead, playing with a high-fashion doll whose legs are so exaggeratedly long and elegant as almost to suggest grasshoppers' thighs. The girl is practising ballerina moves, while talking in a cute, flirtatious, young-adult way, very "Hollywood" and precocious for a five-year-old. She turns to face him. "*Hi! I'm Nutmeg,*" she grates in a different voice, a voice of guttural harshness—and through her veil, Scorpio sees that this five-year-old's face is much older than he thought. It even has lines around its eyes…

Black light blazes and her head rears up, a mass of pulp with several eyes pushing out at odd places. Shrieks cut the air.

He turns and sprints back down the passage, knowing she'll be watching as he runs—but after fifty metres, the barbed-wire around his torso catches on a nail in a door-frame, so he has to turn back in her direction and scrabble at the wire, in a frantic bid to unhook it before she can reach him.

While he fumbles, with tears pricking the backs of his eyes, he feels the tickle of a drip of blood running down his chest beneath his black clothes, behind his crucifix.

The girl scuttles sideways up the length of the passageway, towards him. "*I like to have my eyeballs licked!*" she grates; and a black steel worm curls out from inside the eyeball nearest to Scorpio, as if to invite his tongue to dip down and lick it.

Without any warning, Nutmeg starts scalpelling herself, with her own smiling consent to the process—and inside a moment, a full operation is in progress, performed by Nutmeg using a single deft hand. "*When I'm with you alone, late tonight,*" she grates sweetly at Scorpio, "*I'll let you see me rip my face off, leaving just a slab of flesh—*"

A shot of pain flickers up in Jaymi, from groin to heart (the Scorpio places). Crying out, he springs at his keyboard and starts hammering out multiple batch-reversion commands, until he has reversed Kelly's work, returned his Beast's visual world to what it should be, then sealed off the cockroach-hole Kelly wriggled in through. Sinking back into his seat, he spits through the open bow window.

98 JAYMI CREATES SCORPIO'S SOUNDTRACK

Jaymi rises from his seat, paces up and down like a caged beast, then sits back down at the window. Onward and deeper into Scorpio!

He gazes down at that ring of hairy-trunked palms around the clearing on his left, where his Beast's dancing feet can almost be heard twirling through the scratchy grass, behind the warmth of the breeze up the canyon.

What would be the soundtrack that could live up to this Beast's aforementioned visuals—namely the delicate Scorpionic beauty, sleek depraved face, sulky mouth and luscious darkness of obsession that Jaymi has established in him? What sound would most help the Dreary Ones to hear their own dreariness, through starkest comparison with him?

The answer to this question is a soundtrack sung not in Scorpio's own lisping-snake voice, but in a flat seductive female one—a voice whose sultriness is so dry, whose unimpressibility so effortless, and whose underground presence so privileged in access and enigmatic in aura, as to add up to an icon of quite unreachable cool.

This unnamed vocalist radiates a majesty of downbeat ecstasy, carrying the torch of the whole city's underground, burning with her own laconic magic for a single moment, right here … and then she fades, forever.

Synth-pop morphs into gothic, and a gloomy glamour slides up and flowers in the knowledge there is something alluring in Death, with his princely mien, scythe and spooky fashion sense. Heralding his imminence, clumps of staghorn fungus push their yellow fingers up between the flagstones of the terrace under Jaymi's bow window. Around the kidney-shaped pool on the terrace, kidneys sprout up, ringed by monster-blooms of red rafflesia, the rotting-flesh-scented parasitic meat flower.

The music grows creepier, to keep up with the vegetation. Horror, fat and hungry through the wall of the room, peers in at Jaymi Peek, its sharp little eyes like pinheads.

Peering forward and down, he sees the space on the terrace appears enclosed in walls that swell and breathe, yellow-lit and windowless. Steam coils up from the water in the pool, around a bundle of blood wrapped in velvet that hangs in the air, side-lit through the open glass doors from the lounge directly underneath Jaymi's chair.

In the corner of the lounge, stubble is breaking slowly through the television screen. The image on the screen is zooming in towards a pair of eyes in place of nipples, each one dripping out an icicle of blood.

A chess-board is set upon the glass coffee-table nearby, in mid-game, the chess-pieces modelled out of raw meat: the mitre on the bishop is a shrew's-nose of peering eyes. Beside the board is a contraption of severed shrews' noses; and a hundred baboons' noses fill a sack by the table-leg. Underneath the table, on the wood-effect laminate, a worm-coloured windpipe lies at an angle to a mangled corpse with babbling heart and twitching bones.

In patriotic colour scheme on the dining-table, a cheese's interior is traditionally flavoured with blue veins of mould, red arteries of chilli pepper and white bones. For dessert a bitter jelly has set, like a moat, around the base of a blood-filled sponge-cake; while inside a pineapple, kidney-like and intestinal elements are in evidence.

As an entree there's a stew of battered eyelids, in a range of bacon and citrus tints, around a pale brain-stem. All is carefully laid out beneath a hairy ceiling.

Scorpio flickers up smiling out of Jaymi's screen, takes a dainty bow and claps his hands together—whereupon the terrace and the lounge of the house snap back to their normal state, clean and fresh and cool in the star-lit night across the hillside.

99 JAYMI TEST-DRIVES SCORPIO

Motionless in his chair, Jaymi flicks his eyes to the bottom-right corner of his screen, to check the time, then glances around his bow-windowed eyry. At six o'clock Herb and Ashley will be arriving at the house on Electra Drive. He has also instructed all five incarnated Beasts to gather this evening in the guest wing there, ready to be summoned upstairs to the study as soon as Herb is ready to drop them into the new West Side environment for their mission.

But meanwhile, this final Beast's creation cycle is barrelling forward! For now it is time to test-drive Scorpio—prior to incarnating him, in all his sexy little fierceness, into the big bad world. (Oh, it's dirty work, this, but someone has to do it.)

So, out Scorpio slinks into a test-street on Jaymi's laptop, holding a saucer containing four large snails that he's just picked off a pot-plant at home, where he'd discovered them hiding in its leaves. The snails are climbing all over one another, straining their horns and necks up in all directions, hungry for scents, sights and other information about this new street environment. He turns right, seeking vegetation in which to deposit them. The saucer is now dripping with snails, and he's at an increasing loss to know what to do with it. He stands there anguished under the lamplight, while the flesh of his test-body streams with uncontrollable trickles of fresh perspiration, as it always does so infuriatingly soon after he's just showered, whatever the temperature may be—and what the fuck is he going to do with this snail-dripping saucer? He can't leave it on the pavement, because the snails would slither away and get stepped on...

While he dithers, he's approached by a young man who has been lurking nearby in the manner of a street dealer. "Hey girl, you alright?" he says, peering at Scorpio and the saucer of frisking snails, while continuing to keep a wily eye around him. Could it be a subtle come-on? wonders Scorpio. The man is in his late twenties, perhaps Bangladeshi, and swaggeringly attractive—but Scorpio is still distracted by his snail mission, so makes some indistinct reply, then carries on up the pavement, half-glancing behind him from time to time, half-hoping to be grabbed by the waist and swept away into the shadows, but the man is not following him.

At last he finds a tree with some undergrowth around it. As soon as he's tucked the saucer beneath the leaves, however, he glances around what has clearly become a night-time street full of death, for he can now see evil approaching down the block: a three-wheeled coffin rolls towards him, with vultures on top of it and egg-shaped wheels. On posts around the coffin, small clear plastic bags are nailed, with a fruit-bat in each close-fitting bag, unharmed but wriggling. He shivers, to see that within the open coffin is a supine figure, unmoving until the vehicle draws level, whereupon the figure tilts its head up and its eyes flash red. It extends a hand that's shuffling a tarot-pack, where grotesque clown-faces push out of the blur and whirr of cards, to bite up into the air and snap at Scorpio.

He jumps as a shadowy ambulance streaks past, hissing off ahead towards a hill that's topped by a grand Ferris wheel sprouting spikes around its circumference. Beneath the wheel stands a giant hand made of shadow, menacing; its fingers are curled down except for the middle one, which beckons at Scorpio. Tall figures flank the hand, bending their will at him in silence, to trap him. He feels his feet drawn in their direction … then sets off at a run, to hide. A woman's head peers down from an attic casement at the end of a row of terraced houses on this block, which rear up in giddy shapes with a kind of fish-eye lens effect, so the casement and her head start out at him in shocking prominence. The night-sky is yellow, the houses red and the gardens an ill green. Around the side of the woman's house, fearful faces peer out of windows into a dim courtyard where drips fall through spotlit steam. The face of Mr Punch pokes through a window crack, and something scuttles in the shadows at the courtyard's far end.

He slips through a door into a hallway, to find Punch now sitting inside a windowed box, eyeing Scorpio sharply. Blood is spilling through the ceiling, in quantities that increase in tandem with the anguish arising in Scorpio at his own fear of light-bulbs falling out. "Why is there blood pouring through the ceiling?" he asks the figure in the box.

"Nothing to do with me," squawks Punch, "because I live at an eighty-degree angle!" and convulses in manic laughter.

On the staircase ahead, one rabbit is stroking a second rabbit, with paw-movements that are fully as knowing as those of a human hand. Above them is a girl of about ten, who shrieks in fear and horror at Scorpio's approach. He freezes, not knowing whether to turn tail, to stay still, to dash past her as fast as possible, or (perhaps the least promising option) to "act natural" and try sneaking past her unnoticed. Yet before he can stop himself, he has chosen none of these but instead rushes straight at her, contorting his face so as to cause maximum revulsion between them both, leaping up, up, and over her head, with sudden superhuman buoyancy, leaving her crying far beneath.

—Streaming sweat and shuddering, he lands, as if into a new state of knowing. He is startled to spot Jaymi applauding, up in the world above the laptop screen. "Congratulations, my little Scorpio, you can handle anything," Jaymi enthuses. "And oh boy, *you are ready for your incarnation!*"

Scorpio blinks in confusion, then smoulders ironically up at his creator, and then looks apprehensive. "If you say so," he replies. "I hope this incarnation business is all it's cracked up to be."

"Yours in particular will be exhaustingly electrified," says Jaymi, "but exhilarating as fuck, so buckle up."

100 JAYMI INSTRUCTS THE BEASTS FOR THE REPURPOSING

At six o'clock, soon after Jaymi's two ex-colleagues have finished work, their cars sweep back through the front gates of the house on Electra Drive.

Armed with a Campari and tonic apiece, they settle into the palatial study, where Jaymi bids Herb take the hot-seat before the central monitor. Herb sits and looks with approval at the span of gleaming IT hardware, which is arrayed in a small symphony that echoes the rise and fall of the array of Downtown skyscrapers sitting central in the panorama of L.A. through the windows ahead.

He taps at a few keys, then pushes his glasses up his nose as he reads aloud from the Web: "'The El Segundo refinery occupies a thousand acres, and has twenty-six miles of paved roads, ten miles of railroad tracks and over eleven hundred miles of pipelines.' Big-ass refinery, huh? I see acres of cylindrical tanks there, which it'll be easy enough to reproduce, modelled on a 3D map."

"Does the text refer to the tanks?" asks Jaymi.

Herb flicks his cursor around. "Yes, here's something: 'One hundred and fifty major storage tanks are greater than thirty feet in diameter; and the largest tank has a diameter of two hundred and sixty feet and a height of sixty-four feet.'"

"D'you think there are enough tanks for our different categories of glyphs and pixels to find a home each?"

Herb chuckles. "Yes I do. Three of those real fat-ass tanks will be big enough for the red and green and blue. Then after the RGB is stowed, we'll need quite a few more tanks for all the other items, but there are plenty of dinky little tanks that'll be enough for those."

And so they're off, as Herb takes the reins of the system's full horsepower and gallops his companions forward under Jaymi's direction.

3D maps and many other apps are fired up, numerous parameters are set, and a deluge of automated world-building is unleashed. Such progress is made, all told, that by dinner-time the three of them have created the entire framework for an uncannily sophisticated simulacrum of the West Side: from the refinery, through El Segundo, to LAX and the hidden server farm beside it.

A catered dinner appears at the study door for them. They chow down on it with enthusiasm, while planning how the artwork for this new oceanside landscape can best be made to convey the requisite dirty-cool, stripped-clean flavour, at once retro and futuristic in allure.

After dinner, a further protracted bout of labour results in this artwork being applied across the whole framework.

The first of several pots of coffee is served, which they sip while planning the effects that'll need to be applied to the artwork.

A further intense bout of coordinated labour sees those effects applied.

Another pot is served, as they all conduct spot-checks throughout the landscape they've created. While Herb and Ashley keep testing scattered locations, Jaymi takes over the hot-seat and conducts a detailed inspection of LAX in particular, to ensure it is ready for the Platinum Raven's mission there. He has still to decide the nature of her mission; but he is excited to verify that those retro-futuristic airport stylings are all in place and will live up to whatever agenda she may bring to them.

A third pot is served. Herb and Ashley continue testing and tweaking all over the West Side, while Jaymi conducts another detailed inspection—this time of the refinery, to ensure it is ready for Amber's mission there. The nature of this mission is also undecided, as yet; but with relief he can confirm those refinery visuals have the necessary gleam of steam-wreathed pipes, the requisite squeak of lights and flame against the night sky, and enough all-around metallic charisma, to live up to whatever Amber may bring to them likewise.

And so it goes, with much further beavering by the trio, until late. "And now for the highlight of the night," Jaymi tells his companions. "It is time for the summoning and instruction of the Beasts!" He picks up a remote control and uses it to dim the lights on the ceiling. "I ordered them all to gather tonight, downstairs in the guest wing. Stay here, you two, while I go and fetch them up here." He pauses at the study door. "I'm aware that you haven't seen them all together before, but don't be alarmed, you won't be hurt."

"Well, since you put it like that, now I'm terrified!" jokes Herb, with an undercurrent of alarm.

"You mean they're all going to join us in this room?" says Ashley. "Well! OK then. I mean, I've met them individually. But if they're all here together in the flesh, then they're not going to exact some ghastly revenge on us, are they, for all our … you know?"

"No, they won't do that," says Jaymi. "As long as you both behave yourselves, of course! But no, really, trust me, they're under my command—so just chill. I'll be right back." And with that, he steps out of the study, trots down through the house and raps on the guest wing door.

A few minutes later, six pairs of footsteps can be heard ascending the stairs from the ground floor. Re-entering, Jaymi sees Herb and Ashley have risen from their seats and are standing with a studied and moderately convincing ease that's belied only by their being bunched up together against the wall in a distant corner of the room.

"Do come over and join us," Jaymi calls out to the pair of them, as Amber, Evelyn, Shigem, Kim and the Platinum Raven all enter behind him. The two Bang Dead employees emerge from the corner and shuffle nearer, beaming. Jaymi goes and stands between the pair of them, to provide reassurance to them both. Then he turns his attention to his own creations: five human-seeming creatures, arrayed in their fleshly beauty, facing three humans.

Suppressing the hint of a smile as he glances sidelong at his ex-colleagues, Jaymi can see that in both of them there is greatest alarm at Amber in particular. He is, after all, the Beast who climbed into Herb's home like a giant blond spider and left that unnerving brain-and-knife combination on Herb's keyboard. And he is, after all, the Beast who accessed Ashley's roof garden, spoke at her in a way no one else has ever spoken, then somehow entered her home and squodged that shiversome and dismaying meat around her childhood photograph...

For her part, the Platinum Raven aims an imperious platinum stare at Herb, whose guilty squirm is doubtless in recollection of when he hacked her new-born code on that flat road by the railroad tracks in the Rust Belt heartland of America. His gaze slips away to Evelyn, Shigem and Kim, but there is little escape for him there, as all three fix him with stares suggesting their own vivid memories of his hacking the new-born code of each of them.

The Platinum Raven turns her accusatory look upon Ashley, whose evident embarrassment no doubt derives from her memory of joining Dud in attacking this platinum Beast with napalm that burned into her neck and spread around her shape, up in the Blue Jay Way house. Ashley's gaze flicks away to Evelyn, Shigem and Kim—but there is little escape for her there, as all three target her right back with stares suggesting their own clear memories of her joining with Dud to attack each of them.

"OK then, down to business," murmurs Jaymi with a menacing calm, almost as if he may be about to lash out. The five Beasts release

Herb and Ashley from their chilly reckoning, and turn obediently to their creator. "Evelyn, Shigem, Kim—listen to me. You three already have experience exploring the game-world of *Ain'tTheyFreaky!*: you landed in the Downtown L.A. environment within it. Those seedy streets were a good training-ground for your upcoming mission, which will be the real deal. No doubt you'll be pleased to know that a similarly retro-looking environment has been created, representing the West Side of L.A. Tomorrow, once we've put the finishing touches to the West Side, we'll be dropping you five into it. Amber, Platinum Raven—I'm aware this'll be throwing you two in at the deep end, but that's life. Now, once you've each returned through this monitor here and landed down in that environment in your appointed order, there is a special place where I want you all to converge. This special place is the West Side environment's representation of the real-life server farm where *Ain'tTheyFreaky!* itself is run. You'll find it beside LAX, right where it is in real life; I'll text you its coordinates, as soon as you're down there. Now, this server farm is the money-shot, OK? It's where your combined mission will occur. You'll be collaborating, but all you'll need to do is to follow the natures I've endowed you with. Discuss what you need to discuss, but then just do it—*take action—let it happen—wing it, and take flight!* Evelyn, Shigem, Kim, you've already been inside those servers, as it happens: when you entered Bang Dead's Downtown, I was hacking into them and porting you in there. Tomorrow Herb will hack into those servers again, lay down our new West Side environment in there, and then port all five of you into that environment, where you'll converge on the retro server farm, which is inside the real-life server farm. This time, we have a Russian-doll effect, you see? And this time, the five of you won't just embody my explorations, as in Downtown. This hack will be a much more focused attack on Bang Dead. This time, each of you will embody an element in my repurposing the very substance of *Ain'tTheyFreaky!*'s six Newsfeeds, which reside on those servers. Each of you will embody a part of Herb's hack, and you'll each feel the hack's code running through you like electricity… Let it happen! Dance with it, in grace, if you please, because your appointed mission is nothing more and nothing less than to turn that server farm into one big party!… But here's what you'll be doing from our point of view up here, just so you know: through the Russian-doll effect of the farm-within-the-farm, each of you will be sucking out a particular element from the Newsfeeds, as if through a wormhole. Your demarcation of labour will be as follows. First, Amber—you will be sucking out all the Newsfeeds' letter glyphs, and you'll send them barrelling up those pipes to the refinery, into twenty-six or more separate storage tanks, one tank for each different raw letter of the alphabet so salvaged. Do you copy?"

"Copy that," says Amber.

"Platinum Raven—you will be sucking out all the Newsfeeds' figure glyphs and symbol glyphs, and you'll send them barrelling up those pipes to the refinery, into a bunch of smaller storage tanks, one tank for each different raw figure or symbol so salvaged. Do you copy?

The Platinum Raven nods, and the air in the study flushes with a whirr of pink noise.

"Evelyn—you will be sucking out the red bits and bytes from all the Newsfeeds' pixels, and you'll send them barrelling up those pipes to the refinery, into a capacious refinery storage tank for all the raw red so salvaged. Do you copy?"

"Copy that," says Evelyn.

"Kim—you will be sucking out the green bits and bytes from all the Newsfeeds' pixels, and you'll send them barrelling up those pipes to the refinery, into a comparably capacious refinery storage tank for all the raw green so salvaged. Do you copy?

"Copy that," says Kim.

"And Shigem—you will be sucking out the blue bits and bytes from all the Newsfeeds' pixels, and you'll send them barrelling up those pipes to the refinery, into a similarly capacious refinery storage tank for all the raw blue so salvaged. Do you copy?"

"Copy that," says Shigem.

"Good!" pronounces Jaymi, darting his eyes from one to another of the five Beasts' faces, which reflect the glint of ambitious fire in his own.

"Well, that sounds like an unforgiving schedule, I must say," opines Shigem. "Then again, how afraid one is of being forgiven, especially in profile. I warn you, Jaymi, I'm going to be so tired after this repurposing business, I may just have to be carried off in a heap."

"All right, a little focus, please," says Jaymi, clapping his hands to regain his Beasts' attention.

"Ooh!" says Kim as a sudden thought occurs to him, and he taps Shigem on the arm: "D'you remember that club we went to in Downtown, where that wannabe girl-band was playing?"

"Yes," says Shigem. "What was their name? The Shrill Cows, was it? The Soggy Effusions? Something like that, anyway."

"Er, not sure, I forget their name," says Kim. "Anyway, do you remember the boy who was running the coat-check?"

"Hm, not really. Oh, yes I do. A snippety little thing, he was, right?"

"Yeah, some twee little queen. Anyway, the reason why I'm mentioning him is—"

"He was *so* off-his-face, on something or other," Shigem interrupts, "that he kept mixing up everyone's coats, so every single interaction with every single person in the line became this huge ridiculous drama. It was hilarious. I was just soggy with laughter. Collapsing onto the floor into a puddle of limp semen, I was. I mean, really! Oh yes, it was, er—yeah, it was pretty funny."

"Yup," says Kim, chuckling at the memory. "That's true, it wasn't exactly a Socratic dialogue."

"*Anyhoo*, yes," says Shigem. "Why did you mention him?"

Kim's smile fades away while he reflects on this question, until, several blank moments later, he replies, "I have to admit, I can't actually remember. I'm going to have to come back to you on that one."

"Well then! I'm glad we've established something, at any rate," says Evelyn dryly.

Jaymi claps his hands again. "*Please.* A little focus here. We have important work to do." His Beasts fall silent and turn back to him. "OK, so get some rest now, every one of you. Go home and sleep. You too, Herb and Ashley. Let's all convene here tomorrow evening at around half past six, for you-know-what: the repurposing of *Ain't They Freaky!*!"

101 JAYMI INCARNATES SCORPIO

Late next morning, Jaymi installs himself upstairs in the house on Zeus Drive, in one of the bedrooms not used by the Platinum Raven, and sets up his laptop. Although he conducted the entirety of Scorpio's creation cycle in the bow-windowed room on Jupiter Drive, he has decided to incarnate him here instead, for the simple reason that Amber feels like no kind of house-mate with whom any freshly-fledged Beast should have to find their feet in meat-space. Not that Amber has evinced any specific danger signs in this regard, but he is unpredictable and—well, it just feels like an obvious precaution to take, does it not?

This is the room, therefore, where half an hour later Jaymi clutches the edge of his seat in delirious exhilaration mixed with a sense of electrified solemnity, to see his final Beast slither and squeeze out into meat-space through the laptop monitor in front of him—Scorpio!

Jaymi rises, retreats into the shadows in a corner of the room and stands there watching, with a sensation of burning in his own darkness...

All the fierce beauty he could create from within him, and his very own response to Bang Dead's "Cosy Score"!

Owing to that notional childhood on the south-west margins of Belle Glade, never in fact experienced by Scorpio but incorporated recessively into his code, this Beast already has hazy intimations of what he will experience in his actual in-game childhood and adolescence on the west edge of Asbury Park, to be remembered in *The Imagination Thief*. He can already intuit that much of his growing-up there will constitute a series of struggles against those who will attack him verbally on the streets, who will want to harm him or control him—an atypical growing-up experience, from the viewpoint of most residents of that town, but destined to be his experience nonetheless.

Now that he's standing here in physical space, quivering in this newly-incarnated body for the very first time, Scorpio picks up other snippets of his future life in the two games he's cast for, as if he were a radio tuner catching fragments of sound from ahead through the ether.

Looming large among those fragments are a trio of intimations of when he'll be going by the name Angel in *The Imagination Thief*—a time when he'll be trapped in a fierce love affair with a gangster named Lucan.

The first such fragment happens to be from a moment when the latter's face looks almost gentle. This impression is a deceptive one, as it happens, being caused by nothing more than a momentary still-ness in Lucan, who is sitting lost in thought with his eyelids lowered a little. An unlit cigarette waits in his mouth, while the lighter sits in his hand, which rests on his lap. His big golden crucifix pendant lies against the ever-gleaming tautness of his chest, winking quiet in the sunlight at the movement of his breathing—while Angel's thinner silver cross winks back, lying on the curves of his own little chest over here across the room. The planes of Lucan's face, from his eyebrows and eyes, down his cheeks and nose, to his lips, are so powerful, so beautiful, so effortlessly strong! He's staring into the distance, planning or reflecting on something undiscernible; while Angel stares at Lucan, hot and hard as always, and yet quite tranquil; both lovers balanced in a still minute, sitting here…

The next foreshadowing fragment from the time of *The Imagina-tion Thief* is more representative, being a moment when Angel is filled with an anguishing mixture of insulted rage and horniness. On this occasion the rage results from an instance of Lucan's referring to little pansy faggots on the streets, as he sometimes does—forever knowing himself to be straight, despite being in such a violently sexual relationship with Angel. Yes, Lucan does have girlfriends too, such as Niquelle, every one of whom makes Angel feel insecure and jealous whenever Lucan tells him anything about her, especially when withholding sex. But there's no doubt that he himself, Angel, is Lucan's number one lover by a long chalk, much more than even Niquelle—so how enraging to hear those comments about faggots on the streets. Anyway, in all probability Lucan can't even see down the street, since his view of it must surely be blocked by his own enormous cock.

The final foreshadowing intimation that Scorpio catches from his own future as Angel in *The Imagination Thief* is a strobe-flashing montage of Lucan's descriptions of his childhood memories from Lagos, before his guardian brought him to America: in the mainland ghettos, shadowy figures on the streets, beyond pools of light shed by kerosene lanterns; figures huddled under a concrete flyover; the smell of peppered goat, fried yams and Star beer, floating across the sheer grim scale of the city; Lucan's unwavering Christian faith from as far back as he can remember (an aspect of him that will be shared with Angel, constituting an island of undiscussed harmony between them); and roads that were empty only in the depths of night, glimpsed by Lucan when his guardian's car streaked past darkened warehouses and ships ablaze with light.

But it's not just the time of *The Imagination Thief* from which Scorpio picks up flickers. He also picks them up from the two-year lacuna that will occur after the events of that game and before those of *The Platinum Raven*. His experiences during that pair of "lost" years will be alluded to in the latter game, but only in sketchy terms. One of the flickers he receives is a feeling of the anger that'll have arisen in him during those two years, as fallout from the social victimisation of his growing-up in the former game's location—painful fallout from the constant emasculation of being so relentlessly teased, every day of his childhood and teens, for having qualities of movement and voice that he could never begin to control or quite identify, however hard he tried and however much he prayed at night, and whose meaning he couldn't even understand for many years.

Throughout that two-year lacuna between games, the spines of his anger will turn inward, for the most part, in inevitably internalised self-hate. But not always: for at certain sweeter times, the contrasting sense of empowerment that he'll also find in this anger will turn him into a savage little queen with hot brains, whose fantasy will be to ride the world, battering it with a lash while he rides, and to glory in an event staged just for him, involving a grand, simultaneous beheading of numerous deserving people, all stationed in an appropriate kneeling position in concentric circles around him...

That calming fantasy will rarely fail to put an elfin smile on his face, providing a counterbalance to his propensity for light but persistent self-harming. This habit will prompt him to undergo extended periods of therapy, through which he will find the strength he requires, first to accommodate all the ongoing neuroses he knows will never leave him, and then to flourish within himself in any case, saying fuck-you to all of them. He will even come to pride himself on the beauty of his own damage. It's all his own and nobody else's, after all, so he's at liberty to do just as he pleases with it—and if he wishes to deploy his own daily emotional and psychic scars aesthetically within himself, then he damn well will.

As established in the game-play of *The Platinum Raven*, it will be through his own resources of brute determination that Scorpio will escape being a sex worker on Santa Monica Boulevard, and will propel himself upwards into much greater happiness living in Dubai with Amber and the Platinum Raven. In this escape from work that he wouldn't have chosen, he will lack any outside help, as always, so he will surely deserve congratulations on marshalling his unusual willpower.

Jaymi watches all this with a deep and growing respect, wondering where on earth Scorpio will find this willpower of his. After all, much of Scorpio's inner landscape has been mined from the fractures in his creator's make-up. And Jaymi's own fractures, as he knows from all the sporadic therapy he's had since his early teens, have left him strong-willed in many ways but surprisingly weak-willed in others, such that he just can't see himself finding the same willpower in the same situation.

Perhaps Scorpio is just lucky, then, to find himself in independent possession of such a will? (Lucky ... so does a Beast deserve less congratulation for overcoming adversities, if he turns out to have possessed the necessary equipment to overcome them? But here Jaymi shakes his head, for this question is beyond him.)

Then he has a new brain-wave. Kim and Shigem were paired up during their two creation cycles, before their shared release into incarnated form. But could Jaymi now take things to the next level with a bit of match-making between two separately-created Beasts, after they've both been incarnated at different times? How exciting to arrange for some love interest for Scorpio! That famously delicate Scorpionic beauty, sleek depraved face, sulky mouth and luscious darkness of obsession are delicious things that shouldn't go to waste, after all...

And something obvious occurs to Jaymi. As he knows, Scorpio is already destined to achieve greater happiness during *The Platinum Raven*, when he'll be living in Dubai with Amber and the Platinum Raven. Well, guess what: in that game, Scorpio and Amber are set to be a couple. So, why not give them some practice with each other ahead of time, here in the real-life world of L.A.?

Yes! If anyone has enough voltage to handle Amber, it's Scorpio. If such a dark romance can be made to flower, then aside from the pleasures that Jaymi hopes it will give both of them, maybe it'll earth some of that dangerous voltage in Amber, calm him down and make him sweeter? (It might release some of Jaymi's tension, come to that.)

OK, on the face of it, calmness and sweetness are not what spring to mind from the sketch of Scorpio-as-Angel for *The Imagination Thief*: "spiteful sleek depraved face", "decadence and damage", "obsessive", "jagged", "ambitious will-to-power" … these hardly suggest a playlist of what Shigem might call continuous relaxing favourites.

Nonetheless, there's no gainsaying the neatness and sexiness of this union.

Alright then. Once Scorpio has found his feet in incarnated form, here in the house on Zeus Drive, then Jaymi will steer him back over to the house on Jupiter Drive where his whole creation cycle was conducted, to join Amber.

"I wish I knew why some Beasts are destined to go through the wringer more than others," says Jaymi aloud, addressing Scorpio. "But you'll come through triumphant, in dignity and beauty. You're the only one in both games, apart from me."

Jaymi tails off, realising he is not being heard. For Scorpio is distracted, being gobsmacked, more than any other Beast so far, by his brand-new condition of incarnation—a condition that'll require some serious getting used to, it seems. So aware is he of this newfound buzz and flow of his own body's cells, that he wonders how he'll be able, from now on, to concentrate on thinking about anything very much beyond the lifelong sentence of his own physicality.

There's pleasure in it too, though: looking into a hand-mirror at the full-length wardrobe-mirror behind him, he delights in the stark and elegantly streamlined angel's wings tattooed across the length and width of his back. "Beautiful wings," Scorpio murmurs aloud to himself. "Stay with me forever. See what I do, through the years ahead. See what *we* do. We're on an enchanted adventure together—"

He falls silent, startled to identify the sound of his own voice, which has a degenerate breathiness underlying a fluid steel edge and a slight lisp on every *s*. This is the first time he's ever heard it out loud in the world, he realises … and straightaway feels an anguish of self-consciousness about the breathiness and the degeneracy and the steel, and his lisp, and the whole dark voltage of self-cutting gay narcissistic corrosion and jaggedness, within which he's locked up for life, it would seem, in a grand empowered prison-cell ... and then decides to love this body-prison-cell in any case, forever.

He closes his eyes, to focus his contemplation of the salient aspects of this incarnation he's been dropped into, as best he can identify them. One all-pervasive aspect, he perceives, is an erotic drive that will clearly dominate his life: the continuous urgent pressure and rush of it is so powerful as to be almost pre-orgasmic, with a clean but sultry scent of sex emanating from him, which even he himself can pick up.

Another issue for him, he realises, will be temperature. He finds himself equipped with the advance knowledge that there are varied seasons, but is uncertain how his own internal heating system will work in relation to them, sensing already that his internal temperature gauges are a little messed-up. He has an intimation he will feel permanently overheated throughout summer, no matter how few layers he wears, and permanently too cold throughout winter, no matter he how many layers he wears.

Well then, if temperature is out to get him whatever he does, he will just wear the same styling all the time—and damn well make the most of the equinoxes, when (with a bit of luck) he'll hope to be neither shivering nor sweating, for a day or two at least.

A more specific feature of his incarnation will be perspiration, it seems, which is not quite excessive but certainly constant. That's fine, he'll just shower twice a day. And wear a lot of black. (Never pastels.) At the instant he decides this, he notices the full-length snapshot that's been taped onto his wardrobe-mirror by the production crew's costume department in order to ensure continuity in his manga-like styling; and relief suffuses him, to see what it is.

Not only is he destined to wear the same kind of outfit every day, as he just decided to do by himself. In addition, his entire allotted outfit is black, as he also decided! And accessorised with tastefully simple bits of cool silver jewelry...

He flits across the room to inspect this designated costume from closer, with a fierce attentiveness; and a grin of joy and pleasure lights his face.

He swirls around the bedroom, in a twirly dance of pride.

Then he drops to his knees in prayer, raises up his hands to his creator Jaymi Peek, and lets his eyes close with a quiet seraphic smile.

102 AMBER'S MISSION IN THE EL SEGUNDO REFINERY

Bidding Scorpio take his sweet time in acclimatising to meat-space, Jaymi leaves him in the bedroom on Zeus Drive. Down in the hallway, he encounters the house's resident, the Platinum Raven. "Upstairs you will find a new fellow Beast," he tells her. "His name is Scorpio."

Her pink noise whirrs, in a cautious and provisional joy.

"I'll see you at seven this evening, down the hill at my place," he adds, opening the front door to leave. "I was hoping to tell you to bring him along then, to join the five of you in going down into the West Side. But no, he needs to stay here, for the next day or two: he's still finding his feet in meat-space, so if I sent him back through a screen this soon after his incarnation, I might disorient him altogether. I think you'll get on fine together. Soak up his darkness and infuse it with platinum! See you soon."

At seven o'clock, down the hill, Jaymi welcomes Ashley and Herb into the house on Electra Drive and ushers them upstairs. Entering the study, they see the same five Beasts they saw last night, standing or seated on various perches and surfaces around the room, observing the pair's arrival with a studied calm, all poised and silent in their respective flavours.

"Hey, guys and gals!" pipes Herb jauntily.

"OK, let's get straight down to work here," Jaymi interjects. "There'll be plenty of time for chit-chat later, and maybe a nice newsy catch-up, which I'm sure you're all looking forward to! But first: Amber's mission. Herb, take us there, if you please."

So the three humans take their respective positions in front of the requisite keyboards and monitors. Settling into the central hot-seat as if assuming control of a spacecraft, Herb gets to work, firing out a protracted torrent of commands as precise as a surgeon's incisions. Multiple kinds of graphical user interface and text editor windows full of code flicker up in succession, across all screens; then the entire West Side of L.A. unfurls across Jaymi's outsize central monitor. Adjusting many parameters of its display, Herb revolves and expands this environment, then he zooms in towards a huge industrial area within it, hurtling the viewpoint ever down, until the flatly-styled, retro-flavoured allure of its individual structures and vegetation stands out crisp in the late light of evening. At last, at the appointed moment, Amber is summoned, steps forward and clambers in through the monitor, like a giant blond spider.

On the inland side of the fenced-in corridor of Vista Del Mar Boulevard in El Segundo is the edge of a thousand-acre refinery, looking west through the night to the nearby ocean. Beyond the chain-link fence, a bank of shrubs and palms rises to a line of pale green oil-tanks, each a cylinder some fifty metres in diameter. Across the empty road, Amber's muscular body stands immobile in silhouette, looking away from the refinery across the grand expanse of a concrete field that's lined, like an industrial orchard, with tall metal forms whose cross-bars and finials are strung with a complex vegetation of wires, coils and insulator cones. To his right and beneath him the great bulk of a power station rises on this strip of land, where yellow-white lights illuminate a jet of steam between giant chimneys, with the edge of the Pacific lapping at the beach just beyond.

Amber glances up and sniffs, catching a scent of something burnt and mineral. Thick electric cables sizzle in the humid air above, slanting down across the road towards him from a pylon on the refinery bank, and splaying out to rest upon two frames built below him on the concrete field to his right and left.

He turns and cuts across the deserted road. He is at the dim midpoint between two widely-spaced street-lamps, and the chain-link fence is not too much higher than head-height; so it's the work of an agile minute for his athletic limbs to clamber over the refinery's limits and drop down onto the earth beside the pylon's base, where he springs back upright before vanishing into the shadowy shrubs.

Among the rocks half-buried at the crest of the bank, his shoe stumbles against the fossil of some small sea creature, now on dry land since the ocean-bed rose long ago: a little ammonite-spiral rock whose blood was once the sea. He looks up and onward—and there just ahead of him is a high steel fence. He stakes out its length, finding the point most shadowed by foliage and most adjacent to branches; and with that giant blond spider's metal strength of his, he powers himself up between fence and branches, and over the top.

From here on, the refinery is Amber's. Fizz-lights and gaslights dot the dark shine of a building of black steel, high upon his left.

Keeping in the shadows, he stalks along the low-lit aisles in between rows of tanks on metal fields, stepping over rails and under pipes—a sensuous embodiment of Jaymi's exploration of this brand-new West Side.

The figure of a security guard in the distance stops and stares, down an alleyway of girders. The man calls out, blows a whistle—sets off at a run, coming closer.

Amber ducks from view, jumps up to grab a girder, swings his weight around and upwards, and lands upon a walkway. The man passes underneath, glancing all around, but fails to look above him. Treading softly, Amber runs along this raised level for several hundred metres. He curves up around a chimney base, via a spiral stairway, then curves down again. In the middle distance ahead, he can see the refinery complex's northern edge. He climbs back down from the walkway down a ladder to the ground and sprints towards that boundary, and through a car-park and a gate to the outside world.

Glancing back up at those metal towers behind him, as he trots across the quiet of El Segundo Boulevard and turns into Arena Street, he hears the air-horns of the refinery's alarm system strike up with a long blare and then a short one, four times in succession. Each of the five high flare-stacks emits a roaring tongue of flame at the same time, licking and swaying sky-high into the night, before dying back down into a roil of ultramarine heat-haze around a tiny pilot-light: the first flare-stack's flame is black and blue; the second's flame is mauve and platinum; the third's flame is brown and green; the fourth's flame is apricot and blue; and the fifth's flame is black-currant and black.

Hearing the bleep of an incoming text, he checks his mobile phone. It's Jaymi, sending the coordinates of the server farm! Amber had almost forgotten why he is really here…

OK then. He's done with being a sensuous embodiment of his maker's unfocused explorations around this new West Side land-scape. Jaymi's heart was never quite in this refinery mission despite his best intentions for it, as Amber now perceives. It is time to graduate into being a more bloodlessly precise weapon, thank you. It is time for his real mission.

He zigzags on foot through the quiet streets of El Segundo, locates his car at Grand Avenue and Main Street, fires it up, cruises north to Imperial Highway and hangs a left along the southern edge of LAX. Swinging right onto the desolate width of Pershing Drive, up the western fringe of the airport, he whistles a tune in quarter-tones.

Ahead on the left is that discreet side-turning into Sandpiper Street, where Ashley pulled up in her car while he was tailing her. The security gates that blocked the turning then, which she must have had to unlock, now stand open. Amber turns through the gap in the median of Pershing, then into Sandpiper itself.

Just beyond the top of the slope, invisible from the road down behind him, stands an anonymous, newly-built structure no bigger than a garden shed, on an otherwise featureless stretch of ground. He gets out and locks his car. He approaches the structure and pushes at its door. Unlocked, the door swings inward, revealing a small empty lobby with no signage. He enters and looks around this blank space, where there is little other than a pair of lift doors beside which is a single button bearing a downward-pointing arrow.

103 THE PLATINUM RAVEN'S MISSION ON AVION DRIVE, LAX

At some point during Amber's presence within the footprint of the refinery, Herb opens a new window over the West Side, through which he zooms in towards LAX, hurtling the viewpoint ever down, until the flatly-styled, retro-flavoured allure of its individual runways, terminals and aircraft stands out crisp in the young night. At the appointed moment, the Platinum Raven is summoned forward across Jaymi's study in the house on Electra Drive, swivels up across the desk and swings in through the monitor, just as Amber did.

Moments later, she is standing alone in a windowed angle, halfway down a long, rubber-floored walkway between terminals.

Her mission has as much half-planned ambiguity as Amber's had, but this time Jaymi understands better why he has felt such aversion to the idea of prescribing either of their missions: in both cases, his instinctive hope has been that this unscripted ambiguity will enable his Beasts' identities to flower more than they could if he told them what to do by issuing some creative diktat.

So, how will she act now, left to her own devices? Well, the first thing her nature leads her to do is infiltrate various areas of LAX that are forbidden to the public. Key to the success of these infiltrations is her spotting an airport staff uniform lying spare behind a counter, followed by her boldness in picking it up and donning it as a disguise that'll enable her to move behind the scenes with impunity. Thus garbed, she stalks unchallenged through the corridors and hangars and alleyways, and at last succeeds in finding what she's been looking for: the exact whereabouts of the inflow points where all those tons of jet fuel are pumped into the airport, every hour, from the refinery not far down the coast.

She has fantasised about diverting some of that fuel through the airport's western perimeter, across Pershing Drive and into the server farm one weekend night, so as to flood the underground facility with the fuel before lighting a single match with a gesture of imperious, platinum sass...

But now that those inflow points are right there in front of her, how will she be able to divert any fuel from them? The knowledge of how that pipeline hardware works, *and* the luck in being able to put that knowledge into practice before being interrupted by some busybody: it's rare enough to find just one of those two things in anyone, let alone to find them both together in someone. And she, alas, happens not to be one of the few people with either or both. So her plan to flood the facility is blocked.

—Hold on. Why would Jaymi have equipped her with an intention to take a particular action, but not with the ability to fulfil the intention? she wonders. Was he being perverse there, or just incompetent?

In reflecting so, the Platinum Raven is halfway to intuiting the truth of her status in this LAX scene—but before she can proceed to the second half of that little journey, an airport chase occurs with fitting drama, just as happened to Amber in the refinery. In this case, her hesitant manner and non-engineer's attire arouse the suspicions of a genuine LAX fuel engineer who challenges her, then pursues her when she runs away. Escaping through a freight-loading platform, she emerges on the flat concrete of a deserted loading-bay at the furthest southern cul-de-sac of Avion Drive. A plane taxies past, startlingly close on the other side of the chain-link fence beside her.

She sets off away from it at a run, turning to see that the engineer has spotted her and is in pursuit again. She picks up speed, winding around the rest of Avion, to Century Boulevard and along World Way to where her car is parked on Sky Way. Aware she is still being followed, she makes a quick decision to climb into hiding in the boot of her car—and this she does, taking care to position her foot so as to stop the door from snicking down into the latch and imprisoning her.

Phew! She lies there in the dark, breathing hard. So far, so good.

Running footsteps pass close by the car, two or three times over the next ten minutes, then do not return.

Further minutes pass. Hmm ... how long, she wonders, should she remain in this somewhat undignified position?

At last, after half an hour or so, she decides it is safe to emerge. She extricates herself, first from her airport staff jacket, then gingerly from the boot of the car, casting discreet glances around the car park.

No engineer in sight.

At the bleep of an incoming text, she checks her mobile phone. It's Jaymi, sending her the coordinates of the server farm! She'd almost forgotten why she is really here...

And with this memory comes the further understanding that she is way too transcendent a Beast to be wasted on standard chase scenes through meat-space—and ersatz meat-space, at that. Such staple devices are not her style at all. She was built for subtler things, surely.

OK then. She's done with acting like nothing more than a sensuous embodiment of her maker's unfocused explorations around this new West Side landscape. Jaymi's heart was never quite in this LAX mission despite his best intentions for it, as the Platinum Raven now perceives. It is time to graduate into being a more bloodlessly conceptual weapon, thank you. It is time for her real mission.

So she flits across LAX's western half, through those liminal, mineral spaces that so become her; and slips out through its perimeter, across Pershing Drive and up the lonely bare slope of Sandpiper Street.

Just beyond the top of the slope, two little El Segundo Blue Butterflies dart up out of the wild buckwheat and dance about her, one blue and one a golden-brown. She blows them a kiss.

Ahead of her is a low structure with a single closed door. She gives the door a gentle push. It swings open to reveal a small lobby, at the end of which she sees Amber standing in contemplation of the downward-pointing arrow on a button beside a pair of lift doors.

104 THE BEASTS CONVERGE ON SANDPIPER STREET

Herb opens a third window over the West Side, through which he zooms in on a wide boulevard somewhat east of LAX, hurtling the viewpoint ever down, until the flatly-styled, retro-flavoured allure of its office buildings, street-surface markings and palm trees stands out crisp. At the appointed moment, the remaining three Beasts are summoned forward across Jaymi's study, where they swing themselves up across the desk and slip in through the monitor, one by one.

Shimmering into focus together, Shigem and Kim and Evelyn find themselves stepping up from the kerb of West Century Boulevard, into a bus whose destination is lit up in three letters: "LAX".

Moving down the aisle, Shigem sees the only available seat is next to a surly old man, whose bag is half-occupying the seat. "May I?" Shigem asks, indicating the bag.

The old man moves the bag off, after a second. Shigem nods thanks and sits down, emitting a sigh of fatigue as he does so, since it happens he's been on his feet for quite a while today.

The man mumbles something not quite audible.

"I'm sorry?" Shigem asks, inclining his head towards him.

The old man growls in reply, as he repeats himself: "Is there going to be a lot of sighing?"

Shigem looks at him for a few moments, then realises he must be referring to Shigem's sigh of fatigue upon sitting down just now. The evident assumption, that this sigh was caused by the man's slowness in moving his bag, is so silly that Shigem just speaks aloud his own reflex, "Oh *please*…"

Like a shot, the man rasps back *"Lady—cool it."*

Shigem's mouth falls open. How even more ridiculously silly!… It's clear, however, that the situation is quite unsalvageable already, after no more than a couple of exchanges each.

Reflecting on this unsalvageability, Shigem is bored, irritated and amused in such equal measures that he finds his urge to express each of these three emotions is precisely cancelled out. The only thing to do is to whip out a book from his shoulder-bag and stare into it with a furious cool—which he proceeds to do.

So little is he focusing on the book's pages, however (what with all this ridiculousness, not to mention the flustered indignation beneath his furious cool), that several more seconds elapse before it occurs to Shigem that he should perhaps check whether he is holding the book the right way up ... but too late, alas: "You may want to hold the book the right way up," growls the man dryly.

"Oh, that *does* it," says Shigem, standing up again. "I didn't want to sit down anyway."

"Great, I'll take your seat," says Kim, and sits in his place. "Thanks for warming it up."

Hearing a trio of incoming text bleeps, the three of them check their mobile phones. It's Jaymi, sending them the coordinates of the server farm! It is time for their mission...

"Hold on," says Evelyn, "these coordinates are in the middle of nowhere, beyond the far end of the airport, and this bus only goes to the middle of the airport. That'll be a such a hike. Who *walks* that kind of thing?"

"Not us," says Shigem. "What does Jaymi take us for? We'll catch a cab, from where the bus terminates."

And so it is that a cab glides to a stop, half an hour later, just beyond LAX on a deserted stretch of Pershing Drive. The three of them alight.

Up Sandpiper Street they go, to the top of the bare slope, where they see a low structure. Its unlocked door reveals a small lobby, where Amber and the Platinum Raven are standing in contemplation of the downward-pointing arrow on the single button beside the lift doors.

The five Beasts all high-five. Then they step back in a line, all in character—hands on hips or by their side, or arms folded—heroes on a mission. Amber steps forward, presses the lift button, then turns to the others with his forefinger to his lips. "From now until we get downstairs into the server farm, let's stay silent," he instructs. "There may be security guards."

"Oh boy. No, in that case I think I'd better wait here," says Shigem.
"Why?" asks Evelyn.

"Because whenever I have to be silent, I get hiccups. It doesn't happen straight away, but as soon as the need for silence arrives, so do the hiccups. I feel them forming an orderly queue, until they're all bunched up in the upper part of my trunk. That's a little traumatic in itself, because I have quite a sensitive trunk, as you'd imagine—but the main danger is even worse: just when the room is dead quiet, a violent hiccup pops up, and I have to take aim and stifle it with the right timing, or else it's super-loud. OK, so *that's* all very well, so far, but then all I can do is count the seconds until the next one. And soon enough, I just know that some hiccup is gonna manage to get past me—and everyone'll turn round and stare, and I'll go all pink and have to run out of the room and find upside-down water before it happens again. Oh god, being me is such a *constant* trauma, you've no idea. So no, I'd better be brave and wait here."

"It's true," chips in Kim.

"Er, OK," says Evelyn. "Sorry, I had no idea you have to go through all that. Well ... oh, *Jesus wept*. For fuck's sake, get down there with the rest of us and stop being such a wuss."

"The pain, the anguish—the endless poetry," says Kim.

"*Shh!*" warns Amber fiercely. "*Get* it together please." The lift arrives and the doors open. "OK then—let's hit it!"

In bold-stepping unison they stride forward into the lift, halt, and swivel in formation, so as to face back towards the open lift-doors. Amber presses the down button on the wall of the lift, then stands with his feet planted wide, braced for whatever fast-moving action may be just about to happen...

The lift-doors remain immobile, for several long seconds.

Then slowly, very slowly, they slide to a close.

The lift descends, and coasts to a standstill. The doors re-open to reveal the enormity of the Bang Dead server farm in the hall ahead, thus bringing the five of them to the hilltop crest, as it were, where they're on the tipping-point before sliding down from being Beasts in a decorative landscape, into being programmed embodiments of Jaymi's repurposing the stuff of the Newsfeeds. As that forward-down-sliding takes control of their feet at the threshold of the lift, they feel Herb's code running through them like electricity, along with Jaymi's words when he prophesied this very feeling: "Let it happen! Dance with it, in grace, if you please…"

So they each take an aisle up the warehouse-sized hall, where they stalk and swagger, flaunt and prowl, along between the stacks—still able to feel the weight of their own sexy-Beast physicality on the polished concrete floor, but increasingly able to perceive the dance of billions of glyphs and pixels filling up the servers around them, where the full horror of the *Ain't They Freaky!* Newsfeeds lives enwrapped in Kelly's crude visuals, held aloft in infinitesimal galaxies of impassive ones and zeroes.

They emerge from the far ends of their chosen aisles and converge in the space beyond. "OK, gather round," says Shigem in a stage-whisper; and for want of any competing instructions, the others all obey. "Now brace yourselves for the following suggestion, because it's just a girlish whim and we don't have to do it, but wouldn't this be the ideal venue for a club night? I think this is the ideal opportunity for such a night, and I'm about to tell you why *you* should too. We're sliding into code here, as Jaymi promised. I can feel it happening—can you?" His companions nod, looking more spacey every minute. "We are about to nuke out some hardcore poison from these servers and channel it all along those artwork cyber-pipes and pipelines, into tanks of clean raw stuff. It'll be dirty work, so let's spice it up into a club night, what d'you say? OK, so it'll probably devolve into a scenario of bitchy faggy ironic limp-sassiness, but it's worth a shot. *Or* we could all just plough on miserably instead, if you prefer? Oh, I just can't decide which. You choose."

"Club night!" shouts Evelyn.

"OK, you've persuaded me," says Shigem, "I tell you, it'll be so fierce: I'll float around the club with a constant pout like a kiss, and you'll be all tarted-up like a dyed Chihuahua."

"That's not quite the look I was planning," she says, "but I'm right behind you on the club night idea."

"All right, let's go!" he announces, hugging her and Kim, then pulling the other two into their embrace.

105 THE CLUB NIGHT IN THE SERVER FARM

"So, my fellow Beasts," announces Shigem, leaning nonchalantly against a server stack. "The next hour will contain all the fabulousness of an entire jagged weekend. What's a jagged weekend, you ask? Well I'm glad you did, and I'll tell you. It's a weekend containing spurts of sociability or solitude that are intense and unrelated to one another, all juxtaposed with no time in between them, so one feels not quite in charge of one's vehicle, despite appearances and the lack of any mishap as such. OK? So one more time, as Jaymi said, feel that code inside you, like a current. *Let it flow!* Amber, music please—let's make this server farm sound like the hardest electronic dance music club there's ever been. Platinum Raven, lights please—let's give this server farm a slamming light-show. Then with music and lights, we can frame the next hour as a fantasy invoking the stylised decadence of a whole subculture that never quite was: its flamboyant postures, its eroticism, its utopia of endless nightlife and music and fashion; its extravagant choreography between ambiguous performers, mirroring the artifice of its own behind-the-scenes narratives; and those frenetically-shot and -edited segments, all intercut with fractured footage and colourised images, white-balance cards and onscreen colour-bars. Any questions?"

"I don't know if simple people would understand all that," says Kim. "I mean, of course, very simple people. Unlike Bertha."

"Who's Bertha?" asks Evelyn.

Kim pauses. "Um, I can't actually remember," he admits. "She is someone, but I forget who. Anyway, the point is that I know she's not simple."

"I'm glad we've established that," says Evelyn. "It's good to have something to hold onto."

"A little focus, please!" says Shigem. "Girls—places. So now that the code has spread in us and filled us up, it's time to get repurposing. It's time to draw all the poison out of these servers, and break it down into clean raw glyphs and pixels. So, to every Beast here—my sisters and my brother and my lover, all of you—I say *dance*, through this whole magic server-farm, in grace, if you please!"

While the Platinum Raven sets the light-show spiralling and Amber sends a bass beat booming down the aisles of the warehouse,

Kim catches sight of himself reflected on the shiny black glass of a door, and stares at it. "My god, that blond is tough and unnuanced," he says.

"Just how I like my blonds," says Shigem, coming up beside him, and staring at them both standing there in the glass. "Maybe next time I'll come back to earth as one of those fresh-faced ski-bunnies with perfect skin, who spend all their time giggling and shopping and being adorable, not to mention adora-bubble. You know the girls I mean, they just flounce around flirting and drinking and hic-cupping. That sounds so much fun."

"You have those tendencies already; you just haven't noticed. Most of all, the hiccupping."

The five Beasts separate, stalking up and down the aisles and cir-cling the stacks; and the business of the club night picks up pace...

Amber sucks out all the Newsfeeds' letter glyphs and sends them barrelling through those pipes to the refinery, into twenty-six or more separate storage tanks, one tank for each different raw letter of the alphabet so salvaged.

The Platinum Raven sucks out all the Newsfeeds' figure glyphs and symbol glyphs, and sends them barrelling through those pipes to the refinery, into twenty or thirty rather smaller storage tanks, one tank for each different raw figure or symbol so salvaged.

Evelyn sucks out the red bits and bytes from all the Newsfeeds' pixels, and sends them barrelling through those pipes to the refinery, into a capacious refinery storage tank for all the raw red so salvaged.

Kim sucks out the green bits and bytes from all the Newsfeeds' pixels, and sends them barrelling through those pipes to the refin-ery, into a capacious refinery storage tank for all the raw green so salvaged.

And Shigem sucks out the blue bits and bytes from all the News-feeds' pixels, and sends them barrelling through those pipes to the refinery, into a capacious refinery storage tank for all the raw blue so salvaged.

In an unexpected moment of calm and lucidity amid the general hurly-burly of repurposing, Shigem finds himself shimmering up beside Evelyn. "Hi Lambchop," he says.

"Hi girlfriend."

Somewhere during the course of all this craziness, she must have found a spare minute in which to restyle her hair, he observes. "So, what happened here?" he asks, indicating her coiffure.

"What d'you *mean*, 'what happened here'?" she retorts. "It's *meant* to be like this."

Shigem raises his eyebrows and emits a slow, audible exhalation of breath, shaking his head gently.

She raises her eyes to the ceiling, then tilts her head to one side and indicates Shigem's lips, which he must have found a spare minute to make up, somewhere during all this repurposing. "So is this lipstick a permanent thing, or are you just trying it out for someone else?" she asks.

Kim drifts up to join them, from somewhere. "Evelyn," says Shigem, patiently, "don't fuck with the eagles unless you've got the wingspan—and *you* don't qualify, baby." He turns to Kim: "I don't know, did that sound convincing? Don't answer that. But there is another thing about Evelyn, while we're on the subject: she *always* looks like she's preening…"

"Yeah *right*," she says. "You know, Shigem—you can just lick my fridge-handle, baby, 'cos that's the closest you're gonna get."

"Thanx, sugar."

"Luv you babes."

Shigem looks around him, tipsily authoritative. "Girls, *places*," he instructs, claps his hands and drifts off, back into the club night.

Without warning, Kelly's cursor whisks through the air above the servers, as it did when she smudged Scorpio's visuals in the club where he realised he was surrounded by people who might eat him, just before Nutmeg… The cursor swoops down, scraping pins across the flesh of all five Beasts at once, so they yelp or squeak or bellow out in shock and pain, clamping their hands to their faces in instinctive protection.

Way above them in Jaymi's study on Electra Drive, he and Herb and Ashley can see this whisking cut through space in the server farm, displayed in high resolution on his monitor. Jaymi cries out, as if five different strands of himself have been cut. He pictures Kelly, up in the Sunset Boulevard building or the Factory Place loft, pounding her keys and clicking her mouse all over her screen image of the server farm. She must have managed to break through all

Herb's defences into this West Side, and be wielding some batch command, to target all five Beasts' visuals at once.

Herb pounces at the keyboard and fires out a salvo of commands, many of them more arcane than Jaymi can understand. The whisking stops dead in the air above the server stacks, preventing any more cursor-pin-scrapes from reaching the Beasts' flesh.

Jaymi's upper lip curls in hate, sweating as much as Scorpio's and showing a flash of canines like that Beast's.

Down in the server farm, his creations lick clean the scratches on the backs of their hands, rub the blood-flecked pin-cuts on their faces, then resume their frenzy of repurposing.

Amid that frenzy, half an hour later, Evelyn surfaces again beside Shigem. "This is a bit of a random question," she says, "but I'm just curious: would you like to sleep with Amber? I mean, if you weren't with Kim already."

Shigem halts his exertions and contemplates her, his face now a particular mess from Kelly's attacks. "Well, physically yes," he replies. "When I look at him, I do go a bit melty-kneed and get a hard penis, which are reasonable clues. Though on balance, I'm going to say no—he'd unnerve me too much. But if I were still alive after the sex, then I might enjoy tying a big black rubber spider to his cock at night without waking him, so he'd discover it in the morning."

Evelyn nods thoughtfully. "Interesting. OK. Glad to know that," and drifts off again into the melee.

In due course, the repurposing of all six Newsfeeds is complete, with every glyph and pixel drawn out into an isolated stream of raw material and dispatched up the cyber-pipes and through the pipelines, to the refinery.

On dance the Beasts a little longer then, for joy, down the aisles of the server farm beyond LAX—the Platinum Raven, Evelyn, Kim, Shigem and Amber—while high above their heads, over Sandpiper Street, a cloud of El Segundo Blue Butterflies are starlit in the shrieking of the jet-planes.

Twirling in her punky spikes, Evelyn has the instinctive movements and lost-in-it-ness of the coolest girl on any club-floor, anywhere in the world; while up behind her, floating in a deadness of serious style in the strobe-lights, the Platinum Raven stares out opaquely at the lens and gives a flat, sinister wink without a smile. Incandescent pair…

106 AMBER HEADING EAST ON A MISSION TO MURDER

As the club night nears its climactic moment, it coasts at leisure up the last few metres to that summit, resting easy on the climb that's lifted it there.

The music ascends to a long crest of joy and magic, calling down the spirits to the server farm … then it falls, echoing away, down and back into the past.

The underground warehouse is plunged into darkness; the last little red and green lights go dim on the servers; and just at the instant when the dull flatness of the house-lights comes on, Herb pulls the Beasts deftly out of the West Side environment of Bang Dead's game, propelling them back up into real life. As they streak upwards, the Beasts catch a final glimpse of the server stacks standing dark and inert down the length of every aisle. Then barrelling up into the house on Electra Drive, they proceed to emerge, one by one, through Jaymi's computer monitor, and clamber out into meat-space.

On screens across the world, the six Newsfeeds constituting the bulk of *Ain't They Freaky!* all grind to a halt, within the same minute. Millions of users on every continent tap hyperlinks and refresh pages, with mounting impatience but no success; while a deluge of error messages swells around the world, like a giant tide of deadness laid on deadness.

The Beasts stand scattered around their maker's study, all on a delirious high, aglow with an aura of triumph and excitement, and panting from their exertions. Jaymi darts from one to the next, embracing them in turn, kissing each on the forehead. "*Thank you!*" he tells them all, "I love you!" Then he turns to his ex-colleagues and gives them both a hug. "And thank you too, so much."

Herb's and Ashley's mobile devices both start flashing and vibrating. A sense of comedown-to-reality returns, as the two of them identify the incoming numbers and speak almost in tandem, with an apprehensive weariness: "That's Bang Dead."

"Ah," says Jaymi. "I suppose it would be. I imagine they're wondering why their game just crashed. I think you'd both better scarper. The less you're associated with this house from now on, the better, for all our sakes."

"True. We're out of here," says Herb, gathering his things at speed.

"OK. We'll talk on the phone," says Ashley, gathering hers.

"Let yourselves out downstairs. I'll open the front gates from here."

Five minutes later, the CCTV shows the property's gates closing, after their two cars have exited and turned onto the slope of Electra Drive.

He turns to his Beasts. "So, welcome back to real life. Amber, could you remain here, I need one more thing from you. The rest of you: go home, chill out and rest, if you please. That was magic this evening!"

When the study door has closed behind Evelyn, Shigem, Kim and the Platinum Raven, Jaymi turns to face the remaining Beast, who is looking at his creator with that unnerving perceptiveness of his.

"Amber. I have one more mission for you," says Jaymi. "Kelly broke through Herb's defences, while you were down there, and cut you all, as you won't need reminding. It's late at night now, so she may not have wanted to call Dud at his home, to tell him she broke through. She may not yet have let him know—but as soon as she does, we're all in massive trouble. I'd therefore like you to drive over to Factory Place, gain access to Kelly and terminate her with the very minimum of pain, please. D'you understand?"

Amber considers this, then nods. "Yes."

"Thank you," says Jaymi. "I'll be watching."

Amber gives a calm salute, then leaves the study.

Once the CCTV app has shown the front gates closing after Amber's departing car, Jaymi glances around the room where he now sits alone at his desk chair, closes his eyes, and contemplates his Beast's eastward progress down the freeway.

It'll be a rendezvous from which Kelly is unlikely to come out well. And for a moment, the ghost of that old question hovers: has he been despotic, in acting as he has towards Bang Dead Games and the Dreary Ones?...

No. He has not, because in emanating *Ain't They Freaky!*, Bang Dead's despotism has been much worse. That game kills, in greater number, albeit indirectly; and it will always kill. If left alone, it would never change: such is its nature, and such is the power it derives from its obscene spread.

He directs his attention to pick up where Amber's car has got to, and finds it approaching the northern fringes of Downtown.

As the time ticks away in deadly silence on his screen, he returns to contemplation of what he's doing here. Should he allow his own creation, this dangerous but controllable Beast, to go ahead to that loft and hunt Kelly down? For unless Jaymi takes proactive steps to intervene, Amber *will* now kill her. He's a Beast whose very code was designed to comply with Jaymi's specific instructions to target Dud and the other Dreary Ones. That's just one of the things Amber is equipped to do if commanded to. Like a weapon.

But how can Jaymi ignore the fact that Kelly is another human being, with all that's implied by this status? She's another vortex of consciousness, like Jaymi himself. He shouldn't let her be killed. He knows it would be wrong, in some ways.

Not to mention, Jaymi himself may be discovered to have caused her death. If so, he may be punished hard for it, very likely being found guilty of manslaughter at least. Allowing Amber to kill Kelly may end up landing Jaymi in prison, turning him into some kind of outlaw from society. This would change his life, and not for the better. It would also shut him rudely away from those grand missions of his to leave the world just a teeny tad lovelier, for all its denizens, than it used to be.

But as he contemplates again what *Ain't They Freaky!* does to the world—the destructive and uglifying effects it has and will have on millions globally, and how those people will be influenced to treat one another as a direct result of *Ain't They Freaky!*—he remembers another truth. An equal truth, strong enough to face off countervailing truths such as the aforementioned, and smack those down: that this is a genuine war, in effect.

Owing to her work, Kelly is a general in this war.

As such, she damages and kills, is clearly happy to do so, and appears most unlikely ever to change in these respects.

She's altogether beastlier than Amber is.

So yes: when she is contemplated through clear eyes, it's plain she does deserve to die.

Jaymi's actions have been nothing but legitimate war.

He's glad he has thought this through.

The upshot, at this moment: he will take no action. He will not deflect Amber from his mission. He will leave Amber free to continue it.

He directs his attention to Amber's car again, and finds it on the fringes of Skid Row, on East Fourth Street between Alameda and Central, nearing Factory Place.

The Beast has almost reached her.

He rests his head in his hands, as a new question arises. Why did he not instruct Amber to visit the Blue Jay Way house, instead of the Factory Place loft? Sure, Kelly did need to be prevented from apprising Dud of her breaking through into the club night. Still, Jaymi can't help feeling he was somehow stalling here, in sending Amber towards Dud's employee, rather than towards the ultimate quarry, which is surely Dud himself?

And a further brand-new question pops up: is Jaymi stalling, furthermore, in targeting her through the agency of a Beast?…

He retreats away from this reflection, and bends his attention back eastwards in earnest.

107 VICTORY AND DISASTER (*SECOND DOORWAY OF NO RETURN*)

Amber parks halfway down Factory Place. He licks again at the scratches on the backs of his hands, from Kelly's cursor in the server farm, and glances in the rear-view mirror at the blood-flecked pin-cuts across his face. He pulls a pair of leather gloves on, gets out of the car and locks the doors. The last time he visited here was in the company of a severed pig's head. This time he's alone.

Up in the house on Electra Drive, Jaymi closes his eyes. He pictures Amber accessing the interior of the Factory Place building, somehow, through a combination of uncanny strength, unbeatable willpower, cunning and patience. The details of how those four elements come together on this occasion are a matter of straightforward execution, of little theoretical interest: they come together.

Jaymi leaves his eyes closed, supporting his head in his hands, while his eyes burn on behind his eyelids. How heavy his head feels, charged up by the unique, irreversible journey he has taken to get to this moment, and weighted with this power he's accreted around him like layers of a magnetic field...

He pictures Amber accessing Kelly's loft, with that giant blond spider's metal strength—unpreventable by her.

He pictures Amber stalking through her hallway.

He pictures him turning into her living room, then seeing her there in front of him on the sofa.

He pictures her looking up, seeing Amber, and rising to her feet in terror. As she recognises him, her terror grows. She knows what he's empowered with.

Amber springs forward at Kelly. He pins her down on the sofa, immobilises her and claps a hand over her screaming mouth: beauty caught by the Beast.

How his darkness has grown, beneath that blond hair and behind his eyes! Seeing into those eyes while he holds her down here at arm's length, she is electrified by the extent to which the darkness in them has a "forbidden" quality within it, of an existential flavour rich with sociopathy, body-horror, madness.

For Amber by contrast, her eyes are hard and empty with the things this whole loft is flavoured by: her entrapment in the world of the "Trivia Score: Wacky or Boring?" Newsfeed and its four siblings, the brainless questions that consequently fill her mind, her cosy infantile laughter, her contentment to spend her life creating *Ain'tTheyFreaky!*, and her unthinking pleasure in spreading this game around the world.

"You're a goner now," he murmurs, almost soothing in his manner. "You know that, yes? You've bitten off more than you can chew. You know you're going to lose and bleed... Let's wait and see what will happen in a minute's time, shall we?"

She flails; he contains this. He tilts his head, solicitous. "Oh, Kelly. If only you'd approached things as Herb and Ashley have approached them—going over to Jaymi's side (oh but yes, they have done that!)—then *how* many times fewer problems would have been caused. Ah well. Time to slide lazily away now. Next, watch me kill you, including all that stuff inside your head. Yes! Here it comes, Kelly, so enjoy the rush..."

Keeping one big hand over her mouth to stop her shouting, he throttles her with the other one, easy and calm.

She chokes. She cannot breathe. The same sort of white specks and flecks swim through her vision as Shigem always sees whenever he faints. For Kelly, however, since actual asphyxiation is upon her, these swimming shreds go on to proliferate and thicken and harden, as in speeded-up aerial footage of the spreading of shanty-town slum-roofs up a peninsula on the edge of a city.

As death stoops down towards her, she sees herself as a princess being executed in a Middle Eastern country. As a last indulgence, she is allowed to be carried along in a royal sedan-chair, which turns out to be the mode of execution itself: the chair is lifted to the level of a high balcony, where it becomes air-tight and fills up with red wine (through which she smokes, as if sitting in her own bong), until she is quite submerged, beginning only at the last moment to flounder—

Kelly slumps, lifeless.

Amber feels her neck for a pulse, and verifies there's none.

Then he looks calmly upwards, at an angle, through the air of the loft ... straight into the eyes of Jaymi Peek. And with that mild smile of humorous intelligence playing beneath his features, Amber salutes his creator.

Jaymi wrenches his attention out of Amber. He launches himself up from his desk chair, as if fleeing that mild smile and salute. He crosses the room to the sofa and flops down onto it, breathing hard.

Kelly is dead!

...So be it.

Lying there with his eyes closed, he realises how exhausted he is. So extraordinary have the last couple of days been, he has lost track of when he last slept. He must get back to Amber in a minute; but just for now, just for a moment, he needs to rest his mind...

And of course he falls asleep.

So precipitously does he fall asleep, he is unaware of the dramatic events that next unfold in the Factory Place loft. He almost latches onto those events, while falling past them into unconsciousness, but they sound so much like a distant puppet-show occurring beyond the thickness of several apartment walls, that his attention cannot quite grab onto them.

The first event Jaymi misses is a loud buzz at the front door of Kelly's loft. Amber lets go of her, moves on cat-feet to the front door and peers through the spyhole.

Two cops are in the corridor outside!

Their stance suggests they are poised to draw their weapons if necessary. Amber freezes, as it clicks into place in his head: at some moment after Kelly saw him, she must have managed to trigger an emergency call to the police, using some hidden device that was within her reach on the sofa.

He remains dead quiet, in calculated thought—until he knocks his shoe into something on the floor of the dim hallway, in a rare show of clumsiness, causing a thump and a clatter as something falls over. He swoops his face back to the spyhole. And sure enough, the cops have drawn their weapons and are hollering for him to open the door.

He makes no reply, stepping smartly back up the hall to the sitting-room.

The cops open fire. The door lock smashes. They kick the door in and barrel down the hall, their weapons trained on him.

Retreating into the middle of the room, he glances at the dead Kelly and raises both his arms in surrender.

He offers the cops no resistance when they grab him, handcuff him, escort him downstairs and bundle him into a police car outside on Factory Place.

PART VI

THE JAYMI BEAST'S CREATION, BATTLE AND TRANSCENDENCE

108 DUD'S BAD MORNING

From the moment Dud woke up today, he's had a bad morning. First, the LAPD called him at home, just after his alarm clock had gone off, to inform him his employee Kelly Kandy was murdered by an intruder in her home, late last night. The murderer was captured at the crime scene by two cops, who radio'd the station that they'd arrested him. It seems the perpetrator must have proceeded to over-power them and take control of the cop car, however, because their portable radios and the car radio were tracked down to a deserted Skid Row alleyway, while the car and the cops themselves were gone and haven't been located yet. Regarding the criminal's appearance, the only information the cops had given the station was that he was a white male. As for Kelly's death, it looked like a clean, efficient, high-speed throttling, assassination style.

What bastard could have done that? Poor Kelly. She was a beauty. And Dud never even got chance to have his way with her. He'll have to find a replacement for her now.

Then, as if that wasn't enough, the whole of *Ain't They Freaky!* ground to a mysterious halt last night, as Dud was informed by numerous frantic sources on his way into work. All those thousands of content uploads and scores from players around the world have seemingly vanished from the servers at the LAX server farm. Just wiped away, by some massive glitch. And there wasn't yet any back-up system for those uploads and scores, either, so they're gone forever. Of course there are back-ups of the game's own software itself, so the Newsfeed templates can be reinstalled and reactivated. But until they are, those six domains are sitting blank and idle, while Dud's most valuable advertisers have been contacting Bang Dead all morning to cancel lucrative purchase orders. He'll be slave-driving Ashley around the clock, to work out what kind of attack it was. Then as soon as he's had time to find a replacement for her, she will be sacked.

He groans aloud. All this stress is giving him a headache. Then a thought occurs to him. Could Jaymi be somewhere behind this murder?... If those two cops are found alive, and if they say the killer was tall and well-built and blond and maybe a bit like Rutger Hauer in *The Hitcher*, then Dud will know exactly who it was, having met that very man more than once. In which case, Dud wouldn't hesitate to notify the police, with a view to putting Jaymi in prison for murder, industrial espionage and no doubt other charges.

There's a difficulty, however. To get Jaymi into trouble, Dud would have to point the police towards Amber in one of the advance publicity images for *The Platinum Raven*, so as to identify who created Kelly's murderer. But as yet, neither the police nor the public has any idea that Amber and the other Beasts are capable of breaking out from the confines of Jaymi's games into meat-space—no idea that Jaymi has succeeded in progressing technically so far down that avenue. As soon as they discover this, Jaymi will be the toast of the games industry; and Dud has no wish to trigger such admiration. On the other hand, if people are allowed to continue believing Amber is just an invented character in a story, then Dud can hardly claim that a fictional man killed a real human woman, or he'd soon lose all credibility himself.

He groans aloud again. This is truly a long morning.

109 POLICE ROMANCE AND
THE APEX PREDATOR

The moment he wakes into the morning light on his sofa in the study, Jaymi feels the flicker of a new permutation of guilt, in the question he asks himself. Has he been despotic towards Amber, in sending him after the Dreary Ones like this—first to stalk and terrorise them, then to sabotage their venture down in Westmont, and now to terminate Kelly?

The question nags at him. Wasn't the termination, in particular, a step too far? In the moment before she choked to death, Kelly was electrified by the darkness in Amber's eyes, by the forbidden quality in that darkness, by its authentic nihilism of sociopathy, body-horror and madness. Has Jaymi warped Amber, by equipping him with those things, by birthing as an enforcer destined to wreak destruction? If so, that's hardly fair on him.

Further, has allowing Amber to follow his nature pushed Jaymi himself beyond the pale of civilisation at last?

Well … yes, it has pushed him there, of course it has.

That, however, is the nature of war.

Yes, war. Jaymi was shot at, with three real bullets from a gun-drone, on his own bedroom terrace upstairs. If that didn't count as war, what on earth was it? Mere horseplay? A bit of rough-and-tumble?

No. It was clearly war. So, did the Dreary Ones expect he wouldn't retaliate? Furthermore, Jaymi is certain that not just a ton of suffering but *actual deaths* of random innocent people around the world will occur as a result of *Ain'tTheyFreaky!*'s streaming out globally. Or rather, they would have occurred, had Jaymi not sent his Beasts to repurpose the whole ghastly game—

He jumps, as his phone emits a loud *ting*. Thank goodness, it must be Amber texting him. He'll probably be wondering why Jaymi abandoned him as soon as Kelly died—not knowing, of course, that Jaymi had fallen asleep here without intending to. Oh well, not to worry too much about that. Amber's a big boy. He can always cope perfectly well without help or reassurance, for certain.

But hold on: that wasn't the audio alert that signifies an incoming text. It was the alert allotted to his home security system.

He grabs his phone, with mounting apprehensiveness.

The security app has opened, displaying the same image that has popped up on the CCTV monitor at the end of his desk.

A car has driven right up to his front gates, triggering the app's alert.

It's a police car!

Jaymi jumps up, runs to the front of the house and peers around the edge of a window on the landing. Sure enough, a black and white LAPD car. *How* could this have happened? Every common-sense practicality was set up with precision, ahead of time: Amber's use of an anonymous car with a fake number-plate; Amber's texting with an untraceable phone-card; the whole works. Jaymi isn't stupid, he brainstormed all of that stuff. So what could have gone wrong?

A uniformed cop climbs out of the driver's seat, stands up—a big dangerous specimen, for certain—and presses the button beside the gates. The buzzer sounds in the hallway downstairs, and a churning of vertiginous despair starts rushing up in Jaymi as he contemplates the ruin of his life through a murder or manslaughter conviction, if this carries on in the direction it appears to be going.

His despair spreads wider. Never has he felt so low as he does now, behind all the external drama of this moment. (Also behind the drama, buoyant alongside the despair, is a little hoot of ironic mirth at how incongruous it is for a police car to be entering his life: isn't this the kind of car that pops up in lives that are altogether different from his?)

He strides up and down his landing, at a loss to know what to do. What rage he feels, too, at his own impotence in the face of Bang Dead's massive resources, and the vast global amperage of appeal their crass Newsfeeds will always command, beside the tiny amperage of appeal that his own much higher-voltage content commands. What's been the point of his ever trying, if he's hardly even been able to dent the sheer inertia of Bang Dead's heavy armour? On top of which, it now looks as if he'll rot in prison for murder, while the Dreary Ones continue to vomit up their Newsfeeds around the world forever.

What a vicious fuck-up.

Tears starting in both eyes, he dashes back into his study, cursing in bitter incoherence. He streaks across the room to the CCTV monitor, to look at a close-up of the cop, in case the man's expression should provide any intelligence regarding how best to open communications—and scuds to a halt in utter confusion.

The cop has bent down close to the security lens beside the button outside the gates, so that his face fills this entire desktop monitor, fixing Jaymi with a piercingly perceptive fluidity of humour in a pair of wide-set eyes…

It's Amber!

Jaymi's confusion is mixed with a surge of relief, then a burst of joy. He darts a finger onto the intercom button on the app. "Are you being followed?" he asks in a low voice.

Amber gives a leisurely shake of his head. "No," he replies quietly. "After I was arrested, I pulled the radio off the dashboard and left it in Skid Row with the walkie-talkies and mobiles, before I drove here."

"*What? You were arrested?* And I slept through it! For fuck's sake…" Seeing Amber raise his finger to his lips on the screen, Jaymi speaks more softly: "OK, first of all, let's get that cop car out of sight. Come in and drive straight into the garage." He presses a command in the app, then watches the front gates and garage doors open, while Amber returns to the driver's seat.

With the gates re-closing behind him, Amber glides the vehicle ahead into a space in the triple garage, whose doors Jaymi shuts again as soon as those LAPD insignia are hidden from the potential view of any distant nosy parker across the canyons.

Entering the garage from inside the house, he sees Amber getting out of the car dressed in LAPD uniform. Jaymi is just about to speak, but stops when Amber brings his forefinger up to his lips in a forceful gesture bidding silence. In answer to Jaymi's questioning expression, Amber points towards the locked car-trunk.

Jaymi leads Amber through the internal door from the garage into the house, then through the main hallway, through the little cinema and across the sitting-room to the doors of the ground-floor terrace. He points to the uniform Amber is wearing. "Very flattering. Where's the cop who was wearing it?"

"In the trunk of the cop car, naked, beside the other cop who's still in uniform. Both alive and uninjured, but gagged, blindfolded and tied up with rope."

Jaymi grins. "Wow!" he says, and stands there a moment untangling these events in his mind. "Congratulations on extricating yourself!" Then he taps Amber's chest several times. "Apex predator…"

"I try," demurs Amber.

So, *now* what the hell to do? He's in up to his neck here, and no mistake. There's a murder scene Downtown, a stolen cop car and two kidnapped cops. This big blond Beast here is dangerous company.

"I could assassinate the two cops, to stop them giving out a physical description of me," says Amber. "Advance publicity images have been going out for *The Platinum Raven* already. Either of the cops could have recognised me from those. If so, the LAPD will have an immediate connection from the perpetrator to that game's creator, one Mr J. Peek."

Jaymi winces. "I see your logic, but … I can't have you kill them. That's just not right. Kelly was guilty as hell, but those two aren't. We need to find another way." Then he half-smiles: "In any case, even if your appearance does remind the cops of some publicity image, they'll think it was just a coincidental resemblance. I mean, what else could it be, right? These are cops—they have a practical mindset." He rests his forehead on the palm of one hand, in a manner suggesting exhaustion infused with amusement; while Amber nods slowly with narrowed eyes, as if taking a new step over some threshold of self-understanding. "Did anyone else see you?"

"No. Only Kelly."

Jaymi nods in thought. Then the hint of a breakthrough shines in his eyes. "You know, the cops won't be alone in that reaction. Nobody who worked on these games knows I have the ability to take the final step and actually incarnate you all. So no one will suspect I've done so—provided I put this incarnating business to rest for a good while. The only people who ever knew I could do it are the four Bang Dead folks: Herb and Ashley, who've come over to our side; Kelly, who won't be saying much; and…"

"And Dud," concludes Amber, fixing Jaymi's eyes with a bland, blond smile.

OK then, time for damage control. As soon as the darkness of evening has fallen, the black and white cop car noses quietly back out through the front gates of the house on Electra Drive, with Amber in the driver's seat, changed out of LAPD uniform and wearing a different pair of leather gloves from those he donned on Factory Place. A minute later, before the front gates close, Jaymi drives out in his own car and follows at a distance.

To avoid the myriad camera lenses and crowds of eyes that might witness his driving through traffic, Amber eschews Sunset Boulevard, thereby also eschewing the long ascent of Sunset Plaza Drive up which Kelly once tailed him. Instead he takes the cop car up Laurel Canyon rather than down it, so as to seep unnoticed across the Hollywood Hills along the quiet length of Lookout Mountain Avenue, then Appian Way. By this back-street route, he arrives at the very same hairpin bend where he once peered in at Kelly through her window and gave her a creepy, child-like wave using just the fingers of one hand.

Right there, just above the inaccessible highest cul de sac of Blue Jay Way beneath him, he parks beside the crash barrier at the end of the hairpin, where no nearby windows can see him. He gets out, leans back into the cop car, uncovers the two squirming, rope-bound, gagged and blindfolded bodies on the back seat, and arranges them so that the uniformed cop is sitting upright and the naked cop is curled up on his lap, with the unworn LAPD uniform on the seat beside them. Then he closes the cop car door, steps across to the passenger's seat of Jaymi's car, which has pulled up beside him, and gets in.

Jaymi's car rolls onwards around the east face of the hairpin, and gathers speed as it heads down Sunset Plaza Drive.

His phone rings. "Hallo," he answers.

"Hi, it's Ashley. I still can't get over what an amazing show that was, last night in the server farm!"

"Me neither! Plus, as you'll know better than anybody, *Ain'tTheyFreaky!* remains dead. They haven't started it back up again. Has Dud yet suspected you or Herb of any involvement in that? Or me, indeed?"

"No. He's decided incompetence on my part must have contributed to a security lapse that wiped the game away. But he doesn't realise you were involved, and Herb and I are under no suspicion of any treacherous involvement. As yet. But I'm paranoid he may start to wonder. Which is why I'm calling: I have a suggestion, to help us appear as if this week were just business-as-usual, no different from other recent weeks. I know that gossipy freelancers have informed Dud you've created Scorpio. So I imagine he wouldn't be surprised if you sent Scorpio round to visit him and me, to taunt us with your new creation, because that's exactly what you did after each of the other Beasts was released. OK, Dud may be too distracted to be thinking about that, right now—but if you don't send Scorpio to see us, then in a few weeks' time when the *Ain'tTheyFreaky!* fallout has subsided, he's quite suspicious enough to start wondering why you didn't, and whether anything significant had happened that made you forget to send Scorpio. Better if we stick with our pattern."

"Good thinking, yes."

"Shall I tell Dud that I've heard on the grapevine you're about to inflict Scorpio on the Blue Jay Way house tomorrow, let's say? I know he'll be working from home tomorrow, not in Century City, and I have a couple of meetings at his place with him, either side of lunchtime."

"Perfect! Thank you, Ashley. Brilliant thinking. Keep me updated on the timing of that. I'll be ready to send Scorpio up there whenever's best, as I did with the Platinum Raven. And when Scorpio shows up … can you try not to hurt him more than you have to for appearances' sake?"

"Of course I shall, as far as possible. OK. I'll text you tomorrow morning when I know more."

110 FEINT OF A CO-ATTACK ON SCORPIO

Late the following morning, after the promised communication with Ashley, Jaymi sits in his car on Blue Jay Way, watching Scorpio set off on foot up the hill towards Dud's home. And for a moment, he baulks a little. Ashley will be protecting this Beast as far she can, behind her façade of aggression for Dud's sake. Nonetheless, Dud's attacks will not be pleasant for this newly-incarnated Beast. It may be beneficial to toughen him up for the real world, like this—but again, isn't it perhaps a bit despotic, sending him out to do the dirty work of advancing Jaymi's own ends?

No, fuck that. Life contains much unpleasantness, yes, but that's not Jaymi's fault. There's the work of the angels to do, as it were—so let Scorpio do it!

Slanting his attention up the hill and into his Beast, therefore, Jaymi watches him being let into the house by the housekeeper, then entering the main sitting-room where the Bang Dead duo await.

Within seconds of first taking in this latest creation of Jaymi's, Ashley feels a hot complex of reactions spread through her, starting with a fearful apprehension at him, progressing to a serious admiration for him and concluding with a stab of fierce protectiveness over him. These three things she is careful to conceal from Dud. In fact, she feels a growing anger towards her colleague—for his cruel destructiveness towards the Beasts, and for his forcing her to put on this charade here.

Dud, on the other hand, is somewhat wary of this new Beast, following his unexpected first encounter with the Platinum Raven's formidable strength. Nonetheless, the essence of Dud's scrutiny is the same as it was for the others. He is beady-eyed with the mission to reproduce Jaymi's breakthrough Scorpio-creation, but repurposing him instead into an enhancement for *Ain'tTheyFreaky!*.

Yes, the ugly ambition in Dud's face is clear to Jaymi: he would like nothing better than to incorporate a dumbed-down version of Scorpio into his own tabloid product, so as to entertain customers of the "Cosy Score: Normal-Comfy or Strange-Scary?" Newsfeed, no doubt setting up Bang Dead's cartoony Scorpio as a kind of reference target for a world full of Cosy-scorers to mock and take aim at…

While Dud contemplates all this commercial potential in Jaymi's Beast, it's clear, too, that he's looking at him through the eyes and expectations of an average consumer of *Ain'tTheyFreaky!*. And as soon as Dud looks at him in this way, the main problem becomes apparent: Scorpio is just not reassuring enough, owing to both his darkness and his vulnerability.

To speak plain, as Dud so prides himself on doing, it will need a bit of straightening-out, for normal people. Just as soon as Herb's team have worked out how he was created and have found a way to reverse-engineer him, then that non-reassuringness will be the first thing to fix.

Jaymi pulls his own attention out of Dud, and returns it to Scorpio. Because of Ashley's softened presence, Scorpio's apprehension of Dud's intentions spreads through him with somewhat less of a seepage of pain than occurred in the other Beasts. Yet the prospect of being repurposed does still come at him like an assault, threatening not just to down-convert him into a form that feels cheaper, but to do violence to his own self and truth—to use his precious life for something other than he wants.

Within this prospect, just to kick things off, Scorpio watches in horror to see his own tongue extend across the width of a street, like a meaty baguette, wrap itself around a young man's neck and push its tip into his mouth. There are a couple of further tongues, too: a wagging one, hanging off a doorstep; and then a huge tongue protruding from the upper level of a packed stadium, and curving down to ground-level.

There is a wriggling sack that pursues him up a stairwell. There are disembodied hands, walking down a corridor behind him. And there's a paralysing fear that chokes and nestles on him, grained and grey as dead meat.

He buries his face in a pillow-skin ... and there beside his drowsy head lies a second pillow, made of human flesh. There it is, yes: warm, soft, downy, breathing gently.

Next there is a menagerie of animals. First there are worms, of various kinds: tiny blind worms; worms with hair; worms that mate with him in the grave; and the furry bacon-worm that shoots out of nowhere and bites his arm.

Secondly there are spiders, in diverse situations: lung-spiders; camel-spiders that scream; buying a cactus that starts to move because it's full of tarantulas; a dead pot-plant that sprouts a wriggling horror of legs; the smoking of dead spiders' legs in a joint; and waking up as a purple tarantula.

Continuing on the animal front, he veers into cuisine, with a crème-caramel in a freshly-opened plastic pot. It looks normal, but tastes as if it might wriggle. And sure enough, through the smooth surface of the crème, there twitches up a thin stiff gristly worm with teeth upon its end, champing hard at the air.

For his last animal, there is a scuttling black thing, walking upright but shaped more like a small leggy bag or a spindly little quail. It pursues another organism, before destroying this in a splatter of blood-like fluid—only to mutate into a soft grey-brown snail, whose gnarly little face comes into startling close-up, blazes its bug eyes and bares its teeth in hissing hatred and venom at Scorpio.

He dwells upon the less-than-impressive design feature whereby some pigs' tusks, if left to grow naturally, will curve back and puncture their skulls before pushing into their brains by slow degrees.

And he concludes his session with a late-night screening in a cinema, where he feels an incipient panic attack arising in him. He goes to the washroom, stares in the mirror over the basins, and would swear he can see a great evil grinning out of one side of his face and down that side of his entire body. He gets out a knife … then a man enters the washroom and comes straight to the basins in order to wash his hands. The man fails to see the knife or anything else untoward; and on the way to dry his hands, he accidentally brushes against Scorpio, on the side where the latter saw the grinning evil— and is stabbed in the heart.

Scorpio jolts awake, then sees his own hands holding a stake of wood at arm's length above the organs of his abdomen, trembling, ready at any moment to plunge it down into them—and flings the stake away in terror.

Landing back in clear reality, he finds he is lying alone on the floor of a kitchen. A drone of low conversation drifts in through the open kitchen door, from what sounds like a couple of rooms away: Dud's and Ashley's voices, too far off for Scorpio to make out what they are saying. He must still be in the Blue Jay Way house.

Near him is a back door leading outside. It's closed and probably locked, but he'd be silly not to try the handle. He hauls himself up and tries it. Unlocked!

It's unlocked because, as he cannot know, Ashley has left it unlocked for him. (Later, she will apologise to Dud for her carelessness in doing so.)

Scorpio creeps outside. An alleyway on his left leads to the end of an infinity pool with the cityscape in the distance beyond; while a path ahead leads to an open formal garden with long rectangular ponds and fountains like a miniature Versailles, bordered by low box hedges interspersed with a topiary of tall shrubs shaped into onion-domes, teardrops and twirly cones.

He plumps instead for the greater concealment of a narrower pathway on his right, which he's glad to find leads him away from the house and out of visibility, along the very edge of Dud's land. Along this he flits, between two crisp white stone balustrades that stand in harsh geometric precision against the organic invasion they fend off on either side: the balusters on his right mark the furthest boundary of manicured civilisation, beyond which a thorny scrub of barrel cacti and yucca falls steeply down a rock slope croaking with hidden insect talons; while the balusters on his left forfend a lush overgrowth of ferns and magnolias kept artificially alive with sprinklers.

He reaches a narrow gate—unlocked also! (Ashley's prudent preparations again, as he cannot know.) Shooting hunted glances behind him, he slinks through it and finds himself back out on Blue Jay Way, some way below the main entrance to the house. Relieved to recognise Jaymi's parked car waiting further down, he scampers off towards his creator.

Sitting in the driver's seat, conscious that this is his final Beast approaching him down the hill and getting into the car beside him, Jaymi has a sudden feeling of continental plates drifting nearer one another, on the way to forming some new Pangaea. Then he wonders, as he starts the engine in readiness to drive them both away: does Scorpio *feel* like a Beast, as opposed to a human?

Deep inside Scorpio, *is* there, in fact...?

And somewhere inside himself, he quivers.

111 SCORPIO AS SUCCUBUS IN THE HOUSE ON JUPITER DRIVE

Late at night, as soon as Amber is asleep on his bed upstairs in the house on Jupiter Drive, Jaymi lets himself and Scorpio quietly in through the front door, into the grand hallway of the building. Careful to make no noise, he leads his new creation up the main staircase, along the landing and on down the corridor, stopping outside Amber's bedroom door, which he proceeds to open as slowly as possible, so as not to make the smallest sound. With his finger to his lips, Jaymi turns to his Beast, kisses him on the forehead, then points him into the bedroom, gesturing that Scorpio enter within, on his knees, in utter silence.

Scorpio's eyes are electric with uncertainty, fear and excitement. He does as Jaymi bids: he falls softly to his knees, then slides himself forward, through the door and into the shadows of the room, making not a shred of sound.

Jaymi slips away down the corridor, along the landing, down the staircase, through the hallway and out of the house, to his car. As he drives down the slope of Hercules Drive back home, he can picture what is happening up behind him in the house on Jupiter Drive.

For a long time, Scorpio lies prone on the polished wooden floorboards underneath the bottom end of Amber's bed.

Then by slow degrees, he crawls out from his hatching-place, like Sadako in *Ring*—his palms and nails pressing into the floor. His animal gaze darts about him, through the strands of his black hair hanging down before his face. He freezes, hearing Amber's faint breathing above.

He slinks across the floor along the bottom of the bed, then stops at one corner of it, breathing hard himself. Once he's allowed his breathing to subside a little, he moves just his head, turning it very slowly to look out from between the strands of his own hair, up the length of the bed to Amber's head, which is an indistinct shape against the paler pillow.

Remaining on his hands and knees, Scorpio listens again to the breathing from the other end of the bed. Is Amber asleep? Or is he lying there awake in rigid silence, planning what reaction he will give to the tiny shreds of sound he can hear from Scorpio's movements down at the foot of his bed—planning what sudden violent movement he will make towards that unknown intruder down there?

Scorpio waits immobile, for another half-minute.

Then he slinks onwards, around the corner of the bed, and starts his crawling journey along the side of it, with the wall on his other side, towards the bedside table ahead, prowling ever closer alongside that blond Beast's powerful body lying up there on its back, all uncovered in the hot sticky night, whose electric charge of warmth Scorpio can even feel down here.

In a single bound, he springs up like a cat, lands on top of Amber's chest, plants his claws around the wide muscular heat of it, and crouches there quivering.

Amber jolts awake to see a naked feline succubus, with haunches raised, legs splayed, bottom poised directly over Amber's crotch—and eyes bright and feral in the dark of the room, fixed hungry and murderous on Amber's eyes, inches from his face. But as Amber stares back into their depths, in this first extraordinary meeting between the pair of them, those Scorpio eyes soften, for Amber alone forever, into the dark submissive gazelle-eyes of a houri…

112 THE WEAK TAN FIGURE AND THE VAST TORNADO

Floating in the pool on his back, Jaymi contemplates the sky above Electra Drive. He grins at the palm tree's black asterisk high over-head. It's time to earth that voltage: Scorpio and Amber, tunnelling into the future together…

First, the mental and emotional space Scorpio requires to house and make sense of his own complicated self eats up an unusually large proportion of the space available to him as a whole. If Jaymi had not made him into Amber's lover in particular, it would have been quite possible that Scorpio might have failed to find a long-term partner, despite possessing prolific resources of desirability. For although many men would otherwise have been attracted to him, few of these would have happened to be strong enough to cope with him and stable enough to anchor him without feeling themselves overbalanced; and these few men Scorpio might not have chanced to meet.

Secondly, Amber's own mechanisms are, in themselves, just as demanding and expansive as Scorpio's. But the cold steel of his thinking has enabled him to build the horizons of his entire mental and emotional space at a distance far enough away to enclose a volume more than capacious enough to accommodate both the complexity of his own factory blades and the complicatedness of Scorpio's. That volume is the size of a warehouse, in fact—sometimes leaving Scorpio to feel not just un-cramped from within himself, but positively lost in the space of Amber's hangar-like darkness.

Jaymi's eyes glint, as if the surface of the swimming-pool around his head were crackling with voltage, vermilion flame licking at the glassy-black water…

From that very first time Scorpio saw Amber, after crawling out from under the bed, Scorpio has always had the impression of colossal violence in Amber. The physical power of his presence derives from three elements: Amber's movements, which are quick, unadorned and deadly efficient, as if every parcel of his energy is allotted; his stillness, bespeaking latent force; and his gaze, which sees into whomever it lands upon.

Scorpio has always been aware of this power, to an overwhelming degree; and yet, unlike most others who feel it too, he has never quite been afraid of Amber. There's no reason why he shouldn't be afraid, except that Scorpio knows another truth, too: the sound of the pair of them together, shouting out to the whole world from a shared stage, both emanating an infernally beautiful music wherein the yelps of Scorpio's alto voice spurt up in glee and pride, coiling around the charismatic growl of Amber's bass... No one else has yet heard that music, Jaymi reminds himself—but oh, they will!

Soon: there is machinery in Amber's eyes, glancing back at Scorpio from there in the doorway; and after he walks out, Scorpio has Amber's smile burned into his mind.

Soon after that, Scorpio's delicate head lies in Amber's lap, at peace, with eyes closed: softest touch and after-quiver of desire.

Out in the yellow countryside fields together by themselves, there is unexpected, brightly-sunlit sex—and a sense of foreboding, hanging in the sunlight, looming in the sky above the hillside.

Scorpio is fusing with the hunger of his own libido, licked by the width of the burn of Amber's biceps, muscular chest, forearms and stomach, which all make an animal cage of heat and protection where Scorpio lies curled, coiled in half-sleep around that pole of a penis standing hard and hot while Amber breathes unconscious in the deeps of the small hours.

Their shared music floats back into Scorpio's semi-conscious mind, with those joyfully duetting alto yelps and bass growls. This time, Amber is fucking the music with a thick eighteen-inch boner that pushes up between the bars of the music's cage, drawing the rest of Amber up into it as it grows, until the whole of him is a giant cock straining up between the bars ... and Scorpio moans as that boner is unloaded deep inside him every night, in a Scorpionic love-slave delirium: his anus tightening around the base of Amber's shaft, Amber's stubble scratching at the softness of his open lips, and Amber's arms circling his horny little body where it quivers so electric.

Sinking into sleep, Scorpio sees a weak tan figure imprisoned in a back room, chained like a sex-slave; and out through the window, the rough blond funnel of a vast tornado approaches the house from across a plain...

Catching sight of his own selfhood from above, for an instant, he is shocked at this unexpected glimpse of how intensely sexual his self is, how fiercely sexed his body is—and always, of course, as a bottom, all throughout the years. Could he ever be a top, for the first time, somehow, once, with a man? Or even with a woman? What would it be like?... But this will not be happening for Scorpio with Amber, he can tell. (And Jaymi could inform him, if he wished to, that it won't come close to happening with Lucan either, when Scorpio is Angel in *The Imagination Thief*, though there is the possibility it may at last happen with Jaymi himself.)

Sometimes he compares the enjoyment of having his throat gripped, with his best guess at the orgasm that would happen if he were hanged. For Scorpio, even everyday conversations have become lit from below, by flashes of impalement on a spinning silver metal phallus, cross-lashed with whip scars, with one erect cock in each hand, another in his mouth and others pushing in at him from all directions. Hysterical attacks with a flavour of sexual obsession rise up nearer and nearer to the surface of him, ever closer to erupting uncontrollably out—

"I don't know what sump of my mind this came out of," he says to Amber one day, "but the thought's just flashed up: 'I'd like to be killed by you.'"

Around the floating Jaymi Peek, neon-red flame plays soft across the surface of the water in the swimming-pool.

113 JAYMI'S GAMES *APRICOT EYES* AND *HALLUCINATION IN HONG KONG*

Now that the incarnated Scorpio is securely imprisoned in a meat-space home with Amber, Jaymi can return his attention to Bang Dead Games.

Great though his happiness was to see the entire contents of *Ain'tTheyFreaky!*'s Newsfeeds wiped away, there is no getting away from the problem that Dud can simply fire up the game's software again. All the public's contributions of content and scores and comments so far may have been erased through the intervention of Jaymi and his Beasts, but the blank Newsfeed templates will doubtless just be reloaded and soon start attracting replacement content and scores and comments from around the world, with no greater inconvenience to Dud than having some of his advertisers' and investors' confidence temporarily shaken by the shut-down. Indeed, Dud came back out swinging, only today, by issuing a press release in which he vowed to have the game back up and running soon.

How depressing. How boring and how evil.

Unless Jaymi now takes things to a new level...

The deeper he's gone into the development of *The Imagination Thief*, *The Platinum Raven* and *The Host in the Attic*, the higher he has felt the voltage becoming, between his own output on the one hand and on the other hand his contempt for those who inflict *Ain'tTheyFreaky!* on the world. This voltage is now so high, its crackle and buzz running through him like electric blood, that he almost feels he will fry unless it's earthed.

How will he earth it?

It seems he has got away with Kelly's death, so far at least, in the sense of not getting caught for it. In criminal terms at a deeper level, however, he is in too deep and dark to back out now: in order for her death to have been in aid of more than just a temporary world-cleansing, he'd better go yet further down this tunnel of righteous criminality, to ensure she died for something of greater permanence and grandeur. But how to go further?

He sits immobile, with a deadly gaze levelled on the afternoon cityscape ahead. Whatever this mission may be, Scorpio will be on it, for sure—a Beast aflame with voltage. And Amber, too—the original and most dangerous, fixing Jaymi's eyes with that bland, blond, mild smile and black flames beneath it. But what will be the focus of the mission?

Well … Dud Guy, of course. Who else?

Who else, indeed. On the coat-tails of this clarity comes the question that he recently backed away from: in targeting Kelly through the hands of Amber, was Jaymi perhaps stalling? By his use of a Beast as his proxy, was he trying to fool himself into ignorance of what he himself was doing—killing her?

If he's honest, yes he was.

Well, in this final mission there can be no such wincing. He will stare that darkness cleanly in the face… And the answer appears: he will make a Beast of himself. He will take the lead in this mission, accompanied by Scorpio and Amber—as an incarnated Jaymi Beast!

A Jaymi character is already established as the protagonist of all three games, after all, interacting with a different array of the other Beasts in each one. So well established, in fact, that he'll be able to barrel through this very last Beast's creation cycle and incarnation in super-quick time, so as to create a culmination of the six who are already out in the world. The Jaymi Beast will crown those six by combining the qualities of them all, integrating them into something that feels so natural and clear as to be almost without flavour, rather as the vibrant primary colours of light combine to make a simple-seeming white.

Seeing how much new games material he has amassed, he therefore sets straight to work, feverishly hammering out the outlines of two further games beyond his existing three titles. In their different ways, these two new games, named *Apricot Eyes* and *Hallucination in Hong Kong*, will be created as vehicles for the Jaymi Beast and Scorpio in particular, to bring this final pair of Beasts into a mutual focus that'll kick-start their upcoming Dud mission.

Continuing to hammer away at his keyboard like a fiend, Jaymi Peek jumps headlong from the two games' outlines, to their visuals.

First comes *Apricot Eyes*. Throughout this game, the Jaymi Beast will become familiar with Scorpio's being garbed in his modern visual styling, which has been established as if for a Scorpio manga: the little black pixy-boots, the silver rings on all his fingers, the black leather mini-skirt over black tights, and the slinky black polo-neck, always with a plain and delicate silver crucifix pendant, hanging either high at his neck or lower on his chest, depending on the length of thin silver chain he's chosen on a given day; and one big hooped silver earring, swinging and swaying from his right ear.

But once only in that entire game, the Jaymi Beast will also glimpse an incarnation of Scorpio from long ago—an ancient incarnation as a boy named Phaon, who was dancing on a precipice on the Palatine Hill in Nero's Rome, at sunset, enrapturing a crowd. By the time the Jaymi Beast glimpses him, this Phaon from Classical times will already be long dead, but his dance to Dionysus and song to Cybele will so bewitch, that they will fall sideways through the centuries like a teardrop, to land in the Jaymi Beast's eyes in that game, with the booming of a vast bell...

Next comes *Hallucination in Hong Kong*, in which game the Jaymi Beast will be cast as "I". In a view of Hong Kong from the Peak, the skyscrapers will rise beneath him to the north, with a blackcurrant colouration in the image, and his own eyes reflected back at him where they hang upon the sky above the city.

Also in this game, Scorpio-as-Angel, cast as "you", will be lying on a bench for enormously too long ... or will seem to.

What glacial elevation in the position of "I" in *Hallucination in Hong Kong*—a monstrous elevation, of the kind where all beauty appears as if colourised in post-production. Whereas "you" will be sensual, erotic, fresh—and destroyed by the touch of that glacially elevated, colourised "I".

Jaymi Peek stares up with closed eyes, feeling those continental plates come together down inside him once again, locking tighter than before, with a clang like the asterisk above him on the sky.

114 JAYMI CREATES THE JAYMI BEAST'S CODE AND APPEARANCE

He lowers that deadly gaze of his, from the familiar clump of skyscrapers floating in the distant heat-haze near Violet Street, down to his keyboard.

Here it comes now, then: the code for the Jaymi Beast. Simple and demure in appearance, yes—but a Beast born of balance and serenity, at last.

He opens his design for *The Platinum Raven*, consults the general sketch of the Jaymi character there, then polishes it, so it reads: "On two brief and enigmatic occasions the Chocolate Raven meets Jaymi Peek, who feels almost like someone who might somehow be directing her life."

He opens his design for *The Imagination Thief*, consults the general sketch of the Jaymi character there, then polishes it likewise. In this game the Jaymi character is not presented in the third person as in *The Platinum Raven*, but rather in the first person (although this little guideline sketch itself is in the third): "Narrator Jaymi Peek is an intelligent, humorous lens and a benign observer. On screen, however, he becomes a charismatic and empowered face who projects himself addictively into the imaginations of a global audience. One of Jaymi's missions in his wildly varied projections is perhaps to help himself to transcend all that needs transcending."

So much for the basics that'll be required of the Jaymi Beast's code.

What of the visuals? He returns to his design for *The Platinum Raven*, pauses in thought, then firms up the game's first description of the character's physical appearance: "Dressed in a black suit, white shirt and charcoal-grey tie, he is slim, pretty, watchful, with dark brown hair and big brown eyes, set within a pale face. There's nothing overtly strange in his appearance, yet he strikes her as being somehow larger than life."

He returns to his design for *The Imagination Thief*, and firms up that game's first description of his physical appearance: "As my reflection approaches me, in its black suit, white shirt and charcoal-grey tie, I look at my pale face and I am fascinated to sense something in my brown eyes that I've never sensed before."

In confirmation of the Beast's styling, he navigates to a bit later on in *The Imagination Thief* and clarifies one further little artwork-oriented description of the character: "you start in your chair, to see a figure enter, dressed in a black suit, softly close the door and turn its gaze on you. It's thin, pretty, watchful, with big brown eyes that hold your gaze in silence as it pulses like a cat through the stretch of space between you. 'Forgive me for intruding,' the figure speaks and glides to a halt the other side of your desk. 'My name is Jaymi. You're busy, I'm aware, but I shan't be long.'"

Well, OK then. Bring it on!

115 JAYMI INCARNATES THE JAYMI BEAST

Up looms that ghostly bank of controls against the sky ahead through his study window, with its dials, switches, buttons, faders and small red or green lights set into black metal, hanging over the lower third of the cityscape, while an intimation of the Jaymi Beast flickers in the grain of the upper two-thirds.

First, Jaymi establishes the Jaymi Beast's gleaming detail in *The Imagination Thief* as being his childhood violin, whose visual strings will play throughout the game: "'or have you taken up your child-hood violin again?' [...] the violin I used to own. [...] I used to play it under a favourite tree in the woods near where I lived [...] I'd go to that tree many evenings, alone, to play my violin at dusk; a secret place. [...] they just came up and listened [...] some were even dancing in the clearing, to my music! [...] every few days they would follow me again, and hear, and dance in the clearing at dusk [...] a couple of the parents grabbed my violin and bow, smashed them against my tree [...] Only one woman turned back towards me with a hint of compassion, to say she had heard there were many violins in New York City. [...] I decided that at last I was leaving there forever."

He then establishes the Jaymi Beast's talisman in *The Imagination Thief* as being Dotty, whose visuals will spend almost the entire game-play hidden in his pocket: "I hold up a small, grey, plastic elephant [...] I head back towards the ocean and look at the elephant. 'Hallo Dotty,' I whisper, give her a kiss and put her in my pocket [...] I feel some unidentified object in my left pocket, reach in and pull out a small grey plastic elephant, the one I named Dotty after the woman in the bric-a-brac store, her trunk raised high as if greeting me."

He concludes by establishing the Jaymi Beast's additional motif in *The Imagination Thief* as being three powerful camera lenses, whose visuals will be conduits for much of the game itself: "'Jaymi, let's have you right there in front of the three cameras, on the mark' [...] My outer gaze descends from the minuscule stars, to alight upon the central of the three camera lenses ahead of me [...] Ahead are three cameras; over there, a bank of faders [...] This time the three lenses are angled in relation to one another—one straight ahead of me and one on each side at forty-five degrees to that, like the mirrored panels of a vanity mirror on a dressing-table […] the lights around the three angled cameras are already shining straight at my face […] I can thus see little of what is in front of me, beyond the light that fills the air itself and picks up tiny dust motes. On a level with my eyes I can just about make out those three all-important black circles […] The aperture in each of the three lenses shrinks to a pinpoint, then disappears."

And now the incarnation in this study, for the last time: the Jaymi Beast slithers into meat-space and squeezes through the monitor in front of his creator, whose fingers clutch the chair in a horror of delight to feel his own beat rush away around the world in silence like a mirror-crack fissuring the upper atmosphere.

116   FROM MULHOLLAND HIGHWAY TO THE HOLLYWOOD SIGN

Upstairs in the Blue Jay Way house, Dud hovers his finger over Ashley's phone number, in two minds about whether to call her. Earlier today at work, he asked her for a list of all the IP addresses that are confirmed as being Jaymi's or are thought to belong to him. She agreed, breezily enough, to compile such a list and send it over; yet behind her breeziness, he couldn't shake the sense that she was somehow stalling, as if trying to think of some way to evade his request. Something in her manner set off alarm-bells, as he stood there watching her. Or was he just imagining her strangeness and her stalling? Is he becoming paranoid? So hard to tell.

He scrolls through his contacts and hovers his finger over Herb's number instead. At work today he also spoke to Herb on the phone, to ask him the same question he asked Ashley. A simple request. Those IP addresses belonging to EC1 Digital are, after all, the ones that Herb has been targeting for a while now, whenever he has hacked the code of a new Beast of Jaymi's. Herb will surely have supplied the list to Kelly, for her attempts to smudge each Beast. And like Ashley, Herb agreed to compile a list, but he too sounded oddly awkward, as if he'd rather have been able to find an excuse not to. More alarm-bells in Dud.

Is there some hidden treachery going on here? If those two are betraying him in *any* way, then Dud will uncover this and put the fear of god into them. He will destroy their careers, their reputations, their very homes—

Amber climbs in through the open window beside him, like a giant blond spider.

Dud shouts in terror and launches himself up onto his feet, but is too slow. Amber dives for him, grabs him, overpowers him, pins him down and knocks him out with a massive blow to the side of the head. Amber verifies Dud is out cold, picks him up, drapes him over his shoulder and strides from the room.

Outside, there is no oversight from neighbouring Blue Jay Way properties, and the street is deserted as usual. A car waits at the top of the front drive of the house. While Dud is carried over towards it, the Jaymi Beast gives Amber a nod of admiring respect from the driver's seat. At his approach, the door of the trunk clicks open. Amber deposits the still-unconscious Dud inside, wedging him securely between the spare tyre and a tarpaulin, and shuts him in.

He climbs into the passenger's seat, glances over his shoulder, and lets the menacing fluidity of that smile flicker back at the figure in the rear seat. In response Scorpio bares his teeth at Amber and licks his lips, while a faint glow of perspiration breaks out afresh across his upper lip, soft in the light through the car's side windows.

"Let's hit it!" whoops the Jaymi Beast, banging the wheel, and Scorpio purrs like a rattlesnake behind him.

So down through the exclusive peace of the Bird Streets they filter, emerging from Sunset Plaza Drive onto the raucousness of the Sunset Strip. Half an hour later they have traversed Hollywood and are climbing the slope of Beachwood Drive, with the far-off Hollywood Sign straight ahead, creeping ever nearer to them as they ascend. The Sign swings out of sight while they curve up through the narrower, leafier streets near below it, until they emerge from Ledgewood Drive into the highest cul-de-sac of Mulholland Highway.

The Jaymi Beast parks the car behind a low rise of earth beside a loop of dirt track beyond the very top of the road. Amber opens the trunk, controls a blearily-struggling Dud, ties him up with rope to make a portable bundle, and quells his complaints by tightening the gag over his mouth.

Scorpio changes out of his little pointy boots into tough hiking boots; then he pulls his hand-gun out of his shoulder-bag and passes it to the Jaymi Beast, who grabs another coil of rope and a pair of cable-cutting pliers from the back seat and locks the car. The three of them set off uphill on foot.

A good three hundred metres up the rough hillside of earth and scrub ahead of them, the nine white letters of the Hollywood Sign stand in a wavy array near the skyline. Just above those, and a little to the right, rises the main tower of the transmitter complex on the levelled-off summit of Mount Lee.

The Jaymi Beast leads the way, avoiding the reaches of thicker scrub by steering his companions up the irregular pathways of dried-out watercourses that have been carved by occasional chutes of rainfall.

Amber brings up the rear, bearing with apparent ease the weight of a tied-up Dud in a fireman's lift.

And midway between the two of them, Scorpio climbs with electrified purpose, alert as a fox among the scratchy grass and aloes. Without turning around, he's acutely aware of what's between himself and Amber: a charge of such relentless sexual voltage, from Amber's groin to his own groin and bottom, that he can almost hear the crackle of its power through the warm sunlight below ... and all the way up Mount Lee the three Beasts climb without a word, while Scorpio emits a constant quiet moan, so tight and aching from the pressure of the crackle and the voltage of Amber down behind him.

After twenty minutes of focused climbing, the "D" of the Hollywood Sign comes level with them on their left. The Jaymi Beast bears right and onwards up a further thirty metres, bringing them to the chain-link fence of the complex. He wields the cable-cutting pliers from the ground up, until ten minutes later he has cut a hole big enough to admit them. The three of them clamber in, pulling the fourth, onto the edge of Mount Lee's flat top, levelled off so long ago; and stand there for a moment, panting with exertion.

A few metres across the concrete surface of the compound is the tower: a tapering, metal framework about a hundred metres tall, starting with a red-painted lowest section, then a white section, then again red, white, red, white, and a small further height of red at the top, all sporadically ornamented with dishes, saucers and drums, and bristling with small vertical masts.

As the Beasts step through the evening shadows to the tower's base, sporadic raindrops swing down and splatter onto the red metal beside them, and then fall faster, heralding a storm. They turn and take in the panorama of Los Angeles spread beneath them to the south. Far to their right along the Santa Monica Mountains, a pin of lightning flickers, followed by distant thunder after a few seconds.

The next lightning burst is followed by a boom of thunder, sooner afterwards.

The next flash brings a thunder-clap sooner still.

Amber takes the spare rope from Jaymi. Then with that almost superhuman agility and strength of his, he carries the now-semi-conscious Dud, still in a fireman's lift position, up the side of the transmitter tower, from girder to girder—over red, over white, and so on, for ten solid minutes. When he has almost reached the top, he sits a wobbly-looking Dud on a strut and secures him there with the rope.

Meanwhile, Scorpio scuttles up the tower after him, with the agility of a lemur; then perches in a nearby angle of metal, staring at Amber and baring his teeth, with that delicate silver cross gleaming upon the curve of his breasts, his body streaming with fresh perspiration and rain, and his little tough boots swinging daintily over the void.

Setting off up the base of the tower to join them, the Jaymi Beast hears a faint muffled scream trying to force its way through a gag, weak and tiny in the sky.

Down in the house on Electra Drive, pounding at the keys in the high-tech gleam of his study, Jaymi Peek hears this scream, through the ears of the Jaymi Beast … and for the first time, he identifies within himself the sense of having truly become one apart.

One apart from normality, from society, from the rest, on a journey of his own that no one else could take. It feels as if something jagged and electrical emanates from him, zigzagging outwards across the grand span of Los Angeles spread out ahead through the glass beyond his computer monitors. And far in the distance, at this panorama's right edge, the five flare-stacks burn high for a moment in the sky above the oceanside refinery, with different-coloured tongues of flame.

117 TRANSCENDENCE, VENGEANCE AND FIERCE BEAUTY: THE PRIVATE SCREENING (*CLIMAX*)

The storm has bottled itself back up, refusing to burst quite yet; the air feels close and charged. Lashed to the mast, Dud watches in fascinated terror as the night flickers alive across the city, from the hills on his right, arching up to frame the ocean's width ahead of him, then curving down again to his left where the city-grid runs away south along the coast.

Like a play of lightning through a haze of heat, Herb's script dips at electric speed into the refinery's tanks of glyphs and pixels liberated out of *Ain'tTheyFreaky!*, pulling out only those required to assemble Jaymi's five games in their current state—not one glyph or pixel more than needed, nor one less. That crackling code then plays out the games in sequence. Each spirals up and out from one of the five flare-stacks by the ocean, and spreads in complex flame across the sky in front of Dud. Each game unfolds in the present, self-contained, and at warp speed, but dancing in such clarity that Dud can't look away.

As soon as each game has coiled and convulsed up the shaft of its stack to the flare at the top, it catches aflame from the small pilot light that burns there day and night. Whenever one of the games surges out too fiercely from its stack, through the force of its unfurling, steam is injected as a coolant. Even as far away as here on Mount Lee, the hiss of the steam-jets may just be heard, beneath the audio of the game itself. At the start of each game's play-out, the air-horns in the refinery's alarm system emit their warning signal, one long and one short horn blown four times; and at the end of each game's play-out, they emit their all-clear, one long blast...

First, Herb's lightning script fashions a game-wrapper out of black and blue pixels, and wraps it around *The Imagination Thief*. This game-world unfolds, told in both the first and the second person, as seen by the Jaymi Beast. It stars the Jaymi Beast, and it co-stars Evelyn, Shigem, Kim, and Scorpio in his boy-drag as Angel.

Next, the script fashions a game-wrapper out of mauve and platinum pixels, and wraps it around *The Platinum Raven*. This game-world unfolds in the third person. It stars the Platinum Raven, Amber and Scorpio, with a couple of walk-on appearances by the Jaymi Beast.

Next, the script fashions a game-wrapper out of brown and green pixels, and wraps it around *The Host in the Attic* (whose concept encloses *The Imagination Thief*, as it happens, like a brown and green ring surrounding a black and blue circle). This game-world unfolds in the third person. It stars the Jaymi Beast, and co-stars Scorpio in the guise of Angel.

Next, the script fashions a game-wrapper out of apricot and blue pixels, and wraps it around *Apricot Eyes*. This game-world unfolds in the first person, as seen by the Jaymi Beast. It stars the Jaymi Beast and Scorpio.

And finally the script fashions a game-wrapper out of blackcurrant and black pixels, and wraps it around *Hallucination in Hong Kong*. This game-world unfolds in the first person, as seen by the Jaymi Beast. It stars the Jaymi Beast, and Scorpio in the guise of Angel.

The refinery's alarm system sounds the all-clear once more, with a single long blast. Then the landscape falls silent, as if watching Dud's tiny soggy flailing, up there on the mast.

He blinks, while he flails.

He looks confused by this private screening—even overwhelmed.

His mouth hangs open, displaying a half-chewed piece of gum stuck to his lower-right premolars.

118 TORMENT ON MOUNT LEE (*CLIMAX*)

"When we screen these things for you, Dud, I do wish you'd be more present," Amber coos across at him.

"You mean less vacant?" puts in Scorpio.

"Oh, Dud," sighs Amber, smiling across the width of the tower. "Dud, Dud, Dud. Have you perchance come to recognise that transcendence, vengeance and fierce beauty would seem to have won out over dreariness, laziness and smallness? Could it be that the complexity, unconventionality, beauty and subtlety of truth in this private screening stand in contrast with the simplicity, convention, utility and obviousness of lies in *Ain'tTheyFreaky!*, as an implicit challenge by example? Or is that a leading question, Dud?"

As if battling a new understanding, Dud speaks at last: "Fuck all that shit. Give me *Ain'tTheyFreaky!* every time."

The Jaymi Beast nods. "You may find the following uncomfortable or unnerving," he says.

Dud's scalp prickles, as he senses a scrutiny he knows, from above him on the right. He felt it once before, from a glossy photograph of a motel by a liquor store, where Evelyn was firing out murderous challenge from inside her sunny printed smile at him … and he felt it in Westmont just ahead of him, flitting up the steps to the motel's upper level, was that *her*? but then the walkway was deserted. Glancing somehow down at him now, her challenge from that photo has become more murderous, seemingly equipped with a terrible new knowledge of Bang Dead's attempt to warp her sunlight into brassy, sleazy cartoon-simpleness. And visible in her eyes, despite Jaymi's consigning this to the category of Evelyn's avoided destinies, is the watermark of her standing alone in the bar Downstairs, while her friends all peeped at her from alcoves and corners in search of the girl they used to love before Bang Dead's smudging wrought a weird mutilation of her presence, which none of them could pin down but made them all think "Oh, poor creature, and *what* has gone so wrong with her?"

Another gaze pricks Dud's awareness, from above him on the left, where he cannot stop himself looking up—and there looms Kim's face with its own terrible new knowledge of Bang Dead's having smudged him. Around Kim's eyes is a rubbery ultramarine, the irises an unhealthy orange-ochre, the whites standing out bright against that convexity of skin like egg-yolks in outspread dark-blue blubber. And sad behind these colours, despite Jaymi's consigning this to the category of Kim's avoided destinies, is the watermark of his desire to be close to that girl in Spindle Wood, while Bang Dead's hacking made him frighten her instead with a grimace and a savage snarl of "*What is that meant to MEAN?*", staining both his life and hers forever.

Dud looks down, evasive—but floating up the height of the transmitter tower towards him is the face of Shigem with his own terrible new knowledge of Ashley's and Dud's attack, when a highway of drifters with faces of pain and defeat stretched away in him. And large in Shigem's gaze, despite Jaymi's consigning this to the category of Shigem's avoided destinies, is the watermark of Bang Dead's hack: cowering behind that podium in the nightclub hallway, breathing hard, streaming tears of horror, with the skin of his nape punctured by the end of Krueger's metal fingernail.

From above Dud comes a hiss of pink noise. He looks up ahead, and there are the accusatory eyes of the Platinum Raven, with her own terrible new knowledge of Bang Dead's hack, when she felt like dying: filled with the Black Slab, her guts made of stone, perceiving that no one knew about the diamond-pipe slashing through her rocks, and nobody in future would ever know about it, so that all her platinum transcendence would remain still-born and forever unexpressed. And bitter in her gaze, despite Jaymi's consigning this to the category of the Platinum Raven's avoided destinies, is the watermark of her image on the side of that building on Hope Street, in Bang Dead's smudging of her—fakeness and theft of her, attributed as "Copyright Bang Dead Games".

Dud flinches, as a fifth Beast hisses up before him like a starved baby she-wolf, champing through the sticky air, floating ever nearer, leaking hatred out at him—it's Scorpio, his sexy vermin Beast-face bloodied by a terrible new knowledge of his own incipient panic attack in the fluorescent flicker of that late-night cinema washroom, the evil in the mirror grinning out from the side of his own face and body, and the man brushing against Scorpio on the side where the evil grinned. And harsh in Scorpio's throat, despite Jaymi's consigning this to the category of Scorpio's avoided destinies, can be heard the watermark of that five-year-old girl's voice grating in the corridor—and through her gauzy veil, all those lines around her eyes.

Amber rears up and stands in the floodlight ahead, surrounded by the other Beasts. Central in his insides, a long black heart pounds the darkest drive around him and outward through the humid air. He focuses on Dud, and a negative desire flashes up through his face, with a smudge and flash of anger. His expression splits, a smile beneath his nose but not above it. Seen from one angle, it's a smile like a meat-cleaver; seen from another, there is nothing but a flicker at his lips like a flame beneath a tomb. Words churn in a broth in Amber's skull and then are aimed at Dud, not through the Beast's mouth but through the north side of his face. Unspoken, they're as sharp as a knife through flesh: "How I'd love to kill you off by using noise alone, at just the right frequency and volume, so your frame would disintegrate and soon you would be scooping up your guts from the floor!" Drifting nearer, Amber's face retains his customary wide-set fluidity of humour. Yet under this is an altogether darker energy: disgusted cruelty, insane with revulsion, its eyes scrunched closed and the cords in its neck standing out. Those unspoken words from the side of Amber's face continue, "Your head will be severed, then buried in the garden at Jupiter Drive, facing up toward the house—so I'll always imagine it buried there, staring up at me from the earth beneath my bow window, day and night!"

Despite his slow floating ever closer in to Dud, Amber somehow feels rather to be jumping straight at his face, with fingernails gripping the back of Dud's head in order to do more damage. Guts seem to surge out of Amber's smiling eyes, at the tubby piece of dead meat flailing on the tower.

And yes, with a speeding-up of blood to drive the meat nearly mad, it is time for Amber's nuke-switch to get flicked on—and for Dud to take the highest trip, listening for the sound of his own blood rushing from his head, like a geyser! *What a rush...*

From Dud's viewpoint, the first effects of the nuke-switch's flicking-on seem almost low-key. This will soon be revealed as an illusion; but meanwhile those effects begin simply with a clearer perception of his own stagnant, grey-caging malice, which he sees has infected the rest of him. He sees the lazy cheapness and stupidity of his tabloid output, and the sickeningly dreary evil of this: such busy labour, throughout his years and decades, like a grey-clogged residue pushed out and lain in. (A perverted life, perhaps?... *Nah, no regrets, mate! He'd do it all again—every fucking shred of it, every time!*)

From those opening flashes, Dud's growing self-perception proceeds to a sense of self-allergy. Whatever years might have remained to him from now on, they'd have been irremediably oppressed and greyed-out by the revelation of this permanent stain in him, underlying every other event and leaving everything tainted for him. From here on, he senses, his life would have felt as if he once strangled to death his own identical twin while in the womb, knowing the extraordinary misery and pain the twin would have experienced if he'd been allowed to be born.

The stench of imbalance, failure and wasted resources inside him is now so overpowering as to be incapable of dispersion, it seems. One specific effect of this is to morph his memory of the palatial Blue Jay Way house into a dirty, squalid little apartment instead, with the television always on, a life-size stuffed-toy dog sitting in one armchair and Dud in the other armchair; and on the wall of the poky hallway, a snapshot of Dud when he was young, before the stain arrived.

Half-asleep in front of a game show, he feels his armchair pressing him up against the ceiling of the apartment. Across the room, a green plastic bag of junk on the floor looks like a series of grotesque heads, half-buried under the floor as he stares at it. Near ahead, not far beyond his toes, a corpse looks up at him through the carpet. He jumps up, wailing, and runs from the room, catching sight of a hideous reflection of his face in a mirror, and bolts down the hall, where a faceless head pursues him through a dense maze of furniture that blocks the front door.

But with a jolt he wakes again on the tower, to find the giant face of Amber has floated down upon him. Terrified, he writhes, but his limbs are immobilised, tied to the metal.

Amber reaches out his left hand to the top of Dud's skull, where Dud pictures him running the long nail of his index finger in a hard circle, down into the bone dome, then lifting the resultant circular lid, dropping a wriggly thing inside it, infernal and bestial, then lowering the skull-lid closed again.

The glands of Dud's emotion pump sticky tears out from his right eye first, then his left. His skull tries speaking this aloud, through the flesh that surrounds it and cushions it; but cannot.

As if from above, he can still see himself here, lashed to the highest red-painted band of the tower's framework, with his arms outstretched to either side, his feet together beneath him and his head tilted down to one side—a bag of chemicals and fluid on a scaffolding of pictured pain.

And streaming from this bag of a body, while Dud watches, it seems that a red metal fluid mingles with the rain-spatters and flows down the spreading width of struts and girders, down over the highest white-painted band, over the next red band, the next white band, another red and another white, to the lowest red; until, from the base of the tower, red and white metal tongues run across the ground, halt and harden, then crack open and bleed into earth.

Tiny in the far west, helicopters circle like gnats above Stone Canyon, whose trees sway and screech in a storm that hasn't reached Mount Lee yet. Once it does, thunder and lightning will play about this tower, every bolt threatening to sizzle Dud like a bacon rasher. Meanwhile, splodgy drops of rain spatter down onto the girders beside him, and dogs yelp and howl on the night-time slopes of the canyons below.

119 ONE APART (*CLIMAX*)

Alone on the tower ten metres underneath Dud, the Jaymi Beast gestures at the floating Amber, instructing him to halt his ministrations: from here on, the Jaymi Beast himself will continue.

So now comes the time he must step up to his own appointed mission, as his maker's own Beast, and stare the darkness in the face.

In theory his maker does still have the option to retreat from what's about to happen ... but in practice, both Jaymi Peek and the Jaymi Beast can now see that there really is no such option.

Dud Guy's main contribution to the world has been *Ain't They Freaky!*, having trucked in such content for all his working life. Throughout this career, he's known that his pouring this content out around the globe on an industrial scale has dragged everyone down and backwards. And he's never cared a shit. He'll continue it forever, and he'll never change.

That alone is reason enough for the Jaymi Beast to fulfil his mission here. But the imminent killing of Dud will have a value more sacred than mere reason—more immediate and more ultimate. In the face of Dud's deliberate ugliness, deserving of such violence, the aesthetic value of his death will be sublime.

How fitting it is, then, that Dud's death be meted out by the Jaymi Beast in his own drier, cleaner style than Amber's. The other Beasts have been extended aspects of Jaymi Peek, but the Jaymi

Beast is a culmination of those, combining their embodiments into a double of his creator. Combining those primary colours of light into white, he lacks the tint or flavour of the other Beasts, being simply what he is—another Jaymi. He was always going to have to kill Dud. Here at the end of the line, he was always going to have to walk the walk and do the actual deed.

So the Jaymi Beast looks up, locates his prey, locks it in his sights, and sets off up the last few metres—dark presider and finale of this Temptation of Saint Dud on Mount Lee.

From behind him comes an incursion of enrapturing darkness from Amber's head. Feeling this, while he climbs, the Jaymi Beast grins, whispering to Amber, "You've got a wicked black soul, haven't you? I really should condemn you—you're a wicked boy!"

Amber's eyes hiss back in silence, as the Jaymi Beast clambers onward up the metal girders, absorbing this infusion from his maker's first Beast. Amber is unbalanced, yes, driven by the night from lust to bloodlust—compassion and contempt, like red and white blood cells. Amber is alive to the power of inanimate things to hurt and damage living ones: hard to see a knife without feeling its unused potential. Even just his signature is sinister to witness on a page, so suggestive of a split inside—both halves equipped to identify human limitations. From Amber's point of view, the mutability of his own flesh causes his sense of physical reality to be somewhat tenuous; he feels he can create horrors just by thinking of them. (His favourite early nightmare: visitors arriving to blow down on him with shockingly elongated faces like cones, on an altar-like construction, swooping down at Amber's face to champ and coo and nestle...)

Climbing on upward, the Jaymi Beast turns his face to gaze across the city's span, and feels the Platinum Raven turn her own face inside his, shafting up his image in the way that she alone can do. Rising transcendent through the angles of her face in semi-profile, she floats upon the sky above the hills in his mind. She waits until he reckons she has floated to a finish, then she fires off a last trick: glowing like a vaporous angel of light, she clasps her hands in prayer and emanates a saintly halo, Virgin-Mary-hued in a blue of flaming methane and a white of frozen moonbeams.

A mere two metres from his prey, the Jaymi Beast draws Scorpio's gun from his pocket. At the touch of its black metal, he feels a final

Beast infusion, from the weapon's owner. Within him, Scorpio coils out from beneath the powerful bulk of Amber, then rises in fierce beauty, sexy gun-person and femmy goth-boy that he is, with the moisture shining on his canines and a pin-star squeak of light shining off the silver earring in his right ear. From down beneath those canines comes a blood-voice, amid the rest—Armenian, from two thousand years before the genocide. Incarnate in Scorpio, the basis of life is a union of dying and erotism, with a foretaste of death in the anguishing nudity of each erotic spasm that passes through him like a current every night. He feels himself descended from an ancient time, buried in obscurity but flavouring his cells with the dissolute fever of the priestess-slave he once was. A sacred creature in that former time, he carried an unbreathable heat and febrile glow of death. Enflamed with a flicker both wicked and divine, he casts a spell of dark seduction, embodying transgression, invitation and forbidden fruit—and a walking negation of the crass oaf tied to the metal tower overhead.

Thus infused, the climbing Jaymi Beast luxuriates in his own aloneness. Alone in a grand internal darkness—far removed from the city full of humans in their hidey-holes across L.A. Alone in his own charismatic black midnight, high above the sky that yawns tame upon the suburbs.

Alone with the grinning of his own cells, enclosed in claustro-phobically vast vaults of space and self inside his skull.

Such sensuous, sumptuous aloneness!

Looking up, the Jaymi Beast sees sporadic raindrops falling through the sweaty floodlit air towards him.

Close overhead now, Dud is lashed tight to the metal framework, still uninjured, yet writhing on the red struts in a posture of diseased meat.

The Jaymi Beast centres the prey in his sights. He contemplates his own and that monkey's respective positions and resources here ... and power flows through his insides, rich and smooth and mineral, like petrol pumping through him.

How quiet this moment is.

How exhilarating are his own capacities.

How delicious to be the Jaymi Beast at this moment, so far outside that monkey's narrow world!

How infernally beautiful, to inhabit this particular destiny, outside the limitations of the Dreary Ones...

Once he dreamed of a book whose cover depicted a close-up human eye. There was nothing wrong with this eye at first glance. After a few moments, however, it became clear that its stare was somehow too open, too hard and assaulting, its surrounding flesh too used-up from within, for it to be an eye capable of humanity. In his dream the book's cover stayed shut; but now, as he pictures it here on this mast, it opens at last. And what he sees next, on the pages inside, is his own rising-up from the uncanny valley.

While the Jaymi Beast looks, his left hand strokes his torso unconsciously. His right hand rests upon his forehead, as if to stop damage to a third eye sleeping in its fontanelle. What he sees on those book pages is the pit of horror sinking from the basement of his psyche, through the sump underneath it, and down the well-shaft beneath that. The pit is a perpetual hunger and void, with the vertiginous churn of a whirlpool. It is life-staining, casting a shadow and a sick heat, up through his guts, further up into his brain and down the corridors of his limbs, with an exhilarating shudder of some overpowering forbidden awfulness that will never go away. Somehow his flesh remembers terrible evenings and nights of blood, which he can't quite pull into conscious memory ... and while he moves up the final metal rung of the mast tower beneath his prey, it's as if stains of dark blood are seeping out through his clothing.

The Jaymi Beast feels vertiginous horror and a sensuous drunkenness mating inside him. And yet within this, at the final instant, he elects to continue minimising the dreary monkey's physical pain: he aims the gun at Dud's heart, and shoots him there, with a calm satisfaction ... then he aims it at Dud's forehead, and shoots him there too.

Two clean bullet-holes appear in those places, and the monkey slumps.

In Dud's last seconds of floating semi-consciousness, he sees hellish lands falling away from Mount Lee across L.A., in the style of Mediaeval maps: tar rivers, lead lakes, horrid zones and bottomless pits, across a brimstone ocean, to damnation gulfs beyond. Although so exposed in open sky here, he feels like a dying bison painted on a wall in the very deepest crevice of an ancient cave—down in the rock, where all light has died away leaving prime black silence. Hidden in a sound-crevice underneath the silence, his own last noises are a snuffle, then a croak. Clicks, taps and bubbles, from a fissure in his dying head… He tries to speak aloud, but his voice has died already, so he cannot hear his own scream—

120 BRIDGE TO *THE IMAGINATION THIEF* (*RESOLUTION*)

In a daze of grim ecstasy, the Jaymi Beast climbs back down the tapering framework and rejoins Scorpio and Amber at the tower's base. The three Beasts converge in an inward-facing triangle, their arms around one another's shoulders and their foreheads touching. They stand there together for many moments without speaking, Amber's eyes remaining open and the others' resting closed.

At the sound of distant engines in the sky, the triangle drifts apart, as the trio look up and along the span of the Hollywood Hills. Those helicopters that were circling over Stone Canyon are now nearer, having already curled east over the hillside chateaux of Beverly Park North, perhaps as far as Coldwater Canyon or thereabouts, aiming spotlights onto the slopes as they circle. It won't be long before they approach Mount Lee, where those spotlights will inevitably pick out Dud's corpse lashed atop the transmitter tower…

Peering upwards in alarm, the Jaymi Beast is about to speak, when Amber forestalls him and sets off up the tower. "Amber!" calls the Jaymi Beast, stoops to grab the cable-cutting pliers from the ground and holds them up towards him. "For the rope."

Amber glances down, takes hold of the pliers, then resumes pressing on up the framework, with those metallic-seeming blond-spider movements of his. The other two watch him recede skywards, almost to the top of the structure, where he sets to work with the pliers, extricates Dud's corpse, drapes it over his shoulder and sets off back down.

By the time Amber and Dud are at ground level again, Scorpio has gathered up all the severed rope fragments and other traces from underneath the tower. Then through the hole in the chain-link fence, three Beasts and one corpse sneak out of the transmitter compound and back down the scrubby slopes of Mount Lee, to the car in its hiding-place at the top of Mulholland Highway.

Half an hour later, the Jaymi Beast exits the Harbour Freeway onto Century Boulevard, then travels five blocks west and four blocks south, to the motel by the vacant lot. There, with the utmost speed and discretion, Amber and Scorpio push Dud's corpse out from the back seat, onto the grass verge beside the back of the motel. No witness has been present, as the car slips away down West One Hundred and Fourth Street. But whenever the cops do come to find and identify Dud, it's a fair guess they may conclude that his unknown assassin was probably delivering payback, on behalf of some local gangster, for the recent desecration of those corpses when they were stolen from neighbourhood funeral parlours and dropped into the wet concrete foundations of the Righteous Gun Cockpit, in that outrageously disrespectful publicity stunt by Bang Dead Games.

The car slips away east, then eases back onto the freeway, joining the fast lane northwards to Hollywood.

In his study in the house on Electra Drive, Jaymi Peek lifts his attention out of his three Beasts, leaves it hovering over the moving car, and sits there with a shine of exhilaration in his eyes and a confusion of thoughts and emotions inside.

Three-quarters of an hour later, his phone pings. Checking it, he sees the car has arrived outside. He buzzes open the front gates and garage doors, while it drives in through the courtyard and into the garage.

Another ping on his phone. A text message from Herb: "Hey Jaymi, they're hanging well. Meeting Ashley at the Silver Lake bar for several drinks tomorrow evening at eight. Fancy joining us?"

He smiles, thinks for a moment, then texts back: "You bet. See you there!"

Through his open study door comes the sound of his returning Beasts downstairs…

Later on, around midnight, if a watcher were to be hiding in the shadows at the far edge of Jaymi's middle terrace, peering through the windows at events inside the warm-lit study, then they'd be curious to see the greatest throng of incarnated Beasts ever assembled in that room—no fewer than seven, all slowly converging towards his main computer monitor, chatting among themselves in words that the observer would not be able to hear from across the terrace. Each Beast in turn would then be seen to approach the monitor alone, before climbing up to squeeze and slither into the screen and vanish back into Jaymi's games software, where their respective in-game future awaits. Throughout this process, each Beast would be observed as having an aura of peace and serenity, almost as if embarking on a long-awaited homecoming.

Such a watcher would register Jaymi Peek sitting in the study, alert but relaxed on the sidelines, while the screen of the computer monitor would swallow first the Jaymi Beast, still carrying the gun he shot Dud with; then in due course Amber; then presently Scorpio; and then the Platinum Raven at her majestic leisure.

Tiptoeing across the terrace to the open study doors, piqued by curiosity to eavesdrop on what each Beast might be saying, such a watcher would be just about in time to catch Kim's parting comment to Jaymi: "You know, just sometimes, when I've peered deep into the fabric of life, behind the inanimate structure of things, I believe I've caught glimpses of it, beyond the bars of matter. Yes; I could almost be certain that, at long last, I was actually contemplating … *the bear in the machine!*" And with twinkling eyes, as Jaymi laughs, Kim climbs through into *The Imagination Thief* and is gone.

Evelyn is meanwhile in the midst of some chatty anecdote to Shigem. "I'll tell you the rest in a minute," she says, reaching up to grasp the edges of the monitor, "because we're both headed to the same game as Kim. But basically, what happened was that she gave me this whole pole-up-the-ass routine about her dog needing a passport. I said 'What are you talking about, of course it doesn't need one,' and she said 'But it's a poodle.' I said 'OK swivel-puss, why are poodles so special?' Then she called me a frizzy bitch, so I said 'Well I'm sure your funeral will be a thoroughly tasteless affair, but quite a giggle anyway so it shouldn't matter too much!' OK Shigem—hold that thought, and I'll see you on the other side." And with a quick wave to Jaymi, she climbs in and vanishes.

Shigem approaches the monitor, the last remaining Beast in the room. He turns with affection to look at his creator. "You've been a bit ignored, haven't you, sitting over there?" he asks, and Jaymi nods. "Oh well," continues Shigem, "I'll leave you with this, in case it helps: whenever life gets a bit much and I'm in danger of coming over all unnecessary, I just think of pineapple upside-down cake. As soon as I think about it, all is well with the world. I mean, isn't it the coolest, how it tells you all about itself, in its actual name? And how adorably sweet and lovely, back in those caveman days or whenever it was, that while everyone else from the cave was out somewhere killing other people from other caves, there was one little queen like me who decided it was so much more important to stay back home alone in the cave and invent pineapple upside-down cake instead. I know just why she did that." He climbs gracefully up to the monitor, grabs its edges with a flourish of strength that causes his bangles to jangle in the quiet of the study, and glances back at his maker, one last time. "I'd also like to point out that when it comes to fruitcakes, being heavily fruited is not the same thing as being over-fruited. Bye-bye, Jaymi!" Shigem's warm brown eyes flash the most beautiful smile his creator has ever seen, and perhaps will ever see. Then he's gone, like his companions before him—all sealed into their allotted games forever, never again to run wild through the danger and mess of meat-space.

And so it is, that these seven Beasts are born into the upcoming worlds of *The Imagination Thief, The Platinum Raven, The Host in the Attic, Apricot Eyes* and *Hallucination in Hong Kong*, from their respective origins here in the house on Electra Drive, the house on Zeus Drive, the house on Jupiter Drive or the Melrose Avenue building.

Jaymi Peek looks around the newfound stillness of his study; and a luminous sense of peace expands throughout the room, allowing his mind to breathe clearer than it ever has since he entered this house a few short months ago.

A little of this peace doubtless arises because, by sealing the Beasts forever into his games, he has just consolidated his escape from being identified as the cause of Ashley's and Dud's deaths. For in addition to having managed to avoid any known association with their murders so far, he now has a further safety-net: to wit, neither perpetrator nor murder weapon remains to be found (at least in meat-space, which tends to be where the LAPD restricts itself to).

But his sense of newfound inner peace also derives from something wider than such practicalities, vital though they are. It stems, too, from this final completion of his seven beloved Beasts' creations—each of them born as his response to one or other of Bang Dead's Newsfeeds, but also embodying a particular spell of the most urgent magic he knew how to spin from within himself. Collectively, they are the best contribution he can make to a world that would seem to have been designed to facilitate the likes of *Ain't They Freaky!* instead. They are the highest-quality way he can find by which to integrate himself into the world as it is; to find a home for himself, beyond the steel and glass of this house on Electra Drive.

Now that his five game-worlds are on their way to commercial release, he can feel their casts of Beasts panting at their leashes, impatient to start their own journeys, to spring out into those game-worlds, to run there in pixel form forever more, on screens around the globe...

In Jaymi himself, however, the feeling is rather that of having arrived abruptly home at the end of some gigantic odyssey. He senses the upswing inside him of a new capacity for insight into the world, of a kind he could never have guessed at, had he not travelled such strange paths to get here.

How many contacts he has in the world, and how known he is to so many, for his games; both of which tallies will only increase from now on. And in that context, how striking is the aloneness he feels in his work.

Yet this sense of aloneness isn't *quite* true, or is only a part-truth, because the worldly connections that are most meaningful, most highly-charged and most valuable to him are precisely those made by dint of his game creations' going out into the world—including when these creations are engaged with by people who have never met him, will never meet him, or are not yet even born. Through connecting with his games, many unidentified people will feel less alone for consuming such expressions of his own feelings and visions—even after he's dead, and despite his having created these expressions in the solitude of his houses here in the Hollywood Hills.

For him, that is among the most distilled human connections available.

Moreover, the world is now different from before. For one thing, the whole poisonous machinery of *Ain't They Freaky!* is destroyed, for the present. Its inventor has been assassinated by Jaymi, via the Jaymi Beast's trigger-finger, high above Mount Lee—an act of grandly destructive creation that Jaymi feels almost as grateful for achieving as he feels for being able to create any one of his Beasts. His own truths have thereby taken on Bang Dead's lies and conquered them, firing out a chime of light and sending a starburst of zeroes zinging in all directions around the curve of the planet's surface...

Plus, his own five game-worlds are all set to flame into permanent life.

Magic and enchantment, mined out of dead things!

He sniffs, becoming aware of the scent of a bonfire drifting in through his terrace doors from somewhere across the Hollywood canyons, most likely tended by a gardener at the edge of some hillside estate like this one; and a memory floats back to him. He closes his eyes, trying to grasp it.

Yes: years ago, woodlands at dusk in the late summer, somewhere on the outskirts of Omaha, Nebraska. Nervous on the group's edge, a sixteen-year-old Jaymi plays a violin, and the liquid magic of his music is delighting his audience. An end-of-summer hour, near the end of all their childhoods.

This moving image of him and his audience flickers and slows, as flames from the bonfire flare high, roaring up soundless to obscure the scene. Then they die back down to reveal him anew. An hour after his audience was banished, there he remains in the dark of the clearing: a lone violinist, playing music in the woodlands, as if for all time...

He re-opens his eyes. He looks around his silent study, so recently filled with the excitable chatter of his seven creations in their final minutes of being flesh and blood.

Now that the Jaymi Beast and all his companions have been laminated into their game-worlds, destined to remain locked into pixel form forever, to be played by future gamers, how poignant it is to reflect on what the Jaymi Beast felt during the brief period he was at large in meat-space. Throughout all the urgency and drama of his mission to Mount Lee with the others, did the Jaymi Beast *feel* like a Beast, as opposed to a human?

Deep inside the Jaymi Beast, *was* there, in fact...?

And somewhere inside himself, Jaymi Peek smiles.

At last he can resist the temptation no longer. He jumps up, strides over to his main computer monitor and fires up the world of *The Imagination Thief.*

From a black screen, the three words of the game's opening title fade up, stand for a few seconds, then fade back down into black, before the first scene begins.

"Are you ready for this?" calls Raven to me from the corridor outside my office. "Don't forget we're pressing the button tomorrow!"

I sink back in my chair, my feet resting on my cluttered desktop. "Oh, I'll remember, thank you."

"OK, then. Goodnight." The main door hisses and clicks shut after her, muffling her steps across the stone floor of the outside lobby, where a lift-bell rings. To my left, the sun sinks over the Hudson River, turning its water into twinkly pink vertical strips between the towers of Battery Park City.

THE END

Written in London, 16 May 2014 to 6 August 2017.

If you've enjoyed this tale, then my warm appreciation for leaving a quick rating or just a handful of words of feedback on it, at the online retailer it came from. If you are able to do so, then this really would help me enormously, so very many thanks!

Rohan

Also by Rohan Quine, the following novel is available at most online retailers, either as an ebook (including films and video-book and audiobook) published by EC1 Digital and the Firsty Group, or as a print book published by EC1 Digital.

THE IMAGINATION THIEF
a novel

The Imagination Thief is about a web of secrets, triggered by the stealing and copying of people's imaginations and memories. It's about the magic that can be conjured up by images of people, in imagination or on film; the split between beauty and happiness in the world; and the allure of various kinds of power. It celebrates some of the most extreme possibilities of human imagination, personality and language, exploring the darkest and brightest flavours of beauty living in our minds.

www.rohanquine.com/the-imagination-thief

REVIEWS OF ROHAN QUINE'S
THE IMAGINATION THIEF

See www.rohanquine.com/press-media/the-imagination-thief-reviews-media for all links to the following.

"Rohan Quine is one of the most brilliant and original writers around. His *The Imagination Thief* blended written and spoken word and visuals to create one of the most haunting and complex explorations of the dark corners of the soul you will ever read. Never one to do something simple when something more complex can build up the layers more beautifully [...] suffice to say he is the consummate master of sentencecraft. His prose is a warming sea on which to float and luxuriate. But that is only half of the picture. He has a remarkable insight into the human psyche, and he demonstrates it by lacquering layer on layer of subtle observation and nuance. Allow yourself to slip from the slick surface of the water and you will soon find yourself tangled in a very deep and disturbing world, but the dangers that lurk beneath the surface are so enticing, so intoxicating it is impossible to resist their call."

"*The Imagination Thief* is one of those books that has originality stamped across it with a pair of size 12 DMs. An incredibly dark yet full and balanced with shafts of light picaresque through the recesses of the human psyche, it is an uncomfortable, troubling immersive experience that mixes text, audio and video taking us into places we would rather not go. It could be described as a cubist novel, taking each aspect of the torn mind and laying them out on separate planes through the different media."

"Rohan is one of the most original voices in the literary world today—and one of the most brilliant."
—**Dan Holloway**, novelist, poet and *Guardian* blogger; and see his *Guardian* review at http://bit.ly/13rR45R

"Never read anything like it! Magical realism in NY. Extraordinary."

"An intriguing book that addresses many big issues (love, sex, death, power, the nature and reliability of human memory, history, culture, human potential, the constraints of 21st century society, and more) [...].

[...] described with a larger-than-life intensity that put me strangely in mind of Coleridge's *Kubla Khan*—and occasionally its drug-induced origins too!

It's not an easy or comfortable read, particularly when closely examining mental and physical cruelty and violence between some of the characters. I read with a constant sense of foreboding. However even the most shocking passages are underpinned by the compassion, pity and tenderness of the narrator for all but the most brutal characters. There's also some very welcome, very British understated humour to offset some of the horror. The brevity of the 'mini-chapters' was well-judged—I felt I needed to come up for air after some of the short episodes, and to assimilate the latest action before moving on.

The immediacy of the story is more keenly felt because it is written in the present tense—always more demanding on the reader, I find, and even more so in this case because although most is in the first person, there are also many second-person narratives, where Jaymi is reading the minds of other characters and addressing them: 'You move closer...' That the author is able to keep the reader not only engaged but tantalised by this difficult mode of storytelling indicates the power of his prose.

Though it's very much a modern book, with the constraints of modern life as one of its themes, there are touches of the classic about it too, reminding this reader of Johnson's *Rasselas* [...].

As I turned the pages, I found myself puzzling how on earth this intense tale would end. Without spoiling the plot, I can say I found the conclusion surprising, redemptive and satisfying.

[...] So, here we have not so much an imagination thief, but, to the reader, an imagination expander. Great stuff."
—**Debbie Young**, author and Amazon UK Top 1,200 Reviewer

"It feels like something that will win major awards... I look forward to gritting my teeth and applauding loudly at next year's Booker."
—**Meg Davis**, literary agent, Ki Agency

"Another difficult to classify book, but that's precisely why it works so well. Part literary fiction, part fantasy, it is a surreal experience which makes the most of its equally offbeat location. With a cast of unforgettable characters and a central premise both intriguing and epic, this is what indie fiction does so very well—breaks boundaries and takes risks. In this case, it pays off."
—**JJ Marsh**, novelist

"Rohan Quine not only has several books out. He also has a career in alternative modeling and film to look back on. Naturally, he has gone on to make a series of silent short films to go with an audio track of the author reading from his work. It's flooded with city lights, drugs and darkness. One foot in the New York Nineties, and one foot in today's London, it's both hypnotic and gut-churning."
—**Polly Trope**, novelist and literary editor of *indieBerlin*

"To love some of these characters would be to doom yourself, you are simply asked to observe them; to see them as deeply, as thoroughly as you see yourself, such is the all-encompassing clarity of Quine's descriptive abilities.

[...] Rather than a violation, Jaymi's reading of this motley crew of players is performed with a tenderness and an unending respect for the spectacle of another's soul in its entirety laid bare to us. There is magic in the twisted minds as well as in the sublime.

[...] the decadently rich language of this novel makes it pure chocolate, wine and sex—you will need a cigarette as you turn the last page. This book reads like a musical. The words are liquid and melodic: always entrancing and encaptivating and rising to chorus-line lung-busting crescendos every time Jaymi unleashes his powers and the imaginations of his superbly diverse cast shine out of the page in an explosion of Sound and Vision. Given that he accomplishes this purveyance of the innermost soul with black words on a white page, what is indeed impressive is the sheer level of colour, smell, texture and heat that can be felt during these moments when we are invited to couple our minds with theirs.

As I have stated, this is a piece where the English language is flexed and stretched until it's sweating on the floor in its yoga pants, and yet there are plenty of examples throughout to demonstrate Quine's skill in summing up the state of a character in a few simple words.

[...] there are other characters too, such as Evelyn and Rik, who are able to find light and love in their lives in the same way that Shigem and Kim have, and the warmth and tenderness of these characters serves to further illustrate that in contrast Angel is unable to escape the darkness [...].

[...] Despite Jaymi's authority as our narrator, the English language is the true star of this trans-corporeal, trans-reality, trans-possibility, trans-mindf*$k, all-transcending diva of a debut."
—**Jen McFaul**, author

"Rohan is a dazzling writer [...] 21st century Beat Generation dreamweaver!"
—**Peter Godwin**, musician

"I finished *The Imagination Thief* late last night, and found it ... many things, I suppose, but I know they add up to 'deeply overwhelming'. It took my own imagination prisoner for a long while, and I cannot think of a better accolade for a true novel. I can't recall the details of any earlier version (which is why I've been able to read this as from zero), nor can I find an earlier copy anywhere, but I don't remember that the older version ended the same as this—has it changed? Because now, I read the last few pages—the van trip back to NY—as completely new to me, and I thought you have wonderfully created a quite unforgettably convincingly-constructed exit for the reader from this (again, overwhelming) experience."
—**Dr Michael Halls**, Intercom Trust

"quite brilliantly written. I have now read it twice and think it is full of amazing descriptions—especially those detailing the backgrounds of the various characters as divined by Jaymi in his magic insights. I am not on the whole a fan of magic realism, if one is to call it that, but your prose is so lyrical and beautiful that I felt quite seduced by it. The same applies to your dialogue which is richly colloquial. I am sure that the writing alone will arouse the admiration of the discriminating reading public."
—**Jeremy Trafford**, novelist

"fiery work. How rollickingly it proceeds down to its last bloodily beautiful drop."
—**Willie Coakley**, poet

Also by Rohan Quine, the following four novellas published by EC1 Digital are available at most online retailers, either as a single print book entitled *The Platinum Raven and other novellas*, or as four separate ebooks and audiobooks with the following titles.

The Platinum Raven
The Host in the Attic
Apricot Eyes
Hallucination in Hong Kong

THE PLATINUM RAVEN

A triple convulsion whereby our heroine Raven escalates herself into the Chocolate Raven and then the Platinum Raven, from London to Dubai to the tower in the hills in the desert—then back down again, forever changed

www.rohanquine.com/the-platinum-raven

THE HOST IN THE ATTIC

A hologram of Oscar Wilde's *The Picture of Dorian Gray*,
digitised and reframed in cinematic style, set in London's
Docklands in a few years' time

www.rohanquine.com/the-host-in-the-attic

APRICOT EYES

A cat-and-mouse pursuit through the New York City night involves a preacher, a psychic and a dominatrix, broadcast live on air—until a horror is unearthed, bringing two of them together and the third to a sticky end

www.rohanquine.com/apricot-eyes

HALLUCINATION IN HONG KONG

Sliding from joy to nightmare and back, a plane flight frames
a journey into Jaymi's and Angel's polarised identities and
perceptions, where past and present merge in an obsessive fantasy
of love, death, horror and apocalyptic beauty

www.rohanquine.com/hallucination-in-hong-kong

THE PLATINUM RAVEN AND OTHER NOVELLAS

The Platinum Raven and other novellas comprises four novellas—*The Platinum Raven*, *The Host in the Attic*, *Apricot Eyes* and *Hallucination in Hong Kong*. All four are literary fiction with a touch of magical realism and a dusting of horror, celebrating the darkest and brightest possibilities of human imagination, personality and language

www.rohanquine.com/buy/
the-platinum-raven-and-other-novellas-paperback

REVIEWS OF ROHAN QUINE'S NOVELLAS

See www.rohanquine.com/press-media/the-novellas-reviews-media for all links to the following.

"It would be remiss of me not to take this opportunity to bring people's attention to a truly remarkable book. Rohan Quine writes right at the boundary between literary fiction and experimentalism, and his new collection of four novellas, *The Platinum Raven and other novellas*, is a genuine masterpiece. This guy is as good as [Sergio] De La Pava, and deserves to be the next self-published literary author to cross over into mainstream consciousness."

"Rohan Quine is one of the most brilliant and original writers around. His *The Imagination Thief* blended written and spoken word and visuals to create one of the most haunting and complex explorations of the dark corners of the soul you will ever read. Never one to do something simple when something more complex can build up the layers more beautifully [...] suffice to say he is the consummate master of sentencecraft. His prose is a warming sea on which to float and luxuriate. But that is only half of the picture. He has a remarkable insight into the human psyche, and he demonstrates it by lacquering layer on layer of subtle observation and nuance. Allow yourself to slip from the slick surface of the water and you will soon find yourself tangled in a very deep and disturbing world, but the dangers that lurk beneath the surface are so enticing, so intoxicating it is impossible to resist their call."

"Rohan is one of the most original voices in the literary world today—and one of the most brilliant."

"four stunning new novellas by one of the most exciting literary writers in the UK."

—**Dan Holloway**, novelist, poet and *Guardian* blogger

"Rohan Quine is a master of words, his world is also accessible, and it's a place you definitely need to visit. With echoes of Jennifer Egan's *Goon Squad*, Quine captures all that is beautiful, but he doesn't shy away from all that is ugly. What links the four novellas together is that his characters are all searching for that something beyond the everyday, beyond the ordinary, and Quine is a god, having them dole out kindness and justice. In his world, everything that is commonplace would be annihilated. This is the kind of read you have to give yourself up to. [...] When you emerge on the other side with a greater understanding of what it means to be 'that animal called human', then that will be the time to stop and ask, 'What just happened?'"
—**Jane Davis**, novelist

"Novelist Rohan Quine not only has several books out. He also has a career in alternative modeling and film to look back on. Naturally, he has gone on to make a series of silent short films to go with an audio track of the author reading from his work. It's flooded with city lights, drugs and darkness. One foot in the New York Nineties, and one foot in today's London, it's both hypnotic and gut-churning."
—**Polly Trope**, novelist and literary editor of *indieBerlin*

"A cautionary tale [*The Host in the Attic*] of the potential corrupting power both of vanity and of the internet plays out in modern London's high-tech dockland offices and luxury apartments, with brief forays to lavish West End hotels and country houses. [...] As the story becomes ever darker, gentle touches of humour provide a little light relief. I particularly enjoyed the characterisation of the women, especially the wonderfully petulant Angel Deon [...]. While at first this parable's main purpose may seem to rage against the principles of a high tech, monopolistic, capitalist world that enable individuals to lead unspeakably privileged lives above the law, it is at the same time a cautionary tale against narcissism and the abandonment of love and compassion for others. This broader theme gives the story its true heart and depth. Quine is renowned for his rich, inventive and original prose, and he is skilled at blending contemporary and ancient icons and themes. [...] an interesting approach to dialogue, blending idiom and phraseology from different eras, from Victorian

times through 20th century popular film culture to the modern day. [...] There are some classic moments of horror that are very filmic, including one on a par with the *Psycho* shower scene. Without giving too much away, I can imagine this book might put readers off accessing their own attics for a while."
—**Debbie Young**, novelist and Amazon UK 1,000 Reviewer, writing in *Vine Leaves Literary Journal*

"This is an extraordinary writer. I am going to gorge myself on these novellas as soon as I possibly can."
—**JJ Marsh**, novelist

"cerebral works full of brilliant imagery and invention. This series of novellas are all well crafted and designed to draw the reader in to the shifting realities of their settings. The title novella *The Platinum Raven* in fact has two young women in two narratives [...] very vividly described. There are elements of magical realism and alternate reality throughout. At times the two Ravens appear to communicate but the levels of reality are enigmatic and intriguing. *The Host in the Attic* is a beautifully reinterpreted version of *The Picture of Dorian Gray* set in a high-tech dystopian world and a sinister computer global company—Mainframe Corporation, which appears to permeate every level of society. The hologram corporate image logo is in essence Dorian. All the main characters from Wilde's novel are here in more modern form. It has a tremendous and horrific climax. The horror novella *Apricot Eyes* is a fast-paced horror tale in a nightmarish New York. *Hallucination in Hong Kong* is a mysterious tale of past and present, dreams and waking with horror and love themes. The whole collection is a roller-coaster of at times nightmarish perceptions and strange surreal happenings brilliantly imagined. The tales leave a lasting impression and I recommend highly."
—**Alexander Gordon-Wood**

"a riveting read. The novella *The Host in the Attic* in particular is splendidly Wildean: in it, [Quine's] novel *The Imagination Thief* itself drives forward the plot of *The Host in the Attic*. He is a veritable Imagination Thief!"
—**David McLaughlin**

The following are reviews of Rohan Quine's *Hallucinations* (New York: Demon Angel Books), published in print in the USA only, which included earlier versions of: *Apricot Eyes*; *Hallucination in Hong Kong*; and a few chapters of *The Platinum Raven*.

"I have now been reading *Hallucinations* with great pleasure [...] you are indeed a star."
—**Iris Murdoch**, novelist

"He has no equal, today or tomorrow."
—**James Purdy**, novelist

"Sometimes Quine succeeds with things you wouldn't think language could do, like describing a piece of music with an extended metaphor that reads something like watching the last half-hour of *2001*."
—**Ben Cohen**, *New York Press*

"*Hallucinations* at the end of this millennium is what Lautréamont's, Huysmans's and Wilde's work represented at the end of the 19th century [...] a sadistically svelte structure on top of explosive, primal content that refuses to behave in a linear fashion. It can only be described as literature that strains between ecstasy and bondage [...] one of the chic-est, most provocative things we have read in years [...] one of those seminal works that goes on to be accorded the status of a classic."
—**Wayne Sterling**, *New York Web*

"The imagery is *Apocalypse Now*-era Coppola meets Wes Craven, or *Edward Scissorhands* meets *Barbarella* [...] or Anne Rice (as screenwriter) on an acid trip [...] the lilt and cadence of prose poetry laid end-to-end, resulting in a narrative that is frequently stunning [...] sublime verbal renderings of the emotions and sensations of human love."
—**Hayward Connor**, *Union Jack*

ABOUT ROHAN QUINE

Rohan Quine is an author of literary fiction with a touch of magical realism and a dusting of horror. He grew up in South London, spent a couple of years in L.A. and then a decade in New York, where he ran around excitably, saying a few well-chosen words in various feature films and TV shows, such as *Zoolander, Election, Oz, Third Watch, 100 Centre Street, The Last Days of Disco, The Basketball Diaries, Spin City* and *Law & Order: Special Victims Unit* (see www.

rohanquine.com/those-new-york-nineties/film-tv). He's now living back in East London, as an Imagination Thief, with his boyfriend and two rabbits—a caramel-coloured one with upward ears, and a white one with downward ears.

His novel *The Beasts of Electra Drive* (a Finalist in the IAN Book of the Year Awards 2018) is a prequel to his other five tales, and a good place to start. See www.rohanquine.com/press-media/the-beasts-of-electra-drive-reviews-media for reviews by *Kirkus*, *Bookmuse*, *Bending the Bookshelf* and others. From Hollywood mansions to South Central motels, havoc and love are wrought across a mythic L.A., through the creations of games designer Jaymi, in a unique explosion of glamour and beauty, horror and enchantment, celebrating the magic of creativity itself.

In addition to its paperback format, his novel *The Imagination Thief* is available as an ebook that contains links to film and audio and photographic content in conjunction with the text. See www.rohanquine.com/press-media/the-imagination-thief-reviews-media for some nice reviews in *The Guardian*, *Bookmuse*, *indieBerlin* and elsewhere. It's about a web of secrets triggered by the stealing and copying of people's imaginations and memories, the magic that can be conjured by images of people, the split between beauty and happiness, and the allure of power.

Four novellas—*The Platinum Raven*, *The Host in the Attic*, *Apricot Eyes* and *Hallucination in Hong Kong*—are published as separate ebooks, and also as a single paperback *The Platinum Raven and other novellas*. See www.rohanquine.com/press-media/the-novellas-reviews-media for reviews of these novellas, including by Iris Murdoch, James Purdy, *Lambda Book Report* and *New York Press*. Hunting as a pack, all four delve deep into the beauty, darkness and mirth of this predicament called life, where we seem to have been dropped without sufficient consultation ahead of time.

The six titles are in the process of being released in audiobook and video-book formats too, performed by the author.

CONNECT WITH ROHAN QUINE

If you'd like to be notified of future print and ebook publications, you're most welcome to sign up for my not-too-frequent newsletter at www.rohanquine.com/sign-up. Rest assured, such emails will be at supremely tasteful intervals and your details will be shared with no one else.

And if you wish, thanks for connecting on:
www.twitter.com/rohanquine
www.facebook.com/rohanquinetheimaginationthief
www.goodreads.com/author/show/1089889.rohan_quine
http://theimaginationthief.tumblr.com
www.wattpad.com/user/rohanquine

www.ingramcontent.com/pod-product-compliance
Lightning Source LLC
Chambersburg PA
CBHW051122120726
47905CB00005B/1382